A VIEW OF KEALAKEKUA BAY 1784
Engraving by Byrne after John Webber
Bishop Museum

Published by Ku Pa'a Publishing Incorporated, Honolulu, Hawaii 1995

THE GUNS OF EDEN

A Novel of Hawai'i
When The White Man Came

Ed Sheehan

For Katha and Alex

First Printing 1995
ISBN 0-914916-98-X softs cover
ISBN 0-914916-99-8 hard cover

Book Design by Martha F.M. Smith

For information contact:
Ku Pa'a Publishing Incorporated
P.O. Box 37460
Honolulu, Hawaii 96837
(808) 531-7985

This is fiction loosely based on the lives of Kamehameha I, the king who brought the Hawaiian islands together, and John Young, a seaman marooned in 1790.

An attempt has been made to reflect the times and conditions in the Hawaiʻi of that period but this history has been manipulated and the story is purely an imagining.

Whispering ghosts of the east
Who brought you here
To our land?
Stand up and depart!

- Polynesian incantation

"Life is the owr that God has gvn
To scape from Hell and fly to Hevn"

-John Young's diary

In Hawaiian, a, e, i, o and u would be pronounced ah, ay, ee, oh, oo. In the eighteenth century, almost *every* vowel in a word was pronounced distinctly.

For example, the place-name Kailua would have been said "Kah-ee-loo-ah."

Over the years, many frequently used Hawaiian words have been contracted out of this purity. One encountered here frequently is *haole*, meaning foreigner or stranger (usually white man), and now pronounced "howly."

PROLOGUE

Admiral Sir George Courtney, Royal Navy
Greenwich, London, 1819

I was not surprised when a white man climbed the *Dolphin's* ladder that September morning at Kailua on Hawai'i island, assuming correctly that he was one of the native king's foreign lieutenants. He was a tall dark-haired man in his thirties who introduced himself as John Stone, called Olohana by the *Kanaka*. He served as adviser to King Kamō'ī, he said, and had been dispatched by his majesty to bid me welcome. Stone volunteered that he was an American, abandoned by a New England trader almost two years before, in 1790, with a companion named Tweed. He offered this information with a smile while his clear blue eyes quickly read the state of our ship and its crew.

We had encountered several white vagabonds in touching at other islands, but any expectation I had of dealing here with a brutish and uneducated castaway was immediately dispelled. Stone owned an air of authority and quick tongue. His worn blouse and pantaloons were clean and his sun-browned face with its slightly mashed nose was newly shaven. His gaze met mine in searching appraisal and his attitude displayed neither arrogance nor servility. A fine Durs Egg pistol was at his belt and the staghorn handle of a stout knife protruded

1

from his boot. Both were worn casually and I held no doubt of his skill with either weapon. Here was a man with whom I must move carefully I told myself. A handsome native boy in breech clout, whom he introduced as his ward, watched Stone intently and constantly. I invited them to my cabin and poured wine.

Stone was direct, his tone pleasant but firm. The king hoped we came in peace, he said. This was so, I answered. Our mission was simple and without threat: to chart the Sandwich archipelago in more detail than had been previously accomplished by my late commander, James Cook, and his sailing master, William Bligh. I also told him I had been here before as a seventeen-year-old midshipman with Captain Cook when our great commander had been killed. With others from the *Resolution* and *Discovery* I had been beaten and stoned on that awful day. But I held no rancor, I assured, believing that a few enraged fools had killed Cook and not the Hawaiian people. Now I brought gifts to his king and the cordial greetings of King George III. There need be no fear of mischief from the *Dolphin*.

Stone said King Kamōʻī would be pleased to know this. Ours was the first English naval vessel to visit Hawaiʻi in the thirteen years since Cookʹs death, he pointed out. Thus I could perhaps understand the kingʹs apprehension. This concern had been greatly lessened, he smiled, by fishermenʹs reports of our congeniality and generosity while vising other islands.

I told Stone the gifts I brought were utilitarian: shoots and seeds of beans, squash, oranges and onions, and, principally, two cows and a bull. He said he was not unfamiliar with the care of such animals, but Hawaiians had never seen such beasts and they should cause quite a stir. Over more wine we discussed mutual assistance. Woodworking and farming tools were highly valued, he said, as well as iron, copper and brass in any form. He mentioned the *Little America*, a small schooner acquired from a previous visitor and under the care of his fellow castaway Alec Tweed. She had not felt paint in a long time and badly needed repair in canvas and rigging. I assured him these desires could be satisfied and he in turn made offer of hogs, vegetables, water and firewood. I thought Stone an agreeable man but reminded myself that seamen in such circumstances must be viewed with some suspicion....

Stone talked willingly of his pagan master. A rare man, he said, one he believed would have risen to the forefront if born in any other time or place. A man of immense physical and moral strength, he did not know the feel of fear. No other island leader had so quickly perceived the meaning of white men´s iron, guns and ships to his people. The aim of uniting the separate Hawaiian kingdoms into one occupied his life. Stone went on in this vein and it was clear he was not only the king´s champion but saw himself as a partner in Kamōʻī´s ambitions. Anticipating the question to come I told him firmly that I would not deal in guns, and had refused them to other rulers on Kauaʻi and Oʻahu islands. My charge from the Admiralty was clear: to accomplish my task and bring King George´s greetings to Sandwich Island rulers. For a military man I have an extraordinary aversion to violence, quite likely rooted in the day when our beloved Cook was slain on the dark shore at Kealakekua Bay....

Much of Stone´s information was already known to me. In three months in island waters I had made frequent contact with chiefs and knew of turmoil within the islands. Kamōʻī of Hawaiʻi had become a serious threat to the other rulers. The king of Kauaʻi was confused and fearful, desperately wanting guns against possible invasion. Weeks later I found that the ruler on Oʻahu desired arms for the same reason. I refused both men as gently as one could, setting forth the reason that Great Britain would not contribute to the internecine slaughter.

It became clear, however, that their obsession with Kamō'ī was not without foundation. He had already conquered the districts of his own island—by far the largest of the group and had declared his intention of next taking Maui and its attending small islands of Lāna'i and Kaho'olawe. He had acquired a healthy arsenal from China traders and a fast and sturdy schooner with two cannon. More, he now had the services of Stone and Tweed to teach his people the care and employment of these weapons. The concerns expressed on Kaua'i and O'ahu appeared justified.

But in touching briefly upon northern shores of the big island I found a different attitude towards its monarch. People spoke of Kamō'ī with respect and approval. Men now dared to speak out against cruel and usurious chiefs, it was said, and many wrongs were being rectified. The common people were no longer under threats of capricious punishment for violating minor taboos or displeasing their masters. People were no longer killed for venturing into the shadow of a noble's house or chancing to touch an object he owned. Taxes had been eased and more liberal laws of land and water use put into effect. In many ways Kamō'ī was considered more a liberator than a conqueror....

On the second night at Kailua Kamō'ī arrived to dine aboard the ship in company with his prime minister, an elderly man named "Billy Pitt," obviously named after our own British prime minister. The white counselor, Olohana-Stone, and Kamō'ī's favorite queen, Kahu, also accompanied his highness. She was a woman of startling beauty and considerable height, quite naked above the waist.

My men and myself were in full dress, as were my Marine lieutenant and his lobsterbacks. A salute was fired from our cannon, bringing cheers from the canoes surrounding the *Dolphin*. I greeted the king with a short speech which Mr. Stone translated.

Kamōʻī was impressed with the reception but no more than I was with him. He was a huge and heavily muscled man of great height with a blunt stern countenance and piercing black eyes. He wore a long cloak of fine yellow, black and red feathers that was stunning in its richness and craftsmanship. He moved with a regal aloofness and his attendants treated him with utter reverence, for these island kings are considered akin to gods. I escorted the three men to the great cabin. Meanwhile, Queen Kahu and her entourage were made comfortable with cushions and refreshments on deck, honoring the taboo against dining with men. Elsewhere in the islands I had observed that women meekly accepted this banishment. But there was no doubt that Kahu resented the ordinance....

With Olohana-Stone's help our conversation wandered pleasantly through the amenities. The dinner was the best that could be provided from my personal stores. The king enjoyed everything except sour-kraut, which I told him we found useful in keeping down the scurvy. Kamōʻī said this was a white man's sickness he did not know about and he hoped it would not be another curse introduced to his people. I assured him it would not and also informed him that our men had been pronounced free of the clap by the ship's doctor. This harm had already been done, the king remarked. Hawaiians now suffered many ills never known before Captain Cook. And white men kept making curious introductions—like the hot dust before him. What was it?

Pepper, Mr. Stone told him, and I remarked that a cargo of this precious stuff from far Indian islands had recently sold in London for six hundred percent profit. Kamōʻī said he thought it more an annoyance than an aid to dining. But greater irritation (he smiled as he said this) were the tools white men used to transport food to their mouths.

If he experienced difficulty in handling table silver it was not apparent. His gruff demeanor now relaxed, I thought him a man who easily employed charm and owned considerable natural grace.

He enjoyed our claret and I poured generously. His prime minister, "Pitt," remained quiet, but one was aware that his eyes and ears were sharply receptive. Mr. Stone enjoyed his position with the monarch and was aware of its unique value. I suspected that in his translations to the king he was embellishing my remarks with comment of his own.

Queen Kahu joined us as the table was cleared and brandy poured. This striking lady filled the cabin with the warmth and beauty of her presence. She joined the men without deference, almost immediately contributing wit and infectious laughter, as if her exile of the past hour had been a minor social error best forgotten....

The ponderous bark-cloth bundle the king´s servants brought to the table contained a cloak of feathers only slightly less grand than his own.

A gift for King George, Kamō´ī said, that he might be draped in the splendor of his Hawai'i brother. Another, smaller, cloak was then presented to me. Olohana-Stone explained the significance of these beautiful wraps: only aristocrats of the highest order could wear them. Their manufacture was a painstaking process requiring thousands of rare birds and years of work by the weavers. In thanking the king I vowed that these treasures would be zealously guarded. And now I had a special presentation from King George to Kamō´ī. I passed the polished walnut box to his highness.

He opened it and his expression was puzzled as he lifted the gleaming object to the light. A chronometer, I explained, a very fine one, made by Larcum Kendall, the man who made the instrument used by Captain Cook. Kamō´ī eyebrows still questioned. Mr. Stone explained that it was a watch—a device by which white men told time, the dividing of the day into hours and minutes. I asked Stone to read the inscription:

"In Friendship

> George III
> Great Britain
> April, 1792"

The King peered at the thick and heavy piece almost filling his broad palm. He became aware of its ticking and held it to his ear.

He did not know time made a noise, he said.

As the evening progressed I became more impressed with Kamōʻī's intelligence and desire for knowledge. His curiosity was boundless about what was happening in the world beyond his seas and the kind of men who ruled the great kingdoms. I told him about London; that it now held a million people, creating problems of overcrowding and poverty; that ships crowded the Thames from Gravesend to Chelsea; that shops along the Strand offered goods from every corner of the world. Kamōʻī replied that he wished one day to make a special friend of a great country and King George's land, as he called it, appeared to be an attractive prospect. But, he added, perhaps King George was too occupied with problems in London town with its poor people and crowding. Also, George had recently lost a big war and rich country in America. Kamōʻī now questioned if it was wise to seek alliance with a man so distressed.

Most assuredly yes, I stated. Despite its troubles London was now the capital of the Christian world, center of international commerce and fashion. Not since the heyday of Rome had there been a nation as rich and powerful as England—despite the unfortunate business with the Yankees. Kamōʻī must visit one day and see for himself. I would be pleased to offer him passage.

The king thanked me but said he was too busy with

his own preoccupations and plans. King George's war was over, he said, but his own biggest battles were about to begin. Once the other islands were brought under his rule there would be a Hawai'i united in political and business dealings with the rest of the world. And he would travel, he said with a smile, as the king of Hawai'i-*nei*, beloved Hawai'i, not as the king of the Sandwich Islands. Sandwich was the name of an English lord who had never even seen Hawai'i-*nei*....

I found it a most pleasant evening, murmuring with quiet discourse and good will.

We talked late into the night and those hours remain vivid in my memory: the three handsome brown aristocrats of pagan islands; the arresting music of the native speech; and the trilling laugh of a lovely, half-naked queen over candlelight. The soothing night and warming brandy served to banish formality and Olohana-Stone skillfully provided the verbal link. Obviously Stone possessed power and influence with this ruler and was not averse to strengthening his position. Still I found him a pleasant man and wished he was more forthcoming about himself. I wondered what his life was like as a counselor to this imposing emperor of far islands. I wondered where he came from and how he had arrived at this place....

PART I

O n a tranquil October night in 1790 the merchant ship *Nahant* out of Boston rested at anchor off Olowalu, a small settlement on the west coast of the island of Maui.

In the brig's longboat, which rocked gently alongside, sprawled *Ben Raggs, a slender and freckled boy of fifteen. This was his first voyage and he luxuriated in the soothing air and in the knowledge that he had become a man that afternoon when a young woman of Maui had taken his virginity with enthusiasm and expert performance.*

Ben was not entirely a stranger to sexual matters, being a farm child, but he had never been with a woman before. He felt he had arrived in a sort of paradise and relaxed in the mildly soporific state even though he was on watch to make sure no **Kanaka** *slipped out to pry loose some of the* **Nahant's** *copper bottom-sheathing.*

At long last his choice of a seaman's life seemed justified, for he dreamed these past months of a future filled with romantic ports, alien sights and sounds and exotic women.

In six hours Ben would be dead.

The muffled shouts awakened John Stone just before dawn.

The black-haired and bone-hard bosun of the *Nahant* dressed quickly, knowing what was to be expected on the deck above. Kimi, the ship's lone Hawaiian, had gleefully identified land birds the day before.

Stone felt excitement and curiosity—two emotions long absent from his days. This was his first visit to the islands that had claimed the life of the celebrated James Cook and every sailor had heard of their charms of sweet water, fresh food, balmy air and loving brown arms. And not a moment too soon, after these miserable past weeks of beating down from the northwest. In the passageway he bumped into Blue Bob, the negro mess boy, who was grinning with a stark white mouthful of teeth. Bob was carrying morning tea.

"Topside," Stone said curtly. He climbed the ladder to the quarterdeck. His coxswain, Jake Maul, was at the wheel, peering into the graying dark. Then Stone noticed the smell of land, a tropic spicing of damp earth, wood smoke and greenery, and a welcoming presence after the harsh weeks at sea. How different, he thought, from that of his native New England coast pungent with horse droppings and wharf scents around Boston Harbor. And the silence of the land struck him, for he was a man who had always savored silence.

The islands came sculpted out of dawning light, black broodings on a slate sea. Their great mountains floated high, crisply defined and dominating the western horizon.

Having frequently studied the ship's charts Stone knew the largest mass off the port would be Hawai'i itself, biggest of the group by far. Its nearer peak was miles high, crowned with snow now blushing in sunlight. Mauna Kea, it was called, the White Mountain. Maui island would be the landfall dead ahead—two huge ranges connected by a low, saddle-like isthmus. To the starboard were the lesser heights of Moloka'i, its outline lower and obscured by distance.

Soon terns over the masts seemed to be shrieking welcomes. Higher a fork-tailed frigate bird drifted almost motionless on the wind, pointing landward as if showing the direction.

The mate, Sprague, appeared, lumbering and untidy. After him followed Nathan Quimby, plump and puffing. Quimby's blouse and trousers were soiled and his beard a grayish brush. Under one arm the captain held certain of the ship's charts. He stared coldly, almost haughtily past Stone over the dramatic panorama presented by the islands and the brightening sea. Then he and Sprague spread the maps atop the after skylight. The sheets crackled slightly in a breeze.

These were copies of Cook's charts of what he had named the "Sandwich Islands," Stone knew. They showed very few windward havens on any of the group and none on this side of Maui. A landing here could be disastrous. Even from a distance long swells could be seen crashing against shore cliffs sending spume high over black stones.

Quimby frowned at the sheets, mulling his choices and knowing them few. Kealakekua, the bay Cook had used on the big island of Hawai'i, was at least two days distant, perhaps more. The leeward side of Maui, much closer, offered several fairly safe anchorages. After a few minutes of study he decided upon a place named Olowalu.

All morning the *Nahant* beat back and forth on brisk tradewinds. Nearing noon the channel between Maui and Hawai'i was entered and, with a following sea, the brig fairly flew over the deep wide path.

In early afternoon they were in the lee of the towering extinct volcano, Haleakala. The ship easily plowed through the blue sea about two miles off the land. Long golden beaches could be seen under the feathering of palms. A few canoes were also glimpsed, but too far inshore for their occupants to be distinguishable. The island's aromas were constant now in the gentle trades. A falling sun cast shadows far uplands, turning bronzed lava landscapes into coppers and golds.

The day grew short. It was clear that the *Nahant* would not gain her intended anchorage before dark so Quimby ordered Sprague and Stone to take her out for the night. They were off Olowalu a few hours before dawn. Quimby came above, sulky and quarrelsome. A bastard, Stone thought. Any other master would have been in good humor, given the prospects of provisioning and pleasure in these beckoning isles. Perhaps the captain's foul mood was because of the absence of the *Little American*. The auxiliary schooner had now been lost to sight for well over a week.

Stone refused to be annoyed by the captain's chronic unpleasantness. He had despised Quimby from the first but his choices had been next to none when the *Nahant's* offer had been made.

Life had not smiled upon the bosun in recent years. He was now thirty three and the odds appeared heavily against further advancement, though hope still flamed. One day he would have a command, he vowed again to himself. But of late that day seemed further away.

Stone had spent long and hard years attaining a bosun's grade, and more years practicing it on a variety of vessels. He had studied geography, celestial navigation, account-keeping, even history and military tactics, to be ready for command. But the association of Yankee ship owners was a clannish one bound by family ties and dictated by a tight circle of Boston financiers.

Only once had he come close to success, currying the favor of a shipowner in Malden. Unfortunately he also fell into favor of the man's wife. And one afternoon this starved cow was grazing in his loins when her husband came upon them. The cuckold's fury was apoplectic and his influence considerable. For over two years Stone found it wise to take berths out of New York and Philadelphia.

Then he had killed a man in Jamaica.

The fight was with knives in a palm-roofed tavern over the attentions of a delicious mulatto girl. His assailant had been a "gentleman" of high connections and uncommon talent with the blade. Killing him had not been easy. But the practice Stone had acquired in similar encounters in the dark lanes of Charleston and Boston triumphed.

Stone was not sorry for killing the man, who was intent upon killing him. In truth he had experienced an alien little shudder of pleasure in the act—besides ridding the world of a vile, obnoxious and callous bully. The authorities did not share this latter view, the corpse being one of their own. Stone had finally and reluctantly been cleared of charges, but not before he had spent two hellish months in a furnace-like jail cell.

Back in Boston and near penniless he had met an old friend, Scotsman Alec Tweed, fresh off a merchantman on a Liverpool run. The two were soon pondering their futures over rum at the Bell in Hand. Trade was slack and berths were in short supply. More than one Christian ship had become a Guineaman in the slave trade—and smuggling and gun running were hardly considered vices. Neither Stone nor Tweed was averse to turning a few shillings at the latter but equally neither had any stomach for slaving.

Then Nathan Quimby appeared. The two men had been recommended, he said, by an acquaintance in the Caribbean trade and he had need for two officers. Neither man had warmed to the captain, whose unbathed presence was probably the least of his faults. But relations aboard ships were hardly social and there was no risk of being jailed for the enterprise Quimby planned.

The pay offered was reasonable and a two percent bonus from the China trading could amount to a fairly large sum at journey's end. Bartering seal and sea otter furs from Northwest American Indians to Canton Chinese was time-consuming but highly profitable venture. With any luck Stone and Tweed could be back on Long Wharf in a year with more money than they would normally earn in two. A problem arose in that both men were of equal rank. Therefore which should serve as captain of the *Little American* and which as bosun and third officer of the *Nahant*

Stone had always been the authority of the two, for the big Scot was a trusting and naive soul despite his impressive and cowing bulk. He accepted Stone's decision to place himself with Quimby aboard the *Nahant*. Close to the command, Stone pointed out, he could be alert to any threats and alive to any opportunities that might affect the two men. Tweed agreed without question, trusting Stone implicitly. Since the start of their friendship as youthful soldiers in Boston he had been taking Stone's advice—and never with regret. Neither man had other friends. Tweed's few relatives were scattered in distant Aberdeenshire and Stone was an orphan.

Quimby accepted the arrangement and Stone settled into the bosun's cabin aboard the *Nahant*. Tweed was delighted to be in command of the schooner. It was almost immediately evident during the provisioning period that the captain was a sour and vicious man—which hardly set him apart from others both had served under. Early on there was reluctance on Quimby's part to formally record their agreement on pay bonuses. It was only when Stone threatened to quit, taking Tweed with him, that the captain signed the terms. Another sour note was struck when the mate, Sprague, came aboard. He was Quimby's cousin, a slack-mouthed and beady-eyed man whose family had something to do with helping finance the voyage. It soon became apparent that he was lax and incompetent and would never have rated the post on another ship. Stone decided he had best live with this, though the mate's sneering superiority made relations difficult. Then Stone surprised Sprague one night in the act of buggering one of the Chinese crewmen. Such activities were not extraordinary on ships but were usually manifestations of long periods at sea. Clearly Sprague was a dry-land sodomist as well.

Before the end of the second week of their indenture

Stone and Tweed had come to loath the brutish captain and his repulsive mate. And the *Nahant* and the *Little American* were well on their way to the Indian islands and rugged coastline of northwest America.

Kamōʻi spat.

An attendant crawled to scrape up the spittle. The saliva, beard, nail-clippings—even the skin flakes of the king of Hawaiʻi island were sacred, pregnant with his immensely powerful *mana*. Thus they could not be left about for ordinary mortals to acquire. By possessing even the minutest scrap of Kamōʻiʹs person the lowliest commoner would own part of his noble soul. Even the kingʹs excrement was gathered into a wooden bowl studded with the teeth of his fallen enemies. All this waste was then disposed of in dark blue ocean by a special priest.

Kamōʻi did not even notice the spittoon-bearer groveling in cindery earth. His thoughts were far removed. News had been relayed down this Kona coast of a white manʹs ship in the channel off the north point of Hawaiʻi. These would be the first *haole*, foreigners, to visit in a long time. Perhaps he could expect guests very soon. The prospect was not entirely pleasing.

The massive monarch rested in a clearing on the volcanic slopes of Mauna Loa, gazing over the shimmering tableland of ocean far below. His lone companion was his prime minister, Kalani, an elderly man with white hair over a seamed and serious face. Kalani had been the guardian of Kamōʻiʹs childhood, his tutor in the arts of war and governing and the companion and confidant of his manhood. For almost forty years he had given every waking moment of his life to Kamōʻi.

"So...they come again," he said."You were right, my lord. The *haole* will never leave us alone."

"ʻ*Ae*," the king said in agreement.

He was now undisputed ruler of the five major districts of the island of Hawaiʻi. And he intended to deal with the kings of smaller neighboring islands until he defeated them or they had acknowledged his lordship. Within the island chain he had no doubt of his eventual success. But always dulling the foretaste of final victory was the specter of the *haole* with the power of their guns, iron and big ships.

Complications could only increase as more *haole* came.

He and Kalani had talked often and long about the ways in which Hawaiian life would change.

Once his old mentor had said:"The *mana* of the gods fades beyond our waters, sire. We cannot change this. What you must do is use that *mana* effectively here and now. Your greatness lies in the eyes and minds of our people. *Haole* opinions do not matter."

Kamō'ī's first thought, years ago, had been to reject the *haole*, even to the point of killing them—an action still urged by some of his chiefs. This had seemed the simple solution for the gifts they brought did not appear to justify the problems they introduced.

But harsh truth had prevailed. Clearly the *haole* were numberless and their retaliation to violence could only result in the deaths of many Hawaiians. From the moment when a few natives had traded fish for pieces of metal with Cook's men the islands had been irrevocably joined to a world of dizzying dimensions and strange new meanings. In this world kings of dazzling power ruled staggering numbers of people. In King George's village of London alone there were several hundred times more people than existed on Hawai'i island. Paris town was equally huge, as were the gathering places of Russians, Chinese, Spanish and many others. The English and French kings had scores of harbors floating big ships and many thousands of soldiers, each with a murderous musket. Whole armies with long knives rode on huge dogs, easily conquering kingdoms much bigger than the islands. Even America occupied land so large it defied imagining. All the larger island and seas of Hawai'i could be lost in one corner of its vastness.

From one visitor then another Kamō'ī had learned of the many marvels beyond the horizon: *haole* who looked alike spoke different languages, like the Beretanee-British and the Paniolo-Espanol. Their temples of carved stone reached to the sky. The grand palaces of kings were filled with treasures from the farthest corners of the earth. Other large houses held chambers filled with *haole* markings and colored pictures of people and places.

Haole people had clever contrivances to do their work for them, making clothing, tools and other useful things. The vapors of hot water could be employed to move ships. Certain kinds of earth were cooked to make a red liquid which became iron and copper when cooled. The milk of large animals was drunk and the fur of smaller white animals made into thick tough cloth. The revelations pile one upon the other and evidence of the great powers of *haole* increased with each visiting ship. There seemed no end to their miracles.

But the most vivid lesson had been taught by one of the first *haole*, a young lieutenant with Captain Cook. He had been trying to explain the size of Hawai'i in the world to Kamō'ī and other chiefs. He was not succeeding until he pointed to an outcrop of stone nearby.

"This will be America," he said. He then indicated a large bolder about twenty paces distant in the opposite direction.

"And that will be China."

He then dropped a few tiny pebbles and pointed at them.

"And these are your islands," he said with a smile.

In the scheme of a greater world Hawai'i was but a scatter of gravel.

The enormity was difficult to accept. A rumble of nervous laughter and disbelief had risen from the young man's audience. Kamō'ī realized then that few Hawaiians could conceive this meaning and its importance. They were interested only in *haole* blandishments of luxury and convenience, while the real problem was one of survival.

Closer now to Olowalu, many canoes came alongside the *Nahant*. Their hefty brown occupants appeared friendly, shouting to call attention to small cooked pigs, chickens and green drinking-coconuts. Ignoring this tumultuous floating bazaar, Quimby gave orders that swivel guns be set and manned and muskets be issued to white crewman. He had little trust in his thirty Chinese and their leader, Tan Sing, a thickset and frowning man who commanded his countrymen with curt phrases at appropriate moments. The captain permitted the Orientals to carry knives but was determined he would arm them only in imminently dangerous circumstances. Quimby had acquired the Cantonese from a fellow trader in Boston who said they were docile and easy to feed. He soon discovered that Oriental docility made him uneasy and that Asians ate as much as Methodists.

In the half light the natives´ faces were beaming with excitement and anticipation. They were burly buggers, Stone thought. Most were quite tall and a few downright fat. Several had bluish geometric tattoos like those of the ship´s Hawaiian, Kimi, who was for some reason not to be seen. Their canoes were beautifully carved of single logs, slim and graceful. The men handled the paddles and mat sails with easy skill. But their grins, Stone reminded himself, might be disguising devilish ideas.

"Keep your eyes on the people!" he directed the men along the rails.

"Aye!" Quimby shouted. "These are the dirty cut-throats who killed Cook! They swim like trout and will steal your eyes! See that all sides are protected, Mister Stone."

The bosun moved to follow orders as the brig slipped

into pale green shallows. Now many of the greeters became women, and young girls, wearing only waist wraps, laughing and trilling up at the sailors who understood not a word. White teeth flashed in their brown faces and black hair wisped over the dancing globes of their naked breasts. Stone could not help but compare these comely greeters with the odious bum-boat hags who welcomed ships in New York or Boston, offering themselves and raw whiskey for a few shillings. By dozens the Hawaiian women unwound their skirts, posed startlingly nude in the canoes, then dove into the water. Inland, beach sands brightened over the shallows. High above, beyond a small settlement of neat grass homes, a great cording of violet clouds rested on mountain tops.

The anchor clattered down to clumps of coral on a sandy bottom. Doggedly suspicious, Quimby ordered that guns remained manned until the friendly mood of the natives was firmly established. Canoes crowded closer but none of the Mauians made a move to board the ship. Most were shouting and holding up chickens, fish, yams and coconuts.

"Bring our *Kanaka*, so we can discover what these savages are saying," Quimby demanded.

Kimi had disappeared below and was now summoned, to a greeting of shouts and laughter. The little middle-aged man had draped himself in a bizarre costume for his debut before his people. He wore a threadbare claw-tailed coat with ocean-corroded epaulets. A large and molding beaver hat sat on his dark head and his high boots were several sizes too large. Beneath this accouterment he was his usual Hawaiian self, naked but for a breechcloth. He waved regally to the people on the water though he was by far the smallest of the lot.

On Quimby´s instructions Kimi made conversation with the Olowalu men, first informing the captain that all wished to be friends. Quimby´s reply was that any offensive move would mean Maui people would be killed.

Was this understood?

Kimi relayed this threat to responses of mock groans and headshaking. Everyone understood, he said. But there was nothing to fear. These people came in *aloha*: affection and warmth of spirit. They had no weapons, as one could see.

"No trade until their big chief arrives and proper bargains can be struck," Quimby specified.

When Kimi shouted this edict there were wails of disappointment from the canoes and grumbles when the message became known to *Nahant* crewman who had long anticipated fresh food and sweet water. But it was a wise decision, Stone thought. Indiscriminate barter now could only weaken the serious business of taking on major stores for the long journey ahead. Quimby had Kimi ask if anyone had seen a smaller ship in the past few days.

The answer was no. No other ships for a long time. Almost a year by local reckoning. The last one passed by far at sea. Perhaps her men were afraid, the canoe people said, because some bad islanders elsewhere had killed Captain Cook. They pronounced the name Kapena Kuk .

Quimby asked when their chief would visit his ship.

He was away, was the answer, gone to visit Pono, the Maui king.

Where was Pono?

Far over the mountains, an old man said. The king liked a place called Hāna for its beauty and woodlands and coolness. But their Olowalu chief was expected back the next day.

"We will wait for him," Quimby said."Until then no one is allowed aboard."

Would the captain not reconsider and permit women, at least, to come on the ship?

No, Quimby answered flatly. His porcine face dripped perspiration and his tiny eyes darted everywhere. They would wait for the chief and first settle the business of hogs, water and firewood. Within a few minutes he went below, ordering that he be summoned at the first hint of trouble.

But no trouble came. The afternoon spent itself in the covert consumption of food and fresh water and attempts at talk between the sailors and Mauians. Dozens of swimmers dotted the water, many of them children agog at seeing non-islanders and their huge ships for the first time. Stone puffed his pipe and stared over the scene. This was like a dream after the grim chill weeks beating down from northwest America. The crashing colors, happy voices and languorous air of this landfall were sweet indeed. And the people seemed a handsome and happy race, radiant in health and with an incredible ability as swimmers. But—he reminded himself of Cook—they were also killers, capable of volcanic changes of mood. All hands had best be on guard.

Twice during the afternoon, Quimby came above, his red-eyed stare reading the state of his men and his ship alike. Each time, after growling a few words at Sprague, he went back below.

The sun dropped and the *Nahant* rose and fell almost imperceptibly on light swells. Mountains inland became roseate in falling light. The smaller islands of Lanai and Kaho'olawe darkened across the miles of channel.

Two Chinese crewman were the first to spirit women aboard nearing dark. Then a few whites followed suit. Stone was about to go forward and run the females off when Sprague appeared from below decks.

"Bosun!"

"Aye, Mister Sprague," Stone found it an effort to show even token respect to this bastard.

"Cap'n's changed his mind. Now says only women aboard, and keep the number low." The mate went on:"None with any weapon. No men under no circumstances. And if one canoe so much as bumps the ship the whole lot goes back over the side. Clear?"

Stone nodded. He moved to find Kimi—not a difficult search. The diminutive Hawaiian was near the bow, lecturing a rapt audience in canoes about the wonders of the outer world. Chinese crewmen stared at girls from the rails nearby. The women were fascinated by the braided queues of the Asians, attempting to duplicate them with their own tresses.

Kimi relayed the good news to a chorus of excited response. Stone sauntered aft. Very soon it would be dark. Fiery light over the horizon had died to a faint glow.

The island Venuses and their voices were seductive. It was time now for him to partake of this banquet. He scanned the scattered canoes for a companion to his taste and saw her almost immediately, a lone girl in the bow of a dugout with what looked to be a much younger girl in the stern. Her smile was frankly inviting over a fetching torso with pouting breasts. He motioned to her to come. She tossed her head and without hesitation slipped into the water, leaving the other to paddle back.

In moments, he was lifting the glistening form over the rail. On the deck, dripping, she smiled up at him, her small mouth parted from her exertion, her wet hair clinging to dewed shoulders. A velvety child-woman, he realized, tender, firm and lithe. His senses stirred at the nearness of this nubile loveliness, her glowing skin shedding the sea.

She touched her breast and said, "Namo."

"Olohana," he replied, the first time he had ever used Kimi's name for himself—a Hawaiian approximation of his bosun's cry, "All Hands!"

Her tiny hand was buried in his as she padded beside him to his cabin.

Twice in the night Stone arose to make his rounds. The canoes were gone and all was quiet. Offshore breezes bore the scents of exposed reef and dying fires of the village.

Once Jake Maul spoke to him out of the zone of yellow lamplight on the stern:"Bloody waste of time holding guns on these people, Mister Stone. All they want is fishhooks and fucking."

But the watches remained alert. A half moon silvered cloud edges and the *Nahant* gently rode a rising tide into morning.

Stone stirred awake in Namo´s silken embrace, aware of her woman-scent and the dry warmth of her nakedness. The lightening dawn gave shape to objects in his tiny cabin. Namo sighed and smiled. Her hand traveled his side and her breath was warm on his breast. But now, sexually sated, his duties were more on his mind. Quimby would soon be on deck. He stroked her hair, talking softly in the halting Hawaiian he had learned in nighttime off-hours from Kimi.

"I must go...*Au*...*hele*..." He tapped his chest and pointed above.

"´*Ae*, Olohana."

In the growing light topside canoes were again surrounding the brig. Quimby soon emerged through the scuttle to cough and hawk phlegm over the side.

"Run these dirty sluts off," were his first words.

He allowed small trade and the crew breakfasted happily on melons and roast fish. Smoke strings rose from the grass houses behind the shoreline palms. Mountains were crisp against the lifting sun, giving promise of a warm day. The crowd on the beach was much larger than yesterday, Stone realized, probably containing people from neighboring villages that had received the news of the *Nahant*´s arrival.

"Pretty, ain´t it?" Sprague was at this elbow, round-shouldered and rodent-eyed.

"Aye," Except for ship´s business the two rarely

spoke.

"Got yerself a little bit last night, didn´t yer?"

"Piss off, Sprague."

"Better than spendin´ the night with them books, ain´t it?"

"Aye. And better than buggering the black boy, too."

The mate´s slack mouth tightened. He retreated into his rank.

"See to the moorings," he snapped.

Two hours later a large canoe set out from the beach. It obviously carried someone of importance from the way smaller craft hurried out of its path. Quimby ordered Sprague and Stone to stand with him as a reception committee, with Kimi to interpret.

An old man in white barkcloth was the first aboard. He lacked his front teeth and chanted in falsetto while waving long leaves.

A *kahuna*, Kimi explained, a priest, singing the glories of his master to stranger. He has no teeth because he had knocked them out in mourning for an important ruler. This was the custom.

The Olowalu overlord was a man of middle age with a dissolute face and a large paunch sagging over his breechcloth. He possessed all his teeth and bared them in a grin as the *kahuna* finished his strange song. Then he struggled up over the side, stepped forward, grasped Quimby´s shoulders and rubbed noses with the startled captain.

Hard put to conceal his disgust, Quimby collected himself and offered gifts: two knives, an axehead and several ropes of glass beads. The delighted chief reciprocated: over the rail came screeching piglets, protesting chickens, baskets of yams and silvery fish. There were also several small cooked carcasses Kimi identified as dogs.

"Berry tasty," he said.

Pleasant vowelings of the island tongue tumbled back

and forth as Kimi translated and Stone caught more than a few words now and then. The chief was offering all the good things of his lands and waters. His was a rich district with everything the *haole* might desire. The women of the area were famed for their beauty and skill in giving pleasure. He hoped, in turn, the strangers would be generous with things of foreign metals.

The avid desire of Pacific islanders for metal had been an obsession since Cook's time, Stone reflected. Tales were told of men being killed for a few nails or a chisel. In this primitive civilization of stone and wooden implements iron was magic, a precious and powerful property.

Quimby allowed that such exchanges were possible. He signalled to Blue Bob, the negro mess boy, who stepped forward nervously, rattling a tray of glasses and a bottle. The captain poured a generous portion of madeira for the chief, who tossed it off in one gulp. He puffed his cheeks and rolled his eyes, then held out his glass for more while speaking to Kimi.

This chief would find it desirable, Kimi translated, if the white noble would exchange gifts of six fishhooks or an axe or a knife for each large hog his people brought to the ship. Similar exchanges could be made for casks of water, bundles of firewood or measures to be agreed upon for salt, yams and *kalo* root.

"You thieving brown scum," Quimby muttered through a false smile. Prices had quadrupled since Cook's time. He told Blue Bob to refill the heathen's glass. There was no choice, he knew, but to submit to the extortion. In truth even the inflated prices were greatly to his advantage, considering the value received.

But habit forced him to haggle and he gained small adjustments with the dispensing of more wine. Soon rates of exchanges and delivery times were established. The women, it occurred to Stone, were in the nature of a bonus—free to spread their legs for the sport of it or strike their own bargains.

It was agreed that nighttime hours would be taboo—*kapu* in Hawaiian—for any business activity and thieves would be punished severely. Quimby knew the natives would literally strip his ship of metal, given the opportunity, and the *Nahant's* bottom-sheathing of copper was vital protection against the ravaging toredo worms of warms seas.

Negotiations appeared to be finished. Quimby made another gift of a small cask of wine to the chief but the latter seemed loath to leave.

"Ask if there is anything else he wants," Quimby told Kimi.

The chief pointed at a musket in the arms of the red-headed sailmaker, Scrimmage. It would be an honor, he said, to be presented with such a fine gun.

Quimby became grim. Arming a potential attacker was an unattractive prospect. Stone came to his rescue.

"Give the rascal one without powder or ball, captain. Fair chance he won't know the difference."

Quimby permitted himself a rare chuckle. He seized the musket from Scrimmage, strode to where one of the gift pigs was tethered, and shot the animal in the head. It twitched briefly and died.

The Mauians gasped, then laughed in approval. Quimby handed the weapon to the chief, who brandished it in display to his people in the canoes. He then explained exchange rates to the throng and warned that his agents would monitor all transactions. Nothing not freely given must be taken from the visitors, he said. It was not the stranger's custom to share their goods as islanders did. He pointed at Kimi, declaring that this brother in the humorous costume was spokesman for the captain and must be obeyed. Finally he lurched down into his canoe and made for shore.

Quimby growled orders: Sprague was to form a shore party with casks for water; Stone to have the decks cleared of the litter of mildewed blankets and clothing drying in the sun in order to make room for supplies. Sing and six of his Chinese were posted to make sure no *Kānaka* crept aboard or went diving near the ship. Delivery of hogs would be postponed for a few days. Butchery was messy business, needing plenty of hands and space.

Men heaved lines and the brig's two longboats slapped water. Within an hour canoes were alongside laden with salt, firewood and vegetables. Quimby clumped down from the quarterdeck to taste the coarse reddish crystals, inspect logs for dryness and poke the purplish lumps of *kalo* root. Dripping perspiration in the hot sunshine he soon sought the cool of his cabin. Cheerful now from their satisfactions of food and females, the men worked well. Holds were cleared and the arriving supplies arranged on the deck. Smudge fires were carefully nursed below decks to drive out dampness and the stench of rotted stores. Crewmen and Mauians alike filled the bright day with good-natured cries. Smoke rose from the holds to be whisked away on lazy tradewinds.

At the binnacle Stone surveyed the scene. Tan Sing leaned against the rail nearby, his powerful arms folded, his face impassive but for a glaring white scar across his nose. Alone among the Orientals he wore no queue—his hair was a close-cropped stubble. Stone was certain that he and his lot would vanish as soon as they were paid in China.

Blue Bob brought pork, fish and cold tea. Stone offered the tin dish to Sing, who shook his head, managing to convey thanks with the gesture. Stone was the only one of these foreign devils Sing deigned to be civil to, despite the fact that most his orders—many of them unpleasant—came from the bosun. He thought Stone a hard man but knew he was the only white aboard who would offer to share his plate. Quimby treated the Chinese as he would animals and Sing despised him with a cold passion. He could not know that Stone had early on decided to handle the Asians with respect and fairness. With a captain like Quimby, he reasoned, one never knew when one might need allies...

The black scullery-boy retreated a few feet and stared as the bosun bent to his food. Mr. Stone scolded him, and once had even cuffed him for laxity, but Bob didn't mind. He tried to make himself inconspicuous, hoping Stone wouldn't send him away. Blue Bob was fourteen years old and had no one to talk to.

Stone savored his pipe.

The Olowalu canoes were gone, their owners obeying the *kapu* on nighttime traffic. Lamplight over the side attracted a horde of small fishes, glistening like new silver coins thrown into the water. Other lights were more distant—the glows from village fires and a few torches of octopus fishermen wading shallows of the reef. Now and then a laugh bounced out from land. Most of the brig's men were taking their pleasure ashore. The few who brought their sweethearts to the ship entertained them quickly.

His had been a pleasant afternoon.

Namo had led him among the grass houses, past a pond where fish were raised and under stands of coconuts and plantains. Large-eyed children squealed excitement as they passed and plump women paused at their work to smile and say softly *"aloha."*

Out of the village they had walked shore to a gathering of palms on a little rise above the sea. Dying surf frothed on the black pebbles of a tiny beach. The only sounds were the muttering of the surf and sighs of coconut fronds. They spent the afternoon dining on love and wine, lazing the hours away and laughing at their clumsy attempts to converse. But the seeing, touching and sensing sufficed and soon their bodies trembled, lifted and fell as one in the lacy shade. She was a marvelous lover, without inhibition in an extraordinary innocence....

He drank the cool night air, listening to the soft slaps of water against the ship´s side, gazing at the liquid dance of light on the bay. In a short time this sweet softness would be a memory. No harm now to indulge one's senses; savor fancies of warm flesh on cool pebbles, the sighings of love, leaves and lagoons. This was such a brief caressing of comfort and ease and there were harsh days ahead.

His thoughts moved to Alec Tweed and the *Little American*.

Before departure from Boston the two men had run her down to Cape Cod and back to acquaint themselves with the vessel. She was an excellent little ship—exactly the kind they had idly talked about owning one day... The standard vague dream of ambitious seamen, he thought wryly. And now Tweed and the fine little schooner might be lost forever, victims of some vagary of wind or ocean.

He would miss his friend, should this sad state come to pass. There had been comfort in knowing the big Celt was at hand, ready to share any adventure, meet any problem or join any fight.

King Kamō´i had often pondered the fateful days to come and, in long talks with his old mentor Kalani, had thought carefully to several conclusions.

First, the *haole* would never go away.

But the remoteness that had kept Hawai'i so long a secret would remain an advantage. Only the venturesome trading captains would have reason to visit. In earlier years, when no ships came after Cook, it was thought that the *haole* feared Hawaiians. This, of course, was not so. The bravest warriors with spears, stone daggers and slingshots were like crawling infants against the strangers´ guns.

Second, Hawai'i´s size was in its favor.

Surely none of the great kings or American chiefs

would have designs on so small a place—or the need to conquer it. King George owned many lands, even islands, that he never bothered to visit. America had lands so vast it took months to walk across them. These spaces were inhabited only by lonely bands of red men.

And Hawai'i's wealth.

Clearly the *haole* had riches beyond belief. Hawai'i's wealth was in its lands and sea, scattered among island kings, then parceled out to their nobles and tenants. They could offer only pigs, water, salt and vegetables, along with compliant women. None of these could be seriously coveted by great rulers of the outside world. And this belief gained strength when no ships came for six years after Cook's death. When they did start to arrive all were traders in the animal skins bound for China, visiting in peace.

Nevertheless they brought serious threats to the three hundred thousand people of the islands.

The *haole* derided the Hawaiian pantheon of gods: Kū, of power; Kāne, of creation; Lono, of growth and Kāneloa, of the sea. They had but one god, Kesu Kisto, who represented all things.

And they scorned the sacred system of *kapu*, the ancient laws of social, ecological and religious behavior that kept Hawaiian life in order and balance. They flagrantly ate with women, took fish in forbidden seasons, killed useful trees and plants and burned temple images for firewood. They urinated in drinking streams, evacuated in stone salt-pans and committed other stupid and insulting acts. Worse, ordinary Hawaiian saw these sacrileges and could not fail to see that they went unpunished by the gods.

The changes came too fast. A scant few years ago a Hawaiian would spend weeks chipping a wedge of dense basalt to the sharp edge of an adze. Now he could casually trade a hog—or the services of his daughter—for a superior iron chisel. Medical *kahuna* once spent days in preparing herbs and praying a sick stomach back to normalcy. The *haole* accomplished this in minutes with a pinch of white powder.

The adjustments to be made, the things to learn in order to cope, were a staggering number.

Early on Kamōʻī had made decisions: the ancient ways of worship and rule had served and must not be abandoned. The *kapu* must be kept, and the gods feared and respected. The powder of the *aliʻi*, the rules and high chiefs, as earthly representatives of the gods, must remain unquestioned.

The separated island kingdoms were individually weak and vulnerable, their kings either stupidly scornful or foolishly ignorant of the new threats. They must be joined into one Hawaiʻi of strength and purpose, a single kingdom of power united under one man.

He would be that man.

Thus far he had been successful. His dominance on the island of Hawaiʻi was unquestioned. Five of its six kingdoms were now his, their former *aliʻi* either dead or totally subservient. Kaʻu, the sole remaining district, was poor and a remote area covering lava deserts to the south and posed no problem.

Now his goal was to control all trade and acquire guns, in order to effectively deal with both the *haole* and the neighbor-island kings with whom he must still make war. The ancient dynasties on Maui, Oʻahu and Kauaʻi were powerful and firmly ensconced. Their rule reached back into the mists of time. Their regality was absolute and their blood would not be easy to spill.

Kimi approached Stone on the dark deck. The little Hawaiian was attired only in his *malo*, breechcloth, but sported his ridiculous beaver hat.

"How you, Olohana?"

Stone asked if he was happy to be home.

"This Maui not home. My home, Hawaiʻi." He jerked

his head in the direction of southeast dark. "My king, Kamō´ī." He pronounced it Kah-mo-ee.

Was he an important king?

'*Ae*, yes, Kimi answered. Even before he, Kimi, had left three years before as a stowaway on another trader, Kamō´ī was important. Now the Maui people told him that Kamō´ī had defeated all other Hawai'i island chiefs to assume absolute power on the big island. No man excelled him in strength or courage, it was said. He also possessed great spiritual power, *mana*, and now commanded the *kapu moe*, the *kapu* demanding that all lesser people prostrate themselves in his presence.

"He berry berry big king," Kimi said solemnly.

Quimby labored up out of the scuttle, wearing only boots and a long-filthy nightshirt. His eyes were bloodshot and expression grim. Kimi hastened away.

"Everything in order?"

"Aye, sir. Quiet as an empty church."

"See it remains that way."

Stone eased to windward. The captain's stink was enough to make one's eyes water.

Quimby stared briefly into the dark then went back below.

Stone walked forward to check the watches.

At midship, Delano, the gunner, whined about drawing the duty. He was a thin, sallow man and a chronic complainer. Coldly Stone told him he had his choice of doing his turn or taking ten lashes for breakfast. This was not extraordinary punishment for shirking, nor did Delano fancy it. He fell silent, without malice, having tried and lost. Mr. Stone meant what he said.

The Chinese, long starved for rice, were cooking breadfruit as a substitute on a brazier near the forecastle. Pleasant aromas lifted from chunks of pork and fish grilling beside the plump vegetable. Tan Sing, squatting among his comrades by the rail, nodded curtly as the bosun passed.

Near the cat's head young Ben Raggs was preparing to climb down and take up watch in the longboat for the night. The thin lad greeted Stone with shy respect, his adam's apple bobbing. Stone admonished him to keep a sharp eye for swimming thieves. Raggs answered as he always did, "Yes, Mister Stone, sir."

"And mind you, Ben. No women down there," Stone joked.

Raggs' cheeks pinked. Could Mr. Stone possibly have known what happened to him that afternoon?

"Oh, no sir, no sir," he said.

Stone watched the boy lower himself into the tethered longboat. Raggs was a daily reminder of himself when he had gone to sea at sixteen, orphaned after the horror of the fire. Half a lifetime ago, with forty masters and no equals.

"Now hear me, Ben" he said. "These people might have the look of jolly savages, but in Captain Cook's time they were murderers. Remember that and stay sharp."

"Yes, Mister Stone, sir," piped Raggs. He tugged his cap.

Stone tapped his pipe empty on the rail as the boy settled in the boat's stern. Then he turned to finish his rounds. In a few minutes he was on his way to Quimby's cabin to make his final report of the day.

The lank bosun had to bend to enter the captain's cabin, its air befouled with the mingled odors of cigar smoke, spilled brandy and the rank person of Quimby himself—a man who spent his life upon waters he never willingly allowed to touch his flesh.

"All secure?" Quimby asked in his rasping voice.

"Aye, sir." Stone was a strong-stomached man but this collective stench made him slightly nauseated. The captain slouched at his table, his pig-white paunch abloom through a torn nightshirt.

"I heard shouts," he said. "Any trouble?"

"Bit of a punch-up among the Chinee. Sing took care of it."

"Ugly sod, that one. Anything else?"

"Nothing, captain. No sight." Stone knew Quimby was actually asking if there was any sighting of the *Little American*. He also knew the concern was fueled more by the possibility of losing the auxiliary vessel and its cargo of sea otter furs than any anxiety about its men, one of whom was his son, Tom.

Quimby drew his decanter over the scarred oak table.

"Then goodnight to you, Mr. Stone." There was not a hint of warmth in the words. His pudgy hands closed around the bottle and glass as the bosun shut the door.

Freed from the stink of the captain's cabin, the crisp night air was ambrosial refreshment to John Stone. First stars were glittering specks in a cloudless sky. The ship's planks squeaked with a sound he thought not unlike mutterings of contentment. Someone forward laughed, an uttering not heard in many a week at sea.

Nor was this strange. A tyrant for a captain, a homosexual bully for a mate, rancid water, cheese with the texture and taste of tallow and walrus meat like oak bark hardly made for a merry crew. Thank God for placing these islands where he did....

Jake Maul, a stout and florid man with pantaloons ragged at the knees, was loafing near the wheel. With him was Kimi, his dark skin at one with the night. Stone joined them.

"Ah, Mister Stone," Maul grinned, waving a small bone. "Fresh meat and sweet water are beautiful." Pork grease gleamed on his chin.

Kimi smiled at Stone and spoke in a mix of Hawaiian and English: If fat Maul ate so much pork, he remarked, he would be making sounds like a pig. Stone answered *'Ae* in assent, then asked Kimi in his hesitant Hawaiian if he planned to leave the ship.

Yes, the little man answered. On the big island of Hawai'i. If the *Nahant* did not go there to find the schooner he would use a canoe from Maui. He shook his head. Three years now with white sailors, he said. This was enough. Too much work and worry. Too little laughter among white men.

Perhaps he was right, Stone thought. Certainly laughter had been a stranger aboard his grim ship.

Maul glanced back and forth between the two, not comprehending the exchange.

"You understand this black bugger, Mister Stone?"

"Much of it," Stone said. He and Kimi had spent long hours on watches together. "We've had little to do but talk."

"Me no black bugger," Kimi poked Maul. "Me brown bugger."

After Stone left his quarters, Quimby tossed back his brandy and poured another.

He was annoyed by his discomfort with the bosun, whom he considered little more than one of the bodies aboard ship. Perhaps it was Stone's quiet competence that rankled, or his easy control of sullen and recalcitrant seaman when Quimby's wild rages and savage punishments created problems. The captain was too self-righteous a man to recognize envy.

In truth he cared not a whit for his men as humans. But as instruments for getting his ships and cargos to China he cared a great deal. Rarely had he smiled upon his own son, Tom, now aboard the *Little American*, which he hoped was nearby. He was not unduly worried about the smaller ship's whereabouts. In a voyage plagued by snarling seas, sullen skies and fitful winds his own progress had been unpredictable. Besides, Alec Tweed, like Stone, was an experienced and resourceful sailor. Baring calamity the Scot would bring the schooner to its rendezvous in the islands.

He downed his drink and permitted himself a night-cap. Then he lifted a Bible down from above his bunk. Quimby was hardly a dedicated Christian, though he labored at the pretense when among "civilized" people. Neither was he a man to overlook any promise to increase the odds in his favor. He finished his brandy, made himself comfortable in his odiferous bed and murmured a few pages aloud. In minutes, feeling tipsily virtuous, he drifted to sleep.

In low lamplight Scrimmage, the sailmaker; Delano, the gunner; and the wiry Filipino cook lolled amidships, talking quietly over weak tea and strong tobacco. Forward the Chinese held their own evening's reunion, chattering in a muted dissonance.

Blue Bob stumbled out of Sprague's cabin, having been summoned to his weekly buggering by that dedicated and vicious pederast. Little Bob was crying, but softly, so his shame and pain might be hidden from his shipmates.

On quarterdeck John Stone puffed his pipe and reflected on the time to come with Quimby. The prospect was far from pleasant but certainly irrevocable. Stone tended to believe that a man controlled his own destiny—with reasonable allowance for quirks of chance. Fate had led him to Quimby and would eventually part them. He would fill the intervening time by doing his job and seizing any opportunity for profit or pleasure that tumbled his way. The Sisters of Fate appeared to have determined his directions thus far and he had seen and suffered more than a few of the inconsistancies of man and nature. Perhaps at the end of this venture the Sisters would introduce him to a world without Quimbys, loneliness, dried beef, chill winds and bread alive with weevils. His and Alec Tweed's pay and bonuses might be enough to finance their own vessel. One successful voyage to China would more than pay for it.

Or, they could take the <u>Little American</u>.

It was not the first time the fancy had crossed his mind.

The idea was fascinating, the accomplishment would be easy: he and Tweed, with help from a few of the whites, Sing and the Chinese... a proper time and place...

The thought hinted at madness, of course. Someone could get killed in accomplishing the deed, and Quimby was the likeliest prospect.

They could never go home again... but he had nothing to go home to... They would be doomed to sail distant seas, trade where they could and live as men wanted for the rope. At this moment the British were combing the southern ocean for the sad rascals who had mutinied against Bligh on the *Bounty*.

Still the fantasy beckoned. There was allure in the picture of himself, in command, in freedom, soaring over the blue deep at the helm of the graceful schooner. There was an excellent chance that they would never be apprehended. The Pacific was staggering in size. In ten lifetimes one could never know its far reaches, its lagoons, its promises—or the variety of its women. They were near the middle of a new and unknown vastness of ten thousand islands and a dozen great coasts. There could be furs for China; pearlshell, tea and spices for Russia and Mexico; guns for island emperors and silks for their ladies; the gold of Peru, and the profits and pleasures of a hundred sun-soaked lands of Java and the Celebes. The *hoppos*, the merchant middle-men of Macao and Canton, never asked where a ship was from, who owned the cargo or how it was assigned.

In the ripening night the soprano notes of Delano's fife were a counterpoint to the lapping of waters against the ship's side and the plaint of its tightened shrouds. But the gunner soon ceased his melancholy serenade and joined his comrades in sleep below.

The *Nahant* was safe and sound in soothing waters,

the dreams of its crewmen reprising the day´s delights.

Dawn found the longboat gone, undoubtedly stolen for its metal fittings and nails. Ben Raggs had also disappeared.

Quimby leaped into a fury. He raged and shouted, cursing Stone and the laxity of his watches and commanding the remaining boat to be made ready. Stone, Kimi and eight armed men accompanied him to the beach.

He then led his party to the chief´s compound and shouted demands for an immediate audience. Chickens fluttered away and questioning faces appeared in the doorways of nearby dwellings. The portly chief appeared, rubbing his eyes and bewildered by the commotion. Several strapping men also materialized, a few holding clubs studded with sharks´ teeth. All stared at the ranting captain.

He berated the chief, his retainers and the entire thieving, whoring heathen *kanaka* nation. A quaking Kimi translated as fast as he could. Quimby nearly foamed at the mouth, roaring denunciations and demanding the return of his boat and crewmen. The chief expressed surprise and innocence, in that order. He would immediately dispatch men to discover what had become of the boat and the boy, he said, and the thieves would be severely punished.

Quimby demanded that he be given that pleasure. He became even more abusive, stepping forward and shaking his fist in the chiefís face.

"You, sir, are the head of these scoundrels! It is you I should hang by your fat neck."

"Easy, Captain," Stone urged. "This is how Cook died. There is danger here." He was not without concern for his own skin.

The reminder had effect. Quimby´s shouting subsided. It did not escape his notice that some of the natives

nearby had picked up stones and were talking ominously. He mopped his brow with a grimy kerchief, his hands
trembling.

"We will wait on the ship," he said—then to Kimi:
"Tell this villain he has until noon to return our boat and
the lad."

The warm camaraderie of the past few days had vanished. A muttering crowd of Mauians followed the
Nahant's men to the longboat but made no aggressive
moves, clearly aware of the pointed muskets. Stone
caught a glimpse of Namo among the throng. She
shrugged her shoulders, then smiled.

The whites got away from the beach without incident.
Back on the ship Quimby paced the quarterdeck, continuing his tirade. These miserable beggars would pay for
their treachery, he said. He sent all women off the brig
and personally assisted two over the side with his boot.
Several canoes were in attendance and he directed they
stand well off.

One native tarried, not comprehending, standing in
his dugout and grinning innocently up at the captain. The
madness that simmered below Quimby's rage flared out
of control. He snatched a pistol from Delano and took
careful aim. The Hawaiian's expression turned to terror
before the ball caught him in full in the breast and he
crumpled backward into the water.

Shocked cries arose from other canoes. Occupants in
the nearest vessel waited for the dead man to float within reach, then headed for shore, joined by the others.

Quimby calmly handed the pistol back to Delano. A
quiet descended on the brig, all hands staring at the captain as if waiting for his next move. Shouts from forward
shattered the silence. One of the Chinese had spied a
native boy who managed to remain unseen beneath
Nahant's bow. He was hauled aboard, dripping water
and shaking with fright. Obviously he had been diving
beneath the ship, prying loose its copper sheathing.

Quimby´s rage flamed anew. He ordered the youth to be brought aft and lashed to the mizzen mast. Stone recognized the culprit as one of the chief´s sons. Quimby seized a length of tarred and knotted rope from Jake Maul and began flogging the lad.

He put all his strength into the blows. Five lashes, ten, the fifteen descended and the boy´s head jerked up with each, screaming his agony. Thick blood inched down his buttocks and his back looked like torn liver. At eighteen strokes Quimby was breathless but his anger remained unsated. He stepped back and flung the blood-soaked rope aside.

"Now we will hang this thieving scum, for all his mates to take a lesson!"

"Jesus Christ, Captain!" Stone protested. "You´ve already killed one of these people. And they number fifty to every one of us!"

"Hold your tongue, bosun," Quimby snarled. "Scrimmage! Set a line!"

The sailmaker moved to obey. The young captive hung limp in his bonds, his breathing in tortured moans, his head lolling. Stone stepped between Quimby and the prisoner.

"This is a mistake, Captain. A bad move. For Christ´s sake don't do it."

"Out of my way, damn you."

"He is one of the chief´s sons, Captain. Killing him can mean big trouble." The boy stared at Stone through glazed eyes, not understanding.

Quimby scowled. "The chief´s son, eh?" He squinted at Stone, his thoughts churning, then turned to Sprague.

"Cut the devil down," he said. "And bind him securely."

The remaining morning hours moved like molasses. It was ominously quiet along the shore—canoes drawn upon the sand, only occasional movement among the palm groves. Nearing eleven o´clock a single canoe was seen rounding the eastern headland of the bay. Two men were paddling. As they neared the *Nahant* one stood and waved an oar, recognizable as belonging to the missing longboat.

Once alongside the canoe men were terrified, their stares magnetized on muskets aimed at their noses. Through Kimi´s interpreting one stammered that they were merely messengers for the Olowalu chief, lowly servants commanded to perform an errand. They had nothing to do with the crime...

"Get on with it," Quimby growled. "What do they want?"

The talking-man struggled up over the rail, carrying a bundle wrapped in brown barkcloth. His head lowered, he handed this to the captain.

Quimby peered into the lumpy package and his faced blanched. At his side Sprague mouthed a gargled curse. Stone stepped closer to look. The grisly contents were arm and leg bones and Ragg´s cap.

The messenger chattered frantically into the stunned silence that followed. Kimi translated his explanation that this deed was done by *kauwā*, men who were outcasts and criminals. They had burned the boat for its metal and the blaze attracted attention. Now the chief was holding them for execution, which he desired the captain to attend.

"Sweet Jesus. Did they eat the lad?" Scrimmage wondered aloud.

No, Kimi said, bristling. His people separated the flesh from the bones and buried it. The bones were often kept as tokens, relics. His people were not eaters of other men.

Quimby was pale, his jowls trembling. The canoe man addressed him rapidly, gesturing to himself and his companion.

"He asked if they get reward," Kimi said. "Maybe

knife."

Stone coldly answered, "Tell them they will have knives up their arseholes if they don't get off this ship."

The baleful stares of the crew supported his threat. The obsequious grin of the messenger disappeared. He scrambled over the gunwale and he and his mate paddled hard for shore. Quimby watched, chewing his lip. It was almost a full minute before he spoke: "So. They want a reward, do they? Well, by the Lord God Jehovah we will give them a reward. These butchers must not be allowed to go free with the murders of white men!"

Stone was tempted to observe that the score, tragically, was now even—one murder for each side.

"Sprague," Quimby said. "Take our *Kanaka* ashore and tell the chief we will resume trade this afternoon when we raise the blue peter. Any of our people still ashore?"

"Six, sir. The cook and five Chinamen."

"Find them and return them immediately. Take guns and waste no time, else you too may end up a sack of bones."

Sprague touched his cap and left.

"Stone. Have the larboard cannon below made ready."

"What is your plan, Captain?"

"A reward, bosun. A bloody fat reward."

"Captain. Satisfy yourself with the real criminals. The rest of these people are harmless."

"Do as I say, Stone, and no more impudence. Now, damn your eyes! This is not time for a bloody debate." He looked down at the bundle of bones at his feet.

"And no time for funerals, either." He picked up the grim package and hurled it over the side.

Ben Raggs found his grave in the clear jade waters he had fancied a sort of paradise.

The one o'clock bell sounded before Sprague and the

others returned. Quimby was at the ladder to meet him. The mate reported that the message to the chief had been delivered.

"He's all smiles and simperin' like a priest, cap'n. Got them killers trussed up like hogs. Says you can kill 'em personal if you like."

"Will he trade when we signal?"

"Aye, sir. He can hardly wait. They'll come when we raise the peter."

"In due time," Quimby said. "Guns below ready, Stone?"

"Aye, Captain." Stone had reluctantly followed orders, telling himself the captain could not seriously intend using force. Now, Quimby's face left no doubt. He *wanted* to kill. This son of a bitch was mad—and it was madness to contemplate any future with him.

"I'll have no part of this," he told Quimby.

"Damn you Stone. You *are* part of this!"

"For God's sake be practical, Captain. You can't slaughter hundreds in revenge for one man. And you'll be trading here again."

Quimby's red-flecked eyes bored at him. "I am ordering you," he said slowly, "to get behind those guns and do as you're told."

"No, I will not." To hell with this, thought Stone. I'm not his kind of killer.

"By God I'll have you on a rope in Boston for this."

"No you won't Captain. This is cold, vicious murder you plan, nothing else. Your Christian friends would have no sympathy."

"Be damned then. Sprague and I can hang you here."

"You'll have to do it alone, Captain. If that shit makes one move at me I'll kill him." Stone was aware that Kimi had moved to his side.

"You berry naughty man, Kapena Kimby," Kimi said. "Only two, mebbe t'ree *Kanaka* kill Raggo. Ev'yboby else good people."

"You too, eh?" snarled Quimby. "I'll have your black arse for this."

Sprague piped up. "The others will obey, Captain."

"You're damned right they will." Quimby continued to glare at Stone. "I warn you not to interfere—you or your monkey friend." He stalked aft, Sprague in his trail.

"You berry damn good man, Olohana," said Kimi.

"And you're much more man than I thought, Kimi," said Stone. "Best you get off this ship as soon as you can."

"*'Ae*, him too, I t'ink." The young Hawaiian who had been flogged lay bound in the scuppers, watching through pain-fogged eye.

"Give him water," said Stone. "And fetch Blue Bob with some lard for his back."

Well over a hundred canoes set out from shore when the blue and white pennant ran skyward at Olowalu.

Stone and Kimi watched their approach from atop the *Nahant*'s midship hatch. A few yards away Jake Maul trained a musket on the two by order of Quimby. Jake did not like the assignment but his terror of the captain overcame his fear, mingled with respect, for John Stone. At least the bosun was sane.

Quimby paced the quarterdeck, his triangular hat jutting over a dark scowl, watching the canoes. Sprague was in command below, where the brig's five port cannon had been made ready behind closed ports. On the main deck Delano and Scrimmage manned swivel guns fore and aft. The rest of the crew were strung along the rail, muskets at their feet, staring at the approaching vessels. Sing and his Chinese had also been issued weapons. The canoes came closer.

Lacking Kimi's voice Quimby was forced to converse with hand and arm signals. Shouting and waving he indicated that no one would be allowed on the outboard side of the ship. This was *kapu* and he repeatedly shouted the word, one of the few he knew. When the Mauians understood, they obeyed like aquatic sheep, bumping their canoes into a ragged flock. Only a few faces, displayed puzzlement. About a dozen women and children slipped into the water and splashed about.

Stone watched in growing dread, a chill creeping over his back. An inner rolling of anger and disgust became too much. He started to move to the rail and shout a warning.

"Belay, Mister Stone!" Maul cried. "I have no choice!" His musket was aimed at Stone's head.

The bosun stopped. His gaze went to the captain, who was totally absorbed in the canoe fleet. Quimby stood with a humorless smile on his stubbed face, his eyes shining. The tableau on the water was now exactly how he wanted it.

His arm went up, its hand in a fist. Men along the rail picked up their weapons; others bent over the swivel guns, training the blunderbusses on the visitors. Scrimmage shouted down a skylight and clapping sounds came as the ports snapped open. Nearer natives on the water went silent, many faces showing bewilderment. The eyes of some widened in fear. Several started frantically to paddle away, but this was impossible in the log-jam of the flotilla.

"NOW!" Quimby roared. His hand dropped.

Furious erratic fire exploded: the swivel guns hurling rounds, muskets crackling along the rails. Then, beneath their feet, the five cannon boomed almost simultaneously, their thumping recoil making the brig shudder. Rolling blossoms of smoke bellied out, obscuring the view for moments. A breeze slowly lifted this curtain on a scene of appalling carnage.

Then cannon fire had torn into an almost solid wall of humanity, smashing canoes into splinters and tearing their occupants into pieces. The jagged metal-scrap fill of the swivel gun cartridges had ripped head and limbs from their owners. Terrible cries of agony tore the air.

Women screamed and children wailed. Dozens of the wounded were trying to swim, crying piteously. Other survivors thrashed about in the water, in shock and dazed, not knowing which way to turn. Scores of natives had been killed, many others dying and drowning.

John Stone stared. The abomination had taken less than a minute. At his side, Kimi had fallen to his knees, his hands covering his face. The astringent tang of gunsmoke hung in the air. Suddenly this green and gold world had gone gray.

A babble of Cantonese arose from the Orientals. Quimby was shouting orders. There were clumping sounds as the cannon were withdrawn and their ports slammed shut. Sprague hurried from below to join Quimby. In moments Sing was at the capstan with several of his men, raising the anchor. Sprague shrieked for the steering sails to be hoisted and soon the brig was bearing off.

Behind the lumbering ship a few heads bobbed in water stained with blood. Surviving canoes had pulled away, their terrified occupants huddled down and staring at the horrible flotsam on the bay. The screams had stopped. Now there were only the raking sobs of grief and moans of the dying. And the piteous sounds faded as the *Nahant* gained distance, her canvas blooming in the gentle wind.

Kimi hugged his knees and wept. The Hawaiian boy in the scuppers stared at Stone. The bosun looked about. He drew his knife and stepped to the captive, who watched with frightened eyes. With two quick slashes, Stone cut his bonds then signalled with his thumb. The prisoner eased himself painfully over the side and into the water.

Stone walked aft. Any reservations he'd had about Quimby now disappeared. There was not doubt he was at sea with a madman. God only knew what the rest of the voyage might bring. This daft son of a bitch could get them all killed... The captain's gravelly voice cut into his thoughts: "Bosun! Get up here!"

Stone climbed the few steps to the quarterdeck. Quimby faced him, his flushed face beaded with perspiration and pistol hanging from one fist. Scrimmage was at the wheel behind him, his expression woeful under thick red hair. Sprague stood by the binnacle, his loose mouth wet and eyes narrowed. Quimby spoke deliberately, his words cold and clipped: "There are two choices for you, Mister Stone. Take the wheel and resume your duties with no more lip or go into irons." His pistol lifted to the level of Stone's stomach.

"You will rot in Hell for what you have done here, Captain."

"And you will rot in the bilge for one more impertinence."

Be damned, thought Stone. He would not be buried alive for the sake of an argument he couldn't win with this animal. Nor would he give him another excuse for his insane masthead-justice. On deck and in freedom Stone could further plans for his own future...

Returning Quimby's glare he moved to the wheel. Scrimmage released it with a respectful nod. "South-southeast Mister Stone."

Sprague cackled a laugh.

In a lavender dusk the *Nahant* plowed the choppy channel between Maui and the big island of Hawai'i. All night the brig tacked on brisk trades off her port, making distance sluggishly. At dawn the wind went down in the lee of Hawai'i's northern mountains. With early light tall rounded ranges were seen over dark scabs of ancient lava flows snaking to the shores. With the sun's rise winds over the Kawaihae saddlelands pushed the ship steadily southward. By midafternoon the indigo bulk of Hualālai volcano was being passed beneath the higher, snow-capped heights of Mauna Kea, White Mountain.

Two days after the massacre at Olowalu the *Nahant* was riding gently over the island shelf on the Kona coast off Kealakekua Bay.

PART II

King Kamō'ī paused with his court on the trail overlooking the mushroom-shaped inner bay at Kealakekua. Theirs had been a long march down from the flanks of Mauna Loa, Long Mountain, and everyone was weary. But fatigue had vanished with the sighting of the haole ship resting below. The Nahant lay anchor about a quarter-mile distant. Her undressed spars were sharp against sun-dappled water and she was surrounded by many canoes.

Sunlight crashed on the brilliant gold-and-red feather capes and crested helmets of the highest nobles, those called *ali'i*. Polished spears of Kamō'ī's warrior-guard glinted in the background. The tinted, rectilinear designs of the women's bark-cloth skirts accented their abundant figures and splendid brown breasts. The men were massively proportioned, as were most *ali'i*. Kamō'ī was the tallest of all, half a head above the others, at nearly seven feet.

Only two other nobles held the rank to stand at his side.

One was the elder, Kalani, his prime minister and lifetime companion.

The other was Manu, surviving son of the former king

of the Kona area and Kamō'ī's cousin. At thirty-six he
was a few years younger than Kamō'ī, a strikingly handsome man with features almost European in sharpness
and a classically muscular body. Manu's dark eyes were
without warmth and his every move bespoke arrogance.
He hated the *haole* and stared down at the *Nahant* with
naked distaste.

Kamō'ī called for his "Long Eye." Kai, the tattooed
young giant who commanded Kamō'ī's personal guard,
brought it to him. The brass telescope had been presented to Manu's father by Captain Cook, some ten years
before. Kamō'ī had accompanied the late king to *HMS
Resolution* that day, awestruck as his fellows by the *haole*
magic of ships, guns, tools and cloths. Now he owned not
only his "Long Eye" but the old man's kingdom.

He trained the instrument on the *Nahant*.

Most white *haole* looked alike with their skin fish-belly
color and curious costumes with holes for holding the
hands and carrying things.

This ship did not appear as rich as others, with patches on its sails and discolorations along its sides. But it
would have what Kamō'ī desired most of all—guns.
Guns to make him the supreme ruler of *Hawai'i-nei*,
beloved Hawai'i; guns to balance the strength between
the *haole* and his own people.

"Lako is chief here?" he asked.

"Yes, my lord," Kalani answered. "He is coming to
you now."

The king peered again through the "Long Eye." This
ship also carried many China-*haole* he realized, identifiable by their odd ropings of hair. And there were two
darker men who might be Hawaiians. Or perhaps they
were *popolo*, black ones. There were many kinds of colors
of *haole*. More men would be below, behind the blunt
muzzles of the red mouthed guns poking out of square
holes in the ship's side. And beyond this bay, over vast
stretches of ocean, were infinite number more *haole*.

Kamōʻī had never forgotten the lesson of Cook's young officer and his handful of pebbles.

Lako, high chief of the Kealakekua environs, was brought before Kamōʻī. Lako fell awkwardly, being a corpulent man, to all fours. His head touched the earth as he intoned Kamōʻī's name and professed abject humility in his presence.

The king did not like Lako and recent reports did nothing to alter his feelings.

"This you will do." He spoke precisely. "Represent me before this new *haole*. Discover if his intentions are peaceful, what he desires and how long he will remain. Today let your men do small trade and your women what they will. Tomorrow we will be serious."

"As you command, my *aliʻi*."

"My noble Kalani will decide what prices to pay for their goods. Tell this new captain I think of him as a brother and offer all our blessings of earth and ocean. Do not drink his dark water—for it will steal your wit and snarl your tongue. Stand straight before him and be proud. Return tomorrow at sunset with your report. Remember I have many eyes. Shame or betray me and you will be dead at night time. Now you may go."

Lako waddled away backwards. Kamōʻī stared again at the *Nahant* through the telescope. The brig was surrounded by canoes. He wondered if white women copulated like dogs in heat for baubles of glass and bits of cloth. Perhaps white women were frightfully ugly or extremely unpleasant—the reasons their men did not take them on ships. Or perhaps there was a *kapu* on women aboard vessels. From the talk of previous sailors he had come to believe that *haole wahine* were thin and bony with long necks and small dry breasts. Someday one would come and he would mount her to see what they were like.

Staring again, Kamōʻī now noted that this captain had not yet allowed Hawaiians aboard, indicating he was sus-

picious, cautious. Or it might mean he was waiting for a
chief to arrive whom he could then hold hostage as a
guarantee of peaceful relations. Other captains had done
this. Lako would serve the need admirably should it rise,
being a chief of minor importance. Kamōʻī had not seen
Lako since he had visited this bay with old King Opu to
greet Captain Cook. At that time he had instructed Lako
to take a woman that he, Kamōʻī, had impregnated and
care for her as his wife.

Now the captain relaxed watches on the swivel guns
and the ports on the larger red-mouthed guns closed.

A good sign. Perhaps because surrounding greeters
had no spears or daggers. He would not know they carried slings and stones which they could use with deadly
accuracy. But this was unlikely unless they were pro-
voked to extraordinary anger. The danger was minimal.
Kealakekua people knew Kamōʻī's command that all
ships be welcomed with *aloha* and honest trade.

The king noticed one important inconsistency in the
behavior of these *haole*—they did not appear overly excited by the presence of women. This could only mean they
had paused elsewhere recently. It could not have been on
this island or he would have been informed. If another,
fishermen would soon bring news.

He handed the glass to Kai. The huge guard-captain
was always at his side. Alone among commoners, Kai
experienced physical contact with the king when they
boxed, wrestled or dueled with daggers in daily exercise.
Also nearby was Kamōʻī's rheumy old high priest Pāhoa.
He leaned on a stick, near-senile and confused, his white
cloak snowy in the sunshine.

Kamōʻī rubbed his eyes, irritated by the brightness of
the scene. Kai barked an order and a servant scurried forward with water. The man moved crablike, crouching
and studiously avoiding the king's shadow. The penalty
could be death for polluting Kamōʻī's image with his
own.

Queen Kahu took the small calabash from the attendant. Smiling she dipped a piece of soft *kapa*, barkcloth, and applied its refreshment to the king's brow and eyes. Her touch was loving and the moisture soothing. Three other wives stood near but none moved. All knew their place. Compared to Kahu they were merely conveniences. Second in rank only to Keōpū, his sacred wife, Kahu was first in Kamō'ī's heart. Scarcely a day passed that she did not pique him to annoyance with her irreverence, amuse him with mischief or seduce him with sensuality. They had ceremoniously mated under a wedding mantle six years ago when she was fourteen and he still found her enormously exciting. Only hours ago, while resting in a shelter on the trail, she had teased him to a stony erection and mounted him to a shattering climax. Kahu was mercurial, perverse and disobedient, a woman of shrewd intelligence and large appetites. And very beautiful in classic island style: six feet tall, with a generous wide mouth, luminous dark eyes and a majestic form flowing to remarkably small hands and feet. A slim coronet of delicate golden feathers crowned her black hair and a carved whale-tooth, denoting royal status, rested in the velvet vale of her naked breasts. Kamō'ī's people mirrored his love for Kahu. Wherever she appeared there were delighted smiles and protestations of genuine adulation and pleasure.

"The chief's house is being made ready for you, *ali'i*," said Kalani.

"We will rest here and go down in cool of day."

"'*Ae*, my lord.

Kai shouted orders. His ring of soldiers relaxed their stiffness and moved for better view of the ship. Servants raced about arranging *kapa*-cloth to shade *ali'i*, laying mats and bringing food.

Kamō'ī, Kalani and Manu sat upon the ground for the meal. The women, observing the *kapu* against dining with men, clustered apart. They passed "Long Eye" back and forth with laughing talk about happenings on the ship. *W āhine* were now being allowed aboard and this produced raffish conjectures from Kahu and her lustier sisters. When the wind shifted faint sounds of merriment and happy cries were wafted from the distance.

"This man Lako is weak, sire," said Manu. "I should represent you before this *haole*."

"He is strong enough to talk and I have given him the words." Kamō'ī dipped a thick finger in the *poi* and twirled it to his mouth. He caught Manu's scowl of disappointment. The prince was arrogant and insulting with *haole*, not the man to do his business. Besides, one did not dispatch high *ali'i* on minor errands—or to be taken as hostages.

The prime minister, Kalani, watched the two, his dark grooved face alert. Manu was his sister's son but this attachment did not extend to affection. He wished Manu would temper his speech and behavior. It had been almost ten years since Manu's father, King Opu, had scorned his son to give Kamō'ī the Kū-stone, symbol of power in war and peace. The dying monarch had been wise, Kalani knew. Kamō'ī, his nephew, was the only one with the will, wisdom and bravery to perpetuate his kingdom.

At first Manu's resentment of his cousin had smoldered long, sometimes flaring to the surface. But this was when he was hardly more than a boy with the unchecked emotions of youth. In later years he had quieted considerably, giving his soldiers and lands to Kamō'ī's use and performing valiantly in battle. Only now and then were there hintings of dissidence, a few sour words of disagreement, particularly where dealing with the *haole* were involved. This was not good, Kalani felt. An important *ali'i* who sat in highest councils must be utterly supportive of his king, willing to adapt to the changing ways. Perhaps in days to come it would be wise to keep a sharper eye on Manu.

The monarch made no response. He did not need reminding of the importance of guns to his future. They were vital, the means by which he would gain his power and accomplish his goal. It did little good to reason with the *haole*—and no good to hate them. They were an inevitability, as certain as the moon changing or sun rising. Manu´s loathing of the strangers disturbed him. There would be enough trouble ahead and such attitudes could only lead to unnecessary and annoying complications.

The following day found Kamō´ī resting on pliant leaf-mats in the courtyard of Lako´s compound at Kealakekua. Kahu lay on his left, her attentive head propped on one hand. Attendants surrounding them in late afternoon shadows held the regal *kahili* aloft. These were tall polls topped by luxurious and colorful arrangements of feathers, emblems of the king´s exalted rank.

Kalani squatted at the king´s right hand. As was his custom, Kamō´ī was granting audience to commoners of the district, listening to discussion and complaints about land, fishing and water rights. The petitioners were subdued and spoke obliquely in his cowering presence. Kamō´ī was aware that none spoke of their chief Lako´s wisdom or compassion in governing.

Lako´s woman, the chiefess Līlīnoe, entered the royal presence on her hands and knees. Kalani spoke softly into his master´s ear and the king nodded.

"Rise that I may see you," he said with a slight smile.

She stood, a plump and pretty woman in her late twenties. For an instant her gaze met his then dropped to her feet. He had changed little, she thought, a huge man exuding great *mana*, with eyes that traveled into one´s soul.

"Yes," said Kamō´ī. "I remember you." In truth he had only vague recollection of their few nights together many years ago. If memory served she had been quite satisfactory—a virgin, fresh from the instructions of a woman who taught the many delights of lovemaking.

At his side Kahu examined Līlīnoe with casual interest. Kamōʻī had taken scores of *wāhine* so there was no cause for jealousy. One might as well demand that he eat only a certain kind of fish. Unfortunately Kamōʻī did not reciprocate this generous view, for she too enjoyed a bit of variety from time to time and he resented her easy ways.

"My *aloha* to you," Kamōʻī said. "Do you have trouble?"

"In my heart, sire." Līlīnoe spoke just above a whisper.

"Then speak your heart, woman. We who have made a son are not strangers.

"Mine are the words of a proud mother, my *aliʻi*, but I beg you to believe them. This boy of our making is not ordinary. He lives with dignity among the men and they have respect for him. He is brave and strong with a quick mind." L l noe hesitated. What she was about to ask was most presumptuous. "I have prayed to the gods that he might one day attend you, no matter how humbly."

Kahu glanced sharply at their master. She had never heard such a request. The spawn of Kamōʻī's casual affairs were dispersed over the conquered kingdoms, mostly in ignorance of their royal fatherhood. Their mothers were cared for but there were no ties and petitions like this were never made. The king had entirely forgotten about this child until Kalani placed a reminder in his ear moments ago.

Kamōʻī's first thought was to deny Līlīnoe peremptorily. But something in the urgency of her plea touched him. One must admire a woman who defies rules so courageously on behalf of her child. Additionally, she was a fine looking *wahine* and he was curious. Neither Kēopū-of-Heaven nor Kahu nor any of his other highborn wives had yet given him a son. He would like to see what his son looked like.

"Does he know I am his true father?"

"No, my lord."

"That is best," the king said. "Have you talked of this with your husband?"

"I talk of nothing with Lako, sire." A hint of scorn crept into Lilinoe's tone. "But he would not dare to object."

Kamōʻī nodded. He wondered if *anyone* in the Kona district had respect or affection for this chief...

"We shall see," he said. "Tonight send the boy to the feasting."

Lilinoe's heart leaped.

"How will I know him?" the king asked.

"It will be like seeing yourself when young, my *aliʻi*. And his name is Puna."

Kamōʻī smiled. "Do you have other needs?"

"Beyond this I will never have need, sire."

"Go then and peace be with you."

Kahu watched the woman bow away. How blessed, she thought, to have a son of Kamōʻī's. And this Lilinoe was a *wāhine* of great courage. Very few women challenged the age-old order of things. She often felt she stood along in questioning the *kapu* governing the conduct of females. She saw no valid reason why they were forbidden to eat plantain, pork, certain fish and other desirable foods. The isolation of woman during their monthly bleeding periods also seemed unnecessary. The *kapu* against dining with men annoyed her most. The origin of these prohibitions was lost in time. Priests, when pressed for reasons, could only reply that these were ancient laws, the will of the gods. One day she would openly challenge one of these unreasonable *kapu*, Kahu reflected. She was strong enough and of high enough status to survive an impudent and dangerous act—and it was the only means by which noble women might find a way to more freedom and power.

The prime minister, Kalani, resumed other business, hitching himself closer to the king. He was the only person in the kingdom who did not strictly observe the prostration *kapu*. After nearly forty years of dedication Kamōʻī did not require such gestures from his beloved mentor.

In a few days, Kalani reported, the *Nahant* would have almost a third of the supplies needed. This information came from Kimi and other spies working the fringes of activity around the vessel.

Kamōʻī listened intently to details of the trading. His plan was to see that the *Nahant* was supplied to a point, then hold back on provisions and raise the subject of firearms in barter. The ploy had worked well on other captains.

"This man Kimi," Kalani remarked. "He does good trade for himself, stealing from his master."

"*Auwe*, alas," said Kamōʻī. "He has been too long among the *haole*. What have you discovered about the others?"

"The captain is a loathsome creature. He cares poorly for his men and treats them like dogs. Several times daily he inquires about a smaller ship which was to meet him here. He often reads in the Kesu Kisto Bible-book but does not practice the *aloha* it teaches. He drinks too much, never washes his person and smells horribly."

The king grimaced. Like most Hawaiians he often bathed two or three times daily. Kalani continued: "His number-two man is a *mahu* who prefers boys. He enjoys giving pain, is not the gentle kind. The others fear and hate him."

Kamōʻī shook his head. The *mahu* among Hawaiians passed their days in telling stories, making poems, contriving *hula* and talking with *wāhine*. They never troubled anyone who did not desire their company and were left alone. In his youth Kamōʻī had once permitted a *mahu* to perform on him. The experience was not unpleasant but he much preferred women.

Kalani talked on, "The officer called Olohana is a hard and resolute man but is known to be fair in dealings. Men on the ship seek hiding places when he is angry and it is said he killed a man in a fight. He reads books and makes writing. He despises the captain and the *mahu* and asks many questions about our island and people. He knows a great deal about the use of guns and sailing of big ships."

Kamō'ī nodded and, after a moment, asked, "And the others?"

"There is one China-man who commands his countryman because no others know their tongue. The rest are common men, *ali'i*, who do no thinking or acting without instruction."

"Is the feast ready?" Kamō'ī asked.

Kalani gestured at a nearby attendant. The man reported eagerly, almost babbling with the honor of addressing the monarch. No finer *'aha'aina* could be prepared, he said. Fisherman had brought fat tuna from deep waters and farmers mounds of succulent yams, *kalo* and breadfruit. Plump young pigs, tender dogs and chickens were being readied. The finest dancers and musicians had been assembled from miles around...

The king waived the man silent...

"Now," said Kalani. "What of the guns, sire?" Kamō'ī shrugged. He had not yet decided when to talk of guns with his captain. Best he meet him first and determine his mood.

Queen Kahu spoke with a smile, "Perhaps tonight at the *'aha'aina*, my lord. When the *haole* drink their red water they become more agreeable and generous."

Kamō'ī smiled back. In truth his thoughts had wandered a bit. He had found Kalani's remarks about Olohana to be interesting. Tonight he intended to take a hard look at this man.

While the *Nahant* lay in Kealakekua Bay the *Little American* rode low swells on the water off Kapālehu, some thirty miles to the north.

Alec Tweed, with Tom Quimby and their ten Chinese, had eased the seventy-foot schooner onto green shallows in the rising sunlight. About a dozen canoes came off the small village and pork and drinking coconuts were passed up in exchange for fishhooks and chisels. All hands fell upon the fresh food ravenously.

Curiously none of the natives made a move to come aboard.

Tweed thought this peculiar. Perhaps the tales of wildly enthusiastic greetings from the *Kanaka* were not entirely true. These people were smiling and cheerful enough but subdued. He was puzzled.

Not a man aboard spoke the local tongue so communication was limited to sign language. Tweed posted men on the ship's brace of six-pound cannon and others held muskets at the ready. He cautioned all hands to exercise great care and not fire except on his order.

"Queer," he said to young Tom. Tweed was a tall and heavy man with sandy hair and beard and weather-scarred complexion. "They're pleasant enough but seem verra cautious." His voice, with its burr of Scottish homeland, was soft, in contrast to his muscular bulk.

Smoke curled up from cooking fires among the palms ashore. The trim little ship lifted lazily on long rollers. More canoes came out from the beach.

"Perhaps they ain't seen Christians afore," said Tom Quimby. A pocked-faced youth of seventeen, he was trying to disguise his apprehension.

"Aye, Tom. You could be right. But 'tis queer, queer..." Tweed shrugged. "Ah, well. We'll lay in here a wee while then see if we can find your bloody fayther."

Despite the restrained greeting Tweed felt relief. Having sweet coconut juice and roast pork in his belly helped hugely and this was a bonnie bay. Settled in its sheltered calm he could turn his attention to mending the rudder blade fractured by a floating log over a week before. The chore cold not take long in this gin-clear water over a shallow bottom. Meanwhile he would rig a sail on the ship's boat and search the nearby coast for the *Nahant*.

He made hand motions trying to ascertain if the natives had seen another ship. They only stared and smiled vacantly. A half hour passed. He relieved four men of their muskets for tasks of securing the vessel. The sun climbed, brightening dark lava slopes of distant uplands. A large mountain soared high, its outline sharp above a hazy collar of clouds.

"Hualālai," the canoe people said. *"Nui nui."* They were saying its name, Tweed reckoned, and that it was big, big. Men in the canoes were fascinated by the Chinese and their queues. Men on the schooner were equally entranced by three women who paddled out, as naked as new babies and smiling with bright teeth. Two were in one dugout, both thirtyish, in full bloom with overripe breasts. The third was considerably younger, alone in a small canoe among the others. She was a trim beauty with much darker skin than her sisters. Like rich chocolate, Tweed thought. He would be nibbling this delight by teatime he promised himself.

Within the hour a large canoe set out from shore. Smaller craft were paddled hurriedly out of its path.

"This should be Himself," Tweed said. He and Tom donned jackets for the occasion, the cloaks also hiding pistols tucked in their belts. They stood together as the big craft filled with men came alongside. The chief, a stout grinning fellow wearing a brief cape of yellow feathers, stood amidship.

He was preceded by an emaciated elder in white bark-cloth waving leaves and chanting eerily. For or five of the natives then hoisted their porcine master aboard. There was a moment when Tweed feared they might lose him

in the drink, but the chief managed to claw his way over
the side gasping, grunting and grinning up at the whites.
A dozen gargantuan attendants climbed up to join them.

Tweed suddenly found the immediate deck space
quite crowded. But his guests seemed in jovial humor. He
listened, nodding amiably, while the old priest finished
his wailing.

"He must be their vicar," he remarked to Tom.

The chief stepped forward, his arms lifted. Both
Tweed and Tom recoiled but the man only wished to rub
noses with Tweed. When he stepped back he threw his
arms wide and shouted.

One of the Chinese screamed a warning but it was too
late. The big natives, fanned out around them, were
attacking like furious cats.

Tweed heard Tom cry out "Oh my God!" and saw him
go down from a dagger thrust deep in his chest. He himself was locked in a struggle with one of the giants. The
screeching Chinese were under attack from others. More
men from other canoes were clambering aboard with
daggers and clubs. A soft tropic morning had suddenly
turned incredibly horrible.

Tweed was a powerful man and champion of many a
vicious dock brawl. But he knew in this woeful moment
that his companions were dying and he soon would be
too without a miracle. The arms of his assailant were
thick like masts, surrounding and crushing him. Tweed
summoned his energy to force the Hawaiian away then
jerked a knee into his captor's groin. The attacker grunted and relaxed his hold for an instant. Tweed tried to
draw his pistol but found it knocked from his fingers. The
huge native had bullied him to the ship's side when
Tweed, clutching at his opponents slippery nakedness,
stumbled and lost balance.

Instantly he was in the water with a cool green haze
enveloping him. Coughing brine he fought to the surface
a few yards from the schooner. There was a sharp blow

on his shoulder. A spear thrown from a nearby canoe had grazed him.

A poor swimmer, he thrashed desperately, fighting panic and grasping for breath. For the moment he was beyond reach of the murderers on the ship but several canoes were fast bearing down on him.

He felt helpless in the water, his flailing limbs like lead. A canoe neared, the man in its bow waving a large club. Tweed reached for the outrigger boom and yanked with all his might. The man toppled backward into the water.

Dear God, thought Tweed. I might have a chance. He heard someone laugh, a strange sound in these circumstances. With great effort he hauled himself aboard the canoe.

A girl sat tensed in its stern—the dark young beauty of the earlier trio. Her eyes were round with fright and she held a paddle upraised in protection. She started to rise as if to strike him and he lunged tearing the paddle away. She cowed back, hands up as if to ward off a blow. Tweed jerked his thumb at the water. She comprehended and immediately slid over the side, her cocoa-colored form shivering in the wash. He caught a view of the schooner. Hawaiians were standing on its deck waving their arms joyously over the crumpled bodies of Tom Quimby and the Chinese.

Tweed fell to his knees and started paddling furiously for shore. What he would do when and if he got there did not enter his mind. His only thought was to escape and buy a few more precious minutes of life. His shoulder throbbed with pain and he gulped for breath but he sent every shred of his strength into paddling.

Within a dozen strokes he knew the efforts were hopeless. Pursuing canoes, each with three or four men, easily gained on him. There was a bump when the first overtook his and he turned his paddle to fight the huge brown assassins.

Somehow he beat two into the water before he was overwhelmed. A blow from a club sent him sprawling over the gunwales, his eyes clouded with pain. He fought mightily to remain conscious, clawing for life.

As he slipped into darkness he heard himself rasping the one Hawaiian word he knew; the word for welcome, friendship, good wishes: "*Aloha...Aloha...*"

A face came into being above his own.

A girl's face, a beautiful girl's face, dark in a halo of black hair with gentle eyes, parted lips and breath without taint.

He had seen this face before, he told himself before drifting back to a furry edge of awareness. He clutched for clarity, sight and sound and became aware of the comforting solidity of earth against his back.

He found himself in a leafy chamber with sunlight prickling through fronds overhead. The girl's face came into focus again. She was holding his head, applying cool water to his forehead. He felt the yielding warmth of her bare breast against his cheek.

By the saints he was *alive!*

His shoulder pained him horribly and his head pounded with a thunderous ache but he was *alive*. Blue sky shone through an entrance framed in palm leaves and filled with children's faces, grinning and curious. The girl's face was inches from his and smiling with small and even teeth, her eyes comforting.

He tried very hard to say something but words would not form. He wanted desperately to remain in this beautiful world of speckled sunlight, laughing children and a dark angel's smile. But his senses went liquid again and he dropped back into unconsciousness.

The *Nahant*'s scuppers ran dark with blood.

Almost-human screams of the hogs tore the air as they were seized and their throats cut. The ghastly sounds were an incongruity on the soothing air of Kealakekua Bay.

Sprague reveled in directing the slaughter. Sing's Chinese worked expertly. After the carcasses were bled their entrails and larger bones were removed and tossed to waiting sharks. Frenzied gray bodies darted and wriggled menacingly in the water churning up a reddish foam. The men then butchered the meat into pieces running from four to six pounds. These chunks would be pickled after being salted and pressed for a day. Lastly they would be casked, interlarded with the coarse salt the natives made from seawater.

Supplies would not diminish here, Kimi told Quimby. There was enough food on this long Kona coast for many ships.

The bantam Hawaiian was pleased with himself. Within an hour of meeting the local chief Lako he had been enlisted as a spy for Kamōʻī, with instructions to report everything which happened on the *Nahant*. Kimi complied excepting only revealing the Olowalu tragedy—recognizing he had little proof of his own innocence in the atrocity. He told Lako merely that the ship had visited Maui briefly and supplies had been scarce. Otherwise he was a fountain of information about the *haole*.

"The king will be generous," Lako encouraged.

"To serve the great Kamōʻī is reward enough," Kimi lied, adding not too hastily that he desired to become overseer of farming and fishing in the area of his former home ten miles down the coast. He told Lako he had the wealth in white man's silver to make worthwhile any adjustment the *aliʻi* might find necessary to grant him this post.

Lako answered that he would forward this information to the prime minister, Kalani, then did not. He was hard put to retain his hauteur in the presence of this bumptious nouveau riche upstart. But the order to recruit

Kimi had drifted down from Kamō'ī himself. Anyone derelict in obeying the monarch was sure to be sorry—if he remained alive long enough for regret.

Meanwhile Kimi had the best of two worlds as agent and interpreter for both the *haole* and Hawaiians. He well knew his worth to both sides diminished with the length of the *Nahant's* stay. Olohana Stone was the only man who now knew a little of his tongue but others would learn new words quickly.

For the moment his state was most pleasant and the future looked bright. He plunged into service for both masters dreaming of his return as a chief, even a minor one, in a community where he had once been a common fisherman. He cheated as much as he dared but stole only from the *haole*. With Quimby punishment was the lash, which someone would live through. Under Kamō'ī it was the garrote, which none had survived.

A canoe with a load of salt came alongside. Its owner had made only two trips this day but Kimi told Sprague the man was owed for three. The mate duly counted out the knives and nails in proper payment. Later Kimi and this accomplice would divide the illicit profit. All this was like jelly on his bread since Quimby had promised him fifty cents a day for interpreting services.

By the time the *Nahant* sailed without him Kimi planned on being a richer man. Tonight there was a special honor. He would interpret for Kamō'ī at a feast for the *Nahant's* officers and men. The prospect of acting personally for the great king, actually being at his side and talking for him, was immensely exciting. Kamō'ī could not fail to notice him and take account of him as a man of worth.

The appearance of Olohana Stone cracked his reverie.

The bosun had enjoyed a bucket-bath and his black hair was twisted into a pigtail tied with a red ribbon. He carried his tri-cornered hat and was wearing a blue coatee with brass buttons. Freshly laundered knee breeches and stockings and boots with silver buckles completed his costume. His jaws were burnished from a fresh shave and his light blue eyes seemed to be anticipating the festivities ashore.

This was not the harsh and hard Olohana of the sea, Kimi mused. This Olohana looked like pictures he had seen of gentlemen who owned many horses and cattle on large lands in Virginia and Massachusetts. Despite his slightly mashed nose Olohana was a very good looking *haole*. No wonder the *wāhine* were attracted.

Nourished by their mutual rebellion at Olowalu Kimi now enjoyed a stronger kinship with Stone. Other crewmen had since tried to make friends with Kimi, as if this might somehow alleviate their guilt acquired murdering innocents. The overtures came too late. They had always treated him as odd man out now they could go to their *haole* hell. Soon Kimi would be free of the entire lot of villains and would not miss a one but Olohana.

He greeted the bosun with a pleasantry in Hawaiian discussing the excellence of his appearance.

Stone caught his meaning and thanked him: *"Mahalo."*

Kimi was proud of his student. With his tutoring during nighttime watches Olohana had learned fast. Perhaps this ability had some connection with things the bosun discovered in his beloved books. Perhaps the staring into books made men better.

No. This could not be the reason. The captain often read in his black Bible-book while he got drunk and he remained a vile man.

Within minutes Kimi was following Quimby, Sprague and Stone into the longboat. Four Chinese rowed them ashore in fading light. Little was said. Sprague sullenly licked a drooling lip and Quimby scowled straight ahead. The captain now only spoke to Stone and the Hawaiian when he had direct orders.

This contemptible man would surely make more evil, Kimi thought. He was glad he would not be around to suffer it.

Naked children frolicked around the *Nahant's* men as they walked from the boat to the banquet area. The youngsters were fascinated by the strangers, darting in to touch their clothing then flicking away with cries of excitement. Men and women along the path smiled and spoke *aloha* and these greetings were gay and warm.

The early evening scene under the towering palms was like a fanciful dream to John Stone. At least three hundred people crowded the feasting area. Comely women wore garlands of scented leaves and mahogany-hued bodies glowed from the waning sunset and the dancing flames. The air was perfumed with the incense-like smell of burning coconut husks and aromatic smoke from grilling fish and chicken. Coconut fronds trembled high overhead in gentle breezes and the setting was charged with a holiday spirit.

A fawning Lako escorted Quimby's party to a large spread of leaves laid on smooth pebbles. Wooden bowls brimmed with roasted meat and fish, the *kalo*—mash called *poi*, coconut pudding and condiments of seaweeds and pink salt. Each officer had a servant at his elbow. The *Nahant's* crewmen were happily absorbed in the throng, every tar having acquired native friends during the past few days. Lako took leave to join a nearby spread with chiefs and overseers of the Kona district lesser than himself. A slim boy at his side sat stiffly erect, asserting his right to be among the elders.

Young Puna tried to appear calm and self-possessed while inwardly boiling with anticipation.

Soon he would see the great Kamōʻī for the first time. Before his own eyes the heroic legend would become real. Until a few days ago he had never seen any *haole*. Now he could inspect the officers of the *Nahant* a few yards distant in their strange soft garments and triangular hats—

smiling a bit awkwardly, he thought, perhaps uneasily.

Like other boys of Kealakekua Puna had grown up with stories of Captain Cook and the *haole*: their curious talk, the way they blew smoke from their mouths, their wondrous iron, glass and cloth. He had heard how people thought at first that Cook was a god until he had been found to be only a man like everyone else. Then he had been killed. There were still scars on tree trunks and stones from the red-mouthed guns of the furious Englishmen. Earlier one of Cook's men had died and had been buried near the *heiau*. Puna's friends had talked about digging him up to see what a *haole* looked like. That had been the silly chatter of five- and six-year old children. Puna was now twelve, on the edge of manhood.

This day had begun quite ordinarily but now was in mounting excitement. Puna had spent most of the hours in training in the fighting arts. He enjoyed learning to wrestle, box, fight with daggers and throw spears. But, when forced daily, even such occupations could become boring. Still, as the only son of the chief Lako, it was necessary that he take instruction. One day he would assume his place among the ruling men and he must know the warrior's skills.

For certain he would be a better chief than his father.

Lako inspired no respect or affection, only fear. He governed selfishly and without *aloha*, was giddy almost every day from drinking *'awa*-root liquor and took women on whim from commoners and treated them cruelly. He did not surf, wrestle, race canoes or do other man-things, preferring to idle at bowling, draughts, drinking or womanizing. Puna despised Lako most of all for the disrespect he showed and the pain he gave to Puna's mother, Lilinoe.

Now he sat at Lako's side barely able to contain his excitement. In moments he would see the man he admired most in all the world, the *ali'i nui*, king of kings, Kamō'ī. It seemed unreal.

People were tense and uneasy, craning their necks in the direction from which the king was expected.

The arresting mournful hoot of a conch shell announced Kamōʻī's approach.

Abruptly the crowd fell silent. All dropped to their hands and knees, a movement rippling into a mass genuflection. Stone glanced at Quimby. The captain's face was quizzical, showing his surprise at the power shown by such an obsequious reception.

A doddering old man in a white wrap chanting in a high-pitched voice was first to appear through the trees. This was Pāhoa, Kimi told Stone, chief *kahuna* to the king. He was warning people of the monarch's approach and demanding prostration. The crowd crawled into two sections creating a wide path.

Then the king appeared, walking alone, and John Stone knew he would long remember his first sight of Kamōʻī of Hawaiʻi.

He was everything a king should be, pagan or not.

No mistaking this chap's power, Stone thought. Among a thousand naked *Kanaka* giants one would know he was the leader. The regality showed in the arresting sternness of his blunt features, the piercing dark of his eyes and the set of his massive head and shoulders. This rascal could dominate by silence, Stone told himself, and he looks like one it would be fatal to cross. Without thinking he took off his hat.

Kamōʻī walked without glancing at his subjects, a titanic figure with the tread of a deer. He carried a ten-foot spear as if it were an arrow. A crested helmet of yellow and scarlet feathers adorned his head and his cloak was the grandest wrap Stone had ever seen. Thousands of birds must have died to provide the tiny golden feathers of which it was woven. Like glowing velvet loosely tied and revealing his prodigious muscling, this garment of exquisite beauty fell to his ankles.

Kalani and Manu next appeared, wearing the smaller

capes of their rank. Kahu trailed in the wake of the men with other women of the court. The favorite queen walked tall, her eyes smiling at the people, wearing only a whaletooth pendant above her *kapa*-cloth skirt. Her bronzed skin was flawless and naked breasts shivered seductively. Stone thought he had never seen such a magnificent woman.

He realized that only he and Quimby were standing in the royal presences. Every Hawaiian groveled, head down. Even the irreverent roughnecks of the *Nahant's* crew were on their knees, cowed by the king's potent personality.

The regal figures filed slowly into the clearing. Pāhoa, the priest, walked on. Kamō'ī stopped a few yards in front of his guests and smiled. For a moment his eyes met Stone's and the bosun returned the smile. He felt then that he could like this man. He was imperial, proud and aloof—and probably arrogant and dangerous in the bargain. But there was also a kindness in him. In that instant Stone caught something else. Was it vulnerability? Unsureness? Doubts?

The priest finished. Kahu and the other *wāhine* studied the *haole* with undisguised curiosity. The audience remained on its hands and knees but expectant glances were lifted to the *ali'i*. A thick pile of mats were adjusted for the royal arse so Kamō'ī could sit with no man's head above his.

A sigh went up from the crowd as Pāhoa signalled that the prostration could end. The celebration rumbled back to life in movement and flutters of talk. Kimi crouched, trembling in awe, at Kamō'ī's side. The king spoke to him quietly: "Is this dirty one the captain?"

"'*Ae,* my lord. His name is unpronounceable. His soul is also dirty."

"And the one with the eyes of an eel?"

"Number two man, sire. He fancies boys."

"This other?"

"Number three, my *ali'i*. We call him Olohana, from the cry he uses to summon men on the ship. A brave and good man, sire. He has learned much of our tongue from me."

Interesting, the king thought. Olohana was the one he had liked on first sight.

"And these others?" He scanned the gathering briefly.

"Common sailors, my lord, and lowly peasants of China. Not worth your glance." Kimi gulped his fear. "I am Kimi, my lord, of Ho'okena in your kingdom. I will gladly die in your service."

"Steal from me as you do from this smelly captain and you *will* die," Kamō'ī said matter-of-factly. "Now tell these three I welcome them and say other pleasant things in the English for me."

"'*Ae*, sire."

Shaken to his soles Kimi relayed and embroidered the king's greeting. Quimby made a mumbling response. Stone smiled frankly at the monarch and decided to attempt Hawaiian words. He asked the king how he was, "*Pehea 'oe?*"

"*Maika'i, maika'i,*" good, good, the king answered. He spread his hands in a gesture for the feasting to begin while thinking he must guard his words in the coming conversations. With Kimi acting as his English voice, a nuanced conversation began.

At first Kamō'ī addressed Quimby. He inquired about progress in the trading—a gambit of politeness, since he knew exactly how it stood. Quimby's answers were monosyllabic and stumbling. The man was either barren of social grace, Stone thought, or tongue-tied in the presence of this royal giant. He began elaborating on Quimby's responses and soon the king was addressing himself to the bosun through Kimi. Then Kamō'ī decided to test this Olohana and asked his next question in Hawaiian of Stone directly.

Stone was startled. During the earlier exchanges he had been pleased to discover that he understood much of the king's and Kimi's exchanges. But to be onstage with the intimidating Kamōʻī in Hawaiian seemed something less than desirable. He answered as best he could with a few promptings from Kimi: "The barter is going well, your majesty. Your people deal fairly in provisions of excellent quality."

Halting and labored, Kamōʻī thought, but remarkably good for a white man.

"I direct that all visitors be treated with honesty and hospitality," Kamōʻī said. "How long will you remain at Kealakekua?"

Stone looked at Quimby, who clearly resented his bosun's dealing with this savage in his heathen language. The captain asked petulantly: "What does he want to know?"

"When we'll be leaving."

Kimi busily translated their words. The king must know all that was said.

"Tell him a week," said Quimby. "Perhaps more. But any business talk will be in English. Do you understand, Stone?"

Kamōʻī was amused by the exchange between the two *haole*. Obviously there was no love lost between them. Stone would be the diplomat, the captain an uncouth and greedy man. Kimi had been right in his assessment.

"Are other *haole* coming?" he asked.

"I would think they will, sire," said Stone with more assistance from Kimi. "No one can tell you how many or when. But now there are always ships on the northwest coast of America trading furs from the Indians. As we do they will need food, water and firewood for the long voyage to China. I would say, my lord, that your islands are located in the right place should you wish to profit from such trade."

A judicious answer, the king thought.

"What are these Indians like?" he queried. "Are they like us?"

"No, your majesty. They are short and ugly. They tattoo their tongues black and speak an unpleasant language, as if their mouths were full of food. They are bad tempered, treacherous and foul-smelling from lack of bathing."

Stone stopped abruptly. He might be describing Quimby, at his elbow. Then he remembered he was speaking Hawaiian. He went on: "Like the huge black animals we call bears the Indians seem to be happiest in their own grease. May I speak now in English for my captain to hear?"

Kamōʻī nodded assent.

"Your people are handsome, clean, friendly and generous, sire. It is regrettable that they have the habit of taking things that do not belong to them."

Quimby looked sharply at Stone. This savage before them might not like such blunt talk.

But Kamōʻī only answered through Kimi, "This habit is not always theft, Olohana. In our islands all things useful to living are willingly shared by everyone."

"Sadly, this is not a white man's custom," Stone replied. "Captain Quimby is particularly concerned that your people try to remove pieces of iron and brass from our ship. If this continues soon it will be plucked apart and sink. Surely your highness sees the danger."

Kamōʻī nodded again. He spoke to Kalani directing that the canoe people be admonished. Over the prime minister's shoulder Stone saw Kahu smiling impudently at him from the circle of royal *wāhine*. She sat straight, pink nipples like berries on her bountiful breasts. A marvelous looking woman, he thought, enough for ten men.

Kamōʻī asked Kimi why the captain did not answer questions.

"His tongue sticks unless he is giving orders, my *aliʻi*. He mistrusts and dislikes all men and is without *aloha*".

The captain was indeed cold and graceless, Kamōʻī thought, with the eyes and aroma of a hog. Olohana he liked more and more. The bosun was respectful but with an air of openness and authority. Though he looked like a dangerous man in a fight, his voice was pleasant, manner gracious and thoughts well voiced. He asked Kimi, sotto voce, if Olohana like women.

Yes, and they liked him, was the answer. He had taken much pleasure with Namo, a well-born girl of Olowalu.

Olohana would have a fresh *wāhine* every day if this pleased him, Kamōʻī thought.

He had just made a decision about Olohana's future.

With a pounding of the sharkskin drums the dancing began.

The corps of performers were muscular warriors doing a thudding *hula*. They moved in remarkable precision clad only in loin wraps with necklaces of pearlshell and anklets of dog's teeth. Nose-flute players and drummers sat in a cluster urging the ballet on with a hypnotic steadily mounting rhythm. The big dancers bobbed and weaved as one man, their bodies glistening in the firelight. They finished half-kneeling, with arms extended and palms down in a gesture of dedication to the king. The Hawaiian audience roared approval.

Shouts came from the *Nahant's* crewmen demanding dancing by the *wāhine*. All hands were having a rousing good time. Jake Maul and several Chinese had already disappeared in the bush with their paramours. Delano was gleefully cupping the breast of a serving girl and Scrimmage had been invited to sit with the royal ladies. His flaming red hair fascinated the natives and was the object of admiring inspection wherever he wandered.

Soon it was dark. A sweet breeze from the sea washed the scene. Light from the fire gilded palm fronds above.

His appetite sated with a quart of *poi* and two large

raw fish Kamōʻī turned his attention to the gathering. He found the boy, Puna, beside Lako in the circle of lesser chiefs. The lithe lad sat proudly, seeming at ease among the elders. He had the angular slimness of a twelve-year old but his body promised strength and manly grace. He moved without awkwardness and held himself with dignity beyond his years. Kamōʻī was pleased. Was this what a son of his looked like? He wished he might examine him more closely. Puna turned once and caught the king's probing stare. He flushed and bowed his head, his poise shattered.

In reality the king was everything Puna dreamed he would be. He vowed that one day he would serve this monarch of monarchs even if he were to die in that service.

Stone opened another bottle of port and poured for the king. Kamōʻī tilted the coconut shell and downed its contents in one draught.

The man had enormous capacity for food and drink, thought Stone, and wine did not appear to affect him. This could not be said for Quimby, who had fortified himself for this encounter with several brandies. He was now tipsy, his mouth slack and eyes hooded. Sprague had eased away into the crowd.

A steady warm hum of talk and laughter arose from the banqueters. Stone realized this celebration was more an outpouring of affection for Kamōʻī than a reception for the men of the *Nahant*. The Hawaiians stared at their king as if in the presence of a deity. Stone felt the monarch's eyes upon him. Quite a man, he thought, controlled and strong, one who knows how to handle power. He asked if there were any *haole* things the king desired.

The wine was pleasant, Kamōʻī responded, and he also fancied the *haole* tea. Otherwise his desires were being satisfied by normal trading. He now had a storehouse filled with goods like silks, cottons, cooking pots and other implements. The tools for farming and fishing were distributed by his overseers where they would do the most good. He also possessed a few bags of Spanish and American dollars but thus far had found them useless.

I could bloody well find use for them, Stone thought. He wondered how many. Kamōʻī's face was bland. Was this brown giant playing with them?

"My chief's enjoy the tobacco," Kamōʻī went on. "And my wives are always happy to receive combs, needles, scents, mirrors and other such things."

The king continued to address Olohana Stone but his eyes traveled to Quimby. The last two traders had taken quantities of island sandalwood in part payment for provisions, he said. He had been told the fragrant wood brought high prices in China where it was greatly prized for carving into fans, boxes and other objects—as well as for burning at altars for its aromatic smoke. Would the captain have interest in sandalwood?

Quimby was as close as he ever came to being in an expansive mood. He said he might be interested in a few *piculs*—an Asian measurement of 133 pounds—to see what it would fetch from the Chinese.

"I own mountains covered with these trees." Kamōʻī replied, "and have given thought to their worth in trade."

From what he had heard, he continued, the wood was as profitable in China as the sea-dog skins. And clearly sandalwood was easier to obtain. The discomfort and dangers of dealing with ugly Indians in cold forests would be replaced by barter with friendly Hawaiians in a warm and pleasant land. Distances traveled would also be greatly reduced.

Interesting thoughts, Stone mused. One could almost see Quimby's ears perk up.

The king continued to move with the advantage of the captain's interest.

"I will see you get all the sandalwood your ship can carry," he said. "Unlike pigs and vegetables, which come largely from the stores of my people, all sandalwood belongs to me since I command all lands. But the wood is not easily brought to shore. Many men are required to cut and transport the logs from higher lands."

His voice was a pleasant baritone, firm and authoritative.

"The price will be reasonable. One musket for two *piculs*, and all wood of the highest quality."

Aha, thought Stone. Now he gets serious. He eyed the captain. Quimby stared at the king for a long moment then he nodded his head in agreement. "Done," he said.

Kamōʻī took the assent without change of expression. The bargain had been struck so casually it was not easy to conceal his pleasure. But indicating enthusiasm about the agreement might only make the *haole* uneasy about supplying Hawaiians with guns. Now he must be wary of perfidy from this loathsome man. Quimby might be planning to cheat on the numbers, give him faulty weapons or powder mixed with coal dust. He would not be the first white trader to take advantage of Hawaiian ignorance of firearms.

Stone meanwhile was pondering Quimby's agreement without haggling. This was very much out of character. Perhaps the captain, dulled by drink or in awe of this pagan monarch, was momentarily unguarded. At least six dozen *piculs* could be accommodate on the *Nahant*'s deck. This translated to thirty-five trade muskets, a fair-sized armory for the ruler.

Quimby asked Kamōʻī about possibilities of trade on other islands. With a pint of port atop his brandy he was finding his tongue and feeling expansive.

The king's face tightened. The prospect of unfriendly neighbors acquiring guns did not please him.

His island, Hawaiʻi, was by far the biggest and most prosperous, he said. All things the *haole* desired could be obtained here. He had firmly established rules of fair dealing and friendship to visitors. This condition could not be relied upon elsewhere. He cautioned Quimby about placing faith in other chiefs and rulers. Some of these had *haole* in their service who gave them stupid and thoughtless advice. These men were mostly renegades, drunken deserters devoted to mischief and lechery; men who lived only in selfish interests and were dangerous with guns.

"I desire," he said, "to someday enlist *haole* men in my service to help us learn the new ways and assist in making trade. These will be men of honor. They will be given high rank as chiefs, lands with commoners to work them and high-born wives to bear *ali'i* children."

Not an unpleasant prospect, thought Stone. Being a nabob over a swarm of these *Kanaka* might be amusing—particularly if there were Spanish or American dollars to spice the experience.

The king glanced at the bosun and read only polite attention. Perhaps he had planted an interest, one could not tell. Kalani looked at his master and shrugged faintly. Manu sat half-turned from the whites in disdain.

That man is our enemy, Stone realized.

Conversation subsided. The festivities rolled on. The young girls now dancing were the fairest Stone had yet seen, maidens aglow with puberty, their small breasts quivering and mouths parted from exertion.

The drumming, fifing and staccato clatter of bamboos being slapped together increased in volume as time wore on. Hawaiian men, Stone noted, were as cheerful in sharing their women as they did their food and drink. Scrimmage chortled in his new role as the plaything of queens. Blue Bob had his own circle of admirers marveling at his wooly hair and purple-black skin. Delano and many of the Chinese had disappeared. Kahu sat grandly among her sister *ali'i-wahine,* her eyes wandering to Kamō'ī and his guests, annoyed with the *kapu* prohibiting women from eating with men. Lako, as host, was tensely vigilant, directing servants with impatient gestures. Beside him Puna sat stiff and quiet under the occasional searching look of the monarch.

Only an hour after his arrival Kamōʻī arose to leave. Dutifully his companion *aliʻi* arose with him. The king spoke a pleasant goodbye to Quimby and Stone.

The silence as he departed was like a sound itself, a vacuum in the cacophony of drums, dancing and voices. Again the crowd fell on its knees. As Kamōʻī and his entourage walked into the night there was only the sound of surf thudding on the beach and the old priest's chant clearing his path. As Pāhoa's voice faded the audience picked itself up. In moments the celebration resumed noisier and even less inhibited than before.

He had seen quite enough of this orgy, Quimby growled. He struggled to his feet, stumbling from his intake of liquor and legs half asleep. Stone thought of staying for awhile, perhaps taking one of the enticing young dancers. But he was tired from a long day and uncomfortable from the heavy food and wine. There was a regiment of women, waiting...

He followed Quimby to the beach and the waiting longboat. The Chinese who had drawn rowing duty were sullen as they came to languid attention. Stone wondered if Quimby was aware of how much they hated him.

On their way to the brig Quimby spoke once out of the darkness, "When we deal the guns, bosun, give them no ammunition. You follow me?"

"Aye," Stone said. Quimby was either stupid, drunk or a damned fool to think he could pull such a trick on a man like Kamōʻī.

By the half-mark the captain was snoring liquidly.

"*Puaʻa*," intoned Kimi from the stern. The word meant pig.

Stone was thinking about Namo, the girl of Olowalu. What a lovely thing she was! A quality of innocence, a soothing presence, an exquisite lover. He wondered if he would ever see her again.

Two days later in ashen light before dawn Kalani made his way to the king's sleeping house.

The prime minister clutched a *kapa*-cloth over his shoulders against the chill left by dark. His face was furrowed with concern. Twice within a few hours he had been awakened for bad news. Channel fishermen had arrived during the night with the story of the bestial massacre at Olowalu. Other messengers had come an hour ago with an account of the *Little American*'s capture and the murder of all but one of her men at Ka'ūpūlehu.

He picked his way along the path. There were stirrings around the huts of commoners—fishermen making ready for the day, women coaxing fires to life. He could see pricks of light from the *Nahant* on the bay. Most of her men would be sleeping off last night's debauchery. The king would find it of interest that only Olohana and the Hawaiian, Kimi, had refused to have anything to do with the slaughter on Maui. And he would be upset by Kimi's not telling him about it.

The everpresent Kai greeted Kalani at the king's house, his eyes showing surprise by the earliness of the visit. Four of his guards knelt and dipped spears in salute and Kai bowed low. This noble had access to the king any time he wished.

In moments Kalani was tugging gently at his master's foot. Kamō'ī shuddered awake. Almost instantly alert he listened intently. When Kalani finished he paused only moments before responding. The Olowalu killings were appalling but did not pose a problem. Maui was not his kingdom and he himself neared a state of war with its king Pono. But the massacre did reveal the vicious and unpredictable nature of the man now his guest. Kamō'ī was no stranger to violence but murder for pleasure left him disgusted.

The Ka'ūpūlehu affair, nearby and on his own island,

was a much different matter. The schooner fitted exactly the description of the ship for which Quimby kept searching the horizon, thus the young *haole* killed must be his son. Setting aside this troublesome complication, the Ka'ūpūlehu piracy made mockery of Kamō'ī's declarations of friendship and hospitality to visitors. He pondered the irony aloud to Kalani.

"One cannot decide which of these two villains is the more stupid and dangerous—Captain Quimby or our own chief at Kapā lehu. Both incidents point out the dangers between our people and the *haole*."

"We work against time, my *ali'i*," Kalani pointed out. The messengers are sworn to silence but this news will soon reach the captain."

"We must plan then."

"Another problem, sire..."

"Yes?"

"The guns being sent to us—the captain is not providing the balls with which they kill or the powder which drives them. Without these they are useless."

"Tell him it is not wise to take me for a fool. Stop all trade until he provides these things." He frowned. "And tell this Kimi to never again keep information from me."

The day passed in provisioning and the slaughter of hogs. Quimby sourly accepted Kalani's demand concerning ammunition and trade continued briskly. Under Stone's direction casks containing the sea otter furs were inspected. The pelts were in excellent condition in protective layers of cedar chips.

Sandalwood began arriving in late afternoon and the yellowish logs were lashed amidships. All hands worked cheerfully, knowing the evening ashore would bring more pleasure. Little Kimi, terror-stricken by Kamō'ī's knowledge of his larceny and a grim warning by Kalani, was now keeping accounts scrupulously correct down to the last yam and ounce of salt.

The day waned. Quimby posted men on two swivel guns. For safety's sake, he said, now that the damned *Kanaka* were armed.

The captain ran a muster next day at the twelve o'clock bell and Blue Bob and three Chinese were missing. Rewards of one axehead for each man were offered for their return and many Hawaiians swarmed excitedly over nearby landscapes in the search. The runaways were brought back the next afternoon. Quimby flogged them personally—ten lashes for the black lad, twenty each for the Orientals.

He took his time, swinging the rope with obvious pleasure. The little mess boy went unconscious on the seventh stroke and the backs of the Chinese looked like savaged meat when he finished. Stone watched Tan Sing glaring at the captain, his flushed face highlighting the pale welted scar on his nose. He had rarely seen the headman show any change of expression from bland impassivity—but now his eyes were slits and his face glowered cold hate.

Sprague disappeared near dusk.

Two days later he was found in an outlying hut wild drunk and stark naked, debauching himself with several Hawaiian *mahu*. Returned to the ship he was useless and his chores fell on Stone's shoulders. The bosun was now working from dawn to dark without relief.

There was one other awkward incident. Scrimmage, of the flaming red hair, had been easily enticed into her house by a minor chiefess. This portly wench was consumed by curiosity to see if the bush was equally red in the sailmaker's private patch. Her inspection immediately turned to fondling and the two were rutting merrily when her husband surprised them.

This worthy feigned outrage. His status had been violated along with his wife. Stone read the man easily and mollified him with gifts of some fishhooks and flints.

Sprague slowly trembled his way back to sobriety and resumed his duties. Sandalwood soon covered a large area of the deck and other provisioning proceeded smoothly. The king and his court remained aloof from the whites. Quimby's mood was surly and withdrawn. After morning instructions to Sprague and Stone he retired to his cabin, surfacing only at odd moments to scan for the *Little American*.

Kimi vanished, his belongings with him.

Sprague suggested they petition Kamō´ī to have him returned but Quimby took the defection in stride. Good riddance, he said, and scant chance of finding one *Kanaka* among thousands.

"These blasted Indians stick together. Besides Stone here knows enough of their lingo to get us by."

Another few days at most, Quimby told himself. There had been a fracas the night before between the natives and crewmen over a bottle of wine, indicating relations were no longer warmly fraternal. Other *Kanaka* had begun grumbling that the *haole* were stripping the district of food supplies needed for less productive seasons. There was also dissatisfaction aboard the brig. Loading sandalwood in addition to other chores meant longer days for the seamen. Shore leave had been cut and Quimby feared more desertions. This was a large island and he might not get his men back as easily next time.

Best that he haul out of Kona, he thought. His people had all had their gallops with the sluts and their bellies were full of pork and potatoes. They'd become softened—time the whole bloody lot went back to work, faced reality.

Upon leaving he would run the coast for the *Little American*. If she was not found he would sail on to China. Tweed knew his plan: first up the river to Whampoa for at least a month, then back down to Macao for a few weeks. The Scot could meet him at either port. If he did not Quimby would then accept the loss of the schooner—and his son. In his heart of hearts he would more greatly rue the loss of the vessel. He considered his son a nincompoop and useless and suffered him only because his shrewish wife demanded it.

Yes, he would leave in a few days...

Perhaps between now and departure he would try a woman again.

Sprague had secretly arranged the last one, during a late hour at Olowalu, and Quimby had been unable to perform. But only a few days ago, while lashing the black boy and the Chinese, he had felt a stirring in his groin not experienced for a long time. Perhaps these last few years had been some sort of peculiar phase and he was now coming back to life. He was only fifty, a young man still...

He reached for the bell to summon his mate and his hand stopped.

He was remembering the giggle of the Hawaiian whore as she stared and his own shame and fury as he stood there naked, fat and flaccid before her.

He reached for the brandy bottle instead of the bell. The liquor would not laugh at him.

Stone asked permission to take a day ashore and perhaps shoot some birds for the table. Quimby grunted assent.

After breakfast the bosun tucked a knife and a pistol in his belt and packed a small bag with a pork chunk, a yam and a flask of brandy. He drew a musket and shot from Delano, hailed a canoe and was taken ashore.

The village gave off fitful morning sounds but he saw little activity. Out of the settlement the slow climb over slaggy loose lava was punishing until he reached the shade of the forest line. He climbed higher into the cool green woodlands, now and then catching glimpses of the *Nahant* through the trees. She was neat and small in the distance, like a miniature on water of intense blue in the shadow cliffs. He paused once to rest staring down at the agreeable scene, the tiny canoes moving back and forth, the white line of surf dawdling on the dark pebbled beach. To the north and south hazed distant headlands of the big island eased into the sea. Strange that so few outsiders had seen those benevolent mountains in the sun, a miracle that they had lain undiscovered for so long.

He turned his attention to the hunt. And soon discovered the colorful birds were too small and quick for his gun. Even in a shower of shot they managed to escape unscathed. After an hour of this fruitless pursuit he stretched out in shade. A hawk soared overhead, riding the rinsed-blue emptiness. Stone drank some brandy and ate his potato and pork, cursing himself for not carrying water. No man, and particularly a sailor who had severely suffered its lack, should ever travel without water.

Weariness took him. The soft cushion of mulch and pillow of leaves were too seductive. The silence, broken only by sighs of the greenery, brought drowsiness. The delicate scent of the leaves called *maile* caressed his nostrils...

He was awakened by the heat of the sunshine on his face and knew he had slept hours away. He could not remember such a deep and untroubled rest.

The wind was down and the mountainside in a sublime silence. Not even a bird moved. Clambering back downhill was more difficult than the climb up he discovered, particularly on the slippery, cindered slopes below the tree line. Nearing the bay he noticed there were no canoes around the *Nahant*. Closer still he realized the village fires were dead and not a soul could be seen among the palms. He walked the last few hundred yards with only the sound of his boots scraping rough stones. When he entered the settlement it appeared deserted. Grass houses were silent, mats covering their entrances. Canoes had been drawn high upon the sand. The *Nahant*'s boat was gone.

He went to the water's edge and tried to signal the ship but the distance was too great and the twilight dimmed the view. He felt uneasiness at this strange state of circumstances. There was gloom on the scene not entirely attributable to waning light—a sense of something sadly awry. He fired a shot into the air. Its echo returning from the cliffs was the only response. Soon the setting sun threw the brig into sharp relief about a quarter mile away. When night came, a few lamps pierced the dark from its direction. Stone felt a heavy aloneness, his world plunged into uncertainty.

He walked back to the village and ventured to a hut on its outskirts. He rapped on its doorposts with his musket butt. There was no answer and he knocked again persistently. A low mutter came from within. He took a deep breath and yanked the matting aside.

A man crouched inside, a middle-aged native with frightened eyes. He motioned Stone to enter. It took a few moments for the bosun's eyes to adjust to the dim light from the oily nuts Hawaiians burned for lamps.

"*Kapu la, make la,*" the man repeated, adding Kamō'ī's name. Stone understood that Kamō'ī had imposed a *kapu* on the village and the penalty for breaking it was death. This had thrown everyone into fear and withdrawal.

The Hawaiian offered him water, fish and *poi*. Stone consumed these greedily but attempts to draw the man into conversation were fruitless. Clearly he feared the white man and regretted this contact. Stone spent a sleepless night in the home of his reluctant host.

By the first light of dawning he was exhausted and still apprehensive.

His host had slipped away but there was food left and he gulped some fish. Outside the village was utterly quiet with not a chicken or a dog moving. Nevertheless he felt eyes upon him as he moved back to the beach.

Far off the *Nahant* sat stone-still on the flat water. Stone climbed a rocky outcrop and lifted his kerchief on his musket barrel. He waved this until his arm ached but there was no response from the ship. Perhaps morning light in their eyes rendered him invisible. He waited until the sun shone higher and tried again without success. He fired a shot but the wind in his face drowned the sound and he decided he had best save what little ammunition he had left. He thought of taking one of the canoes but none had paddles and all were too heavy to be dragged into the water. A poor swimmer, he knew he would never accomplish the distance. Behind him the village remained quiet.

He walked to Lako's compound. It was deserted—only a few chickens pecking at gravel and a sow on her side, piglets suckling.

He went back to the beach to wave his impotent pennant and shout when the wind was right—fighting a growing feeling that these efforts were useless. Why was Quimby not sending someone to fetch him? What in God's name was going on?

The sun climbed higher in a pale blue sky. Its heat became uncomfortable. Stone found relief under dripping swordlike fronds of a *hala* tree. His thoughts rioted with his predicament then swam with exhaustion from his restless night. He slept.

It was a marvelous dream, the kind one despairs leaving.

Stone was in command of the *Little American*, at its wheel soaring into beckoning infinity over a sparkling and white-flecked sea. Her tall sails tugged the schooner forward, bellied taunt, glowing like snowdrifts in sunshine. The vessel responded like a loving animal to his slightest touch.

Big Alec Tweed was at the rail, grinning boyishly, his

beefy arm around an utterly naked and beautiful Hawaiian *wahine*. At Stone's feet Namo of Olowalu sat crosslegged, lazily and seductively caressing her coppery breasts and shoulders with a shimmering dark pelt of sea otter. She smiled at Stone, her eyes frank and inviting, her pink tongue flicking over her upper lip. She said something but he could not hear the words.

He would never desire more than this.

It was almost more than one could stand: a sense of sweet freedom, radiant strength, boundless happiness and warm security. Ahead a few wispings of cottony clouds rode an amazingly blue sky. A rainbowed mist floated over inky water in distance. Beyond that rainbow was a stirring of exciting promise—but of what he had no inkling. Soon he would find it. His hands on the wheel were sure and possessive, his body moved in sensual concert with the dipping and sliding of the wiry little ship.

The *Little American* was his. With joy he sailed her into an endless world of rosy light, lovely women, silver and gold and scented tradewinds...

He awoke in the slanting afternoon sunlight.

For moments struggling to wakefulness he was aware only of the cool air and its refreshment. Then he looked seaward and was instantly scrambling to his feet and dashing down the beach.

He watched appalled as the distant *Nahant* rigged out her steering sail booms. He danced on the sand, shouted at the top of his lungs and waved his kerchief frantically. All the while he knew there would be no answer.

Furious, cursing, he watched the canvas rise and the ship bear off. Then he sat on the beach, drained of thought, staring. His connection with the world of civilization became smaller and smaller until it was just a fleck on the horizon and then disappeared.

Minutes later sounds came from the gathering of grass dwellings behind him—pleasant sounds of laughter, people shouting back and forth and children being released.

The *kapu* had been lifted.

At the time Stone could not know he had been deliberately marooned by a plot of Kamō'i's.

Once the king learned that Olohana had trudged off into the hills a well-thought-out plan had gone into action. Representatives of the king went to the people telling them a strict *kapu* was imposed on the bay and its environs and all were to remain in their homes. Kalani was then dispatched with Kimi as translator to deal with Captain Quimby.

The message to Quimby was succinct. Kamō'i, having learned of the captain's cold-blooded massacre of Hawaiians at Olowalu, desired Quimby gone. He directed there be no more traffic with the ship and set the penalty for breaking this *kapu* as death. If Quimby foolishly made reprisal he would be very sorry. He was dealing now with the *ali'i-nui* Kamō'i and his warriors—not with a few pitiful fishermen like the sad souls at Olowalu.

Quimby bellowed outrage. It was not right for the king to quit trading now that he had his guns. He promised that fellow captains would be told of this treachery. Kamō'i would never see another New England ship in his waters.

The implacable prime minister responded coolly. All bargains had been honored. He added that his master was thinking of reporting Quimby's savage behavior to the American *ali'i-nui* Keoki Wakinekoa, George Washington. Surely such a great man would be furious about these senseless killings.

Quimby fought to control his rage. He asked for delivery of his bosun and the other men ashore. Kalani blandly lied that he knew nothing of the bosun but said the others would be returned as soon as he and Kimi returned safely to shore. Finally he told the captain he had only until the next evening to remove his ship from Kealakekua. With this warning he took leave of Quimby and the *Nahant*.

Kimi was beside himself with pleasure at Quimby's discomfiture. Never had he enjoyed the interpreting more.

Quimby did some hard thinking after Kalani left.

He had no doubt this king would do as he threatened. He was a damned big chief and could send men by the thousands, in the night, when the *Nahant*'s guns would be near useless.

His own provisioning was almost complete and posed no serious problem. The absence of the *Little American* was more worrisome but Alec Tweed would surely make a rendezvous in China.

And Stone? The loss of this insolent mutineer would be far from tragic. The situation even had advantages. Quimby would enjoy a windfall gain in Stone's profit-share from the voyage. The bosun was an orphan and bachelor with no whining wife or squalling brats to placate back home. The head Chinaman could take up the slack in duties. And without Stone there would be no one to raise a fuss about Olowalu. Sprague would not tattle. The other riffraff, having helped in the matter, would keep their mouths shut.

He summoned Sprague and instructed him to make ready for sea. Later in the day the mate returned.

"He's on the beach, Captain, wavin' a rag," he said. "Shall I send a boat?"

"And risk losing three or four more men?" Quimby snarled. "Don't be a damn fool."

"Aye, sir." The mate smirked with pleasure and took his leave.

In future, Quimby thought, he would simply take his trade to other islands.

The plan had gone smoothly; the king was gratified. Almost suddenly he had acquisitions of considerable value; the *Little American* with its two red-mouthed guns and two superior white men. Their skill with guns and in handling the ship would make it possible for Kamōʻī to communicate with other monarchs in the world. His fame would spread beyond the islands. Other kings would know his thoughts and plans and he would take his place among the world's leaders.

He had no doubts about the two *haole* enlisting into his service. Blandishments failing he would offer the simple choice—join his court as *aliʻi* of wealth and power or live as best they could among the farmers and fishermen. He had little doubt about their choice. He had heard much of the cruel life at sea and had never met a *haole* who did not find island life most appealing. These two would not be different.

John Stone, pondering his fate during those early hours as a castaway, considered himself a victim of Quimby's warped revenge. He had never tried to hide his loathing for the captain and the rebellion at Olowalu must have sealed his fate.

What was to come next was now the only importance.

Taking stock of his plight he glumly noted that he was a marooned pauper thousands of miles from his homeland with no idea what the next hour might bring. His future was in the hands of a heathen king whom he had seen only once. His possessions were next to nothing: a musket, knife, pistol, a flask, pinch of tobacco and the clothes on his back. His prospects were dim indeed.

If there was a bright side it was that this was a warm and pleasant land with ample food and apparently friendly people—and other ships would surely visit...

Stone was not without experience in adversity nor was he a man to moon over bad luck, even in such a huge dose. Curiously there was even a little prickling of excitement in this adventure.

One day he would settle his account with that pig Quimby. At the moment he would adapt to the present. Only the Sisters of Fate knew how long that time would be.

He turned toward the village. This heathen king might answer a few questions. He had not walked far before a group of men bearing clubs and spears appeared on the path. Stone recognized their leader as one of the chiefs attending the feast a few nights earlier. The gathering did not have a threatening look despite their arms. But he could not tell from the chief's glum expression whether he should prepare for a fight or a parley of some sort. He fingered the pistol at his waist.

Lako stopped in front of Stone and spoke without greeting, "You speak our language."

"Poorly, I'm afraid," Stone answered warily.

Lako's tone was condescending, "Our great king has ordered that you stay here for now. You are free to move within the village but not without. Entry into the king's compound is *kapu*. Do you understand?

"Am I a prisoner then?"

"I cannot answer that. These are the instructions I am to give you."

"I'll give you some instruction. Tell your bloody king I belong to the United States. If he plans any harm to me he will be in trouble." His impetuous outpouring mixed Hawaiian and English and instantly he regretted it. Fortunately Lako only stared without comprehension. After a moment he told Stone to follow his men.

Two warriors with spears led the bosun along the beach. They escorted him to a spacious grass house being cleaned by several women. The *wahine* smiled at Stone but made no talk. After they spread fresh sleeping mats and left containers of food they muttered shy *aloha* and disappeared.

"This will be your house," one of the spearsmen said. Then he and his companion also left.

Stone sat and stared while filling his pipe. A pleasant place, he thought. Surf brushed sand and the shallows sparkled a few yards away. He must be a guest, he thought. Certainly he was being treated as one.

But to what purpose? To keep him for some kind of pagan sacrifice? To fatten him for a roast?

No. Kimi had been appalled by such insinuations, insisting that his people were not cannibals.

Apparently this king wished him comfortable for some reason or use...

He felt he would know soon enough and nothing was to be gained from worrisome speculation. So he entered and found comfort in the grass shelter at Kealakekua.

The little village on the bay resumed its normal routines.

The sounds of women making the *kapa*-barkcloth with wooden beaters punctuated daylight hours. Bearers came from higher lands to exchange melons, yams and firewood for seashore produce of fishes, limpets and edible and medicinal seaweeds. Fishermen went early on the blue, returning in late afternoon to spill their glistening bright-eyed catches into waiting baskets. There was the pock´ing sound of stone adzes biting into log-roughs in the canoe sheds. Children played everywhere, especially cavorting on the shore and dashing in and out of the milky surf. Occasionally there was the unworldly chanting of the *kahuna* as they tended god-figures on the stone platform of the *heiau*-temple.

The king sent gifts to John Stone—a packet of tea, bottles of port, tobacco and once, a surprisingly good razor. The messengers who brought these packages treated them reverently. Kamō´ī himself had chosen the items, thus they were alive with his potent *mana*.

Various women supplied Stone with excellent food: delicious briny limpets, choice fish and lobsters, sweet coconut milk and roast suckling pork.

He was indeed favored, he knew. Though he enjoyed this luxurious rest uncertainty about the future plagued him.

Despite Lako´s warning Stone twice approached the king´s compound. But the big man Kai and the men of his guard turned Stone away. The faces of these formidable retainers held no animosity and they said nothing. But the message of their dropped spears was clear—Stone was not to press further.

Nor did he make friends among the villagers, though all were cordial in daily contact. It was evident that the novelty of the *Nahant´*s visit was a thing of the past. Life was now resumed in seriousness. Skies above the islands were benevolent and the wind gentle, but the land and sea did not give sustenance without resistance.

Every day there were crops to be nurtured, fish to be caught, implements to be made and children to be tutored. When dark came it was without dancing and song. Rather it was a time for a meal to be eaten, problems to be discussed and early and long sleep for the day to come. The villagers had little time to entertain a stranger, particularly one under the king's patronage and eye. The awe in which they held Kamōʻī made them shy with Stone—although a few of the women who brought his food were clearly amenable to satisfying his other appetites. On the third night of his castaway state he asked one of the girls to stay with him. She was one of the younger *wahine*, pretty and shy, and submitted meekly. She seemed more frightened than enthusiastic and for Stone it was little more than brief physical pleasure.

Despite the activity around him he was lonely. He thought of finding Kimi but had no idea where to look. His thoughts frequently wandered to the *Little American*. His tardy friend Tweed might yet be his deliverance. But doubts nagged. Alec was now over two weeks overdue. He had either found a haven elsewhere or was lost forever. There was hope in the knowledge that Tweed was a first-rate seaman—and the schooner was finely and sturdily built in China of their excellent teak wood. Still she was less than a toothpick on the vast deep—and any sailor knew how awful that power could be against puny plank...

He returned to his house late in the afternoon.

The palm grove along the shore was deserted and the warm air still. He peeled off his blouse and splashed water on his face.

Soft light suffused inside the thatching. His eyes adjusting he became instantly aware he was not alone.

Queen Kahu waited in the shadowed space. Fleetingly he noticed she was as tall as he and utterly naked. The mottlings of her nipples were dark against the ample mounds of her breasts. Her arms were upraised, her hands at her hair. She was a woman of huge and flawless proportions and the sight left him speechless. She smiled, amused by his surprise and stepped to him deliberately. Foolishly he was startled when he realized she was unbuckling his belt.

"No," he said. It even sounded silly and his voice was so small...

"Yes, yes," She answered in English, the words like a hiss.

Her surprisingly small warm fingers found his penis and fondled it while she smiled impudently into his eyes. Again he started a protest, thinking of the penalties that could accrue from sporting with Kamōī's favorite but she placed a hand over his mouth. With the other she gently cupped his testicles, her touch knowing, tickling and teasing. Her fingers moved to coax and stroke and the muscle thickened, erecting. She murmured approbation then her fingers encircled the sagging swelling and she pulled him toward the mats.

In moments he was on his back and she was moving to mount him. His penis now as stiff as a stick he had no thought of anything but this moment occupied. Expertly she poked him into her vagina. It was tight and oily warm and his entry was exquisite. He arched into her and she sighed, settling, her head thrown back.

He had never been taken so. This majestic Venus dominated him completely. Her hands pinned his shoulders and her great breasts swayed in her rhythmic rocking ride. Up and down she lifted and ground, haunches rising, buttocks tightened and descending to quiver hungrily upon his member. Her breath was grasping, broken by animal-like throatings as her moist hot tightness gnawed and drew. Her eyes were shut tight and her hair brushed his chest. His nerves rioted and his brain went giddy in the intense climb to pleasure, his very being centered on his taut root in its prison of joy.

He tried to check the approaching climax then surrendered to the gathering, soaring and explosion racked with its ecstasy. She spasmed with him in a violent shudder, whimpering passion, her shoulders hunched and hands in claws before her face.

PART III

She lay at his side.

There was only their breathing in the silence. Her fingers brushed his chest and strolled his groin. She had hands like a child.

Abruptly she patted his shoulder and murmured, *"Maika'i, maika'i,"* good, good. Then she arose, wrapped her skirt about her and was gone.

Stone lay in the blue half-dark feeling the ebb of excitement and staring at the thatching overhead.

He had been virtually raped by a pagan queen. She had taken her pleasure and rewarded him with a pat. By his cock she had tugged him to her bidding, like a puppy on a lead.

Was this his fate? To be the plaything of a heathen Juno?

In the dusk Stone poked at his little supper fire. An apparition appeared through nearby trees Kimi, in his *haole* costume.

"And where in God's name have you been?" was Stone's greeting.

"Kamō'ī my capitan now," was the explanation. "Big news, Olohana. You' friend, Aleka Tweed. He alive, on this island!"

By the saints, Alec Tweed was here. He was not alone...

Kimi told him of the capture of the schooner and

murder of its crew. All were dead except the big *haole*. Tweed had been badly beaten but saved from death by the daughter of the Ka'ūpūlehu chief. She was now nursing him back to health.

"Where is this place?"

"Not far. But no need go, Olohana. Kamō'ī send men. They bring Aleka here. Tomorrow morning they come."

"And the ship?"

"No harm to ship. Kamō'ī send men to watch her."

"Does he speak of me?"

"I hear nothing, Olohana." This was not the truth. Kimi had overheard the prince, Manu, urging the king to kill Olohana because he promised only mischief. Kamō'ī's reply had been that Olohana's future was already decided. Kimi preferred not to unnecessarily trouble his friend with this information. With Kamō'ī's protection Olohana need have no worries.

Stone drifted in and out of sleep that night, his thoughts wandering from his tumble with Kahu to anticipation of Tweed's arrival. Knowing he would soon see his friend lifted his spirits enormously. Together he and the Scot would find ways to cope. And the presence of the *Little American* was most heartening.

He was waiting on the beach before sunrise, sitting hunched against the chill and peering over the dark ocean. Several hours later the canoe appeared around the bay's northern headland. When it neared he recognized Tweed's head and shoulders among the occupants. Tweed turned slowly as the craft gained the beach and his eyes went wide at sight of Stone.

"My God, John! Is that really you?"

"Aye, Alec, and damned glad to see you!"

The canoe paddlers and a dark young woman assisted Tweed to shore. He moved stiffly, his face and arms were purple with bruises. His happiness in seeing his comrade was unbounded as the two embraced and clapped one another upon the back.

Then Tweed stepped back, his face serious. "They killed young Tom and the others, John. And they have the ship."

"Aye, I know, Alec."

"But for this sweet lass I´d be dead too." The dusky beauty at his side smiled at Stone.

"I´ve been told, Alec. Come and we´ll talk."

"Where is the *Nahant*?"

"Gone. The swine left me here."

"Will he be back?"

"I don´t know, that´s the hell of it."

"What will we do, John?" With all his burliness, the Scot showed a child´s perplexity.

"It seems the choices will be made for us. The local king is a very powerful man. Meantime we just keep our heads. Now come rest and eat. We have much to talk about."

And talk they did, of the months and days just past.

Neither man had family or other real friends. They gained shared reassurance being together, the warm and unspoken bond between tried and true companions. Tweed was the more confused and apprehensive so Stone tried to put him at ease.

First, he said, they were both lucky to be alive. Second, there seemed scant chance of harm at this king´s hands, if he´d wanted them killed they´d already be dead. Third, rescue could not be far off, with other ships certain to come to the islands. And finally, they made a strong team, proven by past performance. Stone would be depending upon Tweed´s strength and loyalty more than ever before.

"I think this ruddy king will be seeing us soon," he told Tweed. "When he does, we should hold ourselves cold until we find out his thoughts. Thus far he´s treated me well so I doubt he plans any mischief."

"Aye, John. Whatever you say."

Kalani was reporting to his master. Manu sat hunched near the king´s side and Kahu stretched upon a mat nearby. A male dwarf who served as her attendant massaged her feet.

The *haole* ship had been towed awkwardly by canoes to a small inlet at Honokāhau, Kalani said. There she had been draped with coconut and *hala*-tree fronds to hide her from discovery of any *haole* who might chance by. The vessel was in good condition and her holds remained secured. Olohana and Aleka would know what they contained. Meanwhile guards had been posted.

There was no sight of the *Nahant*, he continued. Quimby had not touched elsewhere on Hawai'i island. If he did he would be made extremely unwelcome. The story of the Olowalu killings and Kamō'ī's banishment of the captain was being made known to chiefs everywhere.

The king asked what the two *haole* were doing.

"It appears they are old friends, sire, and very happy to see one another. They walk and talk a great deal. They need for nothing, as you commanded. Aleka, the reddish one, brought Hina of Ka'ūpūlehu with him. Olohana, according to our man Kimi saddens in the memory of Namo, a well-born girl of Olowalu."

"Send men to fetch this Olowalu *wahine*," Kamō'ī instructed. "Take gifts of *haole* tools. If a pleasant arrangement cannot be made, seize her. I desire he be content in all things."

"Surely these two men plot against you, my *ali'i*," said Manu. "They should be killed immediately."

Queen Kahu rebuked him: "These are men of great value to our master and they have done no wrong. You hate too much, prince."

Kamō'ī often wished Kahu would temper her remarks in meetings of men. But just as often her candid tongue served him good purpose.

"What is their mood?" he asked the prime minister.

"Worried, sire, and curious. They wonder about their fate and ask many questions. Every day Olohana asks to see you."

Kamō'ī paused before responding. The *haole* had been together six days; time enough for them to talk and assess their positions. And he was tiring of this temporary residence in Lako's small compound, as was Kahu. She did not complain but found little ways of letting him know. She missed Kailua and their fine houses in the cove at Kamakahonu. These comforts were less than a day away by canoe.

He might as well settle the question, and now.

"Bring them to me," he ordered.

In three days at O'ahu Quimby had topped off his water casks and taken more vegetables. Now the island lay astern, its Wai'anae mountains disappearing in fading light.

In the forecastle Tan Sing gathered his Chinese colleagues to his plan. The whites were at ease and unsuspicious, he said, fingering the scar across his nose. Weather promised to be kindly. They would do the job next day.

Privately he felt relief that John Stone was no longer aboard. The bosun would likely been a hard man to kill, not to mention the regret Sing would have felt at his murder.

He had no ambivalence about the others. He planned personally to take the pleasure of confronting the captain. It was unfortunate about the Filipino cook and the black boy but Sing's concept of trust required eliminating all but his fellow Chinese.

The watches changed, night descended and the men on the *Nahant* slept.

Sing arose early and studied the dawning sky. It was clear and bright with a steady wind and only a gentle rolling sea. He ate a breakfast of pork, tea and breadfruit then casually signalled his followers. Sing himself made the first move, strolling up to Delano and placing his knife's point under the gunner's chin in the soft part back of the bone. Delano froze and his eyes bulged. Sing tore the armory keys from his waist and tossed them to one of his men. Others swiftly bound and gagged the gunner. Within the same minutes Sprague, Scrimmage and Maul were being seized on the quarterdeck.

Sing and the others silently raced below and opened the arms locker then hurried aft to the captain's cabin. Sing himself threw the door open and entered the captain's quarters behind his aimed pistol. Quimby, sitting at tea in trousers and filthy singlet, started to his feet, sputtering staring into the mouth of the weapon. Soon he too was tied, then dragged, cursing, up the ladder to the main deck.

Maul, Delano, Scrimmage, the Filipino cook and Blue Bob were dispatched mercifully with pistol balls through their brains. Bodies were thrown overboard, spaced a few minutes apart. Sing wanted the sharks attracted.

Sprague was next. He was on his knees, near collapse in terror, his eyes popping and sweat pouring from his face. Whining sounds struggled through a kerchief stuffed in his mouth. He groaned as a line was secured tightly under his arms and tried vainly to scream as he was eased over the ship's side.

The first shark tore off one of his legs, its spade-shaped head jerking from side to side as it gnawed at the bone. The second fish was a giant. The impact of its immense jaws ripped the mate from the line. For a moment the blue water was thrashed into white froth. Then the shark, with what was left of Sprague, was lost in the brig's wake.

Considerably more time was taken with Quimby.

His clothes were torn away and he was forced face down over a hogshead. The flabby naked body quivered over the cask while his legs twitched and trembled.

"Oh please, oh Jesus, oh please," he whimpered. There was not a shred left of the captain's arrogant and brutal persona.

The most recent young victim of his beatings was first. With a back still raw from the whipping he stepped forward and rammed a swab handle deep up Quimby's rectum. The captain spurted urine and shrieked. The next man took a solid grip on Quimby's hair and then slowly carved off one ear. A third Chinese sliced off the other. The captain babbled and writhed, his blood forming a pool on the deck.

The others came, singly at first and then in numbers, to lash at his shaking white form with ropes and chain, stabbing and slashing with knives. For surprising minutes Quimby's screams were constant then, somewhat to the disappointment of the mutineers, he died. A few men continued to beat and cut at him viciously.

Sing shouted. The butchered remains were dragged to the gunwales and tossed overboard. The tattered corpse sank almost immediately, leaving barely a wispy pink stain in the rich blue.

Kimi entered Kamō'ī's presence crawling on hands and knees. His beaver hat tipped precariously and the tails of his shabby coat trailed on the ground exposing naked buttocks.

Tweed, walking behind him, chuckled.

The magnificence of the court sobered him.

Dominating the colorful tableau was the gargantuan emperor, elevated on a thick pile of mats. The voluptuous Kahu lay near his feet, head cupped in her hands. Squatting attendants held the tall wands of feathered *kahili* aloft. Other servants waved woven-leaf fans to keep gnats from the royal torsos.

Kamō'ī wore a rich red-silk Chinese robe over his loincloth. Kalani and Manu sat nearby clad only in *malo* and whale-tooth pendants. The crazed and fading old *kahuna*, Pahoa, crouched in white *kapa*, his usually manic eyes now tightly lidded. Around the edges of this group were Kai and the spearsmen of his guard, lesser *ali'i* and their women. The ladies lolled in fetching nudity, gazing upon the newcomers with raw curiosity.

"*Aloha nui kakou*," the king said. His voice was warm and melodious. Stone felt his tension ease. Tweed remained uneasy. This was his first sight of the stern and impressive monarch.

Kamō'ī smiled, softening his cowing visage. His eyes appraised. Olohana was poised with dignity, he noted, while Tweed was nervous, apprehensive. He spoke to Stone: "Today Kimi will translate for me. I know you speak our language but I wish your friend to understand all I say."

"That will be appreciated, your majesty. Both my friend and I want to know what is to become of us."

"You are my guests," Kamō'ī smiled again. "You, Olohana, showed courage when you refused to take part in the killings at Olowalu. And you, Aleka, proved yourself a brave man at Ka'ūpūlehu. We admire men of courage and compassion. Neither of you are guilty of the viciousness of your captain or the stupidity of our chief at Ka'ūpūlehu. Stay with us in comfort and peace."

He waved his hand in invitation for the men to sit. Kimi remained on his hands and knees, his face pained with the effort of interpreting. The elder Kalani listened intently, watching Olohana. Manu sat rigidly, his arms folded and Stone felt his enmity. Kahu lay stretched on her side, one melony, swelling of breast resting on the other. The corners of her generous mouth curved in a smile. Stone determined he would not look at her.

The king was saying, Kimi relayed, that there might not be another *haole* ship for a long time. They might be his guests for many months, perhaps longer. Who could tell?

Stone and Tweed exchanged looks. They had already discussed this prospect at length. More at ease now, Tweed spoke:

"What has happened to the *Little American*?"

"The ship is safe," Kamō'ī said, "and now in my service. I have taken it in payment for the captain's brutal behavior. Do you think such a price unreasonable?"

The act of a despot, Stone thought. The Maui dead were not his people. But neither he nor Tweed contradicted.

"I am told this is a fine ship," Kamō'ī continued. "Not as large as most *haole* ships, but newly made and strong. And the two red-mouthed guns she carries will be important additions to my armory. Do you men know of my store of guns?"

"Only of those Captain Quimby traded," Stone answered.

He had others, the king went on, and pistols too, made by the Beretanee, British. "These are said to be the best. Is this true?"

"Yes," Stone replied. "But Americans are now making excellent weapons. For a long time the Iron Act of the English prohibited making guns. But the war changed many things like this."

"Why did the war happen?" the king asked. He had heard answers to this question before but was curious to hear Olohana's version.

"King George imposed heavy and unfair taxes. There were many other unjust actions and we had no vote in our own rule."

"I too impose taxes," the king said. "And my subjects accept my rule and the dictates of my chiefs and *kahuna* without question. This is the way of kings."

"I understand this, sire. But I have observed during my short residence here that you are a kind ruler who treats his people fairly and with affection." I must not lay this on too thick, Stone warned himself. "The *kapu* governing the use of lands and water and taking of fishes are laws benefitting everyone. I have learned how your highness moves frequently among his people and knows their needs and desires. King George was a long distance from America, across a great sea. Even in London town where he lived very few of his subjects ever saw him."

"This is not wise for a ruler," Kamōʻi observed. "Does George Washington move among his people?"

"More than King George," Stone guessed aloud.

"Has Olohana seen Washington?"

"Yes, when I was scarcely more than a boy, helping Washington's soldiers. He spoke to me once."

"What did he say?"

"He told me to feed his horse," Stone smiled. Tweed laughed nervously. Kimi translated with sweeping gestures, outlining in air, and Stone realized Hawaiians had never seen a horse. The king laughed too and in that moment seemed only a large and jolly man. Then his face sent serious again. The muskets he had obtained from Quimby. Why were they different from those he had bartered from previous traders?

"Perhaps," Stone answered, "because they possess improved firing mechanisms and shorter barrels which have come into use in recent years. Captain Quimby made a fine bargain about fifteen dollars apiece on the weapons from an Irish man in Boston." He was tempted to add that this was because the Paddy was a notorious villain and the guns were probably stolen.

"How long were you a soldier of Washington?" asked Kamōʻi.

"Almost two years, sire. First carrying messages and ammunition during the battle at Boston. Mister Tweed and I, very young then, met at the time. Later we shipped on private vessels and have been friends since, becoming like brothers."

Kamōʻi nodded approval. "I too have a valued friend in the noble Kalani. This man has been both father and brother to me."

The white-haired minister dipped his head in acknowledgement. Stone thought his face both wise and kind.

Then Kamōʻi drew a pistol from beneath his robe. Kimi sucked in his breath. Stone and Tweed stiffened. But the king merely held the weapon out to Stone, handle first. "Tell me what you think of this."

Stone took it. The piece was of excellent quality, a .22 bore finished of bright steel with carved walnut slabs. Oval silver medallions bore the maker's name, Richards, on one side and "Strand, London," on the other. Under the breech were marks of testing by the London Gunmakers Guild.

"A bonnie barker," Tweed murmured over his shoulder. Stone examined the empty pistol then handed it back.

"An excellent weapon, your majesty. Very well fitted by a good maker. With care, it will have a long life."

"I have ten like this from a British captain," Kamōʻī said. "And many muskets in addition to those from Captain Quimby. I also own four of the turn-around guns." By the latter, he meant swivels. His tone had slightest hint of boasting.

And now, thought Stone, he has the two six-pound cannon of the *Little American* plus the trade muskets she carries that he doesn't even know about. Kamōʻī was searching his face for reaction.

"A fine collection, sire," Stone said. "Your highness now has gun power equal to that of many *haole* ships."

"It is also more than that owned by any other island king," Kamōʻī said. "This is as it should be. It is my destiny to become ruler of all these islands. This prophecy was made by the oldest and wisest of all *kahuna,* a man from Molokaʻi, island of the high priests."

He addressed Olohana, then let his eyes drift to Tweed. *Haole* tended to sneer or laugh at such statements. Here he saw only respectful attention to his words. He went on: "Now that our islands have been brought into the world of other nations it is vital that Hawaiians be joined as one people for common good and protection. But other kings on Maui, Oʻahu and Kauaʻi do not share this vision. They do not understand the perils of remaining scattered kingdoms separated by ocean, each going its own way. They foolishly believe they can face problems alone, deal with each ship as it comes. Some, made witless by their selfishness and greed, even talk of killing the *haole*.

He paused, studying the two men while Kimi translated. He

had never before spoken his thoughts to white men. He continued:

"I was with King Opu and his high chiefs greeting Captain Cook, in this same bay, not many years ago. Only a fool would not then have realized what awful power the *haole* had for destruction and war. And the power was in your iron. We had known iron before only in bits floating ashore in pieces of wood. Until Cook we had never seen guns, knives, axes and chisels. Without iron our strength only is in numbers. If we remain divided in warring factions we will be weak, easy victims of the strangers.

He stared at Olohana. It was the bosun he most desired to impress and Stone's face continued to show interest.

"For many generations Hawaiians have lived under our gods in the comfort and plenty the gods provide. We *ali'i* are their earthy representatives and the *kahuna* priests and master craftsmen retain and practice the knowledge of the ages. The sacred system *kapu* keeps order and dictates proper behavior from birth until death.

These laws are foreign to you *haole*. There will always be the threat of murders from evil men like Quimby. I desire Hawai'i to remain Hawaiian but to survive our people must understand *haole* ways, especially of war. We will not sacrifice our *mana* in making these changes. The *haole* must learn to deal with us as equals, not mindless savages. We are told your *haole* God, Kesu Kisto, said all men were brothers. Is this not so?"

"Yes, sire, this is so," Stone agreed. He thought of Kimi's story about a previous captain who had tried to convert Kamō'ī to Christianity. The man had cited the miracles of Jesus. Kamō'ī had suggested the captain jump off a nearby cliff, if Jesus saved him, Kamō'ī would adopt his religion. The captain had immediately returned to discussion of hogs and salt.

"Teaching my people to place thoughts upon paper that may then be transported great distances will be a fine gift," Kamō'ī continued.

"I will be happy to teach your highness how to write," Stone offered. "With your strong mind you would learn quickly."

"I have more important things to learn first," Kamō'ī answered. "The magic of writing is not as strong as the power of guns and ships. Thoughts on paper would not stop a man like Quimby from killing Hawaiians. Guns and ships will give such people serious thoughts before murdering others. I have seen that men with guns do not always need to use them. Having the weapons is often enough."

"Canny bugger," Tweed muttered. Stone's glance was drawn to Kahu. She was watching and listening while her forefinger traced a circle around one nipple.

When Stone's attention returned Kamō'ī was saying, "Our people know little of guns and large ships. Perhaps Olohana and Aleka will teach my men while you are spending this time among us?"

The two seamen exchanged looks as the king went on: "My gratitude will be large. You will be *ali'i* with fine houses and many servants. You will want for nothing."

There was a pause. Stone was tempted to ask what would happen should they refuse.

"My warriors hurt themselves with guns. Men are crippled and killed by their own weapons. You can prevent this." Kamō'ī's words were polite but their tone near flat. This man rarely made requests, Stone thought.

The *haole* ship required special care and knowledge, Kamō'ī continued.

"You are skilled in handling such vessels and your help will be great. This ship will be the leader of the largest canoe fleet in all the islands. Even now my carvers and *kahuna* are in the high forests selecting the greatest trees for my war canoes. No other *ali'i* in all Hawai'i will have such fleet."

The whites glanced again at one another. The king sighed.

"My best men will be your students. Great warriors will learn well and obey without question.

"Little choice here," Stone muttered to Tweed.

"Verra little," said Tweed.

He remained impressed by the scene in the great house, the massive queens lying about, the bristling of warrior's spears and the nobles worshipfully attentive. "He seems a fair sort, don´t he?"

Stone mused, "God only knows how long we will be here."

"Will they want to hang us if we ever get home?" Tweed asked.

"Maybe. Here *he* is the law. No nation lays claim on this place. If we don´t agree we´re not likely to need worry about the problems of American courts."

"We may find ourselves fighting white men."

"Not likely. He is too shrewd for that, it´s the other islands he´s after."

"Seems so."

"There´s the ship, too." Stone´s voice dropped to a whisper. "With us in command..."

"I ken your meaning."

Stone spoke to Kimi: "Tell his majesty we will do what we can to help until another *haole* ship arrives."

"I am pleased," was the king´s sober response. "Now you are my *ali'i*."

Kalani nodded approval at the whites. Manu stared with ill-concealed animosity. Kahu smiled. The king questioned Stone and Tweed: "Is there anything you desire? I have many *haole* things in my storehouses."

Boots, Tweed said. His own now decorated the extremities of the chief of Ka'ūpūlehu. Stone said his wants were simple and being well supplied. Kimi relayed these answers then pleaded hoarsely to Stone: "Olohana, speak to him of me."

Stone pointed to Kimi. "This man is my friend. He must be treated well and given respect."

Kimi´s voice quivered in translation. The king´s face clouded. Stone realized he had made a mistake. No one made demands of Kamō'ī. Kalani moved to avert unpleasantness: "This *haole* does not know any better, my lord. Forgive his impertinence."

The king´s annoyance passed. Kalani was right and Kamō'ī wanted the bosun pleased. He stared evenly at Stone while directing that some use be found for Kimi at the court.

Kimi´s brow scraped the earth in his joyous thanks. With a few casual words the king had elevated him far from the ranks of ordinary commoners.

Kamō'i crooked a finger and raised his voice to those in attendance. A dozen women resting in the background came to their feet. Kahu made a remark that brought laughter. Kimi said these women were unattached and being offered to Olohana and Aleka.

"I have one who is woman enough," Tweed said, breaking into a broad smile. "But I see no harm in a bit on the side."

"His majesty is most generous," Stone said. "And his kingdom is rich in beautiful *wahine*. I have no wish to take one from his personal store."

Kamō'i uttered a short laugh. "An *ali'i nui* has all the women he wishes, it makes no difference. *Wahine* are easily opened calabashes, containers with removable lids. These are well-born. It is best for *ali'i* to have several wives to make chiefly sons."

"Perhaps his highness will give me time to make a choice," Stone suggested. He had no plans to be here long enough to establish a dynasty.

"As you wish," said the king. "Now I desire that we sit and eat and talk. I have many questions about the white men and their world and the worlds of black people and China people and other *haole*.

The inviting lava depression was fed by cool clear spring water under trees at the village edge. His bath was a delight. Stone sat on flat-worn stones in the delicious wash, luxuriating in the refreshment and recalling the afternoon just past.

Kamō'i´s curiosity was unbounded, his questions tumbling upon one another. How many wives did President Washington keep? Did King George indulge in sports like boxing and wrestling with his nobles? Why were the skins of sea animals more valuable than those of the land? If the Scots and English lived only day´s travel from each other why did they not speak the same language?

Stone answered as best he could, with an occasional assist from Alec Tweed. Both saw their answers being stored in a remarkably agile mind. Their new master would keep them on their toes.

Stone stepped from the pool and mopped himself with his blouse. Then he drew on trousers and boots and started to walk back to the village.

How quickly one´s life could change!

This sudden move into the service of a Hawaiian king seemed a fantasy. But surely it was wiser for Tweed and himself to accept the situation than anger a ruler with the authority of a deity. Even if this could be counted a prison its bars were invisible, food excellent, occupants cheerful and warden most accommodating. The alternative to working for Kamō´ī was a slovenly beggarly existence on the generosity of commoners, if not far worse. One never knew... Within this tenure there might be opportunity for profit in sandalwood, guns, provisions...

Canoes had been drawn upon the beach and small knots of people had gathered by the shore to face the horizon flames of dying day. Soft laughter could be heard, a pleasing counterpoint to liquid sighing of the surf. The scene was tranquil in rosy light, palm trunks bluish in the dusk.

Then he saw her with Hina, Tweed´s woman. Not believing his eyes he walked closer.

It was Namo.

He felt a pleasure he had never before experienced. He spoke her name and she turned, than ran to him with a little cry of joy.

He led her to his house, warmed by her nearness, aware of her clean scent and small hand tight in his. She chattered in her excitement, eyes shining, smiling up at him. When Kamō´ī´s men came, she had joined them gladly and her father and the Olowalu chief had been happy with the gifts of *haole* iron.

Their reunion was tender, loving and long. She would never go away, she said. She would be Olohana´s woman forever.

Stone realized she had said something he wanted very much to hear. This innocent naive island *wahine* who had come so casually into his life had become special to him. Somehow he found her love meaningful and important, unlike that of any other woman he had ever known. There was trust and giving in her smile and immense caring in her touch. He found he wanted to hold her, protect her, make love to her time after time and have her always by his side. Stone found himself, for the first time in his far-from-sheltered life, in love. The feeling was warm and soft and splendid.

PART IV

*O*lohana scratched the king's name in damp sand and Kamō'ī attempted to copy it. He labored painfully.

For centuries Hawaiians had carved stick-figures into lava stone—petroglyphic men, canoes, sails and fish to record births, journeyings and other happenings. These confusing whirls and slants of **haole** writing, which portrayed no objects, proved quite different and puzzling.

Clumsily Kamō'ī tried again. The results remained illegible and he grunted in frustration. Again, Stone spoke encouragement: "Once more, sire. **Slowly.**"

Kamō'ī scowled and bent to the task, his mouth tight. He would not be defeated by the simple manipulation of a stick. This time he made a fair representation of Olohana's large letters.

Kamoi

"Excellent, your highness! There is your name Kamō'ī!"
The king's eyebrows went up. He smiled at Kalani.
"It does not look like Kamō'ī," he said.

The royal court was moving back to Kailua.

As if by magic giant canoes appeared off Kealakekua at dawn. By early afternoon Kamō'ī's party, including the newly recruited foreigners, was riding into the broad bay about fifteen miles to the north. Kailua, Kalani told Stone, was the place most favored by Kamō'ī. He liked its gentle weather, rich fishing and excellent surfriding. Deep in the lee of the soaring volcano the district had a warm and languorous air. Ample fresh water was caught from the uplands. A community of some five thousand souls lived comfortably along its shores.

Stone and Tweed were given commodious thatched residences near the center of the bay shoreline. In typical Hawaiian custom these were surrounded by smaller structures for women, servants and cooking. Small canoes nudged a brief beach. Homes of commoners were strung elsewhere along the strand. The king´s large compound dominated a nearby small cove called Kamakahonu. This inlet was protected and placid, sheltering the king´s splendid canoe.

Kamōʻī lost no time in putting Stone to work.

Midmorning of the next day saw the bosun carefully securing a cocked musket among lava stones, muzzle pointed out to sea. He had tied a length of fine native sennit line to its trigger and trailed this out some five paces behind the weapon. He motioned for the king and Kalani to come to his side. Manu, with Kai and members of the guard, stood a few yards distant watching with silent interest.

Stone yanked the line, firing the piece.

The smoke puff was accompanied by a spurt of flame and a crackling sound as the breech assembly shattered. As Stone had expected, the explosion they witnessed would have torn away the face of anyone firing the weapon in conventional style.

"Who traded these guns to you, sire?"

"An English captain," the king replied. "A man who will not be pleased with his welcome should he come again. I would like to know how many guns are treacherous, like this one."

"It will take time to find out," said Stone.

"I will be grateful. You justify the value we anticipated in your knowledge and help, Olohana."

"Perhaps Billy Pitt will give me a hand?" Stone asked. Billy Pitt was Kalani's new name, given him by Stone from that of his counterpart, the British prime minister. Kalani liked it as did the other Hawaiians. All pronounced it Peelee Peet.

A quick inspection revealed that all Kamōʻi's muskets were the Short Land variety, in use for about forty years. Most bore British Marine and Militia side plates and all had seen decades of use. The Englishman must have acquired them for a few shillings each, Stone mused.

With Billy Pitt's help he began a thorough examination, sighting barrels, working ramrods and inspecting pans and touch holes. All the while, with Kimi's help in Hawaiian, he kept up a running explanation of his actions for his audience, emphasizing keeping the arms scrupulously clean and lightly lubricated. The oil of the candlenut, *kukui*, which the Hawaiians burned for lamps, would serve, he said. This was vital to proper care of the firearms.

When he finished the inspection he pronounced ten out of three hundred-plus muskets to be dangerously faulty. These would be beaten into hoes, daggers, chisels and other implements, Kalani-Pitt said. Hawaiians had learned these tricks at the forges of visiting ships.

Stone turned his attention to the powder casks. Fortunately these had been kept dry in a cave with the guns. He burned samples from several kegs and none appeared to be diluted with alien substances. Examination of the pistols was last. All were of good quality orthodox flintlocks, 22 caliber and made in London. Only one was unusual, a Swiss weapon by Durs Egg. Its appearance was not smart but the precision of its lock mechanism, trueness of bore and excellent balance marked it as a special piece. Also its darkened metal would be less susceptible to ravages of salt air. Stone lingered over its examination.

"Does Olohana admire this one?" the king asked.

"Yes, sire, very much."

"It is yours, with my gratitude," the king said.

Stone thanked him and tucked the pistol in his belt. Manu mumbled something in an annoyed tone and Billy Pitt silenced him with a glare.

Pitt and the king entered into a rapid conversation. Stone was pleased at how fast he was coming to understand Hawaiian. They were taking account of the king's weaponry. With muskets on hand plus those acquired from Quimby, Kamō'ī now owned well over a hundred guns.

"Is there powder and shot enough to supply all these, Olohana?"

Stone scratched figures in the sand with his finger, doing arithmetic. The gathering of brown men watched, fascinated by this curious act.

"A rough estimate, sire, is enough to fire each gun about twelve times."

Kamō'ī nodded satisfaction. He addressed Kai's soldiers, ordering that none of the guns were to be fired without his, Billy Pitt's, Manu's or Olohana's permission. One day soon they would be distributed to worthy men. In the meantime all were to be carefully cleaned and bathed in oil as the *haole ali'i*, Olohana, had instructed.

The trim schooner had survived the Ka'ūpūlehu piracy without damage.

She rode buoyant and level on the near-hidden waters of Honokōhau, indicating that none of her copper sheathing had been torn away. The two cannon and swivel guns were in place and none of her metal fittings were missing. The holds had not been tampered with but the small forecastle and after cabins had been looted of everything moveable. Tweed said the losses were not serious—tools, galley gear and the men's sea chests. Her principal cargo lay intact. Therein lay her value.

"What is this cargo?" Billy Pitt asked.

"Three hundred otter skins," said Tweed through Olohana. "All full pelts and top grade. Along with fifty trade muskets and ammunition, and knives, tools, blankets, flints, skillets and the like." Tweed and Stone had agreed that Stone would speak Hawaiian when dealing with the king and others. Kimi was always with them on important occasions and could keep Tweed aware of what was being said.

"Your king is richer than he knows, Billy Pitt," said Stone. The old man smiled, still adjusting to his new name.

Stone went on: "Nothing else must be taken, particularly the bottom sheathing. And the cannon must be under guard day and night."

"This will be done," Pitt assured him. "But what Hawaiian would be able to steal an object as large as these guns?"

Stone did not answer. He had heard of natives who had thrown a massive anvil over a ship's side then brought it ashore by diving down and pushing and pulling it along the ocean's bottom.

Voices rose from the attending canoes. Kamō'ī was approaching. In minutes the big double hulls of the royal canoe were bumping the *Little American*.

The king jumped aboard without ceremony, lithe as a greyhound despite his dimensions. He strode the deck, tugging shrouds, stroking guns and uttering grunts of approval. Despite his towering figure, thought Stone, he was like a small boy with a new plaything.

Pitt informed his master of the cargo and Kamō'ī was pleased.

"But the ship is more important than what she carries," he said. "This is the first *haole* ship under command of a Hawaiian king, therefore a symbol of great meaning. I will stay here tonight so I may better know this vessel."

Tweed smashed the hasps of the hold with a maul and chisel brought for the purpose. The king was delighted with its contents. The muskets were British Army weapons with the Tower of London stamp. Stone assured him all were in good condition. The sea otter furs were beautiful, rich, dark and thick, almost five feet long, silvered at their bases and turning to exquisite dark brown. The fur rippled voluptuously, glistening even in the waning light.

He would sell these off to the next visiting captain on his way to China, Kamō'ī said. They should command a high price since the purchaser would not have to suffer hardship and danger to acquire them in the Indian lands.

"Your majesty is growing rich in *haole* goods," remarked Stone.

"I will be richer in days to come," Kamō'ī said. "And this wealth will be used wisely. But the value of guns and ships is only as great as that of the men who command them. They must be men of special skills, like you and Aleka."

Mats were brought to elevate the royal buttocks. The others lounged around the king on the after deck. Tweed had jimmied open a locker containing brandy, tobacco and pipes and all but the king lighted up. Stone had heard Kamō'ī once say that he had no desire to take the smoke of dead leaves into his breast but had no objection to others doing so. Twilight was deepening and food was brought from the small settlement on shore. Honokōhau was a small and picturesque inlet. A few fishermen's huts nestled under palms along the shore. Shallows over the coral reef were glass clear. Far inland Hualālai volcano soared above its slopes of dark brown lava.

During supper the king had many questions, mostly about guns. Guns, he said, would greatly change the Hawaiian way of making war.

"What is the Hawaiian way?" asked Stone.

"First the enemy kings announce they are ready to fight," Kamō'ī explained. "Special *kahuna* of war are then consulted for interpretation of signs in the winds, stars and moon. Certain religious formalities and rituals are carefully observed along with proper sacrifices to Kū, our god of power. Much time is spent in preparation. War is a test of skills and courage. Attacks are not made upon an unprepared enemy."

He rinsed his hand in a calabash offered by an attendant before continuing: "When a time and place are agreed upon, the main battle is always preceded by contests between the best and bravest warriors. Champions of both sides meet in boxing, wrestling and spear-throwing duels. When these are finished, the main bodies of troops lock in battle. In the final stages, the conflict is always hand-to-hand with clubs and daggers often chief against chief or king against king and always to the death. Women and children are spared, except for *wahine kaua*, war-women who fight with men. Vanquished soldiers are sought out and killed or banished into the *kauwa*, or slave, class."

Kamō'ī paused. "What is the *haole* way?"

"Different, your highness," answered Stone. He glanced at Tweed, who was shaking his head in wonderment. "White men's countries do not fight with religious ritual, though religion causes many wars. Armies and navies almost always attack without warning and strong countries overrun weak ones without notice. Kings, admirals and generals do not personally fight, but direct their men from behind the lines. Often, many women are raped and children killed. After the battle, conquerors usually loot and burn the villages and lands gained."

Kamō'ī exchanged glances with Billy Pitt. It appeared that the *haole* were even more savage than he had believed...

"Is this the way Washington fought?" he wanted to know.

"No, sire. He and his generals fought and suffered along with their men. There was no raping or burning because it was our own land we fought upon and among our own people."

"But the Americans were weaker," Kamōʻī said. "How is it they came to win?"

"The slow process of wearing down a stronger opponent," Stone explained. "King George had to send men and supplies across a vast ocean and this cost time. Much fighting was done on ground unsuitable to the English way of making war. Their battalions marched shoulder to shoulder in files three men deep and this was suicide against riflemen in forests and deep brush. The English tried to adapt but their basic moves remained the same a massing of troops, delivery of volleys at the last possible moment and shortest range, then a final bayonet charge. Such tactics played into rebel hands. The Americans moved in small groups, sometimes alone, and were excellent shots. Scarcely an American household did not have a gun and a man with experience in using it for game. These marksmen picked off the red coats of the British with ease then dissolved into the landscape like the Indians they themselves had earlier been fighting."

"The old ways are not always the best, sire," Stone finished.

Kamōʻī thought a moment before answering: "They are best in respecting what man cannot change," he said. "Nothing can alter the flight of the sun, waxings and wanings of the moon, the movings of tides or shifting of winds. The spawning of fishes, growing of *kalo* and making of sweet water are in the hands of the gods and forever will be. With all the startling new knowledge and changes, the workings of our gods remain the same." His voice was low and forceful, his eyes bright with his belief.

"I am willing to consider new ways of commerce and war and governing," he continued. "But our gods and *kapu* must remain unharmed. Iron, guns, glass and cloth may be touched, their magic explained. But the *haole* offer no proof that Iesu Kristo is a god above all others. Rather your people make mockery of your Bible-book. You kill senselessly, like Quimby, cheat like the Englishman with guns and, clearly, do not love your fellow man. Further, I have been told that many China-people bow obeisance to a fat smiling god and those of another country worship one called Allah. Thus Iesu Kristo is not the god of every *haole* and I am not alone in doubting him." His black eyes stared evenly at Stone.

"Do you believe in Iesu Kristo, Olohana?"

Stone was tempted to lie. Perhaps it would help to ingratiate him with the monarch and, in fact, he had not seen the inside of a church since he was a boy. But the truth would save possible future subterfuge: "Yes, your highness. But I make no demands that others believe."

Kamō'ī waved his hand skyward, dismissing the subject.

"There is space for all our gods," he said.

Stone and Tweed settled into a comfortable existence, their every need fulfilled.

Daily, farmers brought melons and vegetables and fishermen deposited choice catches at their doors. The king's storehouse provided luxuries of tea, tobacco and wine. Each man had a platoon of servants. Kamō'ī's edict that they be treated as *ali'i* was strictly observed.

Their women were attentive and loving. Namo and Hina supervised households with the firm authority of women raised as chiefesses. The lives of both ladies revolved around their men, though Hina's enrapture with the big Scot was manifested more openly. She took delight in combing his sandy locks and massaging his back. Often when they sat together she idly stroked his genitals. Hina was considerably darker skinned than any of her sisters, moving Tweed once to remark: "Faith, she is as fair as the driven charcoal."

The two men soon assumed a loose routine. Both arose early and after sunrise were off, Tweed to the ship and Stone to join his diminutive army.

Stone strolled inland where a fallow yam field served as the parade ground for his loin clothed infantry. He was met by the royal captain, Kai, who called the soldiers to their feet at Olohana's approach. All were young, tall and strong hand-picked by Kamō'ī and Billy Pitt. Every morning Stone ran them through marching drills as a disciplinary exercise. He followed these efforts with instruction in the care and handling of muskets. The troop was about one hundred and fifty in total, bright and burly warriors who responded well to his teaching. His principal problem was to convince them to take the training seriously, for they were seemingly conditioned to the idea of war as a sport. Every man obeyed with alacrity, respecting Stone's *ali'i* status, but few seemed to fully comprehend the awful power of the weapons. This problem was solved on the fourth day when one of the men shot off the toes of a comrade.

The carelessness stopped.

Tweed spent his days aboard the schooner with his neophyte sailors. The king had moved her to Kailua for the Scot's training sessions. Tweed had two sets of pupils, schooled on alternate days. All hands were learning well and fast, he said, natural sailors because they were natural water-people. Soon he would take them out to sea and test their skills.

Stone raised his eyebrows when Tweed said this.

"Himself and Billy Pitt will be aboard," Tweed informed.

Neither man had mentioned the possibility of leaving the islands for weeks.

When last the subject had surfaced, they found themselves in agreement that life with Kamō'ī had decided advantages over life at sea.

What would they do when another ship arrived?

"If we signed on it's back to being seamen again," Tweed said.

"A bit of a comedown for big Hawaiian chiefs," Stone

thought aloud.

"Aye. I like being a grand man," the Scot smiled. "'Tis a long way from that miserable wee croft in Scotland. And what about you? Dinna ye think about return to Boston?"

"It crosses my mind and lately as quickly leaves. There's nothing there for me but time to kill until another sailing. Home is wherever I'm happy." Stone tamped his pipe.

"Alec, I believe Heaven or Fate or whatever has a plan for each of us and being here is part of it. I enjoy being a noble and will play the part as long as it's comfortable. One day the Fates may send us back to what we were. Meantime, this is a ruddy good life with interesting duties and loving ladies. I swear I've never known the fondness I feel for this one. So let's accept the plan as long as it lasts and no matter who made it, be it God or Fate or Quimby or this king. We'll see what our mood is when the next ship arrives."

"Aye and we see what kind of tub she is."

"If things go wrong we can find a way to take the schooner, Alec."

"I've thought of that course also."

"Yes. We could do it, wouldn't need much help, a half dozen good men..."

"Where would you choose to sail her?"

"It's a large ocean, Alec, a world all its own. We are not criminals, would not have to hide." The only awkwardness, Stone thought, would be in a return to Boston and the need for explanation...

"What could go wrong here?" Tweed asked naively.

"We could lose favor with this king. He could lose the fights he plans. There might be trouble with some visiting ship, even some great nation taking a fancy to this place."

Unspoken thoughts of the disagreeable prince, Manu, also crossed Stone's mind. "Not everyone here welcomes us with open arms, Alec. We'll be wise to watch our backs."

Kimi visited, seeking relaxation and fellowship with the *haole*.

The novelty of attending Kamō'ī's court was wearing thin and he was finding life on his hands and knees quite trying. As a minor functionary he had no task other than teaching English words to the king, Billy Pitt and Kahu or answering their queries about *haole* ways.

He was fed and housed well, living on the fringes of regality. It had too quickly become all a bore. Nothing had been said about the homestead he coveted.

He had already offered a bribe in white men's tools and silver to a neighboring chief for the acres he desired. But such transfers needed the approval of Kamō'ī, arbiter in the use of all lands. Daring to broach the matter to the king would be a serious breach of etiquette so Kimi had hinted strongly of his desires to Billy Pitt. Now he waited, there being nothing else he could do.

One late afternoon he gratefully accepted a tin cup full of port from Olohana then sprawled with a sigh. In the embrace of wine, Kimi became voluble with news of the court so Stone always poured generously for him. At the moment the little Hawaiian needed no priming.

A very important *kahuna* had arrived at Kamakahonu Cove, he reported. He was the oldest and most revered member of the colony of high priests on Moloka'i island, the same who had earlier prophesied that Kamō'ī would one day be *ali'i nui*, the highest chief. The old man was also known as the wisest of all priests in reading and interpreting of signs and omens of war.

He told Kamō'ī that the time of his greatest glory drew near. But he must heighten preparations, finish large numbers of war canoes and learn the use of the *haole* guns. Pono, the ruler of Maui, Moloka'i and Lana'i, had taken residence at Hana on Maui. This was an ominous move, for Hana was just across the channel from Hawai'i and Pono had brought many soldiers with him. Despite Pono's reputation as an invincible king, all the signs of moon, winds and stars pointed to a victory for Kamō'ī. First, however, there were certain things the king must do.

Kimi interrupted himself: "This man very big *kahuna*. Old Pahoa look at ground when this one talk."

"Go on," urged Stone. "What must the king do?"

Most important, Kimi relayed, was to build a great temple to Kū, god of power.

The site had already been chosen by priests rigidly trained for such efforts. They had studied many places and decided on a hillside overlooking the bay at Kawaihae to the north. The *heiau* would be called Koholā, from its site, known as the Hill of Whales. Specialist *kahuna* were now working on the proper design. This must be the grandest of all *heiau*, built to the glory of Kū and his earthly representative, Kamō'ī. Its size would make all other temples in Hawai'i seem like mounds of stones gathered by small children.

Kimi talked on. Other edicts had been imposed by the Moloka'i high priest: Everyone capable of lifting a stone must participate in the construction of Koholā, from toddlers to the very old. The king himself must pay respects with humble labor. Only one person would be exempted from the toil and he must be a close relative of Kamō'ī. Through this *ali'i*, unsullied by labor, the immense power of Kū would pass into the *heiau*, giving it the strongest possible *mana*.

More, the sacrifices of twelve men were to mark the building, the *kahuna* specified. Eleven of these could be from the outcast class or be common criminals. But the twelfth man must be a person of considerable significance, an *ali'i* of the highest rank. Koholā could be considered sacred and appropriately dedicated only when these instructions had been scrupulously carried out.

"When does all this begin?" Stone asked.

"Already begin," Kimi answered. "King give order today."

The walk over the lava flow was long and hot. But

Manu had disguised himself as a commoner and his cape of leaves protected him from the relentless sun.

It was noon and he encountered no one. About a mile from Kailua village he headed shoreward. The sea surged and boomed against bluffs, sending sheets of spume into the air. There was one place without these clouds of spray. The tiny beach would be there, he knew, the place of his secret rendezvous.

Soon he was picking his way down the slippery loose lava. A canoe had been drawn into the inlet and four men held it, the surf washing their thighs. A fifth man stood on the glistening dark pebbles. He bowed deeply as Manu approached but did not fall to his knees, indicating he too was an *ali'i* of importance.

"I am Palila, sire, sent by Koa, lord of the Ka'ū plain. I bring you my master's greetings and love." The words were formality, having little import.

"My message to Koa is brief," Manu said. "Tell him it is too late."

"Too late, sire?"

"Yes. Kamō'ī now has a fine *haole* ship with large guns, and many muskets, and sober white men to teach their use to his warriors. Even with the help of my troops, your master's cause would be lost. Tell him his kingdom is doomed, finished. He is too weak. It is only a matter of time before he will fall, like the others."

"Kamō'ī and Koa are old friends. As children they lived like brothers, sharing mats and *poi.*"

"When I was a child, *I* was Kamō'ī's prince," Manu reminded the man sourly. "All this has changed. He is becoming like a *haole.* He remembers our past only as it serves him."

"We too will acquire guns and white men," Palila stated.

"No, you will not. The Ka'ū lands have no harbors for large ships. Your earth is almost barren of vegetables, your water bitter. You are too poor in provisions to trade for guns. You will attract no *haole* ships at Ka'ū ."

Palila squared his shoulders. "There are no finer or braver warriors than ours, sire."

"They will be blown off the earth. They will be like old feeble *wahine* against the guns of Kamō'ī. Tell Koa this."

The face of the Ka'ū emissary darkened with disappointment.

"What are we to do, prince?" he asked.

"Make no aggressive moves, make no annoying talk. Remain in contact with me. I have not given up all hope."

Forced to crawl when approaching his sacred wife, Kamō'ī did not visit her often.

She was named Keōpū-of-Heaven, and her lofty status emanated from her birth as the daughter of Pono, king of Maui, and his half-sister. Thus her *mana* was so potent that anyone of lesser blood had to prostrate themselves in her presence. The slightest contact with a commoner was a pollution. No ordinary Hawaiian dared to handle an object she owned or defile her with his shadow. To stare at her was unthinkable and to touch her meant death. Because of the penalties for such transgressions, and the dangers thus imposed on the populace, Keōpū rarely ventured from her house in daylight hours.

Her marriage to Kamō'ī had been arranged by the high priests ten years before, when she was fourteen. He had then been considered the wisest and bravest of the young chiefs. A wife of highest stature was necessary that he might have sons of the purest *ali'i* strain. So far, Keōpū had only borne him two daughters, impish creatures with large brown eyes, shamefully indulged by their mother and treated with detached affection by the king. A son by Kahu would be almost equally acceptable, but despite her lustiness, she was thus far barren. None of the other women of his court had the necessary eminence, and none had borne males in any case. A great *ali'i* needed sons and Kamō'ī kept trying to make one with Keōpū.

He did not find her unattractive, despite the fact that she had far less flesh than Kahu and far less skill in the love act. But even when he visited her for copulation the *kapu* dictated that he approach on hands and knees. He did not find this avenue to sex exciting. And, unfortunately, Keōpū had never been schooled in the ways of making love. She submitted pleasantly but passively, unlike the enthusiastic and imaginative Kahu. Kahu was capable of delightful surprises. Keōpū knew none of these ways of pleasing and was keenly aware of her shortcomings.

Once, seeking knowledge, she had arranged to watch the indoctrination of a Hawaiian boy into the techniques of making physical pleasure.

The teacher was a young woman named Lā, a widow at the court. Her student was Puna, son of the chief, Lako. Keōpū watched the proceedings through a slit in the *pili*-grass wall of Lā's house.

The twelve-year old lad was only vaguely aware of what was about to happen. He feigned bravado and tried to behave in a manly fashion but his eyes betrayed his nervousness.

Lā was the soul of understanding, her low voice soothing as they sat on mats. She crooned admiration for his good looks, her hands petting his calves, fingers brushing the inside of his thighs. She asked him to stand, that she might better admire his manliness. Kneeling before him, her hands fondled his shoulders and arms, stroked his legs. The boy's eyes widened as she unwound his malo. The cloth dropped and his stiff *uli* was erected like an upraised brown thumb. Gently she massaged the taut sac of his testicles. Then her hands moved to cup his buttocks and she bent to fellate him. Puna moaned his pleasure at the shock of her wet, tugging mouth.

Clearly Lā took delight in her craft. Her pouting mouth totally enclosed his eager stiffness and she sucked hungrily, with throatings of enjoyment. The boy swayed, his eyes shut tight and his body arched. His hands fluttered at his sides and his knees almost buckled. Lā gave a strangled laugh and disgorged his penis.

Now she urged Puna down to the mats and began caressing him expertly from head to foot, murmuring endearments. She took his hand and led it between her thighs, moving it back and forth on the moist fruit of her vagina. Puna looked so thin and small against her, Keōpū thought. Lā seemed twice his size a voluptuous bulk leaning above the boy, smiling, the nipples of her hanging breasts pricked erect. With her fingertips she gently teased the tip of his quivering member. Her head dipped and her pink tongue fluttered over his legs, his stomach and groin. The boy gasped and his back lifted. Watching them, Keōpū became wet...stretched full on her back, drawing the lad on top of her, muttering encouragement. Her thighs lifted and parted, her knees thrown wide as she guided him into her body. Puna panted and shuddered with his mounting excitement. His hands clawed the mats as he plunged and writhed in his passion. Then he climaxed with an exultant yelp.

Tenderly Lā caressed the small form collapsed upon her own. Her large arms enfolded Puna and her soft voice spoke compliments and admiration.

Keōpū withdrew. There was a film of perspiration on her brow, and a Hawaiian queen never perspired.

She, Keōpū, could not behave so. The daughter of an ancient and lofty dynasty could not so shamelessly perform on a person of lower rank, even a husband. She could not fawn, no matter what promise of sweet reward. True that Kamō'ī was now the most powerful *ali'i* on Hawai'i, but this did not alter his bloodlines. She was still his aristocratic superior.

Perhaps someday her feelings might somehow, miraculously, change. Perhaps if they had sons their relationship might be different. Perhaps then she could permit him to come to her as a master and she would be able to do things to him with her tongue and hands like Lā, the teaching woman.

She thought of Kahu. Kahu was always in Kamōʻiʻs company and everyone knew they enjoyed a vigorous sex life. Sounds from Kamōʻiʻs mats in the night and often in daytime were evidence enough. It was also no secret that Kahu took other men from time to time. Perhaps she should sit and talk with Kahu. The two enjoyed warm relations, and something useful might come of a chat.

A prisoner by day, Keōpū walked the beach at night. She enjoyed the release from confinement, the feel of damp sand between her toes, the dark breeze on her face. Nocturnal strolls were one of the few freedoms she knew. Ladies of the court trailed her steps and guards attended the group listlessly, wanting sleep. Keōpū informed her entourage that she wished to walk by herself. Disobeying the elegant little queen never occurred to her attendants.

Olohana, sitting on a patch of beach grass and puffing his final pipe of the day, saw her figure approaching on the sand. As she neared, he spoke: *"Aloha. Pehea ʻoe?"*

Keōpū was startled by the figure in dark and the accent of the greeting. This was one of the *haole*, she realized. She had seen them before only from a distance and was curious.

"Whose woman are you?" Olohana asked pleasantly.

"Kamōʻiʻs" she answered.

"I have never seen you, and I know all his women except the sacred one."

"I am she."

"Greetings, your highness." Stone came to his feet and bowed. Her features were obscured but he noted her slimness, her slightness, compared to the monumental Kahu.

"Are you happy with us?" she asked.

"Yes, my lady. Life here is very pleasant compared to the one we left."

"Are we strange to you?"

"No more than we are strange to you, highness."

"'Ae," she said in her gentle voice. She hesitated before deciding: "I will sit and we will talk."

Stone said he was honored, or offered an equivalent. His Hawaiian came painfully, a search for the right words.

She settled near him on the coarse littoral grass. Dim moonlight revealed her sharp nose, dainty mouth and slim neck. She sat straight, the soft balls of her breasts resting on her crossed arms. What did one say to sacred Hawaiian queens?

"What are you called?" she asked.

"Olohana, my lady."

Her brow wrinkled, uncomprehending.

"It is the Hawaiian way of saying the words I shout at men on the ship." He mocked the cry: "All hands! ... Olohana!"

She smiled and her nose crinkled. "And the other man?"

"Aleka, madam, from his name, Alec."

Keōpū felt quite at ease with this first *haole* she had ever spoken to. They were not so strange, other than in color and clothing. She liked his voice soft, firm and polite, without reverence or fear. And Olohana was curiously attractive in his pale, slim *haole* way.

"Why do the *haole* never bring women to Hawai'i?" she asked.

"Some captains carry their wives aboard ships, children too, sometimes. But this is not the usual custom. Life is harsh and dangerous at sea. Women remain at home, keeping their houses in order, waiting for their man."

Kahu's constant complaint crossed Keōpū's mind: "Do the wives of *haole* chiefs eat with their men?"

"Yes, they are treated as equals in that respect."

"Does the queen of Washington go to war with her man?"

"No, my lady. She also stays at home and waits."

Crouching figures moved on the sand nearby. The queen spoke a curt command and the guards immediately halted.

"Are any foods *kapu* to *haole* women? Such as the plantains, pork and certain fishes denied us?"

"No. *Haole* men and women eat the same things."

"I have heard that the *wahine* of you and Aleka flaunt the *kapu*, eating openly with you." Her tone was chiding. Stone shrugged noncommittally, knowing himself an encourager of the sacrilege.

"Are any *haole* women possessed of great *mana*?

"There are those famed for their great spirit and power over others, my lady. Elizabeth, a queen of England in years past, was such a *wahine*. And Marie Antoinette, now queen of France, has great *mana*. An important Englishman has said she glitters like the morning star, is filled with life, splendor and joy."

Keōpū pursed her lips. She had heard much the same thoughts expressed about Kahu. She envied Kahu's carefree ways and her ability to move and laugh in freedom among the people. But she held no bitterness.

"Did Washington's wife have *mana*?"

"Of a sort," Stone answered. "Hers was a *mana* born of wealth and high position and she placed these riches at her husband's disposal. Much of Washington's lands and money came from his wife. Usually it is these blessings that make *ali'i* in America, not the fortunes of birth and bloodlines."

Stone was suddenly anxious to avoid being led down endless, twisting lanes of explanation. Keōpū's curiosity could keep him defining these complications for days. At first her presence had cowed him a bit, but now this exalted queen of Oceania seemed little more than a friendly and utterly naive young lady trailing her fingers in the sand and asking childish questions. And it was a struggle for him to make proper answers with his limited

Hawaiian.

Distraction came with her attendants drawing nearer. All were vague shapes in the moonlight, listening quietly.

"Will you and the man Aleka stay with us?" Keōpū asked.

He would tell them what they wished to hear, Stone decided.

"Yes, your highness. Kamō'ī is kind, generous and wise. He loves his people and wishes their protection. We will remain and help, at least for a while." Mutters of approval arose from the audience.

The queen came to her feet and Stone stood to face her. He bowed, then on impulse reached for her hand and brought it to his lips.

Guards growled and moved forward but Keōpū waved them away. She was never touched by commoners but she had been pleased by this strange *haole* gesture.

"My *aloha* to you, Olohana," she said.

"And my thanks to you, dear lady."

He watched her walk away into the night.

This innocent girl was a woman of considerable stature, he was thinking. One never knew when such friends might be useful....

Kamō'ī took only from the *haole* that which was useful or comforting to him.

His interests were utilitarian, his questions concerned practical matters. He frequently wore the red silk Chinese robe given to him by one of Cook's officers but just as often discarded it for the comfort of a simple *malo*. He owned a brass bed but preferred his couch of mats. He eschewed tobacco but enjoyed wine. He thought *haole* music an abomination after Tweed had croaked a few chanteys for him one night. The idea of fashion brought him to laughter. How could one tell what *wahine haole* looked like under the layers of clothing they were said to wear? And why did men employ wigs? He had seen these on previous captains and they appeared to serve no purpose other than to provide home for fleas.

He had great respect for writing but believed it would take too long for him to learn it properly. He would have a young subordinate acquire this skill for him, he said. Personally he would master his own signature, which he could then affix to documents dictated by him. He would concentrate on the learning of numbers. Except for guns, this was the *haole* skill most useful in executive matters and decisions to come.

His liveliest interest was in the progress of his soldiers and sailors. On several occasions he visited the yam field to examine his troops personally and demanded daily reports of their progress. He had also taken an afternoon cruise on the *Little American* and was delighted with the performance of its crew. Later, ashore, Stone ran his infantry through a brisk marching drill and parade for their monarch. All hands, aship and ashore, were becoming adept in their new skills, giving Kamō'ī considerable pride. No other island king could boast such a force, he said. And his fleet of war canoes was well on the way to completion. Soon several hundred of these huge craft would be gathered at Kailua. A few would then have blunderbusses mounted on swivels amidships.

At the end of two months Olohana was able to assure Kamō'ī that he commanded a company of excellent musketeers and two schooner crews who could expertly handle the vessel and its cannon. Additionally all weapons were in top-notch condition and the *Little American* glowed with care. The king was pleased.

Both Stone and Tweed had chosen native lieutenants, bright young pupils with a talent for leadership. Billy Pitt soon pointed out that a few of these were not of the *ali'i* class, thus might not meet the king's approval. Olohana asked to plead his own case.

"Sire," he argued to Kamō'ī. "Superior men must be

respected for their ability, not the accidents of birth."

"Such actions go against the customs of centuries," the king replied. "*Ali'i* have always commanded. Your choices place several youths of high birth under the direction of commoners. This cannot be."

"I am a farmer's son," Stone retaliated, "and you have chosen me to lead your fighting men. Your old ways are in question, sire, and you should consider some changes. This is a minor adjustment in the order of things."

Not minor, the king thought, but he would find it difficult to debate Olohana's point. There was his own experience: If he had not been chosen over the higher-ranked Manu by Manu's own father he would not now be custodian of the *Kū*-stone. Olohana was right, as the late King *Opu* had been right: the wisest and strongest must lead. Still it was difficult to ignore the dictates of centuries...

"This could cause trouble," he said.

"There could be far worse trouble should we choose weak men, sire." Stone was enjoying the strength of his argument and the king's discomfit. And he had a hunch that Pitt was on his side. "The men are trained to follow my orders without question," he added. "I can handle any trouble."

The king glanced at Kalani-Pitt, whose face was impassive. Then he sighed and shrugged his massive shoulders.

"Very well, Olohana. But make your selections carefully."

"Thank you, sire. You will not regret this."

"It will be best if I do not regret it." Kamō'ī smiled crookedly, and there was a wisp of threat in his rejoinder.

Stone felt annoyance. A tough piece of meat, he told himself, and likely a bit of a bastard in the bargain.

The bosun no longer had doubt that Kamō'ī had arranged his abandonment and the *Nahant*'s departure. All the pieces fit from the king's earlier reference to enlisting white men through timing of the *kapu* on the

Kealakekua district, right up to the cajolery of Tweed and himself into the monarch's service.

He also knew that displaying anger over this manipulation of his life would avail him nothing. A protest would be like complaining.

"You did not always find me unpleasant," Manu said to Kahu.

"We were scarcely more than children then," she answered. "I have thought you unpleasant for many years. I want no more overtures from you. Relieve yourself with the fishermen's wives."

"As you do with the *haole*?"

"I am a queen. This is my business." She wondered how he knew. Perhaps one of his men had seen her visit Olohana...

"The king would make it his business, should I tell him."

"He knows I have amused myself with others. He knows there is no importance in it."

"Yes, but it still makes him angry and unhappy."

"Then why would you wish to hurt both of us?"

"Why would you wish to refuse me? We once made great pleasure together."

"That was long ago." To tell him she now loathed him and thought him dangerous to her husband would only make matters worse.

"Leave me alone, prince. Leave me alone."

Hawai'i island covered some four thousand square miles and the royal summons had been carried to its farthest corners.

From every village and cove, highest hamlet and remotest *ohana* commune, people arrived to labor on the temple of Kū at Kawaihae.

Some came for a few hours, some for a day, others for a week. They came first in hundreds, then thousands.

Within a month after Kamōʻīʻs command that the *heiau* be built the slopes surrounding its site above the bay were dotted with grass shelters and aswarm with workers.

From dawn to dark long lines of men, women and children passed stones to the builders for placement under direction of the troop architect—*kahuna*. Smooth stones for stairs and flooring were brought from beaches and stream beds. Rough stones for shaping into walls came from the jumbled lava flows of higher lands. Even higher, in moist forests, other craftsmen and priests labored at carving specially selected logs into scowling god-images to decorate the *heiau*. For miles along the coast farmers and fishermen were pressed into service to feed the multitude. Canoes plied back and forth from Kailua bringing additional supplies. Hundreds of men backpacked vegetables, *poi* and pigs over cold saddle-lands of volcanos from the Hilo and *Hāmākua* districts on the windward side of the island.

Slowly the foundation of the *heiau* was filled with rubble and leveled. Slowly the massive platform rose to dominate the hillside. Over two hundred feet long, rising twenty feet into the air with fifteen-foot-thick walls, the *heiau* of *Koholā* was becoming the most magnificent temple in all the islands. It was a fitting tribute to the supremacy of Kamōʻī, earthly representative of Kū, god of power and the rising son.

Stone had seen the *Kū*-stone only once, and then surreptitiously, for it was believed only the highest *aliʻi* should gaze upon it. He had persuaded Billy Pitt to show it to him. The prime minister had been a reluctant guide, clearly doubtful he was doing the right thing.

Pitt had chosen a late afternoon for the visit, leading Olohana to the rear of the king's house. There the image was kept under guard day and night by Kai's men.

A small, high-peaked grass structure housed the sacred figure. Pitt took a deep breath and stepped inside, motioning Olohana to join him. His eyes adjusting to the gloom, Stone saw a bulbous, fine-wicker container atop a large flat stone. Reverently, Billy Pitt lifted this cover.

Stone was astounded.

This font of terrible power, this symbol of symbols, was nothing more than an eggshaped lump of gray basalt smaller than a man's head. Rounded, smooth and finely pored, it rested on a bed of fresh fanned *ti* leaves, decorated with a few scarlet feathers.

Stone stared in the silence. Pitt was bent to the waist, his eyes to the ground.

In moments he said, "Enough," and carefully replaced the cover. He drew Stone outside.

Its origin was lost in antiquity, Pitt said, but the stone had given strength to kings long forgotten. It came, he explained, with the first settlers in Hawai'i many centuries ago, from Hawai'iki, the motherland, far in the southern seas. Kū's mana had helped the brave voyagers find a path over a vast and unknown ocean; had sustained them through awful days of storms, thirst and hunger; given them the courage to build life anew on these raw lands then known only to birds and fishes.

Since that far time the stone had breathed its potent *mana* on many great leaders. Those who possessed it acquired regality over all others. Kamō'ī had carried it in the wars that won him Hawai'i island. He would carry it to victories over the kingdoms on Maui, O'ahu and Kaua'i. One day soon, with Kū's blessing, Kamō'ī would command a single Hawaiian monarchy. Such had been the prophecy, Pitt said. Soon it would be a truth.

Pitt sipped tea and studied Olohana's face over the evening fire. The old man was perceptive; this *haole* had much on his mind.

"You are troubled," he said softly.

"Yes, *makua*." Stone often addressed Pitt as older-one, in respect.

"Ho'oponopono." Pitt's hand made a circle. The expression meant to talk problems out.

"We did not make agreement to kill," Stone said after a moment.

Pitt shrugged slightly and answered calmly: "You are not teaching our men to shoot at birds or sail the ship to Indian lands for animal skins."

"I am no stranger to fighting or death, *makua*."

"'*Ae*," Pitt nodded. "The life of a *haole* sea man must hold many ugly moments."

"Aleka shares my thoughts. This war you plan; the fight is not ours."

"Have you ever killed a man, Olohana?"

"Yes, once. Have you?"

"Many. Always, it had to be done, and I have never known regret. Why did you kill?"

"He was drunk, insane and would have killed me," Stone said.

"Would you kill again?"

"If I had to, in good cause."

"Our cause is good: the *salvation* of our people; our safety and future in this immense and strange new world. Make it yours."

"I am not long from that world and its people, Billy Pitt. In many ways you remain strangers to me. And how long will I be among you? These are thoughts I struggle with."

"You are becoming like one of us and may stay as long as you like. The king respects you and considers you of great value. You and Aleka have already taught us new ways of killing. What comes next is a short step. In our victories there will be much reward. You will then be a man of power and station, at the right hand of a supreme ruler. Stay with us and share the glories."

Stone fell silent. Small flames consumed another twig, crackling with frenetic blues, greens and oranges.

Power, stature, glory...the goals at which most men aimed their dreams. Now he enjoyed these endowments, such as they were in this little kingdom in a great sea. And the rewards of land perhaps even gold would soon be forthcoming, if the king was to be trusted.

Was he willing to pay the price? A scant few months ago he had refused to help Quimby in killing—now he was about to become a partner in slaughter. In truth Kamōʻī was as much a despot as the captain, the difference being that his tyranny was benign and his violence had reason. Nevertheless his ambition involved mass killing.

Should Stone case his lot with such a man? Could such a commitment mark him as an outlaw to the American government or any other nation with an eye on these landfalls? Was he to spend the rest of his life as Olohana, advisor to a pagan king, marshall of a half-naked army and sometimes cuckholder to the royal court? The prospect of another ship arriving had lessened in importance.

Under these present seductions of warmth, ease and a loving woman he was losing any thought of spending the rest of life at the pleasure of captains like Quimby. The London wit, Samuel Johnson, was right: A man was better off in prison than at sea, for being at sea was being in prison with a good chance of being drowned.

For the moment his choices were clear: He could deny Kamōʻī, then wait in a squalid beachcomber's boredom for return to an uncertain existence, or gamble his very neck on the king's success, with its promise of stature and wealth. There was always the *Little American* for escape, should conditions turn sour.

But could Tweed be counted upon for support? Alec was wallowing in the pleasures of being the admiral of Kamōʻī's navy and a cock among the plump Hawaiian hens.

Was all this actually happening to John Stone, late of Wakefield, Massachusetts and bosun of the *Nahant*, out of Boston? Perhaps this was, indeed, a dream.

Somewhere there were teeming cities, wharves with tiny shops and tall ships, inns and taverns on noisy streets and little houses on distant farms. Somewhere there were crowds of pale people with pink cheeks, burning autumn trees, first snow, snorting horses, forests of scented pine and carriages clattering on cobbles.

Or perhaps all *that* had become the dream...

PART V

"Consider," Kamōʻī said to Olohana.

"A very short time ago we were alone in the universe. The horizon was the end of our world. The things we knew were all we would ever know, about ourselves, our way of life, our land and our sea.

*"In one day Captain Cook and his men completely changed our lives. In **one** day they brought iron, guns, the wheel, writing, strong drink, the sexing disease and a strange new God. Even," he smiled faintly, "a kind of time marked by the ringing of bells."*

His expression again became grave.

*"But the deadliest gift the **haole** brought cannot be seen or touched. This is **doubt**. Doubt about our gods and beliefs and ancient customs. We will not only never be the same, we will be different in terrible new ways. Changes come with each ship, making us less Hawaiian, asking us to believe less in ourselves, to deny the gods and laws that have given us dignity, order and meaning. These doubts will spread over our islands, to eat at us and destroy us just as swiftly and surely as your **haole** sicknesses of lungs and genitals."*

In April of 1792 Kamōʻī moved his court to the Koholā *heiau* site to take temporary residence along the Kawaihae shore.

It was now time, as the priests had instructed, for the king and his nobles to participate in building the temple. In this way they would infuse its stones with their *mana*.

The king first ordered that the *kapu* demanding prostration be relaxed. Nothing should be allowed to slow the work. He set the example personally. Wearing only a *malo*, he went out to labor the next morning with his subjects.

Olohana found the effect astonishing.

He had never seen such esteem and affection. Stones the king lifted were passed on like the sacred objects they had instantly become. Many commoners continued to prostrate themselves before their ruler.

Even Kamehameha's queens were pressed into service. The sight of these personages moving humbly among them spurred the crowds to uncommon effort. Olohana and Aleka stripped off their blouses and fell to with the others, pleasing Kamōʻī. Most *haole* had piled scorn upon Hawaiian ways, prattling on about their True God. The king heard no proselytizing from these two. Beyond dining with their women, they broke no *kapu*. The eating with women attributed to Christian eccentricity. It posed no problem unless the habit spread. Neither man prostrated himself before the king, but Kamōʻī had not expected this of the *haole*.

Kamōʻī himself rigidly adhered to the sacred laws. That didn't mean he had never questioned the necessity of some and the stringency of others.

The *kapu* stood for order in living and spiritual being. But killing a commoner because he strayed into an *aliʻi's* shadow or touched a possession of a high noble did not seem to serve justice. Nor did women eating with men appear to threaten social virtue. Kahu annoyingly provided frequent reminders of this. She was offered the *wahine-kaua*, the women of war, as examples of feminine equality. Such women went to battle with men, she pointed out, serving as paddlers and organizers of food and supplies. Many also fought side by side with men. How could it be said they were inferior? Even now several hundred *wahine-kaua* prepared for the Maui invasion.

With their public exposure at Koholā, Kamō'ī was reminded of how much Kahu was loved by the people. Affection for her people poured from the tall beauty and they responded in kind. She moved among the throng with ease, petting children, making jokes and smiling encouragement. Keōpū-of-Heaven remained shadow-like in her seclusion, barely seeming to exist.

One other ali'i was sequestered, exempted from toil by order of the priests.

A half-brother of Kamō'ī, the harmless dolt giggled euphorically for no apparent reason and was happiest romping with children. Such shortcomings did not lessen his high caste. Through the vessel of his person unpolluted by labor the spirit of Kū would pass into the stones of the heiau. Such was the belief inherited from far time.

Eleven of the twelve to be sacrificed on the Koholā altar were criminals and kauwā outcasts. The twelfth had to be of considerable importance, an ali'i of highest rank and an enemy of Kamō'ī.

Thirty miles south such a man waited.

Koa, the king of Ka'ū, stared seaward deep in thought.

When he was a tiny prince he had taken playmates from among ali'i cousins. Kamō'ī became his closest friend when both were five years old. For ten years they shared mats and food, fished and surfed together and learned the arts of ali'i behavior. They were taught governing by the man Kamō'ī now called Billy Pitt. The two were even indoctrinated in copulation by the same teaching woman.

Those halcyon days were an eternity distant.

Years had come between them as the play of boys turned to the business of ali'i. Kamō'ī, a promising warrior at fifteen, had been summoned to the court of Opū in Kona. Koa stayed in Ka'ū attending his ailing father. He and Kamō'ī communicated only rarely by messengers, sending greetings back and forth. In time even these contacts stopped. On his father's death Koa became king at twenty.

After Opū died Kamō'ī began the war campaigns bringing other island districts under his rule. One by one Kohala, Hāmākua, Hilo and Puna had fallen. Only Ka'ū had remained unthreatened. It seemed Kamō'ī desired to avoid unpleasantness with his boyhood comrade.

Now this truce was coming to an end. Time and circumstance were forcing a showdown.

Koa knew that Kamō'ī needed a united Hawai'i island before he challenged any other island. Kamō'ī could not permit any exceptions. Koa was equally determined not to subject his dynasty and personal honor to another. Twenty generations of his family had governed Ka'ū. He would die before submitting to domination, even that of an old friend. Years back he had made this clear to Kamō'ī through an envoy. There had been no response.

He had sought one other avenue of survival—the overture to Manu through the chief Palila. Koa now saw this as a desperate and doomed effort. He had suspected that Manu's hatred of the *haole* could form an alliance against Kamō'ī, but rejection by the disinherited prince had been quick.

Even in his arrogance, Manu had been right: without guns Koa had no hope of winning. Without a good harbor he could never attract the *haole* traders who supplied the weapons.

Ka'ū lands were large, encompassing the entire leaf-shaped southern potion of the big island but they were arid and poor. Farming was minimal except on uplands where water trickled from the flanks of Mauna Loa. Only fishing was good, deep sea tuna could be taken from shore bluffs rising above the blue ocean. The greatest resource of Ka'ū had always been its fighting men. But, as Manu had harshly pointed out, they would die like infants against the guns of Kamō'ī.

Koa's invitation to the dedication of the Kohola *heiau*

meant that Kamōʻī could no longer postpone assumption of complete power. Koa understood full well that he had been chosen as the principal sacrifice to Kū. His alternative was a brutal war he could not win which would ravage his lands and see his soldiers executed or enslaved. If Koa accepted Kamōʻī's summons, much of this grief would be spared.

Perhaps he would find a purpose and honor in death which had eluded him in life. He had not been a strong king nor had he produced sons, a knowledge which shamed him. But he could die well that his ancestral line might end in glory.

His heart was heavy with sadness for the times and conditions bringing him and his childhood comrade to this melancholy impasse. He did not blame Kamōʻī. They were equally captives of circumstance. Fate alone had made them enemies.

The gods had decided. His time had come. He summoned his closest advisor and companion, Pūkuʻi, and told him to make preparations to leave for Koholā.

The monarch of Maui gazed across the channel at Hawaiʻi. Pono was a large and heavy man in his mid-fifties, his brow narrow over a truculent face with a slightly hooked nose and cold dark eyes. From head to ankle, the left half of his body was tattooed in a crosshatch design of blue-black, heightening his forbidding appearance.

Brisk winds whipped a fine mist over the water. Distant mountains of the big island loomed high and dark above this gray blanket. Behind those mountains Kamōʻī was raising a large army to attack Maui. Pono knew Kamōʻī was building a massive *heiau* to give his cause justice and sacred strength.

Upstart, Pono thought scornfully. He considered Kamōʻī an *aliʻi* of only second rank who had acquired power through deviousness and marriage. Now Kamōʻī had the arrogance to believe he could add Maui to his realm. He would find this far more difficult than conquests of the weak and scattered kingdoms of his own island.

Pono vowed to see Kamō'ī humiliated, beaten and killed. Pono would then slaughter his enemy's nobles and have his wives and children garroted to obliterate the line and stamp his memory into oblivion. It mattered not that Kamō'ī's wife, Keōpū, was one of Pono's daughters. It mattered even less that Kamō'ī was rumored to be one of his sons, spawn of a casual adventure in his boyhood. One did not keep an accounting of such bastards.

He broke wind, as much in scorn as relief. It was a sustained and explosive fart, demanding attention. His attending soldiers shifted their feet one sycophant murmured admiration. Pono's spittoon bearer dropped his eyes. One could not capture and bury exudations at sea...

Pono's thoughts turned to the schooner Kamō'ī had taken. A fine ship, from all reports new and fast, with two powerful red-mouthed guns. He also knew of Kamō'ī's *haole* and their training of the Hawai'i warriors and shiphandlers. But Pono also had guns—sixty-five of them and a *haole* named Pavão. This man had deserted from a visiting ship over a year before. Since then he had suffered a steady decline from his excess of *wahine* and 'awa-root liquor. But he knew guns and had managed the training of a select cadre of musketmen. When not narcotized from 'awa, Pavão often made good sense. His scheme to send large numbers of canoes into the schooner's guns to overwhelm it could conceivably work. Many fighters would be lost, but the speed and weight of the attack might accomplish the capture. Pono was very keen to seize the schooner. Next to the heart of Kamō'ī it was the prize he most desired.

He commanded that his *haole* be brought.

In moments Pavão was in his presence. A bone-thin swarthy Portuguese in his late twenties, round seaman's hat was cocked over his bloodshot eyes. His trousers were caked with dirt and one shoulder was bared through a torn blouse. Pavão´s face was blue with beard and he leaned insolently against a coconut trunk. Pono decided that one day he would take pleasure in personally strangling this dog. In the meantime, when he was sober, he would put his *haole* to as much use as possible.

"The men with guns," he said, "are they being made ready?"

"Yes, yer honor."

"They no longer throw away shot at rats and birds?"

"No, yer highness." In truth, Pavão had neglected to order his troops to stop such waste of ammunition. He would tend to this today.

"Messengers have been exchanged," Pono said. "Soon there will be battle."

"We´ll be ready for ´em, *ali´i*." Pavão rooted between his buttocks. He was anxious to get back to a still he had improvised to make strong liquor from Hawaiian *ti*-root. He and his native cronies had sampled the stuff in large quantities the night before and he badly wanted a medicinal dollop to ease his recovery.

Pavão refused to take this talk of war seriously. Most of the fighting, he reckoned, would be between screeching mobs of *kanaka* armed with sling-stones, spears and knuckle-dusters of sharks´ teeth. Personally he planned to stay safely away from any such fracas with the protection of a musket or two, pistols and plenty of ammunition.

He counted the days waiting for another ship. When one came he intended to wheedle himself aboard, no matter her flag or destination. In the meantime, he would get along as best he could by humoring this nigger king.

Olohana bowed before Keōpū.

The sacred queen stretched upon mats in her special house. Servants waved cooling wisks above her pretty head. She was naked except for a piece of supple *kapa* tossed casually across her middle. In the soft light her skin glowed like a buffed copper. Stone was struck as before by the delicacy of her features and trimness of her figure. Her wistful dreaming air was incongruous against her nudity.

"Olohana!" she greeted him, "welcome. I have a gift for you."

"You are very kind, your highness."

She crooked a finger and a slim boy, moving forward on his hands and knees, detached himself from her entourage.

"Stand," she ordered.

"The *boy*, your majesty?"

"'*Ae*. You have no children. He is yours. Is he not fine looking? So straight and strong."

"Yes, my lady. A handsome lad indeed."

"Take him then."

There was nothing unusual about this, Stone knew. In Hawaiian custom, childless couples were often given children by those more generously blessed. Such youngsters were called *hānai*, to be raised and loved as one's own. Of the thousands of *hānai* children, scarcely a one was troubled by the circumstances.

"He is called Puna," the queen said. "The son of my cousin, Lilinoe, and the chief, Lako, of Kealakekua."

The boy squared his shoulders and looked bravely at Olohana. He had seen Stone at the feast for the *Nahant's* men, but since then Olohana's reputation as a chief and adviser to Kamō'ī had grown large. Puna did not wish to appear timorous before him.

Keōpū went on, "He is trained well by warriors and *kahuna* and has already been with a woman. His mother desires he serve with Kamō'ī and the king has granted her wish. Now he will be yours to care for."

"Thank you, my lady. I am honored." Stone knew he was without choice in the matter, the decision already made. He smiled at Puna and offered his hand.

"Grasp Olohana´s hand," the queen instructed. "Such is the *haole* way of greeting. You must learn these things."

Olohana´s clasp was warm and friendly. Puna felt more at ease.

"Do you wish to come with me, young chief?" Stone asked.

"Yes, *ali'i*."

Keōpū smiled. "He will be a fine big chief one day," she said. Tonight she would pray again that she might give Kamō'ī a son as fine as this boy.

Dutifully Stone took Puna to his house. Dutifully Namo welcomed the lad. Clearly the boy pleased Olohana, thus she was also pleased despite a nibbling of what she knew was jealousy.

Still he seemed an exceptional youth obedient, well mannered and courteous and respectful of his elders. Besides, a gift from Keōpū-of-Heaven was a very special gift.

"You have seen the boy?" queried the king.

"'*Ae, ali'i*," Olohana replied. "He is with us now."

"I have plans for him and wish your help."

"Sire?"

"Teach him to speak in the English and to write the *haole* way, and the numbers used in trade and counting silver and gold. Also the behavior of better *haole* people."

"My lord, I am but a rough soldier and seaman, not very familiar with the ways of better *haole* people. And I am not a teacher."

"You have taught our soldiers well, and you teach Kalani Pitt and me many things. The boy is quick. I desire that in time he may write for me, be able to speak for me and represent me before the *haole*. Perhaps one day you may be gone. Is this not so?"

"Yes, *ali'i*. This is so." This was the first time the king had mentioned the possibility.

"I will confide in you, Olohana. He is my true son. I wish to know if he will someday make a strong king. This is important."

"I will do my best, your highness."

At Kawaihae the *heiau* of Koholā neared completion.

Kahuna studied the sea, sky and winds of omens. In inclement weather the work was halted, for it could only go forward under the most benevolent conditions.

Other priests and workers brought roughly shaped god-images down from the mountains for refining and finishing on site. The firepits and altars were well begun and the tall supports of the oracle tower had been raised. At every stage there were pauses for chanting and incantations by the priests of Kū.

Each aspect of the effort was rigidly organized and directed by the *kahuna*: food supplies for the laborers, times of work and times of rest. No one laughed and even talk was minimal. From dawn to dusk lines of people passing stones stretched off from the site, like spokes of a gargantuan wheel. The *heiau* was now visible from miles at sea, a magnificent platform of dark splendor over the sparkling bay.

During the final days of construction the high priests decreed that work should be finished under a *kapu* of speech and in complete silence. Dogs were muzzled and chickens jailed under baskets. Children were shushed. Sounds came only from feet shuffling on clinkered lava and the thud of stones being placed into position.

Only once was this stillness broken.

Nearing dark one evening Stone, Tweed and the boy sat by their crude shelter while Namo and Hina prepared food. An uneven line of men approached from the shore below, moving up slowly through the brush and boulders. Several priests of Kū were identifiable by their white *kapa* shrouds. Soldiers carrying spears followed. As the file came closer the naked, staggering forms of eleven men joined by bonds of sennit became clearly visible.

The women averted their faces until the forlorn column passed. Puna stood erect, staring.

"These are for Kū," he said, then fell silent.

Soon the first awful screams came from the *heiau* above.

"Jasus God," said Tweed. The tortured shrieks bit at Stone's nerve ends. Namo clutched his arm in a steely grip.

Eleven agonies tore the air. When there was silence they knew the last man had been sacrificed.

Their flesh would be stripped away and burned, Puna said, and their bones buried in corners and at other key parts of the temple. Firelight glowed all night, outlining edges of the huge platform as the priests completed their grisly work.

In days following less gruesome rituals were observed.

God images were raised into proper positions. The cluster of tall carvings were stylized male figures with flowing coxcombs of headdress and grinning malevolent mouths. The Kū figure was the most intimidating of all, a fearsome and commanding presence with baleful pearl-shell eyes and a snarling wide-curved mouth. Meanwhile the skeletal stanchions of the oracle tower were draped in white *kapa* and the last smooth beachstones of flooring and altar carefully laid.

A morning came when the people were told to rest and wait.

At midday old Pahoa mounted the rise of stone and began to chant.

His message was charged with emotion the people had labored reverently and well. The priests finished their ceremonies of inspecting the *heiau* and blessing it with prayer and turmeric water. Now, Pahoa proclaimed, the time approached for the temple to be dedicated to Kū. Physically it was finished and the people were free to speak and move in normal ways.

Sound erupted like a clap of thunder.

Sharkskin drums rolled the news along the shores and into the mountains. The Kawaihae hillside erupted with shouting and laughter in the relief of the laboring throngs. The night brought feasting, dancing and not a little fornication, for that too had been *kapu* during construction. Under a cruel sun the work had been tedious and exhausting. The release was sweet and the accomplishment a pride and joy.

To make Koholā truly the *heiau* of Kū only one final rite remained.

In one day a fast south wind had carried King Koa's canoes far from Ka'ū .

Late afternoon found the five craft drawn upon glasslike shallows of Kiholo Bay. Ashore, Koa's companion and high chief, Pūku'i, ordered preparation of an evening meal while the monarch and several lesser nobles sat quietly without words.

Kiholo was their camp before arrival in Kawaihae the next day. Koa had yet another purpose for this visit, a final important duty to perform in a sacred pool in the area. A few of his soldiers had gone ahead to clear the environs of people in order that when the time came, the king and his priest might be undisturbed.

He need have no fear of being alone, Koa mused wryly. All nearby residents had fled at first sight of his canoes, terrified of the death-curse he carried.

Silence was heavy around the supper fire. Koa watched until its coals grew faint then swathed himself in a *kapa* for sleep. That relief would not come. Through most of the night he stared at the stars, thinking of the immensity of the universe, the smallness of his island world, the vagaries of man and the transports of destiny. At dawn he roused his priest. Pūku'i offered food, his strong young face loving and troubled. Koa refused, desiring that these last hours be sharp in consciousness, not dulled in the slightest way.

He rose, urinated, then abruptly ordered his *kahuna* to lead the way. The two walked inland, out of the shore grove. Pūku'i followed, five paces behind. A path of smooth beachstones wound through the lava field, twisting to avoid blister-like risings and ragged crevasses. About every ten feet white chunks of dry coral had been placed to mark the route.

With rising light a small gathering of coco-palms could be seen over the arid waste, indicating the pool. Soon they gained the brief shallow fed by leachings from distant hills.

Koa did not pause. He immediately unwound his *malo* and held out his hand to the priest. The *kahuna* handed his master a steel knife, then fell to his knees and began a wailing chant.

The Ka'ū king walked into the water to his thighs. A thought crossed his mind, he was naked except for this knife, his one possession from the world of the *haole* the same *haole* who had changed everything, had made even this moment necessary. He would not linger on the irony, he must accomplish the deed.

"The Death of Uli," sorcerers called the act the severing of that part of a man which his followers could then use if they wished to find and take revenge upon his assassin.

Koa did not hesitate. He held the head of his penis firmly with one hand and tugged it outward. With one quick slash he cut it off beneath the glans.

The detached piece felt curiously soft and strange between his fingers. Blood gushed from the stump, clouding the clear water. The priest, with a guttural cry, thrashed into the basin with herbs and soft *kapa* to bind the wound. On the bank Pūku'i crouched with his head in his hands, trembling. Koa made his way out of the pool and sat, staring, his shock subsiding.

In another half hour the trio had returned to the beach camp. The Ka'ū soldiers waited quietly by their canoes. Pūku'i reverently helped Koa don the golden helmet and cloak of his rank. A spear bearer knelt, offering the long polished staff to his monarch. Koa instructed that only those who would be his proper ali'i companions in death need accompany him to his canoe. All others were free to return to Ka'ū.

Pūku'i made the response, "Every man has begged to follow you, my ali'i. Grant them this honor."

Koa nodded. He said nothing but his eyes revealed his pride and gratitude.

Three hours later they had rounded the southern headlands of Kawaihae and were upon the bay. The thick rising of the Koholā heiau stood blunt and stark against lifting land above the shore.

Men in the canoes tensed. Koa rose to stand tall with his spear on the central platform of the doubled-hulled royal canoe. As they neared shore he realized that bluff and beach were filled with a crowd of thousands, watching in an eerie silence. Kamō'ī and his nobles, with a white man, soon came into view in a grouping on the sand. The cloaks of the king, Kalani-Pitt and Manu were burnished by sunshine. Koa's canoe grated on the shallows. A ramp was dropped and he stepped ashore.

For a long moment the two kings eyed one another with the half smiles and studying eyes of men who had not met for years. Then, Kamō'ī stepped closer. Kalani-Pitt and Manu moved with him, but the haole, who was Olohana, held his ground

Kamō'ī halted a few paces in front of Koa, his face now serious.

"I greet you with a heavy heart, old friend," he said softly.

"I come in sadness, O companion of my youth," Koa replied.

Kamō'ī's gaze traveled from Koa's face to remain fixed upon the horizon. There was not a sound from the watching crowds.

Kamō'ī raised his voice. "Do it now."

Manu, who had begged for the assignment, stepped past Kamō'ī. His spear flashed forward and thudded into Koa's heart.

The Ka'ū king fell back. His mouth wrenched open in a strangled sound and his fingers clutched briefly at the sand. He died almost instantly, his blood pulsing out over the velvety feathers of his cloak.

Kamō'ī stared with a grieving face at the limp corpse. After a moment he spoke to Billy Pitt. "You, Kalani, will see that his flesh is burned and ashes taken to the deep sea. His bones will be buried beneath Kohola's most sacred altar."

He scanned the remaining men of Ka'ū, kneeling unmoving behind the body of their beloved ruler. Only the young chief, Pūku'i, had his head raised, returning Kamō'ī's look. His face was stricken and his eyes wet with his grief.

"Spare these others," Kamō'ī said. "Kū has now been honored."

He turned and strode away.

That night the bones of the last ruler on Hawai'i to oppose Kamō'ī were laid on the main altar of Kohola. The attendant procession and chanting proclaimed that the noblest possible offering had been properly made. The prophecy of the Moloka'i wise man was fulfilled. Kamō'ī was now truly *ali'i-'ai-moku*, sovereign above all others on the island of Hawai'i.

By a fire on the slopes below, Olohana and Aleka listened to the sounds of ritual and smoked their pipes. Only the highest *ali'i* and most important *kahuna* joined this final ceremony.

The night was starless and the usually steady winds of

the area had dropped, as if in deference to the solemn occasion. Fires on the *heiau* above sent reddish smoke billowing into listless air. The Moloka'i priest´s tenor drifted down, a piercing dissonant vibrato defying translation by the *haole*.

Namo told them what the decrepit old *kahuna* was chanting:

"O Kū , Kū of all power and force,
here is our supreme offering to you
Curse
the rebels within and without
and traitors everywhere
who would betray our land
Grant
Long life to the great Kamō'ī
and to all his chiefs
and to all his people
and the kingdom that is
and the kingdom that will soon be.
This is finished."

PART VI

O n a September morning in 1792 goodbyes were said to
Captain George Courtney and his men of **HMS
Dolphin**.
Lustrous in their feathered finery, Kamō'ī and his
entourage gathered on the shore at Kamakahonu Cove.
Longboats crowded the shallows of the tiny beach and the scarlet jackets of British marines punctuated the scene with raw
color. Courtney and his officers were authority personified in
their dress blues with the gold piping.

From deeper water the **Dolphin's** cannon boomed a final
salute to Kamō'ī, belching orange fire and blossoms of pungent
smoke. Thousands of Hawaiians in canoes and along shore
cheered as the captain and king embraced, calling each other
brother. Courtney shook hands with young Puna, serious and
prideful in his new midshipman's uniform. A gift from
Courtney and the ship's tailor, its glory was only slightly
diminished by Puna's bare feet.

Olohana and Aleka spoke their farewells. Kahu was regal
and beaming in her white silk, basking in admiring stares from
the lobsterbacks and sailors. Many crewmen were bidding
goodby to distraught **wahine**. Olohana wondered how many
little half-British bastards would be popping up nine months
hence. He was also wondering if politely refusing Courtney's
offer of passage to London was an act he would regret...

The piercing notes of a bosun's whistle lifted over the
crowded inlet. The longboats set off, Courtney erect, his hand in

salute to the king mentally congratulating himself that he had managed to not give arms to any Hawaiian king, despite the many pressures. He would be leaving all islanders the better with gifts of tools, seeds, shoots and animals. No matter the political turns in days to come, Great Britain and George Courtney need feel no guilt about encouraging internecine slaughter among these naive islanders. A decent man, he felt this sincerely. Beyond its moral righteousness, such a stance held pragmatic benefit from these actions. England should enjoy cordial relations with the winner of the Hawai'i power struggle no matter the outcome.

Within an hour the <u>Dolphin</u>'s sails lifted and she trudged out to blue water. Women along the beach wailed mournfully as the ship shook out full canvas and bore away. Soon she was gone over the northeast horizon.

In a rosy twilight Kamō'ī summoned Olohana.

He held out the watch presented to him by Courtney on behalf of King George.

"This thing has died," he stated.

Wondering, Stone took the heavy timepiece from the king's hand.

It had simply run down. He wound and then shook it and handed it back to the king.

"It requires the winding, sire. This forces the small round irons within to press against one another. In expanding, they exert the power to make the watch work."

"Ah..." said Kamō'ī. He thought for a moment.

"Nothing else stopped," he smiled. "The sun and clouds traveled on and the sea rose. Time did not stop."

Less than a day into Kamō'ī's invasion of Maui, the forces of Pono were largely routed.

The Maui king roused on that fateful morning to an astounding sight: Hana's bay was dark with war canoes discharging a horde of thousands upon its rocky shores. The surf was alive with warriors struggling in to land. At nearby Hamoa Beach hundreds of canoes brought in a second legion in a totally unexpected flank attack. Offshore, the *Little American* plied ominously on the deep, surrounded by more canoes, waiting.

Wave upon wave of warriors came in to mass above the shores. A few challenges were thrown and accepted by wrestling and boxing champions, but these ritual contests were brief, with a roughly equal number of winners on each side.

The assault which followed was devastating.

Kamō'ī's musketeers performed with deadly efficiency. Disciplined, they fired only when shots would count, taking their orders from a white man who deliberately trod back and forth. The regal figures of Kamō'ī, Kalani-Pitt and Manu could also be seen, their golden feather cloaks glowing among their dark troops.

Stunned and demoralized by superior gunfire and numbers, fumbling Mauians quickly gave ground. The invaders easily broke their line in dozens of places. Those defenders with guns soon ran out of ammunition and fled, abandoning their weapons among the stones. Meanwhile Kamō'ī's schooner had been brought closer inshore, belching frightful fire with its cannon and blasting grass houses and boundary walls into the air.

Pavão's gamble to send many canoes against the *haole* ship proved a disaster. Tweed's ring of defending craft was almost impregnable and the few Maui canoes actually breaking through met a horrid fate. Olohana and Aleka had devised cannon loads filled with metal scraps. These vicious missiles tore canoes and occupants to shreds. After several suicidal attempts the remaining attackers stayed well clear. Pavão watched this debacle from a safe vantage point above the bay.

Facing certain destruction if he tried to hold, Pono ordered a withdrawal. Now fighting valiantly from less exposed hillsides, the Maui men only slowly gave ground. Near the end of the day Pono and his personal troops escaped to trails along the gully-slashed coastline leading northward. This tortuous terrain slowed both retreat and attack.

Kamō'ī's fighters followed tenaciously with an added threat—their cannon had been brought from the ship. Pono's few remaining guns were now almost ineffectual.

Pavão seized a canoe and escaped. Even in retreat, the king ordered a party out to find him and bring back his head. Not his heart, Pono specified. Curiously, a *haole* heart looked just like a Hawaiian.

Pono's anger was a raging fire. Humiliation weighed upon him like an enormous stone. He cursed the *kahuna* who had not foreseen his inadequacies. He cursed white men and their new ways of war. He cursed his chiefs and soldiers who could not hold their lines. And he particularly cursed the day on which he might have planted the seed that had become Kamō'ī.

For six dreadful days Pono retreated over harsh lava fields and ragged ravines. Kamō'ī's devastating cannon and musketmen murdering his troops all the way.

In the night Olohana led raids on the camped Mauians. Such nocturnal activity was before unknown in Hawaiian warfare. Each sunup Pono's men faced, and many failed in, dangerous and desperate escapes through snipers Olohana had sent ahead. Each day Pono became more shaken with doubt, plagued by inadequacies. His monarchy shattered, his dignity with it, his confidence fled.

Seven days after the flight from Hana he stood with his surviving chiefs, some two thousand warriors and a small scattering of musketmen at the mouth of a deeply cut valley named 'Īao.

He sent a message to Kamō'ī. Here he would make a stand, he said. It would end in victory for Maui.

His claim was utter bravado and Pono knew it. The high walls of 'Īao behind him formed a trap and the situation was hopeless. His troops were now reduced to the best and wiliest, but exhausted only pride kept them from flight. None knew that Pono had secretly made plans for his own escape. He did not intend to become another sacrifice on the altar of Kū .

He ordered the premier champion among his fighters brought before him. This warrior was Luna and he was Pono's last chance to salvage the honor of his monarchy. His instructions were simple and clear—kill Kamō'ī.

Dawn of the seventh day revealed the Hawai'i army in a large curved line, sealing the mouth of 'Īao Valley. Cannon from the *Little American* had been carried and rolled to positions near its center. Olohana arranged fifty muskets to complement their fire with remaining guns strung on either side.

Kamō'ī had nothing to fear from the ground already captured. Villages along the route of Pono's retreat had been abandoned. Tweed's alert canoe fleet guarded ocean approaches and surrounded the schooner in the harbor of Kahului a few miles below. Pono's disorganized flotilla was scattered, no longer a threat.

On the eve of the 'Īao battle both armies rested. On the Maui side all was quiet, but the mood around the campfires of Kamō'ī's troops was festive. About two hundred *wahine-kaua* were with the men, joining their fellow warriors in *hula* and laughter. All sensed victory, with little time before Maui belonged to their monarch.

The king summoned Pitt, Olohana and Manu.

He would lead the attack on the morrow, he said. The time now came for his personal engagement with Pono.

After he killed the Maui king, Kalani-Pitt and Manu would move flank troops forward behind Olohana's guns until all resistance was wiped out. Guns would be used only when necessary, for ammunition was in short supply. Women and children would be spared and any surviving enemy soldiers taken prisoner.

The king was utterly relaxed and supremely sure of himself. Stone was struck by his calm certainty. Clearly there was no question in Kamō'ī's mind about killing Pono and taking his island.

What manner of man had Stone indentured himself to? Could Kamō'ī be mad? Was he, Stone, also mad in following him? Only a few weeks ago he and Alec Tweed had been playing at general and admiral, their chores an amusement, the days carefree and easy. Now they had survived a week of shot and flame, broken bodies and the screams of wounded and dying.

At the very moment he heard the insane incongruity of laughter and song on the eve of another day of blood and death. Would he survive another day? Another week? Was his reward worth such a gamble?

He stared into the fire, only half listening to his companions. Manu's tone was peevish. The Hawai'i troops were too concentrated, he was saying, vulnerable to being surrounded.

Billy Pitt shook his head. Stone came to full attention and the king looked at him. It was on Olohana's advice that the men had been drawn into a single mass.

"There is nothing to fear by having them gathered together," Stone said. "Our scouts tell us there is no opposition anywhere else. One more strong drive and this battle should be over. Leave the troops as they are, with all our fire power in the one place."

The king paused only a moment. "We will do as Olohana says."

Manu glowered, bowing obedience, then left to join his men. Pitt departed to order his soldiers to rest for the day ahead. Kamō'ī and Olohana were alone.

Sounds of merriment faded in the camp. The king moved closer to the dwindling flames, for a long time silent.

When he spoke his voice was soft and confiding. "What do you think of Manu, Olohana?"

"I have never liked him, sire, a feeling he returns many times stronger. Surely you know this."

Kamō'ī nodded. "In many ways he is still a boy, head-strong, who will not listen. He remembers things best forgotten."

"I sense something wrong in him, *ali'i*. I think he may fail you one day." Perhaps he was treading where he should not go, Stone thought, but to hell with it. Kamō'ī had asked and he would answer straight. "There is a hollowness in the man. Something missing."

The king shrugged slightly, not wishing to admit his own doubts. He also told himself it might well be Olohana's jealousy showing. A moment later he said: "Manu is the first son of Opū, who made me a king and whose memory I must honor. Manu has pledged his lands and men to me and fought well."

Stone did not reply.

"And you, Olohana. You fight well for a man who does not have his heart in it."

"It is not the first time, my lord. And not without purpose." This was as good a time as any to tuck a reminder in the king's ear. "There is the future and the lands you promised."

"In time, never fear." Kamō'ī would rather have heard some expression of support for his cause. "First we must finish this unpleasantness. In days to come we will use guns only for protection and to keep peace. I pray you will be with me then."

"You have changed my life greatly, sire. Now my ambition is to live long enough to enjoy it."

"You will, Olohana. The gods favor you."

"How do you know such a thing, *ali'i*?"

"Because I decided not to kill you after you lay with Kahu." The king delivered the words evenly, without malice.

Stone jerked in surprise. He must never underestimate this man. Kamō'ī arose, tugging a *kapa* around his towering form.

"Now we will rest," he said. "Our enemies must die tomorrow."

Save for a barkcloth pouch cradling his genitals, Luna of Maui lay naked as a servant massaged his torso and arms.

He was the supreme fighter of Pono and had trained all his life for the approaching combat; prepared for it with a hundred deadly contests. To kill such an enemy *ali'i* would elevate him to the most celebrated ranks of island warriors. To kill the great Kamō'ī would bring him honor transcending his dreams.

Early sunlight slanted into the clearing at the mouth of 'Īao Valley. Behind Luna the eastern walls were in shadow. Farther back and soaring high, a solitary rounded peak rose sharply, its plunging sides bright in sunshine. Nearer, Luna's comrades were half hidden in low growth, tensed in anticipation. On a nearby knoll Pono and members of his court stared down at the dark and ominous champion. The attendant finished his massage and Luna stood, starkly alone.

For long minutes there was silence. All eyes fixed on Luna's statuesque figure holding a large spear. Then sounds of the approaching Hawai'i army rose up from the slopes below.

A priest was first to appear out of the trees—Pahoa, infirm and limping, his hands upraised, chanting the genealogy of his master.

In moments Kamō'ī himself appeared, striding surely, his head high and golden cloak rippling in his wake.

This was Pono's first sight of the man sworn to destroy him.

A giant, he realized, truly a giant among men. His had been a prudent decision not to fight Kamō'ī personally no matter what others might think. Best to *insure* that he died, if need be by the hands of a man in his fullest physical power, like Luna.

The brush broke in hundreds of places as other Hawai'i men entered the clearing. Pono recognized Kalani-Pitt in the foreground. The prime minister was accompanied by a white man in a tri-cornered hat who directed soldiers with hand signals. Many Hawai'i soldiers held muskets with expert familiarity, but overwhelmingly the foreign troops were armed with the same spears, daggers and clubs as the Maui men.

Kalani-Pitt and the *haole* stopped. Kamō'ī's cloak was removed and he was handed a spear. He walked forward until he faced Luna across a few yards of gravelly flat ground.

He would not take Pono's substitution as an insult, Kamō'ī had decided. In truth the insult was to the Maui king. By fighting this surrogate Kamō'ī scorned Pono's need for such assistance.

He studied his adversary calmly. A mountain of muscle; he would have his hands full. This was no surprise, he could be only the finest Maui could produce.

Gazes of the two locked, Kamō'ī smiled slightly, acknowledging the commoner. Luna bowed his head briefly in deference to the *ali'i-nui*. Both splendid bodies glistened, thick shafts of spears held athwart facing chests. Watchers on both sides fell silent, the rustling of leaves in fitful breezes the only sounds.

Olohana climbed a stone for a better view. His mouth was dry and he was taut with excitement. It was the stillness, he told himself that and the vision of these powerful giants facing one another. What would his future be if Kamō'ī was killed? He touched the pistols at his belt for reassurance and glanced at Billy Pitt. The elder's face was drawn, his lips pressed together and his eyes riveted upon his beloved student and master.

For interminable moments the two fighters were motionless then, by some signal known only to them, they moved forward. With the harsh crack of wood upon wood the deadly duel began.

Stone held his breath. This clash of giants was a sight he would never forget—two magnificent warriors dedicated to the kill. Lunging, thrusting, parrying their huge bodies leapt with alacrity from harm's way, handling the thick and heavy spears as if they were broomsticks.

Silent minutes offered a brilliant display of the killing art. Then Kamō'ī, with a clever fast feint, teased his opponent off balance. Luna stumbled to recover. Groans escaped from his comrades. Declining to lunge with a death thrust, Kamō'ī slashed at the Maui man's spear with every ounce of his strength. The weapon clattered free to the ground. Stricken with surprise and shame, Luna crouched, facing the king, arms out from his sides, fingers flexing.

The king's next move surprised everyone, Luna most of all.

Kamō'ī tossed his own spear aside. He beckoned Luna to approach, challenging the Maui man to fight hand to hand. Excitement erupted from both sides.

Luna took a deep breath and moved forward. Kamō'ī waited, legs spread and hands out. The thick muscles of his shoulders flexed in anticipation.

It was a collision of mammoths.

Sounds of the scrape of feet and grunts and exhalations as the fighters clutched flesh for holds came clearly through the silence. Gladiators of ancient Rome could not have matched such a struggle, Stone thought. In a sylvan setting two utterly fearless men locked, swayed and rocked, each dedicated to the death of the other.

Inches were given, inches taken. For long minutes neither had command. Suddenly Kamō'ī, with a gargantuan gathering of effort, managed to trip and throw Luna.

The fallen battler frantically tried to regain his feet. Kamō'ī with astonishing swiftness, scissored the Mauian between thick haunches then caught and trapped one of Luna's arms behind him. The king's other hand darted to find a pressure point between Luna's neck and shoulder and his steely fingers dug in savagely.

Barely holding himself on one hand and both knees Luna shrieked pain, nearly senseless. Kamō'ī controlled him as if pinching the gills of a flopping fish.

Billy Pitt moved forward and handed Kamō'ī a dagger. The king released the fallen man and stood over him. Painfully Luna struggled to raise his head, still on his knees. Glazed eyes cleared as he stared up at his conqueror. Kamō'ī placed the tip of the knife to Luna's breast. The Maui champion closed his eyes and tossed his head back in a last gesture of pride and defiance.

Kamō'ī jerked a short shallow stroke with the dagger's point. The Maui warrior shuddered in reflex. A few drops of blood appeared on his breast.

The dagger rang on stones as the king tossed it aside. "Join me, brave one," he said.

Luna prostrated himself fully in a gesture of submission and loyalty. A great cry welled up from Kamō'ī's troops. Stone laughed his relief. Billy Pitt threw his arms in the air and shouted. Stone raised his musket high and roared for the charge at the top of his voice. As one man the troops surged forward in a shouting mass, engulfing him and Pitt.

With the defeat of their champion the spirit of the remaining Mauians finally broke. For a few minutes they held, then, faltering broke scattering.

Relentlessly the Hawai'i men pursued the Mauians up the valley. Its terrain was rough and pitted, strewn with boulders and outcrops and slashed with a stream that soon ran with blood. Survivors not killed were bound and led out as prisoners. Nearing nightfall the carnage at 'Īao subsided and the island belonged to Kamō'ī. After eight days of fighting Maui and its thirty thousand people had a new king.

Pono made his escape.

With a small band of nobles, priests and soldiers he used an unguarded gully to slip through the Hawai'i lines. By late afternoon he was being in the chop of the inter-island channel, tossed about heading for the island of O'ahu and the protection of his half-brother, King Pule.

In the night great waves broke over his canoe and pounding cold rains came. These discomforts were lost in the depth of his shame and the blackness of his depression.

PART VII

*L*ess than a week after the 'Īao battle Olohana was with the king when Billy Pitt brought news that two nearby district chiefs were plotting to kill Kamō'ī. Pitt's informant was Luna, now devotedly Kamō'ī's man, who told the king the conspirators were meeting at that moment in a near by cave.

"Are they indeed?" the king asked.

He ordered Luna to take him, Pitt and Olohana to the meeting place.

A quarter mile from the village Luna pointed to a hole in the lava, scarcely large enough for a man to enter on hands and knees. Kamō'ī motioned the others to silence and moved quietly to the opening. His companions watched as he strained to listen. His face darkened with anger.

He delicately placed the spear he carried across the cave's opening. Then he padded back to the others and signalled them to join him in returning to the site where he was holding royal audiences.

"What does all this mean, Billy Pitt?" Olohana asked.

"It is forbidden under pain of death to touch the king's spear. Those men cannot leave the cave."

But a few hours later, while Kamō'ī was meeting with several administrators, the would be murderers appeared. The king fixed them with a cold and unblinking stare.

The taller said, "I am Hoku, sire, your servant in all things."

His companion added, "And I am Nana, my lord, desiring

only to serve you."

With a sardonic smile the king answered: "Alas, you cannot be these men, for they are dead."

He lifted a hand and jerked its thumb down.

Massive guards behind the two chiefs moved with practiced swiftness, snapping garrotes around the necks of the two and tightening them with vicious muscling. The culprits fell to their knees with brief, gargled sounds—hands clawing and eyes distended. For only a few moments they thrashed in silent mindless terror, then they were still.

Conquering Maui had given Kamōʻī one of the lushest and most hospitable of the Hawaiian islands, with grand valleys, beckoning beaches, a long sloping central lowland and two soaring mountain ranges. One of these was mostly the awesome and extinct volcano of Haleakalā, into whose crater, Stone reckoned, both Boston and Philadelphia might easily be placed. The victory also brought the smaller islands of Molokaʻi, Lānaʻi and Kahoʻolawe under Kamōʻī's regency. These smaller islands traditionally obeyed the ruling dynasty of Maui, thus they were now his.

Celebration of this immense victory was intense but short lived. His monarchy must be firmly and immediately established, Kamōʻī said. He would waste no time in taking the proper steps.

Manu was dispatched with the main body of troops back to Hawaiʻi. He left reluctantly, unhappy about any move that removed him from Kamōʻī. With five hundred select soldiers Kamōʻī began traveling his new dominion—weeding out dissidents, laying down tax laws and appointing new and cooperative chiefs. Where acceptable Maui men could not be found his soldiers who had distinguished themselves in battle were made administrators.

Everywhere villagers grumbled, though never loudly, at feeding the victorious strangers. But quickly there was scant objection to Kamōʻī's presence or edicts. Pono had been harsh in his taxing and when the new king's more moderate demands were known the fears of most Mauians evaporated.

The *Little American* served admirably as the royal yacht. A month following ʻĪao it was off Lahaina town on Maui's somnolent lee coast.

Here Kamōʻī was to meet with the rulers of Molokaʻi, Lānaʻi and Kahoʻolawe. For the occasion he donned his feather cloak and helmet. He ordered Tweed to ready the ship's two cannons—knowing how firing these guns would impress the minor *aliʻi*. As the ship slipped into Lahaina shallows the guns were discharged, their booming echoing against the distant hills, their large smoke rings trembling over the water.

Billy Pitt had become Olohana's tireless instructor in all matters Hawaiian. From him Stone now learned that Molokaʻi, with its deep windward valleys and rich fishponds on a lee shelf, was the most valued of the Maui neighbor isles. Lānaʻi was smaller, with good farms on its higher lands and excellent fishing on some shores. The smallest of the three, Kahoʻolawe, was also the least attractive. Arid and wind whipped, it lacked the high peaks to capture life giving rains.

Kamōʻī went ashore over a watery avenue bordered by canoes parted to let him pass. Chiefs of Lahaina and the three islands waited at the head of the shoreside crowd with their retinues of women and attendants. All fell to their hands and knees as Pono's conqueror stepped upon land.

Time was not wasted. As soon as Kamōʻī was ceremoniously seated on a dais of raised mats Pitt motioned for Molokaʻi chief to approach.

Like the other chiefs he had come with appropriate gifts: supple mats, rare shells, lineny *kapa* and suckling pigs. His walk was old and palsied, his wrinkled skin scaly from years of addiction to *ʻawa*-root liquor. Kamōʻī well knew the man's incompetence as a ruler. He had already chosen a replacemet—a chief from Hilo who had fought well in his service. He crisply offered the quaking Molokaʻi man a simple choice—retire to a place of refuge and receive care and respect for the rest of his life or be strangled. The old man accepted exile eagerly.

The *aliʻi* from Lānaʻi came next, a heavy man in his forties whose great belly touched the ground as he crawled forward.

He did not look like a fighter, Pitt whispered to Olohana, but this man had a conspicuous record of brave acts in opposition to Pono. Additionally he was a wise ruler who treated his people with compassion.

He would continue governing, Kamōʻī decreed, then attached three of his most trusted men to the Lānaʻi court. Constant surveillance would insure that desirable conditions continued to exist.

Next came the chief from Kahoʻolawe.

He was a handsome young man who had only recently inherited the rule upon his father's death. Thus far he had been generous and just to the two thousand commoners on the small island. He too would retain his position, Kamōʻī said, but also under the eyes of three men from the king's court, and a *kahuna*-specialist in irrigation and farming.

Finally the Lahaina chief was brought forward. His protestations of love and loyalty were patently insincere and Stone felt certain he would be replaced. Kamōʻī's crooked smile confirmed the thought. Pitt murmured that the man had a long history of doing whatever Pono had desired, no matter how cruel or immoral the act.

Kamōʻī asked that Mohu of South Kona step forward from the rank of his *aliʻi*. The burly warrior fell to his knees. His thick shoulders and arms were scarred from years of battle at his master's side.

"Here is the new lord of Maui," the king said. His eyes swept the cringing audience. "From this moment, Mohu speaks to you with my heart and tongue."

In the greathouse of the ousted Lahaina chief almost two weeks plodded by before details of governing and taxing Maui and its three lesser isles were settled. Defeating Pono had added over a thousand square miles to Kamōʻī's monarchy, with all the problems attendant to such a space and its population. A steady stream of minor chiefs came to visit the king, arriving with reports and leaving with instructions.

Guns had won the lands, Kamōʻi remarked to Olohana, but only a fair and paternal rule would keep them.

"We cannot rule by guns alone. We need loyal subjects, not frightened people. With peace and justice, *haole* tools and the smiles of the gods we will be united and strong."

To his remaining lieutenants on Maui, Kamōʻi made a brief speech: "We will soon weave the islands now won into a great cloak. This cloak we will use to smother Pule of Oʻahu. But Pule is a wise and courageous man and this will not be easy. The humiliating defeat of his brother will only stiffen his resolve. He has guns and may acquire more, for Oʻahu with its good anchorage and plentiful provisions attracts *haole* ships. We will need a large and strong army and a huge fleet to defeat him. Our plans for the days ahead must be made with wisdom and keen foresight—but with our own comrades governing here such plans can be accomplished as well in Kona as elsewhere. It is time to turn again to the chores of peace and pleasures of our families. Now we go home."

Two days later the *Little American* and its flotilla of canoes sailed back into the bay at Kailua. Within a week the canoe fleet had been dispersed and most craft returned to fishing. Except for the musketmen and others of the king′s guard, the soldiers were released, returning as heroes to their farms, fishponds and *kalo* patches.

Kamōʻi declared a rest period for the men of the Maui expedition and took time himself for fishing and surfing, the latter in company with Kahu. Olohana often watched them from the beach—two naked and magnificent bronzed figures, skimming the frothing surf like dark gulls.

Hina informed Tweed that two of the ladies in his harem were pregnant and the Scot was overjoyed by the news. Puna begged Olohana to tell him every detail of the Maui battles and listened with fascination. Namo watched these two in their earnest and often happy conversation and could not help but envy the time Olohana spent with the boy.

Peace shown upon Hawaiʻi island like the sun.

Women welcomed their men home and many babies were

conceived. Children romped, swam, laughed and learned the skills of their parents. The moon changed with little alteration in the weather—not an unusual circumstance in the islands. Days melted gently into one another.

It had been little more than a year, Stone reckoned, since he and Tweed had been abandoned on Kona shores. In that brief time they had been transformed into the general and admiral of a Polynesian king and helped win a war on his behalf. They were "married" to beautiful and aristocratic island women. In the near future, their new master promised, they would own large plantations with many workers to manage them. They lived well in a soft land and wanted for nothing. But, sooner than either man desired, a new and larger conflict loomed in the taking of Oʻahu for Kamōʻī. The fact that this might cost him his life did not escape John Stone's reflection.

Thoughts of New England came to him only rarely now, rising at odd moments with flashes of distant sights, sounds and voices that as quickly slipped away. Even less since Maui. The Maui experience, for both Stone and Tweed, had given an aura of permanency to their residence—an initiation suffered and passed. Tweed no longer spoke of his former life. It was as if he had known none before the attack at Kaʻūpūlehu. The Scot had become a dedicated islander, fluent in Hawaiian and utterly happy with his home, the ship and the women who happily satisfied his satiric appetite.

Then, early in November of 1791, the brig *Sarah* appeared in a pasteled dawning off Kailua Bay.

She was a stout and scarred three master of some two hundred fifty tons carrying eight guns. As their canoe approached, Tweed wondered aloud to Stone what her commander might be like.

"From her look, a Yankee, I'll wager," was Olohana's answer. "So he'll be pious or a hypocrite or a bastard—maybe all three. I don't give a damn so long as he has what we need."

Most of Stone's surmise was correct. The *Sarah's* master, Adam Cox, was a desiccated and crusty Marblehead man who took one look at his two welcomers and leapt to a conclusion. With shaven faces, clear eyes, clean blouses and nankeen breeches they were not the sort of white men he usually encountered in these infidel seas.

"Praise the Lord!" he exclaimed. "You are here in His work."

Stone was tempted to reply that in truth he and his friend were quite actively engaged in the heathen's work. But the words that came were, "Sorry, no, Captain. We were stranded when our ship left hastily after a dispute with the big chief. She was the *Nahant*, out of Boston, Captain Nathan Quimby. Do you know him?"

He did not, Cox answered, his face sobered. But he had heard of him only recently from a captain at Nootka. Quimby and the *Nahant* were apparently lost, many months overdue. Hope had been abandoned for the ship and her crew.

Stone and Tweed stared at one another.

"He was your friend?"

"No." Stone's thoughts raced. He and Tweed were on this ship to do business with Cox, thus it was best that he not offer his true opinion of Quimby. Cordiality must be the keynote... The faces of the other members of the *Nahant's* crew moved across his mind—Maul, Scrimmage, Blue Bob... Nevertheless, 'tis bad news."

"Do you wish to be delivered from these pagans?" Cox motioned at the excited crowd of natives surrounding his ship.

"No, thank you, Captain," Stone said. "This king treats us with generosity and we live handsomely as chiefs. We have decided to stay for a bit." He knew Tweed would agree that life with Cox on the long haul to China and back to America would be a dismal alternative to their present condition. Surely there would be a better opportunity one day...

The captain did not pursue the subject, having no genuine desire to feed two extra mouths for six to eight months. He had done his Christian duty by making the offer and now considered the amenities observed. He turned the talk to trade. He needed water, meat, salt and firewood, he said. He did not deal in sinful spirits, he added loftily, but mentioned no scruples concerning guns. Stone said he did the king´s business and that tools, cookware and fishhooks were among the items desired. He could supply all these, Cox answered.

"Yon schooner," he nodded at the *Little American*, riding inshore water a quarter mile distant. "Will she be another trader"

"No," Stone said. "She belongs to the king, purchased from Captain Quimby." The truth, he reasoned, would only cause awkwardness.

Cox stared sourly at the naked girls in the water being cheered by seamen along the rails. Fresh water, plantains and baked pig being hoisted aboard were contributing to the pleasure. He invited Stone and Tweed to take a cup of tea in his cabin. Settled in these stuffy quarters Stone asked for news of the outside world.

Cox´s idea of news was anything of current interest in the fur trade. The northwest Indians were raising their demands in barter goods, he said. And the Russians were more numerous, with trading posts as far south as the Farallone Islands off New Albion. Many British captains were now flying French and Spanish flags in order to trade free of throttling restrictions imposed on them by their own East India and Hudson´s Bay companies. Abruptly he asked when he would meet the king.

"This must be at his convenience," Stone answered politely, knowing that Kamō´ī would not wish to see this man. "He is now the king of five of the seven largest islands. Governing his domain keeps him quite busy."

"Perhaps he will join me in a Bible service," Cox said. "I serve proudly as a lay member of the New England Missionary Society, and seize every opportunity to join souls to Christ."

"Commendable, Captain. But it is unlikely he will attend you. He holds very strongly to his native beliefs. He respects the white man´s religion but refuses to accept it for his own."

Cox appeared shocked. "Has no one told him of the glories of Jesus?"

Stone said that Jesus had been frequently mentioned by

previous visitors but with little effect on his highness. Tweed smiled behind his hand. Stone turned the subject back to trade. Provisions were in lean supply, he said. A recent excursion to Maui had depleted stores.

Cox's eyes narrowed in his suspicion that this claim was an excuse to inflate prices. Sensing his reaction Stone assured him terms would be fair. Kamōʻi desired visitors to leave his islands content with their treatment.

"Do you have guns for trade, Captain?" Stone asked. He suspected that an immensely greedy man lurked behind the pious facade of this Bible thumper. It showed in the way Cox made tea—a miserly pinch in the pot.

The captain was taken aback by the directness, his cup arrested in midair.

"Aye, Mister Stone. I carry arms. But I take care who I trade them to. And when I do it calls for an extraordinary kind of bargain."

"Would three hundred otter skins in prime condition be extraordinary?"

"Three hundred skins? *Here?*"

"Aye. His highness made an arrangement with an earlier vessel some time ago. The pelts are finest quality, sir, still safe in cedar chips."

Cox carefully put his cup down. Stone could feel his mind churning.

"What sort of trade do you have in mind, Mister Stone?"

"One musket for two skins. Plus five kegs of powder and five thousand ball."

Cox pursed his thin lips.

"I am thinking that one gun for *four* skins is more within reason," he said. "These are choice weapons, first rate Brown Besses."

The reference, Stone knew, was to standard British Army infantry muskets, made by the thousands in English midland cities like Birmingham. Blunt and brass fitted, they were simply designed for simple care. But they were hardly accurate, with lateral error as much as three feet, thus useless except for close fighting. Still, even these would be better than none...He decided to stand firm, certain his assessment of Cox was right.

"No," he smiled. "My offer is fair, Captain. I know your profit on the pelts in China."

"I'll do some thinking on this," Cox hedged. "In the meantime, perhaps you can show me the goods."

Trade started at midday.

Stone and Tweed acquired blouses, boots and trousers. Cox had other items needed: flints, axes, drills and iron hooping with which Tweed desired to band wooden cannon wheels carved by canoemakers. The *Sarah's* men grumbled through their duties, denied release to the seductions of the shore. They were kept in order by the mate, a bowlegged martinet with close set eyes and an unkempt beard.

In the afternoon Cox took a longboat to inspect the pelts still stored aboard the *Little American.* He wanted to ask more questions about this neat ship but restrained himself, suspecting this might embarrass his hosts. Successful trade at Kona was far more important to him than satisfaction of his curiosity. The furs were top grade, no cubs and full pelts, exactly as Stone had represented, and would fetch at least one hundred dollars a piece in Whampoa or Macao.

Back on the *Sarah* Cox broke open a crate of muskets for Stone's inspection. Olohana plucked out a random few, noting guild marks, clicking locks and looking for evidences of rust or other damage. All had seen considerable use but were in good condition. Neither man mentioned the gap in negotiations, each playing a waiting game.

Stone invited Cox to come ashore for supper and was relieved when the other pleaded weariness and refused. Before Stone left Cox, without comment, handed him a Bible. Stone thanked him. He had long been starved for reading and the very feel of any book was a pleasure. Besides, he reasoned, it would serve admirably as a reading text for Puna.

On the third day Cox allowed some of his people to go ashore and scattered like sparrows through seaside settlements. The captain remained aboard and neither Stone or

Tweed saw him all day. Kimi reported that the mate had nego-
tiated for a *wahine* to be brought to Cox the night before. She
had been taken aboard surreptitiously and sent quietly home
before dawn. Cox's precautions were of no avail. By sunup the
girl's friends had heard every detail of her toss with the old
cock and were admiring her new skirt of bright red cotton.

Later in the day Olohana again called on the captain.

They sat to thin tea and, after brief discussion of trade, Cox
suddenly turned the talk to Stone's personal activities.

"Have you no desire to leave this man's employ?" he
asked.

"He is an important king, Captain. Mister Tweed and I
enjoy every comfort, are treated as nobility." Stone was tempted to tell this skinflint to mind his own bloody business then
thought better of it. "These are cheerful islands. The people are
kind and generous. I have a loving woman, many servants and
know the trust of a powerful ruler who has promised me lands
of my own. These are excellent prospects for a humble sailor,
Captain."

"I question the price, Mister Stone. You fight and kill for a
pagan ruler. You could meet a terrible death in this heathen
place."

It was one of those moments for John Stone. The New
England twang, rather than the words, of the captain's speech
caused Stone a small wave of nostalgia. Perhaps one day he
would walk the webbed byways of Boston again, enjoy a
tankard of dark ale, grainy bread, sweet butter and a juicy beef-
steak. It would be pleasant to hear the sounds of English in a
smoky tavern, feel spring's promise, a crisp autumn, a white
winter...

And how would he return? As an indigent seaman—or
master of a rich Hawaiian plantation? He yanked himself back
to the present, eyeing Cox's gaunt face in the dim light of the
cabin.

"This king's campaign is just, Captain. As right in its way
as the cause for which we fought not long ago. For myself the
dangers are no more than I have faced for years. One can die

cruelly in a gale, from thirst or fever or the knife of a Nootka Indian or Chinese cutthroat. All factors considered, life here improves my chances of experiencing old age, not to mention enjoying it."

"There is a far greater reward," Cox said. "This life of yours can only lead to eternal damnation."

"You may leave the care of my soul to me, Captain," Stone said. He'd be damned if he'd take such criticism from this randy old hypocrite.

On the morning of the sixth day ten of the *Sarah's* men abandoned a water casking detail and disappeared into the hills.

Cox urgently summoned Stone and Tweed and demanded that the deserters be found and returned.

"Disgraceful, isn't it, Alec?" said Stone.

"Aye, that it is, John. The lassies nae doot. Tarts, every last one, tempting these poor lads."

"Hussies," Stone agreed solemnly. "Agents of Satan himself."

Cox stared from one to the other, the truth seeping in.

"We'll see what can be done, Captain," Stone said briskly. "But there's a great deal of ground to cover and this will take time. Perhaps while our people are searching for these sinners we two may have a serious talk about the guns and furs?"

There was a charged moment of silence before Cox answered, "Twas three skins for each weapon, as I recall.

"Your pardon, sir. I offered two for one. *With* the ammunition."

Cox's face flamed.

"Very well." He almost choked on the assent. Whoring women were not the only agents of Satan here.

"Thank you, Captain. I'm sure you'll see good profit." Stone knew Cox would cheerfully have had him flogged within an inch of his life had he been under his command. But all he could do now was to nod curtly. He enjoyed the captain's discomfort. In his own way Cox was another Quimby, smoother and less vicious.

The errant seamen were duly returned, every man giddy from feasting and fornication and wishing the caper might have gone on forever. The captain delivered the ammunition and muskets, one hundred fifty pieces in excellent condition. Stone had the pelts ready for transfer to the *Sarah*. It would have been difficult to ascertain which man conducted a more rigid examination of his goods. Each was coolly polite during the exchange.

Further trading proceeded smoothly. But the twelfth day Cox had all the provisions required for a long journey and the king's storehouse was considerably enriched. Cox had also bargained additional powder and ball for a deckload of sandalwood. He too had heard of the huge gains to be made by taking the fragrant logs to China.

More, his bony nose sniffed other possibilities in this archipelago. For all his narrowmindedness Adam Cox was an imaginative businessman. The success of Cox and Pinkham, Ltd., of Cornhill, Boston, attested to this. China trade, he reckoned, was opening at a faster rate than anyone had envisioned. Interest in the Orient could only accelerate in the counting houses of New York, Boston and London. More ships would traverse the Pacific and this halfway point at Hawai'i would be vital for food and water. A post for ships' supplies and service in the islands could make one rich, not to mention the profit from supplying the heathen with tools, cloths, mirrors and other gimcracks they so passionately desired.

Another thought ran parallel in his mind. He would alert his friends in New Haven and Boston to the sore need for Christian guidance in this pagan place. Its women were wanton, the men dissolute and weak and their idols outrageous. The islands cried for the voices of God's servants—and the calming influences of decent businessmen could only help in His glorious work.

Two huge canoes rode bright water, tugging the *Sarah* seaward by lines snapping spray. Naked muscles strained as the paddlers dipped and drew in unison. Tweed directed the tow from one of the canoes. Olohana was aboard the ship bidding

Cox farewell. Puna was with him, astonished at the sights and sounds of the immense *haole* vessel.

He trusted, Stone said, that Cox was satisfied in trade and that his stay had been pleasant.

The captain thanked him. Since the distrust engendered over the gun exchange he had been suspicious of every move on Stone's part. But the barter goods had been of excellent quality and agreements strictly adhered to. Not above a trick or two himself, Cox even had a grudging admiration for Stone's intrigue. He could never be comfortable in the presence of a man who served a savage king so diligently—but one scarcely choose one's business associates in such places and it was wisest that they part on friendly terms. This man Olohana might serve some use in future plans... He made a gift of writing materials and paper to Stone's young ward and, with his goodbye, gave Stone a new blue coatee and an English cutlass.

The *Sarah's* sails crackled up and filled with a warm breeze off the Kona slopes. The ship wore away on deep green swells, her men glancing sorrowfully at the shores of their pleasures.

As the dark blue mountains of Hualālai and Mauna Loa dropped beneath the horizon Cox called all free hands together. He exhorted them to pray for the souls of Stone, Tweed and their pagan host—a man, he realized, whom he had never seen.

PART VIII

"Why is *haole* skin white?" Puna asked.

They did not live in constant sun, Olohana explained, thus their skins were not burned dark. In the land called Africa, where the sun was always overhead, natives became black. But this apparently took many years, more time than one could reckon.

"Why are the eyes of China men long and narrow?"

Fumbling, Olohana said that the way men looked was most likely related to the way they lived, long long ago. Indians of northwest America had the same kind of eyes.

Abruptly, the boy changed the subject, "Why do men make war?"

Despite the size of this query Olohana found it easier to answer than others leaping from Puna's nimble mind. He replied after a pause, "Because they want land or wealth held by others or wish to impose their power and will upon people."

"Why do you fight for us, Olohana?"

Could he tell the truth? That he had been given but little choice and had chosen fighting as easier for himself than not fighting? At first this was true. But he had violently underlined the choice on Maui, in blood.

"Kamōʻī has made me one of you," he said. "He offers me a rich and pleasant future, gives me honor. I believe in his cause." The statement seemed vague and evasive-he hoped Puna would not probe further. Soon enough this youth would understand the blandishments of ease and comfort, power and station.

"He has spoken to me three times," Puna said proudly.

"He sees you with favor, otherwise he would not bother."

Puna´s eyes studied his feet. His next question would be difficult but he had put it off as long as he could bear.

"Is he my real father, Olohana?"

Stone had been whetting his knife, and stopped. It was only a question of time before the true story reached the boy. Nothing would be gained by avoiding an answer.

"It´s said he is, lad."

His arms folded, Puna stared hard at the ground, absorbing this candid information.

"Do you understand the reasoning?" Olohana asked.

"Yes. My mother is of the *ali'i* but not noble enough for the *ali'i nui*. He cannot recognize me."

"Ah, but he has. You are here, at his court, with his chiefs and queens. No other young man is so honored." Olohana grasped the boy´s hard slim shoulders. "Stand proud and respectful, learn and be loyal. You must earn his attention. Then he will speak to you more."

Puna forced a smile. "One day I will show him my worth. One day I will show him I am a true *ali'i*. He will want me always at his side. I will be like you, Olohana."

"Yes, my hearty. For certain, one day you will." Stone sheathed his knife. "Now come with me. A young chief must know reading and writing in this new world he will face, and it is time for your lessons."

Puna´s shoulders squared. "An "*ali'i* need not know these things."

"An "*ali'i* needs knowledge more than other men. Now come. For the time being I am in command."

Kamō'i had been in higher lands, helping select trees for war canoes and at the sport of snaring birds. Upon his return he was delighted with Olohana´s trade for the guns. Henceforth, he told his chiefs, Olohana would regularly act as his personal representative with full power to deal with visitors. Stone made appropriate thanks for the honor, fully aware that the king had not the slightest intention of relinquishing his own role as arbiter in such matters.

Nevertheless Stone was gratified, not expecting to be recognized so publicly. He was, after all, a foreigner, someone naturally to be distrusted. The gesture gave him added dimension as counselor to Kamō'ī in trade and fiscal matters—a relationship to be desired if he was to advance himself.

The king and Billy Pitt had been discussing the *haole.*

"Pono was foolishly unprepared," Kamō'ī noted. "And we had superior gun power. But Olohana trained and led the men well and bravely and Aleka handled the ship and canoes with skill. We owe much to these two."

"It was wise, *ali'i,* to leave the trading in Olohana's hands and absent yourself while the ship was here."

"If I am to continue trust in them it was necessary to know if they would leave—and they did not. Or rather, Olohana chose to stay. It appears we will have this man Aleka for the rest of his life."

A silence followed, broken by Billy Pitt, "You must reward them, sire. Olohana has hinted impatience to me."

"'*Ae.* In time we will find the proper lands for them, but this is not urgent. Aleka is content with the ship and his household, most particularly, his women. I am told he is endowed like Captain Courtney's bull animal, with much the same philosophy. But Olohana *thinks* and we do not know what is in his mind. I will do him honor and keep him busy so he does not become restless."

In months following Kamō'ī drew Olohana more and more to his side, asking questions on a multitude of subjects having to do with the *haole* world and its workings. He also began making Stone privy to court matters of every nature, even to discussions of political and land problems of which Olohana knew next to nothing.

A sampling of the air that pervaded the court had brought Stone to an early decision—it would be in his best interest to move discreetly. Several of the lesser *ali'i* attending the ruler obviously resented Olohana's new status. Others were courteous but wary. Stone knew none of these men would dare make objections about him to the king. Kamō'ī's actions were religiously justified by his extraordinary *mana*. Anyone who doubted the monarch's wisdom kept such sacrilege to himself. Royal decisions went unquestioned and, if violated in any way, harsh and often fatal punishment followed.

But Stone stood well outside this system of *kapu* and his own person was very far from sacred. In short, he was vulnerable game for anyone who disliked or envied him. His wisest course, he determined, was to minimize friction by keeping silent and listening hard in the king's assemblies. It would be a fool's game to offer opinions on matters which were purely Hawaiian and he physically withdrew from discussions concerning religion or the *kapu*. If he had any suggestions about future trade or military matters he made them privately to the king and Pitt.

Kamō'ī desired that Olohana be present at the frequent court sessions held in the royal greathouse.

During these conferences Billy Pitt always sat on the king's right and Kahu on his left. The king frequently murmured in consultation with his favorite queen. Unlike most aristocrats, who held themselves aloof from the people, Kahu had an unusual grasp of social and political goings on. Kamō'ī respected her thoughts and more than once Stone observed her influence changing the course of his thinking.

His own relationship with the grande dame was cordial. He was properly respectful, she responded in an amiable fashion and they conversed easily. Never, even in rare moments when they were alone, had she hinted of their brief sexual frolic. Apparently she considered such capers to be minor indulgences, a perquisite of her rank. Clearly she approved of him and his inclusion in the top scale of her husband's advisors. Stone vowed he would nourish this support, realizing that anyone who dared step between Kahu and her master would surely and sadly rue the indiscretion.

He quit attempting even lukewarm attempts at polite relations with Manu. The prince made his hostility overt, though he softened the attitude when in Kamō'ī's presence. When Manu was ordered to *Ka'ū* to make an inventory of its lands, wealth and men—and find a replacement for the district's weak chief—he complained bitterly. He told Pitt that he was being removed from Kamō'ī's inner circle, strongly insinuating that Olohana had conspired to have him sent away. The vicious *haole* was robbing him of the king's affection and trust, he said, and Kamō'ī was blind to this.

"This is not true," Pitt had reacted. "The *haole* keeps himself apart from such matters. The king sends you to Ka'ū because he trusts you and values you. But if you persist in these foolish notions you will rob yourself of his confidence."

Pitt could see that Manu remained unconvinced. After long experience with his nephew's stubbornness, he could only hope that Manu might one day see things as they truly were...

In the still air of a warm afternoon the two women lay nude upon mats in Keōpū's house.

"We give birth to men," Kahu said to the sacred queen. "In agony we bring them into the world to suckle at our breasts. By what reasoning do they come to command and humiliate us?"

Keōpū had no reply. Beyond reflecting that this was the way of the gods—and that Kahu had never experienced birthing pain—she could think of no logical answer. Indeed since all people groveled in her presence she had little understanding of the complaint.

Like other subjects Kahu entered Keōpū's presence on her hands and knees. But once this *kapu* was honored and the servants dismissed the royal *wāhine* found ease and amusement in each other's company. They shared their master without petulance or jealousy and scarcely thought of his lesser wives.

Kahu could never completely relax with her exalted sister but the two much enjoyed these frequent chats. Kahu was everything Keōpū could not be: mischievous, gay and lusty. She was also in constant touch with happenings in the kingdom and thus Keōpū's only contact for news of the court. These reports were bountiful and lively, spiced by Kahu's vivid imagination and risque nature. She now temporarily abandoned her favorite complaint, the subjugation of females, and offered Keōpū her morsel of gossip for the day, "Aleka, the *haole* called The Cock, has impregnated *three* of his women."

"*Auwe*," alas, Keōpū said. "He is named well." She poured sweet Canary into small glasses. "And Olohana?"

"He walks on clouds since discovering he too will be a father. He and the Maui girl have great *aloha* for each other, whispering and laughing a great deal, always touching when together. They will quarrel no more."

Keōpū's eyes questioned.

"She was jealous, my lady. Olohana was spending so much time with the boy, teaching him the reading and writing. She shouted and threw things, but all that has changed."

Keōpū nodded. Kahu went on, "The king draws Olohana to his side more and more. He has great faith in him, seeking his thoughts and advice on problems."

"Is this good?"

"'*Ae*. Olohana knows more than ships and guns. He has read and studied and has much knowledge of the world outside. When he counsels it is to help us, not the other *haole*. Kalani Pitt pronounces him superior and trustworthy. And what Kalani says our master believes."

"Do you believe?" asked Keōpū.

"Yes. These are men of value. Both have had opportunity to betray, or lie—or escape with the Boston captain. Both have been honorable and dutiful."

"And Manu? What does he say?"

"Nothing, but his eyes and manner speak. He hates them. Kamō'ī has sent him to Ka'ū to arrange the peace, an errand of honor and importance. But Manu sees this as a plot to remove him from the court."

"He is a puzzle," Keōpū murmured.

"'*Ae*. He has no *aloha*. I have seen him amused only when someone is hurt or humbled." Kahu finished her wine. "I have warned the king that there is evil in this man, that he must not place too must trust in him. Do you think I did right?"

"Yes. He respects what you say." If Keōpū had one envy it was of Kahu's ability to communicate with their husband. She and the king rarely conversed beyond pleasantries and small talk about their daughters. "What was his answer?"

"That Manu had served him well, had fought bravely in our wars and on Maui and, as the son of Ōpū, would continue at his side."

Keōpū shrugged. This appeared to settle the matter.

Kahu sighed. "Men remain blind to things a woman sees instantly," she said. "I think our inner sight is a gift from the gods. But sadly the gods have not told men of this blessing. Otherwise, *wāhine* would enjoy more respect and freedom from humiliating *kapu*."

Keōpū was so restricted by her status she hardly knew what freedom meant. She wanted to turn the conversation back to more interesting subjects. She refilled Kahu´s glass with the potent wine, knowing it tickled her bawdy nature and lubricated her tongue.

"These *haole*," she ventured. "Are they different from our men? Are they... *made* differently?"

Kahu paused. She was not supposed to know the answer, despite the fact that she had ridden Olohana—and, more recently, Aleka—and Keōpū might conceivably know this.

"There is no difference, my lady, except for the color. Both men have large pieces—I am told." Olohana was splendidly equipped but Aleka had one of the biggest *uli* she had ever taken. The women of his household had composed a little song in its praise.

Keōpū nodded. She wondered if the instruments of the *haole* could be larger than that of Kamō´i—the only one she had ever experienced. When fully erected the king could lift her off the mats with his *uli*.

Kahu talked on, "The size of a man´s tool does not make him a better performer, dear sister. Men who enjoy *giving* pleasure as well as taking it are best, making the experience last longer. Others finish in moments, like chickens, leaving a woman gasping in desire. But to give a man greatest joy, an admiring of his *uli* is best. There is no fascination, no love greater, than that of a man for his *uli*."

"Alas," said Keōpū, her eyes down. She could hardly contribute to this discussion without mention of their master-and the two never spoke of Kamō'i's sexual performances. The silence became awkward and she felt need to say something.

"So... The women of these *haole* are happy?"

"'*Ae*, my queen," said Kahu. "Their men are generous and thoughtful, their houses want for nothing and they are not humbled or beaten. And they eat with their men—coconuts, plantains, pigs, everything—and the gods have not punished them."

Perhaps, she thought, she could persuade Keōpū to make a bold move in the same direction, "One day we too should sit and eat with the men, my lady. If you and I made such brave gesture it would have important meaning."

"One must not be arrogant," Stone said to Puna.

"What is arrogant?" the boy asked.

"Too much pride, the attitude that one is much superior to others."

"I *am* superior, Olohana. I am *ali'i*."

"So am I, laddie, and your *hānai*-guardian besides. So take heed of what I say. A truly strong man has no need to bully or boast or parade his strength. You never see the king behave badly like that."

"Listen well to Olohana," said Namo. "He speaks wisely."

A maid brushed her hair as she sat, enjoying the idle talk of the two men. Namo was happy, warmly aware of the budding life within her.

"'*Ae*," Puna said. He wished to please. Olohana was now of a hero's stature with the success of his men and guns on Maui. Puna was immensely proud to be his *hānai*—and the envy of every young man of the district.

"Walk and talk softly," Stone said. "This befits important men. Think before you speak. And it is wise to always be prepared for the worst."

"'*Ae*, Olohana."

Stone stared into the large brown eyes.

Words, he thought, only words. He will have to make his own mistakes, just like the rest of us.

PART IX

*H*e wished to tell a story, Kamōʻī said. The gathering of chiefs around the small evening fire fell silent.

This was said to have happened in islands far to the south, the king began. Probably in the lands of Feegee, for they were many and rarely visited by white men.

Once, not long ago, a *haole* ship appeared off one of these islands and a tall young man was put ashore. He was pale and unsmiling and dressed in dark clothes. He carried nothing but a black book. The ship which brought him immediately sailed away.

The young stranger was greeted warmly, given a spacious house and food and coconut milk to drink. The high chiefs personally honored him, seeking to know if there was anything they could do to make him comfortable and happy.

But communication was difficult. The young man only waved his black book and pointed to the sky. On the second evening a beautiful young virgin was sent to his house. In moments, she had been driven out and was weeping, while the young man shouted and waved his black book.

It soon became clear that the book dominated the man´s thoughts and dictated his actions. Everywhere he moved he held it aloft, proclaiming its contents. In time he came to be understood. He interrupted the women at their weaving and men at fishing to tell them its messages. He told people they should not go naked, despite its comforts; that a man must have only one wife; that young people should not be taught the many beautiful ways of making physical love—and that the sacred marriage of a high chief to his sister was an evil act.

Kamō'ī moistened his narrative with a sip of port and went on. The stranger and his black book became a constant irritation. He interfered with the priests at their rites and once seized and threw several god images into a fire. He derided the beliefs and customs of the people and sneered when they protested that these ways had served them well since time began. He caused trouble between husbands and wives. He terrified the children, telling them they would go to a land of eternal flame when they died.

So, Kamō'ī continued, one night the chiefs and elders of the island held a meeting to decide what to do about this despicable man.

He did not fish, or grow or make anything useful. Nor was he entertaining. He had never done anything to make anyone laugh or be joyful.

He would not lie with a woman, therefore he could not make children.

He spent his days annoying people who were his generous hosts, causing them to be fearful and unhappy.

The novelty of having him as a guest had long since worn away. And the ship that brought him had not returned—indicating he was not wanted elsewhere.

The gathering of elders decided he was good for only one thing.

So, Kamō'ī smiled, on the next day they ate him

A week after his arrival in Ka'ū Manu had its presumptive heir strangled. Fortunately the pretender was an ineffectual fool who would not be missed. His assassination accomplished three purposes: it marked Manu as a man of power, eliminated the only blood heir to Koa's monarchy and jolted the remaining chiefs into a more compliant state.

As Kamō'ī's regent Manu ruled without question, his presence inviolate and his word law. Kamō'ī's instructions to him had been clear. Manu was to exile or kill unreliable chiefs or others loyal to Koa's memory, organize an army responsive to the new rule and find a strong *ali'i* to install as high chief of the district.

Before a second week had passed Manu's initial resentment of his commission became realization of how it could be turned to his advantage. At home in Kona he had a personal force of some thousand men drawn from his ancestral lands. Here in Ka'ū he could turn a much larger army to his will without its awareness. His census was encouraging. Ka'ū being more dependent upon the sea than other areas, was rich in canoes. Its fighting men were quiet and tough, products of their harsh and lonely environment. The chiefs were veteran warriors with skills refined in a dozen battles. Manu felt certain many of them nursed a secret hatred of Kamō'ī. Surely none hid the emotion more successfully than he. One day soon this first son of Ōpū would assume his rightful position.

His immediate need was to win the confidence and support of the Ka'ū leaders. This he proceeded to do by taking individual chiefs aside, flattering them and hinting that they had been personally chosen for important roles in the new order. Great rewards would come to those who served faithfully, he promised, never suggesting this loyalty was not to Kamō'ī. He became kindly and confiding and none of the *ali'i* he approached sensed his true objective. He urged them to hone their Ka'ū fighting men to their finest edge. When time for their employment arrived all must obey without hesitation. Manu had not yet decided when that time would be.

He summoned Pūku'i, the young chief who had accompanied Koa to his death at the Koholā dedication. Thus far Pūku'i had been subdued and distant, coolly respectful. He was held in highest esteem by his peers and was a champion among fighters. If manipulated properly he could well be one of Manu´s most effective lieutenants in the days to come. Certainly he was a man to be handled with care.

High in the rain forests the *kāhuna* of canoe building studied the *'elepaio* birds. If the brown and white creatures walked the length of a tree trunk without pause it meant the wood was sound. If a bird stopped to peck this indicated a flaw or the presence of insects and the tree was not suitable.

When a desired trunk was thus found free of imperfection a camp was established and offerings were made of fish and *kapa* cloths to the gods of the canoe maker´s art. A pig and a red fish were cooked and eaten with proper ceremony. Only then would felling of the giant begin.

Stone adzes thumped and *kāhuna* voices lifted in chants to Kaū of Power as the tree came crashing to earth. For days work went on removing branches and crudely shaping the huge bulk. Weeks followed in the bruising, backbreaking labor of hauling, pushing and easing the ponderous roughs over valleys and down cliffs to the seashore. There, in large shelters called *hālau*, painstaking work continued to shape the immense log into a graceful and magnificent *wa'a peleleu*, war canoe, for Kamō'ī´s fleet.

Slowly the thick trunks were tapered, their sides trimmed, tops flattened, bottom rounded and insides hollowed. Workmen waded in scatters of curled chips as the tedious chore of refining the hulls plodded on. Others tended only to the constant process of disassembly, careful flaking and relashing of the stone adzes to their wooden handles. Still others were engaged exclusively in the finer carvings of graceful outriggers, booms and bow and stern fittings. At every stage time was spent in additional ceremonies and prayers to Kaū of Canoemaking. In the leafy sheds men worked every minute of daylight.

These scenes were repeated in hundreds of *hālau* along the Kona coast and elsewhere on the big island. The *wa'a peleleu* armada of Kamō'ī would be the greatest flotilla for war ever built in the islands.

Olohana often watched, fascinated by the infinite patience of the craftsmen. Only a few had iron tools and most work was accomplished laboriously with adzes of stone, drills of sea urchin spines and other implements of basalt and shell. Coarse stone rubbers were first used to smooth the hull, then buffers of finer stone and soft coral. Final touches were made painstakingly with rubbers of densest lava and abrasive shark skin. A dye paint, made from plant juices, *kukui* oil and plantain buds was then applied with brushes of beaten fibrous root, and the dried finish was polished for days with more *kukui* oil, creating a gleaming and water repellant surface. Gunwale strakes and bow and pieces were carved and fitted with precision, secured expertly and neatly with lashings of fine native sennit.

When the crafts were finished they were masterpieces of their builders' art, many forty to fifty feet long, slim, beautiful and immensely strong to carry many warriors and supplies. In a final blessing they were eased into the water and rocked back and forth to the accompaniment of more chanting and ceremony. This act was called "drinking the sea" and served not only to wet and expand lashings and timbers but to confirm the *wa'a peleleu* in the noble cause of Kamō'ī.

Adzes of the craftsmen filled the air daily with sharp hollow exclamations. Coupled with the wooden beaters of women pounding *kapa* cloth from bark, these filled the somnolent days with erratic drumming.

But Olohana Stone did not find the noises unpleasant. They seemed rather like the ticking of many clocks, marking hours in a land where time scarcely mattered and seasons flowed gently, one into the next.

In this serenity of tropical life the years before Hawai'i

seemed another lifetime. The days to come were only spiced by the hintings of excitement and danger. All Stone had to do was stay alive to enjoy them.

At Kealakekua two men walked the shore at dusk.

Manu was well over six feet, his massive shoulders squared under a cloak of finest *kapa*. Lako was short and stubby, stumbling in the wake of this regal figure.

"He gave a *hānai* son to me then took him away without a word," Lako whined. "This is but one of many insults I have suffered."

Manu did not answer. He had no curiosity about Lako's motives for joining him and held the Kealakekua chief in contempt. His only interest was in using him. As an *ali'i* Lako could travel freely without exciting comment. He would serve as a courier and an organizer with important contacts. Additionally he had fighting men under his control, some with muskets. Manu disliked placing confidence in such a fellow but the number of his co conspirators must stay small and his choices were limited.

"Never once has he given me the respect or kindness he grants others," Lako puffed on. "From you, my lord, I would have the treatment due a fellow *ali'i*."

Manu's answer was cool and the words precise, "From me you will receive everything I promise. This does not include a personal relationship. You are now only the chief of a small district but, if you serve me well, you will be much richer and more powerful."

Lako fell another step behind. Manu stopped to turn and face him.

"How many men do you now command?"

"Three hundred, *ali'i*. Good fighters, and loyal to me." Lako's soldiers were loyal because he bribed them lavishly and they lived well on the labor of others.

"Tell no one of our pact. Do you understand? *No one.*"

"Of course, *ali'i*."

"Betray me and your tongue and balls will be fed to

the crabs while you watch. Is that clear?"

"Yes, my *ali'i*." Lako wondered if he had not exchanged one intolerable situation for another far worse. This young prince's stare sent a shiver down his spine. But it was much too late for any change of mind.

"Now," said Manu. "We will talk of what must be done."

The springtime months passed uneventfully. Summer waned, vivid and warm. September came, bright and dry.

The most desirable food fish spawned on the reefs, their fingerlings swarming in dark clouds over golden shallows. *Kapu* were imposed, limiting the taking of the delicious fry in order that large numbers might survive and grow fat for the leaner times ahead.

Ashore newly harvested lands were left to life fallow and enrich themselves. Fishponds were cleaned of unwanted weeds and the stock depleting carnivorous barracuda caught and killed. Soon it would be the season of *ho'oilo*, that half of the year when the sun retreated to the south and days became shorter. Grass houses were repaired and reinforced for times coming when the winds would shift, bringing harsh gustings and briny air. Fishes were salted and stored, *kalo* corms dried and hogs and dogs fattened with yams and *poi*.

Priests tidied the important Kona coast *heiau* at Kailua, Kahalu'u and Keauhou. At Kawaihae the Koholā temple was quiet, for Kaū was at rest. Commoners tended their family and fish god shrines along the shores. Walls were mended and trails cleared and canoes drawn upon the beaches for repairs and caulking. *Hālau"* sheds reverberated with the biting adze sounds of work on the great canoes. Other occupations might turn gentler and more reflective but work on Kamō'ī's *wa'a peleleu* remained constant.

Then time came for the *makahiki*, the annual post harvest period of rest, games, feasting—and payment of tribute.

The banners of Lono, god of life and growth, were hoisted, white *kapa* flowing from a crosspiece atop a long pole. These glowing pennants were carried clockwise around the island, accompanied by Kamō'ī's tribute collectors. It was Lono's banners, Pitt told Olohana, that the Hawaiians had confused with the sails of Captain Cook's ships. They thought he was the god returned after centuries of self imposed exile. This was why they had at first idolized the English captain when he came at the time of Lono's *makahiki*. Only after one of Cook's men died, and others proved quite mortal in their greed for women and debauchery, had Hawaiians sensed the truth. When blood was drawn from Cook on that final day, the aura of his godliness vanished and a few fools killed him.

Were any of these men still about? Stone asked.

Yes, was Pitt's answer. A few lived in sorrow, regretting what had been done. But others were proud and boastful about it.

Manu returned to Kailua and reported to Kamō'ī.

He had appointed the chief, Pūku'i, as the king's regent in Ka'ū.

Pūku'i was by far the strongest and most dependable man, Manu said. He had been like a brother to the late Koa but appeared to have accepted his king's assassination and adjusted to the new order. Other Ka'ū chiefs had fallen in line behind Pūku'i. A few strong dissidents had been eliminated. Others less fanatic had been banished to the sanctuary at Hōnaunau where time would neuter them as threats.

A force of some fifteen hundred men had been raised for Kamō'ī's army. Their lack of firearms was somewhat compensated for by their excellence in hand to hand combat. Many were counted among Ka'ū's champions in spear throwing, wrestling, dagger fighting and sling stone marksmanship. Canoes were available to transport this regiment when Kamō'ī issued a call.

Manu went on into detail: numbers of farmers, fishermen and craftsmen, kinds and skills of *kāhuna*, water supplies, canoe landings, produce of shores and uplands, concentrations of people and the health and wealth of villages.

The king listened intently. Ten years of his boyhood had been happily spent in Ka'ū and this was news of remembered places. When Manu finished Kamō'ī thanked him for a work well done. The new army, he said, would be assigned to Manu's command when the proper time arrived.

Inwardly the prince sighed relief. He had not betrayed a hint of anything awry. Surely the gods were on his side.

Massed tribute goods piled up in the storehouse of the king.

Comfortable with their annual forfeit of pigs, dogs, mats, *kapa*, yams and taros, people paid, then played, rested and laughed, performing only those duties necessary to daily life.

Almost every afternoon there were games. On the water there were canoe, swimming and surfing competitions—an aquatic carnival of color and happy shouting. In less exacting endeavors there were dart throwing, stilt walking, kite flying and a Hawaiian variety of checkers called *kōnane*.

Districts as far distant as Hilo and Puna sent their finest athletes to compete before the royal court. These champions attracted large crowds to contests of foot racing, boxing and wrestling. One bright afternoon Kamō'ī strengthened his legend with an amazing display of courage and skill. Standing alone in a small field he deflected five thick spears thrown at him by burly warriors. He caught the sixth, its force spinning him around, then held it above his head. The roar from the multitude witnessing this feat could be heard in the hills.

The *haole* were not to be excused. Tweed took on a wrestler from the Kohala area and, after a bruising twenty minutes, referees called it a draw.

Stone's challenge came from a gargantuan boxer from Puna. They fought back bare knuckle and the big Hawaiian's terrifying roundhouses whistled past Stone's ears. The man was like a bull, relying far more upon brute strength than science. Olohana knew instantly that his only chance for victory lay in outboxing his opponent. Stone bobbed, weaved, ducked, backpedaled and bent almost to his knees in contortions to avoid the wild and brutal fists. Meantime he managed to land short jabs now and then, knowing they did only scant damage.

Then the big man caught him with a glancing punch that tore at his ear and set his head to singing. Stone faltered and staggered back but his assailant didn't follow the advantage. Desperate, Olohana rushed and caught the Hawaiian in a bear hug, holding tenaciously until his head cleared. Leaping away he realized his opponent was breathing heavily, tiring fast. If Stone could keep him moving and throwing impotent blows, he might finally wear the Puna man down. From the side he heard Tweed shouting urgently, "Box him, John! Box him!"

Such strategy seemed to be working. As they danced Stone found another vulnerability in his nemesis. When Stone feinted with a right the Hawaiian's hands spread apart and the hole in his guard widened. Stone played upon this reflex and each time the opening grew wider. Feinting a final time he gambled and won, throwing a vicious left through the gap which caught the man full on the mouth. He dropped to all fours, head waggling from side to side in his struggle to keep consciousness. Stone stood above him, waiting. There was only one rule in this contest—fight to win.

The gladiator struggled to his feet, hands dangling. Stone hit him twice more with all his strength before he went down again, this time spread eagled upon his back.

The onlookers broke into cheers. From his seat under the lofty plumes of the many royal *kāhili*, the king smiled. Olohana could not know he had ordered this match arranged, to test the mettle of this *haole*.

In the *makahiki* nighttime there was feasting and dancing, story telling and the introduction of new *hula* and chants. Dark came with a loving air, stars snowing the dome of sky, mountain breezes floating scents of sweet *maile* leaves and moist greenery. It was the time of year when weather was best, days shortening and night a caressing coolness.

Lono of Growth had been generous, Kanaloa of the Sea, fruitful. Kū of War was at peace and Kāne, the god of man, sent happiness over the land.

News traveled fast, Olohana reflected. In this bartering society talk seemed to be the stuff most eagerly exchanged.

The pastime extended out over the ocean channels. In their fraternity of interest fishermen from neighboring islands often joined their canoes on the deep to discuss movings of seabirds, winds, dolphins and tuna, and exchange gossip of home shores. From such sources, Kamō'ī received disturbing intelligence about O'ahu.

A captain named Broom had visited there recently in a big ship mounting twelve guns. A fur trader out of New York, he had been generous with gifts, currying the favor of King Pule.

While at O'ahu Broom had taken his vessel into a harbor hitherto unknown to foreign ships. Protected by a flat coral islet, this spacious bay indented a lowland on O'ahu's lee side at a place called Kou. Because of its warm weather and listless winds Kou held only the small huts of a few fishing families.

But Broom had declared this water to be the finest and safest anchorage yet found in the Pacific Ocean for big ships. He named the area Fair Haven or, in Hawaiian, Honolulu.

The canoe men with this news were brought before Kamōʻī, who demanded more details.

Captain Broom had at least fifty men, they said. His ship, the *Mystic*, was a fine craft which flew like a bird. He had given Pule many muskets and two of his large guns. And he had offered Pule the use of his ship and men to fight Kamōʻī. In return for this aid Pule would grant Broom exclusive rights to deal with future foreign ships in the harbor of Honolulu.

First it would be necessary for Broom to sail to China and trade his sea dog skins. Upon his return the bargain would be struck.

Kamōʻī gave his informants gifts of steel knives and dismissed them. Pitt, Kahu and Olohana were at his side.

This was the first outright offer of a *haole* to interfere in Hawaiian affairs, Kamōʻī noted. Therefore it deserved full attention.

"Pule is making a mistake," Pitt said. "One should not trust a man like this."

"Perhaps it is not so," Kahu speculated. "Perhaps he will only use the *haole*ʹs help, then kill him."

"He is too crafty," the king said. "There is no profit and big trouble in that. I think Pule wold only use the *haole* to kill other *haole*." He turned to Stone. "What do you think, Olohana?"

"Broom is a private merchant, sire, acting like a pirate. He has no right to talk war with a Hawaiian king. This is against the law."

Kamōʻī did not appear relieved.

Kahu spoke what was on his mind, "*Haole* far

from their homes pay no attention to laws. They make laws to please themselves."

"It will be many months before he returns," the pragmatic Pitt observed.

"Yes," replied the king. "We must speed work on the war canoes, and make ready to gather the men."

"I could go to O'ahu," Olohana offered. "Talk to him, explain the dangers in his ambition."

"You might not return," Kamō'ī smiled.

"I will return, sire."

"It is not you I doubt, Olohana. Pule could hold you, Pule could kill you. I can give you no protection on O'ahu."

"I wish to talk to you of protection, my *ali'i*." This was an opportunity for Stone to speak of something much on his mind. "Broom is but one of the first, sire. The China trade is very rich and other ships will surely come with men who plan mischief. One day soon it will be wise for you to make an alliance with some powerful nation for protection against such villains. You will agree to favor their ships and merchants here and in return they will guard you against troublemakers like Broom and murderers like Quimby."

The king looked at Billy Pitt and Kahu before responding "Which country do you think this should be, Olohana?"

Stone ha already decided not to let patriotism stand in the way of practicality. The American war fleet had been comprised mostly of privateers, their valor considerably inspired by profit. Almost all these merchantmen had long ago returned to trade and no longer resembled a navy. America was a new country, faced with the many vexing problems of youth. It would be a long time before she could offer protection to a colony as distant as Hawai'i.

France was said to be in turmoil, near bankrupt-cy and anarchy. The Russians represented arro-gance and a Draconian rule. The Spanish king had his hands full with troubles internally and with the British.

But England still had a large navy, with ships scattered far and wide, their crews highly trained and rigidly disciplined. The power of the Crown and its Admiralty remained strong throughout the world, despite the humiliating defeat by the Yankees.

Olohana had his answer ready, "King George's country, sire."

Stroking his chin, the king was silent for moments. "First, we must have O'ahu," he said.

PART X

Niho had been carefully chosen for his assignment. He was an enormous man, well over six feet, with a chest like a hogshead and limbs like coconut trunks. Hidden, he waited as Olohana finished his bath. The path Stone would follow back to his house was deserted at this late afternoon hour.

Niho's chief had promised considerable reward in axes, knives and fishhooks for this service and had hinted broadly that elimination of the *haole* would greatly please someone in highest authority. But Niho needed little incentive for this chore. He despised the strangers and was simply anxious to do as quick a job as possible and make his getaway.

He hunched behind large boulders beside the narrow trail, twirling a sturdy sennit garotte in his fingers and watching Olohana's approach over the surroundings of tossed lava. Only Stone's head was visible, bobbing as he neared. Niho could not see the boy Puna accompanying his intended victim, dawdling a few yards behind, because of his lesser height.

As the *haole* passed Niho leaped out at him, garotte whipping through the air. Only the scraping of arid cinders as Niho jumped gave Olohana the needed split second to barely evade the deadly attack. Ducking, the line lashed across his forehead. His head was snapped back by the assassin's pull before the braided cord slipped away. Then he was stumbling under the weight of the huge attacker frantically trying to rectify his miscalculation.

Already it was too late. Niho's chance had flown. Olohana was fighting for his life, kicking and slashing furiously with feet and elbows at the awful hulk upon his back. Both stumbled and fell, still entwined-and then Puna was upon the big Hawaiian with his knife.

Puna likely killed Niho with his first vicious thrust into Niho's back, but he stabbed again and again until Stone pushed the dead man aside and struggled to his feet.

Puna stared back and forth from the limp corpse to the bloody knife in his hand, stupefied by what he had done.

"Steady, lad, steady," gasped Olohana. The boy was now trembling. Stone, too, was shaken by the assault, leaning against one of the boulders and gulping air. Niho's blood glistened on the slaggy rubble of the trail. His body was on its face, arms akimbo and back ripped from Puna's frantic thrusts.

"Why?" Stone wondered aloud. "And who is he?"

"Kealakekua man," said Puna. "One of Lako's."

Some two hundred miles to the northwest Pule, king of O'ahu, sat under a leafy shelter above the sands of Waikīkī.

This long curve of beach was his favorite resting place. On a clear sunny day like this its waters danced and sparkled. There was shade from the royal pavilion and tradewinds provided a comforting rinse of refreshment.

Distant, over twenty miles or so of wind whipped channel, the island of Moloka'i could be seen in soft silhouette rising from the sea like a basking whale. Near Pule, at water's edge, several men were tugging at a surround net. Silvery fish jumped and swirled in panic within its confines, boiling the shallows. Three naked girls waded nearby with neatly woven coconut leaf baskets to pack the catch.

Ocean mullet, Pule thought. Tastier than the brackish pond variety. The *wāhine* would bring him the choicest of the haul.

An attendant announced the arrival of Lako, of Hawai'i island.

At mention of the name Pule's half brother Pono raised himself from the mats upon which he had been lying.

The rotund Lako entered their presence on all fours. Pule impatiently acknowledged his fawning greeting then asked the news.

"Kamō'ī's preparations near an end, my *ali'i*," Lako said.

"When will he come?"

"Makali'i, my lord, at the time of *Akua*." This meant December, when the moon was fully round.

Soon, Pule thought, only the waxing and waning of two moons. The *haole*, Broom, would not return in time to help. Pule was glad he had insisted on guns before Broom left, particularly the two large guns of burning fire, his cannon...

Pono was at his side. A sullen and bitter man since his shameful defeat, his eyes now brightened with interest.

"Where will he make his landing?" he asked Lako.

"That has not been decided, my *ali'i*."

"And his strength?" Pono pursued. "How many men, guns, canoes?"

Pule felt resentment at the interruption. Since Pono's humiliating escape from Maui the man had been obsessed with the dream of smashing Kamō'ī and regaining his kingdom.

"Very strong," Lako replied. "Ten thousand men, over nine hundred canoes and the *haole* ship with its big guns."

Strong indeed, thought Pule. He could not float a canoe force large enough to repel such a fleet. He had best lay plans for a long battle on land.

"We will crush the scum," Pono sneered.

Hate swallows his common sense, Pule thought. He walked to the edge of the pebbled *lānai*, desiring to think. His inadequacy was worrisome. Kamō'ī was said to have twice as many muskets but the two cannon from Broom would help enormously. Pule wished he had held out for more.

He also wished he was not standing alone against the big island king.

Only two weeks ago he had made the mistake of dispatching Pono to enlist the aid of Kaumu of Kaua'i. Kaumu had refused and Pule suspected that his brother's intemperance and lack of subtlety was partly the reason. Pono's ravings about

Kamōʻī had probably only served to make Kaumu more apprehensive, determined to tighten his own defenses and depend upon his distance-some ninety miles from Oʻahu-to spare him from Kamōʻīʹs ambition.

This thinking was foolish, of course. Kaumu lived a wishful dream. If Kamōʻī was not stopped at Oʻahu it was only a matter of time before Kauaʻi would fall.

So much for cousin Kaumu, Pule thought. He had best turn to his own organization. Time grew short.

His chiefs were loyal and his men in total would be at least ten thousand. In this, at least, he was equal. If his arms were used wisely the effect of Kamōʻīʹs superior firepower could be minimized. The defection of Manu with a large number of soldiers and a good number of guns would have a demoralizing effect on the invaders.

He spoke to Lako, "How do you know these things?" Lako was a minor chief and would not be privy to discussion between Kamōʻī and his advisers.

"My son attends the court, *aliʻi*, as a *hānai* of the *haole* chief Olohana. Thus he hears much talk of plans from the mouth of Kamōʻī himself."

"How old is this son?"

"Thirteen, my *aliʻi*."

Pule was incredulous. "You use a boy as a spy?"

"He does not know my loyalties, *aliʻi*. He is merely a boy making boasts to his old father-a man he now treats as an inferior. He seeks to impress me." Lako decided against telling Pule that Puna was not his natural son.

"How can we trust his word? Many children enlarge on the truth!"

"He has not lied to me, my *aliʻi*. I am certain."

Stupid man, Pule thought. If Lako was not useful as a contact he would have had him strangled before sundown. Using a child in these matters was very dangerous. Pule often had doubts about the men around him. One of the benefits of killing Kamōʻī would be ridding himself of Pono, sending him back to Maui where he would be less an annoyance.

He stared over the bright beach sands. The wall of Lē'ahi crater rose over the eastern end of Waikīkī, its serrated sides green from the nourishment of recent rains. Lē'ahi served as a lookout point for the area. Beyond the crater were more beaches and other observation posts. The best of these was atop the plunging sea cliffs at Makapu'u, giving excellent viewing of the channel approaches from Moloka'i and often of the neighbor island itself. He would double the number of sentries and take no chance of being caught unprepared.

Kamō'ī would make his final massing of troops on Moloka'i, launching his assault after a brief rest. Campfires on Moloka'i would be seen from Makapu'u. Many fires would mean he was on his way. The invasion would come somewhere along this southern coast of O'ahu.

But where?

Probably not at the long bay of Maunalua, he reasoned. Outside its reef the waters were exposed to channel winds, which could easily be dangerous in this season. Conditions worsened as one moved around windward shores of the island. With a large *wa'a peleleu* fleet Kamō'ī would want to minimize problems and keep the canoes together. This suggested landing here at Waikīkī where there was no reef wall to present danger and the steady rollers would surf large canoes swiftly into shore.

He asked Lako if Kamō'ī would send messengers to give the traditional declaration of war.

"The *haole*, Olohana, urges him to throw old ways aside, *ali'i*. He wants Kamō'ī to attach swiftly, with full force of cannon, muskets and spears. Kamō'ī listens respectfully but has made no decision."

"He will choose the *haole* way," Pono interjected. "As he did against me, with tricks and stealth and attacks in the night."

Fool, thought Pule. He would have fought back in the same fashion.

"What news of Manu?" he asked Lako.

"All is well, *ali'i*. He has chosen Pūku'i as his minister. The Ka'ū forces will obey him blindly."

"Who is Pūku'i?"

"He was Koa´s companion and chief of guard, highness, and accompanied him to his sacrifice at Koholā."

"Does Pūku'i know of Manu´s plan to desert to us?"

"No, *ali'i*, he does not."

"And Kamō'ī's *haole;* could they be lured to our service?" Pule had not yet met a *haole* who could not be bought.

"They are dedicated to Kamō'ī, my *ali'i* They want for nothing. He has promised rich lands, fine houses, servants and *haole* silver. They are happy and work well."

Pule thought ruefully of the many *haole* scattered about O'ahu. Only two were worth the costs of their keep. Both of these had been left by Captain Broom as an implied promise of his return. One, named Murray, was a gunner, said to be English. The other was a black man, believed to have escaped from slavery in America. He was called Poni, from the purplish hue of his skin. The remaining whites were the rubbish of previous vessels, deserters or castaways living off Hawaiians in remote villages. A few minor chiefs thought it a mark of stature to have a *haole* lounging about. One of the few intelligent moves Pono had made recently was to kill his traitorous *haole* Pāvao, when he struggled ashore on O'ahu after the Maui debacle.

When the time of his victory came he, Pule, would strictly regulate the movements of *haole* in all Hawai'i. Only a few would be allowed to take residence in the islands and these would be carefully selected: craftsmen to serve him, business men in supplies and sandalwood and representatives of friendly foreign governments.

He stared reflectively out to sea. Moloka'i was invisible now, behind a vagrant drift of rain far out on the channel.

"Let me kill him when he comes," Pono said at his elbow.

"No, brother," Pule answered. "This is my land. It is I who will have his heart."

Late at night Billy Pitt joined Kamō'ī in the king´s sleeping house.

"We are now ready, my *ali'i*," he reported.

"What do the priests say?"

"The weather will be kind and Kū sends all favorable signs."

"At the fullness of the moon, then. Two weeks."

"As you say, *ali'i*."

The king lay back against mats, hands behind his head, staring at the thatching above. A tiny fire gave light to the enclosure, its smoke escaping through a hole in the peaked roof.

"We have come a long way, old comrade," he said.

"You wailed in my arms as an infant, my lord."

"I have held you in my heart since, Kalani."

"I may not return from this battle, *ali'i*."

"Nonsense. We will go on to even greater days."

"I am aging, exalted one. Over sixty *makahiki*.

These bones no longer quickly obey my head."

"Fight like the *haole* generals then, and stay in the rear," the king smiled.

"I could not do that, *ali'i*."

"I would not think it ill if you chose not to go, Kalani."

"To stay with the children and old ones is unthinkable."

"Never fear, father of my heart. You are still better than the young cocks."

"You are kind, my lord. Sadly, this is not so."

"Enough of this talk. You are an extension of my right arm. You will come and you will be splendid, as always."

"Yes, my *ali'i*. Now-let us talk of plans. The men are being gathered and instructed."

"And Moloka'i and Maui?"

"They will join us on the way."

"How many?"

"With ours, over ten thousand."

"And the O'ahu numbers?"

"Last report was eight thousand, almost a month ago. We have heard nothing since."

"Numbers are not always of most importance. The way in which Pule uses his men and weapons can mean more."

"True, *ali'i*."

"He has a clever mind and the knowledge of many battles. He is without fear and will fight hard. We will earn every stone and tree on O'ahu."

"'*Ae*, my lord. This is so."

"Where are our *haole?*"

"Olohana is fitting guns to the *wa'a peleleu*. Aleka remains on the big ship, making it ready. Olohana tells him what to do."

"Good men, Kalani."

"Yes, *ali'i*, we are fortunate, considering the kinds of villains we might have acquired."

"I think they will remain here for a long time."

"Aleka is now like one of us, *ali'i*. And I have less doubt every day that Olohana will leave. I think he knows we arranged his abandonment here-and itches with the knowledge. But he enjoys the power of being an *ali'i* and commanding your army. I have assured him you have not forgotten your promise of lands and this prospect sustains him. Perhaps he wrestles with thoughts of his homeland but he has no family there-and his best friend is here, becoming a Hawaiian." Pitt paused. "You have given both these men power and station they would never have known on ships or in America, my lord. They accept their bounties as nobles and will perform the killing as the price they must pay."

"Cold words, Kalani Pitt."

"The truth is often chill, my lord. I mean no unkindness. I have no doubt of their loyalty to you or their contentment here. They now use many Hawaiian words in speaking to one another. Olohana knows great pleasure in his wife and the *hānai*"boy and will soon have a child of his own."

"Olohana will have as much value in peace as he does in war, Kalani. He conducts himself well with these traders."

"'*Ae, ali'i*. He moves comfortably with men of rank. *Haole* seamen employ strange conversation, with no poetry and little subtlety."

"He is right about the protection of the English. This is good thinking."

"Yes. A pity we do not have such support now, when it is needed."

"So be it. One cannot press these needs with great nations as one does with private sea captains. Once O'ahu is ours we will have many friends, you will see. The children will know a world very different from ours, old friend."

"Who could have dreamed of these changes, my lord? The gods gave no signs..." "The *haole* do. We must be alert, recognize signals, interpret their meanings, then act in our best interests."

"Yes, *ali'i*."

"The boy, Puna."

"'Ae, *ali'i*."

"He will come to O'ahu with us. He has already killed a man and I desire to see how he behaves in circumstances to come."

"There are many years ahead, *ali'i*. Keōpū will give you a son or Kahu will bear one."

"Despite her enthusiasm I fear Kahu is barren, old comrade. Further, a son by either of these women may not be right-as Manu was not right even in his father's eyes. Puna is of good age and of my blood."

"As you wish. I will tell Olohana. He is very watchful of the boy and there is much respect and affection between the two."

"Good. What is known of this Niho, the man Puna killed?"

"Little, *ali'i*. He came from Kealakekua and was one of those who killed Captain Cook. He lived alone, abhorred friendships and hated the *haole*. Perhaps he was mad."

Kamō'ī studied the small fire. Moments passed before he spoke, "Perhaps there is something happening here that I do not know about, Kalani."

"If *I* know *you* will know, my lord. The *haole* have enemies among us, mostly inspired by jealousy. Our *kāhuna* feel particularly threatened by their knowledge and cleverness. But we find no evidence of a plot to kill Olohana or a compelling reason for one. I remains a mystery."

The king paused only a moment before turning to another subject, "The men from Ka'ū. Have you seen them?"

"Yes, *ali'i*. They are here. Most impressive. A fine addition to your force."

"And their chief, Pūku'i? I know nothing of him."

"Young, strong, a proud and aloof man, *ali'i*. I am not at ease with him. Something in his eyes disturbs me."

"You think Manu has made a mistake in selecting him?"

"Perhaps it is my own mistake, exalted one. Perhaps because I cannot forget Pūku'i's face when his lord, Koa, was sacrificed to Kū."

Runners were dispatched over the mountains, messengers in canoes found their way to the most remote 'ohana. Their message was simple: gather now in Kailua. Join Kamō'ī for the taking of O'ahu.

All over the big island men began leaving their farms and lagoons to join the king.

On the long Kona coast activity heightened in the canoe sheds. Soon almost a thousand large wa'a peleleu would be ready for the invasion. Many were double hulls and some had blunderbusses mounted in swivels on midship platforms. A few of the larger canoes boasted canvas sails, bartered from Captain Cox, giving them added speed and maneuverability.

In the night fires flickered on the heiau at Koholā and Kamakahonu. Priests chanted, offering sacrifices of dogs, pigs and chickens to Kū of Power and Kanaloa of the Sea, pleading that omens of winds, waves and stars might tell of safe passage and ultimate victory. Special incantations were composed, the wisest kāhuna studied and interpreted the slightest signs.

Every day at twilight Kamō'ī gathered his ali'i for reports and discussion. Scarcely a day passed that another Hawai'i island chief did not arrive to prostrate himself and declare his loyalty and devotion. Even Kimi arrived from the little plantation he had finally been granted through the help of Olohana and Billy Pitt. He led twenty awkward "soldiers," five with muskets. This ragtag squad was absorbed into Pitt's command.

Aleka Tweed spent most of his time aboard the Little American, sharpening the skills of its crewmen and organizing a signalling system for the canoe fleet. Billy Pitt, with Manu's help, was organizing and tending to the care of the gathering army. Olohana busied himself with blending smaller groups into larger battalions and a final inspection and testing of weaponry. Many of the uninitiated volunteers from faraway districts had to be warned not to stand in front of guns being fired.

The gathering on the water of Kamōʻī's strike force gained momentum. A few days after the summons went out Olohana counted some three dozen new craft on the emerald bay. A week later many hundreds of canoes nodded on swells offshore or were drawn up on the Kailua sands. Meanwhile crowds had swollen in temporary campsites over the district's lowlands. In the night men and women talked long around fires in the palm groves. There were bursts of music, *hula* and not a little love making.

Daylight activity was also spirited. Spears cracked as warriors dueled in practice. Sling stones thudded into target trees. Boxers and wrestlers exercised and were massaged. Muskets were given thorough cleanings, rubbed with *kukui* oil and rolled in *kapa* against the ravages of sea air. Gatherings of people around beached canoes talked of the journey ahead. Naked children romped about, the boys carrying sticks of make believe spears, the girls teasing, preening and laughing. Constantly lines of women and men brought supplies for stowage in the canoes: dried fish, *poi*, yams and coconut meat. Gourds and large bamboo joints were filled with water and sealed with pitch.

With good fortune the expedition would be in sight of other islands all the way to Oʻahu, almost two hundred miles distant. But many of these miles were across deep and wind beaten channels. Hawaiians were acutely aware of the vagaries of ocean travel. Any voyagers blown into the open sea would have crucial need of food and water. When these were gone such sailors would drift on forever into the dark realm of Pō, the infinite land of night, darkness and obscurity.

At Waikīkī King Pule lay nude upon mats, his tattooed form dark and heavy. A handsome woman wearing only a waist wrap knelt at his side. She had long serviced the monarch with *lomi*, massage, and responded to his other desires. At the moment his thick penis only drooped like a sea cucumber between his legs.

To Pule now she was merely a pair of hands. He closed his eyes in the cool start of pleasure as she applied coconut oil to his thighs and calves.

This was a good time for thinking.

His *kāhuna* had studied the omens of stars, moon, waves and wind. The time was right. Kamō'ī had sent two stones, one black and one white. Pule had returned the black, signifying he was ready to make war. The invasion should come on the next full moon.

He sighed in contentment as the women's strong fingers probed, uncoiling his muscles. There was still power in this flesh that had served him so well for over fifty years. And war was the proper occupation of an *ali'i*—the supreme test of a noble man, marvelous outings of excitement within which one's courage and intelligence were put to the severest demands. In his time Pule had won many battles large and small, always at the head of his troops and personally facing and killing several upstart challengers. Now he would right a grievous wrong. For centuries, Maui and its lesser islands had been under the unquestioned domination of his family. In the space of a few days they had been lost through his brother Pono's stupidity.

He, Pule, would make no such mistakes. Kamō'ī would soon discover he faced a wily and dangerous foe. Pule had fewer muskets but he could match Kamō'ī's big guns with the two cannon obtained from Broom. In numbers of men they would be near equal. Even now his troops were gathering, long lines of men coming over the mountains from windward O'ahu, the central plains, the north shore and the leeward coast of Wai'anae. Soon there would be thousands on the plain of Mō'ili'ili and the marshlands of Waikīkī, good men all, strong and loyal.

He turned to lie on his stomach. The *lomi* woman began kneading the backs of his legs. No walking, he told her. He did not feel equal to her usual treading on his spine.

Pressed upon his penis, he felt its warm thickening. A satisfaction, he thought. Very reassuring when the *uli* perked so easily on a man who had seen fifty *makahiki*. He exhaled, taking pleasure at the thrusting of the woman's fingers and in the thought of pleasures to come. After the battle he would personally sacrifice Kamō'ī and his nobles on Pule's dynastic *heiau* at Lē'ahi crater. Then he would roast and eat the heart of this presumptuous bastard.

Perhaps he would send Kamōʻi's head to Kaumu on Kauaʻi. Such a gesture would give new fear to that vacillating fool. One day *all* the islands would be under the rule of Pule, this crafty old boar who fought and killed all the fine young challengers. His indeed would be a glorious kingdom—one in which the *haole* would be treated as exactly what they were: dangerous interlopers tolerated only for the services they could perform or good things they could bring.

He spread his legs in invitation. The woman's hands moved up the inside of his thighs, gentler, caressing.

One day soon he must decide which of his three sons would be chosen as heir. None of those born to his sacred wife had turned out as Pule had wished. The oldest was more interested in riding surf and pounding *wāhine* than in learning *aliʻi* ways. The second was passionately devoted to poetry and dancing, diminishing himself in his father's eyes. The youngest boy had only recently become a dangler—that stage in life when the penis first begins to droop. This son showed promise of being manly and brave. Perhaps Pule would elevate him over the older boys. Of a certainty his heir would be only from him and his sacred wife. He would not be like that doddering old fool, Ōpū, who had chosen a nephew, Kamōʻi. Pule believed strongly in proper *aliʻi* succession. Only those of the oldest and purest blood lines should rule.

The masseuse parted his buttocks with one hand and applied oil to his sphincter with a warm finger. For a few moments he floated on the pleasure of her touch, then grunted at the delightful shock of the digit slithering into his anus. For several minutes he gave himself completely to her expert massage, then rolled over on his back. Now he was fully hardened, the pillar of dark flesh lying wooden stiff on his belly. The woman dutifully whispered admiration of the royal erection, but he paid her no attention.

Muffled shouts came from a nearby clearing in the grove of palms—the voice of his gunner, Murray, haranguing his men.

A useful man, Pule thought. He was fortunate to have him.

And Poni, the black one, too. Clever with guns—surely as clever as Kamōʻi's *haole*. The defection of Manu with his large number of soldiers would be devastating to the big island warrior chief.

The *lomi* woman used only her fingertips now, trailing, teasing...

A *kōlea*, golden plover, fluttered to the earth a few yards away. The bird stood stone still, tensed on its long thin legs, its black eyes assessing the surroundings and its speckled coat gleaming dully in the sunshine. In a moment, sensing no danger, it ran a few feet and began pecking at the ground.

Like the cursed *haole*, Pule thought. The *kōlea* came out of nowhere every year, fattened on the land, then emptied his bowels upon it and disappeared.

With one hand the woman gently fingered his testicles. The other gripped his taut *uli* and moved up and down, warm and slippery with oil. Pule shut his eyes and commanded her to suck.

PART XI

The stars were obscured, the night soft. Cool of late evening crept shoreward from the upper reaches of Mauna Loa. In the dim light of a ship's lamp Namo and Olohana lay talking in murmured tones.

"I am afraid," she said.

"Do not be, ku'u ipo." The words meant "my sweetheart."

"Many men will be killed. You may be killed."

"We are very strong and we have more guns."

"It needs but one gun to kill you. I will die if you do not return."

"Nonsense, girl."

"It is true. I will kill myself."

"Don't say such foolish things. You are young and beautiful and a chiefly woman. You would live as you did before I came."

"I was nothing before you came. I will be nothing if you die."

"Put this fear out of your mind. I will be back."

She was silent for a moment, then, "Will you take other women over there?"

He chuckled at this sudden shift of her concern. "I feel no need for other women."

She pressed her lips to his breast, not answering. Some day he would wander... After a moment she said, "The boy goes with you?"

"The king wishes it. That is a command."

"You must watch him carefully. It is not enough that he has already killed a man. He still seeks to prove himself, fancies he is a warrior. I see him striving to be like you in many little ways."

"Boys are impatient and foolish, they cannot wait to take on the troublings of age."

"Do you have trouble, Olohana?"

"Never when I am with you."

She lifted herself on one elbow and smiled down on him. "Soon you will have a young man of your own."

"How do you know you carry a son?"

"How do I know the sun will rise tomorrow?"

Kamōʻī had been true to his vow.

Never in Hawaiʻiʻs history had there been an armada like this. Olohana thought he had never seen so grand a sight—a thousand prows aimed at the northwest horizon.

In rising light the *Little American* fussed steadily along, her canvas shortened so she would not outdistance other craft. The tugging sails and rhythmic bodies of the paddlers gave the scene a quality of power and purpose. Early sun lent brilliance to the vista—the gleaming torsos of the men, the canvas snapping and strings of wake on a peaceful sea.

On this first day there was one pause to pick up men and canoes from the Kohala coastal area. Here other warriors, too, joined from the Hilo and Hmkua districts across the mountains. At dusk the fleet was heading into the broad channel dividing Maui and Hawaii islands.

On this inky deep the calm ended. In the dark crews fought to keep their craft on course under brutal, battering gusts. Canoes lifted and plunged on vicious chops and the schoonerʻs deck was frequently awash. Three canoes were lost on the crossing, blown into the vast wastes of the western sea never to be seen again.

Dawning glowed dully after the nightmarish dark. Kamōʻīʻs force was more than halfway across, widely scattered by stiff winds. Endless hills of waves rolled in six-foot swells, their tops churned into grayish froth. Kamōʻī, Pitt and Olohana clutched shrouds on the heaving deck, watching nearby canoes rise to plunge and disappear in troughs. Tweed was on the wheel, teeth clenched and feet planted far apart, glorying his control of the reeling sliding vessel. Puna held the rail with both hands, his eyes bright with excitement. He had never been so far at sea or experienced such wild deep water.

A heavy rain squall exploded, the stinging assault obscuring their view for almost an hour. When it passed the winds also diminished. The huge upsurge of Haleakalā volcano on Maui was now distinct, a majestic presence commanding the southern end of the island. Once in its lee they would know calm and comfort.

As the sun dropped the canoes moved under the protection of the land mass and the sea quieted. A long and low crescent of rainbow appeared in an exquisite glow over distant lowlands. The quaking voice of old Pāhoa was heard in a chant of thanks, for the rainbow was a sign of heavenly blessings. Angry chops of water, as if in corroboration, subsided to gentle heavings. A large school of mahimahi scattered ahead of the *Little American*, ripping the surface for hundreds of yards. The fish suddenly broke water in panic, flying from wave to wave like thrown knives.

Slowly the scattered canoes came together, their occupants near exhaustion. But the men's spirits had risen now that they were out of the backbreaking demand of the channel. Those on the schooner heard shouts of happy relief and saw paddles raised and flourished in salutes.

Supper was spread on the midship hatch and eaten with relish. As night fell the armada melted into dark. A steady wind wafted down the slopes of the massive volcano, nudging the fleet steadily northward. In the early morning roofs of Lāhainā village were in view under a beautiful backdrop of the west Maui mountains.

A mile offshore Mohu, the new Maui governor, came alongside in a large canoe. The dark and glowering battler genuflected deeply to Kamō'ī and Pitt. In a brief formal speech he said he was proud to offer the best of Maui's men to the king's cause. Kamō'ī greeted him warmly, bidding him to rise. He grasped Mohu's arms and the two rubbed noses.

"Every man will die for your glory, my ali'i," said Mohu.

"They will fight and conquer for their own glory," the king gently corrected. "Now come, old comrade, sit and eat with us."

Manu and other chiefs reported that men and craft were in excellent condition despite the cruel crossing. Except for the loss of the three canoes a few fractured masts and some torn sails were the only casualties. With a little rest the warriors would soon be able to resume the journey.

Kamō'ī decreed six hours respite. This would have the fleet crossing the Moloka'i in the night. It had been arranged for fires to be lighted on the island uplands if an overcast hid the moon and stars.

The army rested well in their canoes. The signal fires were not needed on the approach. The night was clear, the moon a glowing disc and the Milky Way a dusting of crisp jewels. Gentle trades blew at their quarter all through the crossing. Before dawn the first canoes were approaching their final rendezvous off the long western beaches of Moloka'i.

They had seen few signs of life on this island of the wise men—only here and there small houses among trees or huts of the 'ohana-families which tended walled fishponds on shallows inside the reefs.

Billy Pitt told Olohana that on the far shore behind Moloka'i's distant mountains deep basins of green and bountiful valleys rolled down to the sea. In contrast the shore they now paralleled held only the emptiness of tumbled lava, an arid and treeless waste scarred by ancient flows. Stone thought he had never seen such a barren and inhospitable coast.

Once around the cape called Lā'au, Moloka'i's western beaches were beckoning. These raw deserts offered miles of golden strands upon which canoes could be drawn up and men could take rest. These sands were also the closest landfalls to O'ahu, visible now in the ragged blue silhouette some twenty miles distant.

First in dozens then by hundreds the *wa'a peleleu* rode great waves to shore—sterns high astride the foaming crests, bows down and plowing green water. Olohana rode in with the king and Pitt, his breath arrested in the thrilling surge as the craft lifted and flew forward, sharing smiles with his companions as its bottom ground the sand.

By noon the entire flotilla had taken these flights and the canoes were dry upon the broad beaches. They stretched as far as the eye could see, a scatter of dark scratches on the bright littoral, their crews making rough camp on the dunes above. Offshore Alec Tweed tacked the *Little American* back and forth on the deep. There was no haven the for the schooner on this surf-pounded shoreline.

Most of the army slept through the afternoon, bone-weary from the days past. Nearing twilight all were up and about—some to bathe and others to wade with nets for fresh food. Mohu came to Kamō'ī with the news that Moloka'i soldiers had joined them, about three hundred sturdy men who had hiked overland from more pololous areas. The Maui high chief also voiced a veiled request. Most of the fish being caught in these shallows were mo'i, a delicacy reserved for ali'i consumption only...

"Tell them to eat," Kamō'ī smiled. "Tonight all my men are princes."

Fires were lighted, a necklace of small flamings on the long shore.

Men ate and speculated on the morrow and what it would bring. There was little laughter or joking and almost all soon rolled into their kapa for the night. Guards were not needed on this desolate land's end. Lights of the *Little American* pierced the dark as she trudged back and forth offshore, often disappearing behind swells.

But there was activity at Kamō'ī's campsite. A stout wahine kaua fed sticks to the fire. The chiefs had gathered and now sat in a half-circle, the flames lighting their somber faces. Their voices murmured until Kamō'ī arrived then every man but Olohana prostrated himself.

From now on, the king said, there would be no prostration until O'ahu was taken. Nor would there be a kapu against approaching or speaking to an ali'i. There was no time in war for such formalities. He sat on mats with Pitt, Manu and Olohana at his sides. His audience sprawled but was tensely attentive. Kamō'ī signaled Olohana with a flick of his hand. Stone arose.

"It is decided," he said. "We will leave at sunrise and all at once. The kāhuna of weather say the crossing will be easy, we can remain together and be at full strength for the landing."

Several heads nodded. Kamō'ī studied the faces of his followers. Puna sat huddled and listening outside the circle of ali'i.

Olohana continued, "Our last information is that Pule expects us at Waikīkī, where conditions are ideal for landing our many wa'a peleleu. In this he will be disappointed."

He stood and scratched a long crescent line in the sand with a stick. "This is the bay of Maunalua, east of Lē'ahi crater running about three miles long from Lē'ahi to Kawaihoa."

He indicated an area in the left center of the curve. "If

we land our forces here, on the Wailupe, Wai'alae and Khala beaches at the high tide we can ride over the reefs with little trouble. Ashore the lands are largely flat and strong points can be quickly established. Pule will have most of his men and weapons elsewhere, at considerable distant. Through the rest of the day we can take more land and bring in more canoes. On the following morning we will have our entire army on shore, ready to drive ahead."

The chief of a remote Maui district addressed Kamō'ī, "Ali'i, why does this haole tell us what to do?"

"He speaks with wisdom and he is my brother," the king replied crisply. "Does anyone find this too difficult to accept?"

Silence was profound. Only the thump of surf on the nearby beach could be heard. For the first time Stone felt affection for this man.

He spaced three Xs in the sand. "We will divide into three sections," he said. "The king will command the center and I will accompany him with our heavy guns. Kalani-Pitt will lead our troops on the left and Manu those on the right. Aleka, with the ship and two hundred canoes, will guard the water approaches. But it is unlikely we will meet any challenge at sea."

Listeners muttered agreement; there was no fleet like Kamō'ī's.

"Almost ten thousand men, landed over a few miles, should easily drive a weaker force back into the hills," Olohana continued. "But Pule will react quickly and strike back. Tomorrow night we will meet on O'ahu and discuss further moves. By then we will know where his strength is placed and this will dictate what we do next." He turned to Kamō'ī. "Have I spoken our plan correctly, ali'i?"

"Yes." Kamō'ī addressed the group, "Orders from Kalani-Pitt, Olohana and Manu are to be obeyed immediately, without question." The gathering rumbled assent.

Kamōʻi arose and the chiefs bowed their heads. "Good fortune to you, brave one," he said. "Now we rest."

The chiefs dispersed to their camps. Olohana rolled his blanket about him. Thoughts of Namo crossed his mind. Far to the south she would be sleeping now, her far in repose, her hair cascading upon her mats. Puna stirred beside him on the sand. The lad had fallen asleep immediately. In the moonlight his face had the innocence of a small child. And no wonder, Stone thought. He is a child, despite his cocky pride and affectations of manhood. He should not be here.

Stone stared up at the vast powdering of stars. Fires along the beach were dying now, dull glows in the dark. Flames nearby leaped briefly to life. He saw that Kamōʻi was quite awake, sitting and peering into the fire.

Stone had been touched by the king's expression of faith in him, the words lifting his spirits considerably. He watched the monarch now, sitting statue-still, his thick arms over his knees as he stared into the struggling flames, their light flickering on his tawny skin. He had heard Kamōʻi called "The Lonely One." Now indeed he looked lonely, his expression curiously pensive.

I've become his man, thought Stone, the commitment made without conscious realization.

At some point this past year he had crossed a line and had no desire to turn back. He had found a home in these islands with these people. If he lived through this expedition he might well know peace and well-being and contentment for long years to come.

He gazed long at the motionless figure by the fire.

Damn your eyes, he mused. You kidnapped me, then bribed me to your service and as yet have not even paid my price. Stone found he was no longer even vexed about it.

And tomorrow I will kill for you again...

The canoes were off the Molokaʻi beaches in the pre-dawn calm and well into the channel as the first slants of sunlight dazzled on the ocean behind them.

The sky was clear, only a few wisps of clouds floating high, and the wind a sure and gentle promise of a fair passage. It would be about six hours to Oʻahu, the peaks of its two mountain ranges hazy now on the northwest horizon.

Kaiwi, the channel they crossed, was a broad deep cut. Many were the tales told of its treachery. But this morning it was at rest and the canoes rode a following sea that surfed them to their goal. With the sun's climb distance shortened and Oʻahu came into sharper detail: miles of serrated cliffs plunging to the windward plain, the rocky offshore islets where only birds lived and the rise of Lēʻahi crater like an inverted platter obscuring Waikīkī on the left. Dead ahead and nearer were the breastlike loomings of Kawaihoa headland and its blunt inland crater, marking the beaches of Wailupe, Waiʻalae and Kāhala where they would land.

Olohana stared at this island bastion dozing into day. A skein of clouds nuzzled the peaks of its windward mountains. Valleys nearer ran miles inland, delineated sharply by morning shadows and etched vertically by white strings of waterfalls. So peaceful looking, he thought. But plantings of coconut palms alongshore seemed like sentinels and the approaching land somehow exuded an ominous air.

By late morning they were close enough to discern movement but saw none. Beaches and the intervening waters remained empty. Only sea birds moved, wheeling out from land to dip and flutter at their feeding. The wind had dropped to fitful breezes and the sails of the schooner and the waʻa peleleu flapped and bellied as they pressed forward. Men in canoes bent to their paddles, their vessels spread out in an uneven front over two miles of water. The warriors now labored in silence—there was no shouting or chanting. Faces were grimly serious as the distance to land shortened.

Beyond the fact that battle awaited, the ordinary soldiers knew nothing. They had been told simply to move straight ahead and stay together, their chiefs would give further instructions at the proper times. These orders were to be obeyed quickly and without question.

It was this that made Manu´s defection so easy. About a mile and a half from O'ahu he passed his order. Within minutes some two hundred canoes of his command veered from the main body of the armada off to the right.

They were nearly a mile distant before the desertion was realized aboard the *Little American*. The masthead watch, the only man who could actually see the movement, had not at first believed his eyes. He shouted at Olohana, who scurried into the rigging to verify the astounding report.

The lookout was right. Manu´s canoes were off in the distance, growing smaller, heading for the windward coast.

Stone descended to face a puzzled Kamō'i.

"It is true, ali'i. He has taken his men and those from Ka´ū and deserted. There is no mistake. He has abandoned us."

Kamō'i stared at him, struggling to absorb the truth. His eyes were large and unblinking and his full lips tightened to a straight line. The muscles of his jaw tensed as the fury crept in. He looked as if the blood had been drawn from his face.

"Dear God," said Tweed from the side. "Over two thousand of the buggers."

Kamō'i turned and walked to the rail, a towering brown giant clad only in a breech cloth. He bent to grip the wood, his head up and looking in the direction of the traitor´s flight. The muscles of his thick forearms flexed as he kneaded the rail. Olohana and Aleka could feel his turmoil.

Tweed spoke again, "We could chase them down and kill the son of a bitch, ali'i."

Kamō'i exhaled a heavy sigh and turned, his face more composed.

"No, we will go as planned. Move canoes to strengthen that side and be sure some have guns." He looked again over the glittering sea.

"Manu is already a dead man," he said. "Only his killing remains."

PART XII

*F*rom his lookout point high under the seaward lip of Lē'ahi
crater Pule could see the swarm of canoes far out in the
channel.

*He stared, knowing he did not have long to wait. Once they
were nearer O'ahu their goal could be almost pinpointed.
Beneath him on the Waikīkī flatlands his army waited behind a
wall of palms lining the beach.*

*The sun burst from behind clouds, its raw sparkle on the
water obscuring the far fleet. When the light was again dulled
by drifting cumulus Pule saw that Kamō'ī had made his choice.*

*The landing would be on the beaches of Maunalua bay,
some three miles east of Waikīkī.*

*He cursed his miscalculation, gruffly ordered assembly of
his companions and began the descent to join his soldiers.*

Sails reefed and paddlers idling, the canoe fleet rode
at ease about a quarter mile off O'ahu.

There was still no evidence of activity along the beaches. Beyond the pale shallows near-blinding sandstrips
remained empty in the sunshine. Closer, breakers curled
over the submerged coral shelf in the eternal encounter of
sea and land. The Hawai'i army would have to ride these
tumblings over the reef into calm water. But Kamō'ī and
his khuna had reckoned correctly—the tide would be
high enough to give the vessels draught and take them
swiftly to shore.

Olohana relayed the king's orders: Half the canoes
were to form a line spaced two boat-lengths apart and

then head for land at the firing of the schooners cannon. The others would heave to behind this striking force and serve as a reserve against any reprisals from the water. While there was still no sign of enemy craft, these might exist out of sight behind the blunt cape two miles to port where Lēʻahi crater flared high then dipped sharply into the sea.

"Very quiet, aliʻi," said Stone.

"There will soon be much noise," Kamōʻī answered. He signalled for his waʻa peleleu to be brought alongside. Nearby Pāhoa began a chant, his aged falsetto quaking.

"Aliʻi," Olohana said. "I wish to leave the boy here, with Aleka."

"He has been behaving like a man, Olohana."

"He is still a boy, too young to face guns."

"I wish to see how he conducts himself."

"To hell with your wishes," Stone said. "This is not a new spear you are testing. This is a small boy who saved my life. I wish to save his."

For a long moment the king stared at him with baleful eyes. Stone glared back, his jaw set in determination.

"Do as you will, Olohana," the king said.

Stone made his way aft past Tweed's breech-clouted gunners, their gazes riveted on the silent island. He wondered how long it would be before he could accept the sight of half-naked brown men manning a trim New England ship. The ruddy Scot was leaning against the quarterdeck rail, directing his helmsman. He smiled wryly at Stone.

"I've been thinking, John," he said.

"Yes?"

"We're bloody daft."

"We're paying the piper, Alec."

"Aye, but we haven't been enjoying his tunes that long, have we?"

"There's another old saw: 'In for a penny, in for a

pound.'"

"I thought we'd settled up on Maui," Tweed said.

"Maui was a lark compared to what might happen here."

"I fear you're right," Tweed said softly, then shrugged. "Ah, well... It's a bit late to be having doots. And it's been a bonnie year, hasn't it?"

"Yes, it has that, Alec."

They looked at each other, smiling. Such a short time since all this began and so much had happened... Olohana voice a thought more on his mind, "Alec. There's a chance I might be done in this time..."

"Fiddlesticks. Stay behind the bloody cannon."

"There's something I ask of you if it happens. See that Namo is cared for, and the lad, Puna."

"My solemn word, John."

"And the child when it comes. I wish for it to know our ways too."

"I understand," said Tweed. "Now hear me, John. I ask the same."

"Done."

The two shook hands. Pāhoa's chanting stopped. Kai, of the king's guard was shouting orders.

"Time to go," said Stone. "The boy stays with you, Alec."

"Fair weather my friend," said Tweed.

A cannon barked a brief bass. Thousands of paddles stabbed the blue waters. The canoes shot forward and the invasion began.

It was necessary that Kamō'ī set a proper example.

He stood imperially on a platform athwart the double hulls—a thick spear in one hand, the other on the mast. Attendants holding aloft the tall *kāhili*—batons of his rank knelt on either side. The only sounds were the gruntings of paddlers, pipes of seabirds and a muted sing-song from Pāhoa. Olohana crouched near the king, eyeing the shore and preparing his pistols. Glancing back to right or left showed the other canoes coming in, but the king´s was well in advance of the rest.

The dark water became green, lifting into swells as it neared the barrier of reef. Shouts of the steersmen were heard exhorting their companions to paddle faster and catch the waves. Then the canoes were being carried like twigs hurled forward on the boiling peaks, soaring in over the miles-long shelf of coral. Steersmen fought to keep the ponderous craft bulleting straight ahead. Olohana grasped both gunwales in an iron grip. Kamō´i´s only concession to the sliding plunge was to clamp tighter his one ham-sized around the swaying mast.

The liquid roaring of the wave turned to a whisper as it subsided. Olohana realized they were now safely into the lagoon. Pink and purple clusters of the living stone moved beneath in glass-clear shallows. A few voices spoke satisfaction. Men were soon jumping over the sides to help guide the vessels through waist-high water. More canoes came in on both sides.

A first splatter of musket fire erupted from the jumble of brush above the beach. Three wading men went down, faces forward in the water. Another ball splintered the shaft of a *kāhili* beside the king. But Kamō´i stood tall and calm, ordering his men to hold fire. He would not waste ammunition on a foe so well hidden.

Olohana remained in the canoe until it scraped land. A pistol in each hand, he scrambled over the side. Again there was a splatter of fire and two of his companions crumpled in the shallows. He felt a sudden wash of fear at being such a naked target and trashed forward, cursing his boots heavy in the tugging water and almost falling on the slippery clumps of coral.

For what seemed an interminable time he floundered on the beach´s damp granules. Then he was crouched, racing up into the beach. He felt he had scarcely breathed during these few moments and now gasped for air. His initial fears lessened as he found himself still alive and now under cover.

The growths ahead were low and spotty, without signs of life. He heard a rustling nearby and watched one of his soldiers stepped into a clearing, his spear upraised for the throw. A musket ball slammed into his chest and the weapon fell to the ground. The warrior collapsed to his knees, a surprised expression on his face before he pitched forward. Olohana fired both pistols in the direction of the shot then scrambled for still heavier cover.

A waste, he cursed. He had seen nothing.

He waited but there was no response. Hurriedly he reloaded his pistols, hearing sporadic fire, distant shouts and the crack of spear on spear. He found a place of comparative safety in nearby coconut trees. Here there was a clearer view of his surroundings. To his right and left several of his musketmen were partly hidden in brush. He shouted at them to keep cover and fire carefully.

The king was now approaching through waist-high brush some twenty yards distant. Kai and a phalanxof guards moved cautiously, peering, muskets at the ready, keeping themselves between Kamōʻī and the unseen enemy. The king stared into the landscape, seemingly unaware of his prominence as a target. It was incredible, Stone thought, that Oʻahu gunners had not concentrated fire upon him.

Silence only now came from the defenders. They must be pulling back, Stone thought. Kamōʻī had reckoned correctly—this area had been thinly defended, likely only a guarding force now in retreat from overwhelming numbers. Pule had expected their landing elsewhere.

Kamōʻī joined him, striding as if immune from harm. Kai was near his side, gaze darting from his master to the threatening greenery inland. The silence continued. Olohana realized he was soaked in perspiration.

Scarcely a half hour had passed since the landing but it seemed to those there an eternity. Then more shots snapped out and two of Kai´s men went down only a few yards distant. The kin rapidly joined the others in a crouch.

It would be foolhardy to blunder ahead, Stone told him. The O'ahu fighters knew this terrain and its hiding places—and might have more guns than shown so far. However few, the guns could cause considerable loss. It was best now to strengthen positions won then advance carefully, firing only when targets were clear.

After a moment Kamō'ī nodded. Olohana muttered instructions to a messenger then dispatched another to signal Tweed they were ready for another wave of canoes and the two cannon. Within half hour messages arrived from Billy Pitt and Mohu on their flanks. The lines were unbroken. A long stretch of shoreline had been taken with only light losses. In most sectors Kamō'ī's troops were two hundred yards inland and meeting little or no resistance. Still Olohana and the king could hear occasional musket crackles and shouting, evidence that minor encounters continued.

The second wave of canoes landed without incident. Warriors already ashore moved steadily forward. There was only token opposition of sporadic fire from thickets and a few hand-to-hand engagements by the more zealous warriors. The advance was cautious, steady and unchecked.

Kamō'ī was quietly pleased. Two miles of beach had been taken in the brief battle. He had read Pule´s plan correctly. He knew there was great conflict ahead but within two hours of the schooner´s cannon signal he had successfully placed almost eight thousand of his fighting men on the shores of O'ahu.

The sun rose to its apogee.

Silence hung over the humid rocky slopes stretching from beaches to the foothills of the Ko'olau Mountains.

Hawai'i troops moved steadily inland.

Kamōʻī agreed with Olohanaʻs suggestion to pause for rest, consolidation and assessment. His army remained an unbroken mass but unchecked advance over unfamiliar earth would create separations and dilute its strength. Hawaiʻi men were shaped now in a large crescent, center bellied inland and ends curved toward the ocean. The *Little American* and her attending canoes guarded sea approaches. All craft studiously dispersed, moving outside the long platform of coral reef.

Billy Pitt and Mohu arrived from their commands to consult with the king and Olohana. Losses remained light, they said, and spirits were high. Mohu said his men were grumbling about the slow advance, "This is all too easy, my aliʻi."

It would become less easy, Kamōʻī answered testily. He pointed to Lēʻahi crater, about a mile to their left. The rise was low, only some five or six hundred feet. But its steep sides formed an effective barrier against access to Waikīkī and the Mānoa lowlands beyond.

"Puleʻs main army is behind there," he said. "These men we fight are the sentinels and farmers and fishermen of this area."

"Each with the courage of three men," Pitt observed.

"Men who fight for their homes fight fiercely," said Mohu.

"There is only one way he can come," spoke Pitt. "From behind Lēʻahi, over the ridges of Kaimukī."

"He will not come," the king answered. "He will choose that we go to him, on the other side, where he has his strength."

"Alas," rued Mohu. "It would be better here. The spirit of our men is high and they now thirst for a fight."

"They shall have their fight," the king said. "But no foolish moves, no blundering ahead. Do you agree, Olohana?"

"Move carefully until nightfall, my aliʻi. If Pule chooses to battle on the Kaimukī rise tomorrow, so be it. If he does not, all the better. We will have the advantage of moving downhill against him."

"Kalani-Pitt?"

"I agree, heavenly one."

"Mohu?"

"I fear a trap, most exalted."

"How?" the king countered. "He can come only from one direction on land. Aleka will signal any danger from the sea. And I doubt he will fight in the night."

"I have lookouts forward, ali'i," Olohana said. "They will give news of any unusual movement."

Kamō'ī nodded.

"We are not fighting in the Hawaiian way," Mohu thought aloud. He was a man much concerned with tradition.

"We will never again fight in the old way," Kamō'ī said. "Guns have changed the old ways."

Stone breathed relief. There would be no time-consuming contests among champions, no chanting by priests about the superiority of their masters. Unhampered by such ritual, and with some luck, they might make short work of this bloody business.

He glanced at his companions: the contemplative heavy features of the king, Pitt's walnut-seamed visage under his white thatch and the savage countenance of Mohu. Not one hinted at the prospect of losing. Thoughts of retreat did not exist. Their confidence was infectious.

Discussion about supply lines and deployment of men, as the front narrowed on the uphill march continued. Soon, Kamō'ī said, they would draw their force more tightly together, forming a great blunt wedge aimed at the Kaimukī saddlelands. The system of communications Olohana had devised was working well. Using men and wahine kaua immediately behind the leading lines messages could be relayed over the entire front in minutes. Most of the war-women were busily carrying supplies and ammunition but others had pitched into the fray. One, an expert with a dagger, had accounted for three O'ahu men. Several had one or two corpses to their credit.

The king arose, signalling the end of the meeting. Staccato musket fire and shouts of men could be heard from distant pockets of engagement.

The big guns were now ashore, a messenger reported. The king and Olohana went back to inspect them. Stone checked the tackle for training the weapons then ran his men through the motions of loading and raising and lowering the breeches. Kamō'ī watched silently then ordered that more men be brought to make moving of the cannon faster and easier.

Skirmishes spluttered on like brush fires through the afternoon.

Higher slopes became rougher, troughed with gullies and strewn with ragged lava outcrops. These afforded O'ahu snipers good cover. Their harassment was constant, using their few muskets to deadly advantage. Other O'ahuans made suicidal dashes into the Hawai'i lines with spears, clubs and daggers. As the day waned these encounters became fewer and finally stopped.

In dusk the Kaimukī uplands had been reached by a vanguard of about three thousand Hawai'i men. Lē'ahi crater was now on their left, a jagged peak silhouetted by a claret-colored sunset over the distant western sea. To the right hills like tilted plateaus rose to be lost in scrub under high peaks of the Ko'olau range.

Kamō'ī and Olohana climbed a hillock.

The entire southern and western expanse of O'ahu stretched before them in twilight grandeur.

Soft lift gentled its vastness, the green convolutions of valleys into mountains, the sweeps of plain and nibblings of blue ocean on far shores. At least twenty miles distant, the long sawtooth loom of the Wai'anae mountains obscured the western sea.

Closer, broad central lowlands swept down between the mountain ranges. Still closer they could see the dull silver of landlocked waters at Wai Momi, Harbor of Pearls, and the nearer smaller indentations of the bay at Kou, the place becoming known as Honolulu.

Below them to the south slow-motion rollers of surf left long lacings, curling indolently on the sands at Waikīkī. Above the beach puddlings of marsh could be seen under thick groves of coco palms. Miles of flatland stretched inland to disappear in the floorings of deep valleys at Pālolo and Mānoa.

This was the prize and it was beautiful.

The two men stood quietly, gazing down. Clouds over the mountains turned violet as daylight dimmed. Dark came quickly to the island world. As they watched they saw tiny points of firelight appearing on the plain below, a few at first, then hundreds.

Kamō'ī was right, thought Olohana. Pule was down there and in great forces, waiting for them.

Manu paused on a narrow ledge of the trail, his back flattened against wet stones of the dizzying cliff, called a pali.

Icy water dripped from clumps of clinging lichen and brush above. Beneath his feet the pali plunged over a thousand feet almost straight down. He leaned out as far as he dared and looked up. Less than two hundred feet to go, he estimated.

From this height the trees on the lowlands far beneath looked like tiny buddings and groves of palms were like a flooring of small green stars. The distant view was one of arresting beauty—almost the entire windward O'ahu coastline stretched out with its beaches and green shores and the splendid serrations of the Ko'olau mountains rose abruptly in a long pleated wall. But he had no time for such musings... Darkness was coming soon and surviving this terrifying climb was all that now mattered. Three men, perhaps more, had already fallen to their deaths. But scaling the Ko'olaus on this ancient pali trail up into Nu'uanu valley had been Manu's only choice. His only alternative route for joining Pule's forces had been a long march around the mountain wall—and that would have consumed days.

The muddy path beneath his feet led up in zig-zags around indentations in the face of the pali. In places there was room for two men abreast but most of the footing would accommodate only a single file. Every inch was treacherously slippery. Beneath and behind him his followers formed a long and straggling line. Pūku'i, the Ka'ū chief, was leading the file. He was visible only now and then, moving slowly in Manu's path.

Manu started climbing again, testing the solidity of each step before placing his weight upon it. His kapa cloak was soaked, despite its treatment of kukui nut oil and he stopped in one of the wider places to shake it out. Cold wind cruelly blasted his naked torso. He shuddered in the trashing mist, working his toes and fingers to restore circulation, hearing muffled voices as the nearer men approached. He could now see Pūku'i beneath, his scowling face streaked with mud and his arms scratched and bleeding. Manu peered up again. Low clouds raced through a gap between two sharp rises. Between those peaks was rest and safety in the broad vale of Nu'uanu. Soon they would be at the summit. This knowledge lifted his spirits. He replaced his kapa, trembling at its chill, and shouted to Pūku'i, indicating by gesture that their goal was near. Then he pressed on, planting his feet carefully, moving crabwise where the path narrowed.

Higher, he was in clouds, whipped and shrouded by a driving mist. He picked his way very slowly, hearing voices of the others on the lifted wind.

Then, startlingly, there was no climbing. He was inching ahead into a gray wall. For several minutes he was unsure, apprehensive, until a brief break in the cloud revealed flat land ahead. He had gained the top of the pali! The treacherous climb was over! He shouted the news to the men below and their excited voices responded.

Within a half hour the first hundred men were up and over the precipice. Clouds rose higher, racing along the fluted walls of the huge valley. The wet had risen with the clouds and the men rested, drying their wraps. Despite the winds the setting sun offered welcome warmth. A steady stream of men struggled up into view. Manu noticed idly that all were Ka' warriors.

Pūku'i sat among his comrades, talking softly. In a few minutes he detached himself, walking slowly toward Manu. Something in his manner was disturbing. Manu rose to meet him. Always before, the Ka'ū chief had approached in deference, with a courteous bow.

"We will no linger here," Manu said. "When the men are gathered we will march down to a drier and more comfortable camp for the night."

Pūku'i said nothing. Moisture glistened on the knotted muscling of his powerful shoulders. His dark eyes bored into Manu's with a steady and unblinking stare—as if seeing something for the first time which he found extremely unpleasant. Several of the Ka'ū men moved to places behind him, silent and watching the two ali'i. Manu's misgivings became fear.

"Do you mark what I say, chief?"

"Mark this, prince," said Pūku'i. He drew an iron dagger from his malo and held it upright, inches from Manu's face. The damp blade shone dully. Pūku'i's voice rose, words meant to be heard by the companions at his back.

"This is the dagger of Koa, our lord of Ka'ū. With it he took the Death of Uli. We use it now for his revenge. Mark this, assassin!"

His hand dropped and the knife shot forward, plunging into Manu's stomach.

Manu gasped. Pūku'i brought the knife up with both hands, supporting the dying prince for moments. Then he stopped back, released him, and Manu crumpled dead into the mud.

Kamō'ī's regiments descended the Kaimukī slopes at the first hint of morning light. The army was over an hour into its advance as the sun brought brightness to Waikīkī lowlands.

Along a mile of front the Hawai'i soldiers plodded among clumps of palms and slogged through shallows of kalo patches and marshland. Lē'ahi crater was now above and behind them, its plunging sides in sunrise shadows.

The first attack from O'ahu's defenders exploded at about nine o'clock.

Thousands of waiting warriors burst from cover to engage the invaders. Sling stones and spears flew into the Hawai'i ranks. Thumping cannon ripped ghastly spaces in the massing of big island men. Pule had wisely arranged his heavy weaponry where it would best counter Kamō'ī's guns.

Kamō'ī's army buckled but held. Billy Pitt's flank took the initial brunt of the attack and met it full on. Fighters wielding daggers, spears and clubs met and clashed in savage fray. The air was torn with the crackle of musket fire, cannon bursts and the cries of the wounded and dying.

Olohana raced back and forth between the big guns and his muskets forces, directing fire at the heavier concentrations of defenders, cursing the time and struggle used in moving his own cannon over swampy depressions. The king ranged along the lines in great strides, shouting encouragement and leaping in to join the fight. More than one O'ahu battler met his end at the point of Kamō'ī's spear or dagger.

Time crept through the hellish morning. The battle

pulsed and swayed, each side gaining and losing yards, feet and inches. The biting smell of gunsmoke mingled with the steaming scents of dank earth and brackish water. Tradewinds dropped and the warm air stilled. Slowly, imperceptibly at first, the superior musketry of Kamō'i's men began to show effect. Skirmishes became fewer, the armies more separated. Darting raids into the Hawai'i lines ceased. There were lulls in the fighting.

A runner arrived from Billy Pitt. His men had driven forward to Waikīkī beach. He had captured Pule's sacred family heiau at the foot of Lē'ahi. Seizure of his temple was a grave loss and personal insult to Pule. The courier also reported that Aleka had brought the *Little American* and her canoes around Lē'ahi point without incident. All their craft now rode the low swells outside Waikīkī's surf line. There was no indication of opposition on the water—hundreds of O'ahu canoes lay abandoned on the sand.

"Only two things Pule can do, my lord," said Olohana. "Stand or retreat."

"He will stand," the king said.

In the afternoon Kamō'i's army gained more ground.

Along the beach Pitt's men took and burned Pule's pavilion-retreat by the shore. Inland Mohu's troops slaughtered a hundred men trying to creep around to their rear. Kamō'i's forces now held a rough line running across a mile of Waikīkī plain from the beach to foothills of the Ko'olau mountains. Olohana reckoned gains forwarded by the movement of his cannon—at least a quarter mile since the first encounters in the morning.

Later in the day weak points became evident in the O'ahu front. A few eager Hawai'i chiefs wanted to dash into these soft spots but Olohana commanded them to stay and move with the main body. With night coming ventures forward at odd points could only create weaknesses. Good sense dictated that they remain together, a solid wall of soldiers advancing as one, always in communication.

Hand-to-hand fighting ceased with fading light. Both sides settled in wherever cover was available. Men camped where twilight found them—along stream beds, behind boulders and under scrubby trees. Olohana ordered the cannon rolled back to be cleaned and guarded. O'ahu's big guns had been silent for almost two hours. Was Pule running out of ammunition? Or had he simply drawn his guns back for better placement? A scout who had seen the weapons said they were almost exactly like Olohana's red-mouthed guns and commanded by two haole, one black and one white.

Olohana sought out the king, who had refused the comforts of captured houses to stay with his men. Kai's guards had cleared ground litter in a lava depression for the monarch's comfort and were now squatting on its edges, alert and peering into the surrounding landscape. A young wahine kaua was handing gourds of water to the king, who dashed them upon himself, rinsing away mud and perspiration. He motioned Olohana to sit.

"Three hundred warriors dead," Kamō'ī said. "And fifty more wahine kaua."

"Pule has suffered twice that number, ali'i."

"He will lose many more before he breaks," said Kamō'ī. "Are the wounded being cared for?"

"Yes, ali'i. All have been taken to safety and the medical kāhuna."

A commotion was heard nearby. Soldiers dragged three men into Kamō'ī's presence. Each was naked and bound at the wrists. They were thrown to the ground and groveled before the monarch, their eyes furtive with fear.

These three dogs had run from the fighting, Kai reported. They had been caught trying to escape into the hills.

"Is there any doubt of this?" Kamō'ī asked.

"No, ali'i, none," answered Kai.

The king shook his head sadly. Kai would not mislead him. He made a cutting motion across his throat.

Garbled pleas for mercy burst from the culprits— sounds arrested as sennit lines whipped around their necks. In moments the bodies were limp and were being dragged away.

Poi and fish were brought and the king and Olohana sat to eat. The royal spittoon-bearer squatted nearby, his gaze never leaving the monarch. The tiniest scrap of waste must be recovered. If the enemy could possess a shred of Kamō'i's mana the results would be catastrophic.

Minor commanders arrived with reports and questions. Kamō'i listened intently, making almost instant decisions and referring all questions about guns to Olohana. When the last visitor left he feel silent, lost in thought. Night came as a dark void, for the moon was clouded and fires forbidden. Olohana passed his brandy flask to the king, who drank and sighed. He tugged his kapa around his shoulders in the growing cool. The only sound was the scraping of Kai's crude straw sandals on cinders as he walked guard a few yards away. The man's devotion was fanatic, thought Olohana. He wondered if he ever slept.

The king spoke softly, "You will not regret following me, Olohana."

"I have never regretted it, my ali'i," Stone answered, thinking, Not yet, not yet...

Kamō'i settled back against the porous stone.

"The haole captain, Broom, is right. In years to come trading ships will choose this island over others. O'ahu is rich in things they need, and the harbor he called Honolulu is excellent. Ships sheltering there will not have the open sea at their backs." He drank again. "Yes, this is where the haole will come."

He handed the flask back, almost hidden in his massive hand.

"It will be necessary to have a chief here who can deal properly with these people. One who knows their ways, but is loyal to me."

He paused.

"You are that man, Olohana. You will rule Oʻahu for me."

Reclining, Stone brought himself slowly to his elbows, the import of the king's words sinking in.

"I am greatly honored, my aliʻi," were the words that came, and with them a tumbled rush of thought: This was the reward—not a few hundred acres of seashore and farmland on Hawaiʻi Island but a rich and beautiful island of his own. The prospect was dazzling. He would lord of this splendid little kingdom, with its mountain ranges, grand sweeping plain, deep and dozing valleys and lovely beaches. Its thousands of people would be his subjects, his word instantly obeyed, his wish a command. He would make rules, command trade, know power he had never dreamed of. As Kamōʻī's regent, his influence would be enormous...

"I don't know what to say, aliʻi."

"Say nothing then," the king said. "But I wish you to think of it."

That night was a misery. Heavy rain, born of thick clouds westering against the Koʻolaus, drifted down to dispel itself in sheets over the lowlands.

Guards rigged a square of ship's canvas to shelter the king and Olohana but this was scant relief from the slanting wet which soaked their wraps. They sat, huddled against aerial roots of a hala tree, and dozed fitfully. Both arose before dawn. The king ate heartily, Olohana with disinterest. Still in dark they were off, the king to visit and encourage the men, Olohana to bring the cannon forward.

When fighting resumed it was in chill mists over a terrain of mud and slippery stones. Gains were small, gunfire sporadic. Neither side used cannon, for targets were obscured by gray shrouds of moisture. The broad flatland with its tumbles of lava, scrub brush and trees gave ample cover for both armies. Swollen streams out of the valleys meandered over the plain, feeding shallow pools and marshes. When the rain stopped and sun broke through this landscape steamed. There was no breeze and the humidity caused the fighters to drip with sweat.

The captive brought before Kamōʻī in midmorning was a white man, about thirty, with a hooked nose, lank black hair and a remarkably cheerful expression. He wore nondescript seaman's clothes and was shoeless. He stared boldly at Olohana and Kamōʻī before guards pushed him roughly to his knees. He made a protest and Olohana told him to be quiet.

"What is your name?"

"Murray, cap'n. What's yours?"

"This is the aliʻi-nui, Kamōʻī. Bow to him."

"Anything you say, squire."

"Where are you from?"

"Off the Mystic, Cap'n Broom, 'bout a month or more back."

"Your position is not to be envied, Murray."

"Fair times till now," Murray tried a smile.

"How many other haole are there with Pule?"

"Only one in the fight, squire. Black lad named Poni Toole. But four or five others on the island. All whites and proper rascals every one. Thieves and murderers—two from Botany Bay."

Kamōʻī listened hard. He knew enough English to catch the drift of this interview.

"You have a simple choice, Murray," Olohana said. "Give me honest answers or feel a rope around your dirty neck."

"I'll tell you anything you want to know, chief. The fight's over for me, ain't it?"

"That's the truth, Murray. How many guns does Pule

have and how are they spread?"

"'Bout a hundred and fifty, and all close by. And the two cannon. But there's more coming, down Nu'uanu with your friend, Manu."

"When is he expected?"

Murray shrugged. "Today, tomorrow. 'Tis a fair march down."

"Does Pule have any reserves to the rear?"

"No, guvnor, the whole lot is within a mile."

"Lie to us and you're a dead man."

"Nothing but the truth, I swear." Murray raised his right hand in a gesture of oath, a movement made awkward by his lashings.

"I can talk a lot friendlier without this." He held up his bonds.

"We don't want your friendship, bucko, only information. What is Pule's plan?"

"I ain't close to his lordship, chief, and I don't know his lingo. But as far as I can figger, he plans to fight any place you are."

"Can you get a message to the black man?"

"Should be easy, yer honor."

"Without taking it yourself?"

"There's ways."

"Tell him to bring the cannon to us and you'll both be spared."

"Ah, now. That might be a hard trick."

"I take you for the tricky sort, Murray. You'll find a way. In cold fact, you'd better find a way."

Murray's unctuous smile was gone.

"I'll give you a few minutes to think it out," Olohana said.

"You don't have much aloha for white men, guvnor."

"You reckon wrong, Murray. You are the enemy. I choose to be loyal to my man."

"I can fight for him too. Don't matter to me what side I'm on. 'Twas Cap'n Broom give me to this kanaka's service."

"When will Broom return?"

"Two months at the least."

"Take him away," Olohana instructed the guards.

"Can we believe him?" Kamō'ī asked.

"I think so, ali'i. He knows he'll lose his head by lying."

"If his shipmate brings their cannon Pule will be gravely weakened."

"Yes, ali'i. that will make the rest easier"

"No, Olohana, only perhaps faster."

Tweed accompanied some supply canoes ashore and went directly to the king. He had seen a bit of action, he reported. In the night a canoe with fifteen daring O'ahu paddlers had slipped through the schooner's guard fleet. But the ship's watches were alert and the canoe and its crew had been destroyed before doing harm.

"Foolish men," the Scot said, "but brave... brave."

Kamō'ī told him to keep the large ship and canoes on sharp and constant patrol. O'ahu canoes abandoned along Waikīkī might be a ruse. It was possible that Pule had a hidden fleet at Wai Momi, the pearl harbor, or even around fringes of Mmala Bay at Kou-Honolulu.

"Aye, m'lord," said Tweed, then to Olohana, "John, the boy is gone."

"Gone? Where? What do you mean?"

"Ashore, I reckon. He went over the side at first light this morning. Not to worry. Little nipper swims like a salmon."

Kamō'ī's eyes were on Tweed.

"You wish that I have men look for him, ali'i?" Tweed asked.

"Olohana will answer that."

Stone hesitated only a moment. It was difficult, but there was only one thing for him to say, "No. He is but one of many now. We cannot take time."

"As you say," said Tweed. "Nevertheless, I'll keep an eye cocked. But I think, John. that you'll see him before I do."

PART XIII

*B*y the fourth day the forward drive and relentless pounding of Kamōʻīʻs men and guns had exacted a dreadful toll.

Pule of Oʻahu took an accounting.

Its stark truths were deeply distressing. He had been pushed back three miles in so many days. His gunner, Murray, had been taken. Then the cursed black haole, Poni Toole, had absconded with the two precious cannon. Pule had no doubt these would soon be used against him.

Invaders swarmed over the lowlands of Waikīkī, Kewalo and Kakaʻako. Smoke rose from burning canoes and the few huts of fisher folks at Honolulu. Other canoes along Māmala Bay had been pierced with holes and their crews routed. Old people, women and children had escaped the area a few days before. His queens and his sons were in hiding, miles away on the leeward coast at Waiʻanae.

His dilemma worsened by the hour. He occupied less than a half mile of front on the slopes of the blunt crater of Puʻuowaina, the Hill of Sacrifice. His back was against its wall and escape to the sea through a massed enemy was impossible. On its inland end Puʻuowaina fell to the ridges of a saddleland. Soon he would be forced into a retreat through this narrow corridor.

In the rising light of early morning he stood under a kou tree. Its orange-colored flowers were daubs of warmth in the brisk air. Pono of Maui snored on the turf nearby. A few yards distant guards with muskets rested against jagged stones, yawning from their all-night vigil as they stared down over the wooded landscape. The scene below was eerily quiet, showing no evidence of the thousands of warriors facing one another, waiting.

A servant offered food. Pule ate listlessly, pondering what this day might bring. His men had fought heroically—but how much more could they give? The odds were now appalling, the loss of the cannon disastrous. Manu's failure to appear was another disappointment. The Hawai'i traitor should have joined him two days ago. Pule had initially counted on Manu's treachery more as a blow to Kamō'ī's morale than anything else. Now he sorely needed the extra guns and the famed fighting men of Ka'ū.

Pono grunted awake. In these past three days his bravado had disappeared and he rarely spoke. He stared at his half-brother with reddened eyes.

He is but a shell, though Pule, an *ali'i* in name only. Strange how a man can live a lie for a lifetime.

"Take men and find Manu," he said. "Go now."

Olohana awoke and massaged his stiff limbs.

A soldier hunched a few feet away, grasping his musket and peering uphill. The warrior shivered under his cape of leaves in the morning damp. Olohana told him to fetch tea and food and asked if the king was awake.

Yes, said the musketman. His highness had just finished extruding a magnificent bowel movement.

"Bring both the black and the white haole to me," Olohana ordered.

"'Ae, my *ali'i*," said the soldier, then, "The young chief is here, *ali'i*. He crept in the night through enemy warriors and was very tired and hungry."

Thank God, thought Stone. "Where is he?"

"There, *ali'i*." The man pointed to a clump of brush several yards downhill. "He would not permit us to awaken you."

Puna lay in deep sleep under the cover, his hair matted and face smeared with soil. His *kapa* wrap had worked loose, revealing a slim shoulder and arm liberally scratched from his passage through brush and thorns.

Bloody little fool, Stone thought. Sheer luck he hadn't been shot or run through with a spear. Annoyance swelled in him, temptation to wake the lad roughly, speak harshly about the worry he'd caused, perhaps even cuff him once or twice to emphasize the point...

But the irritation soon passed. Stone rolled his *kapa* into a pillow and eased it beneath the boy's head. Then he covered him.

Puna stirred, sighed and fell back into exhausted slumber.

The sun came up in the cradle between Lē'ahi and the Ko'olau range and Kamō'ī struck.

He attacked savagely with every man and weapon, sensing correctly that Pule was now at his lowest point, physically and mentally.

The O'ahu lines trembled and held only briefly.

Kamō'ī's volcanic assault could not be stopped. Scenting victory, his men fought like demons, pouring into breaks torn open by the horrendous blastings of the four cannon. Olohana's new gunners, Murray and Toole, performed with expert alacrity, knowing the slightest false move would cost their lives. Special guards with pistols watched their every motion.

Under the cannon and musket fire hand-to-hand fighting raged everywhere along the front. The viciousness of the attack stunned the O'ahu fighters. Many were isolated and killed, others panicked and fled. Several hundred, seeking safety in the small valley of Pauoa, were pursued and slain along its walls. Billy Pitt led a thousand men up the sides of Pu'uowaina, and slaughtered half that number of enemies in the shallow crater. Inland Mohu's charging troops scattered opponents in disorganized escapes into the nearest foothills. Kamō'i's legion became a juggernaut, crushing everything in its path, every soldier fired to a fever of confidence. O'ahu soldiers began to break and run even before actually facing Kamō'i's legion. These flights of panic multiplied, becoming mass desertions.

Within two hours Pule's lines had broken in dozens of places. By midday his defense had disintegrated into a disorderly flight. The major part of the O'ahu army was in chaotic retreat, citizen-soldiers fleeing back toward the deep valleys and small villages. Only the fulltime warriors of Pule's personal battalions remained doggedly together. The sounds of struggle waned, then ended; the smoke and smell of the turmoil drifted away on tradewinds.

In the dying day Pule and his thousand remaining fighters were withdrawing to a refuge on the land above the wide valley of Nu'uanu. Before them the long gorge stretched for miles between steep walls to the Ko'olau peaks. Behind them Kamō'i's army settled into a long bow-shape, denying any escape seaward.

In his dank camp that night the O'ahu king sat alone, a monarch deeply humiliated, a man on the run. Nearby his few remaining chiefs huddled in silence and soldiers gloomily made beds upon the ground. In the dark below they could see the celebratory fires of their invaders, flaming like gestures of scorn.

When the wind shifted bursts of laughter and snatches of song lifted up from the camp below. More than once jubilant shouts of the Hawai'i men echoed clearly as they hailed their king on the eve of his greatest and richest victory.

But the triumph would not be complete, Pule knew, nor the victory a true one, until Kamō'i killed him.

Kai brought the news, "Five men approach from the far side of the valley, my ali'i. One wears the cape of an *ali'i."*

Kamō'ī beckoned to Pitt and Olohana. Following Kai the party picked their way through tangled brush to a rise over the bank of the main stream of Nu'uanu. Kai pointed across to where a woodsmen's trail became lost among trees. They waited.

The first man to emerge walked straight and purposefully. Sunlight caught the golden feathers of his shoulder cloak. He carried a spear with a piece of white *kapa* tied to its end and held aloft. Under his other arm was a bundle wrapped in dark barkcloth. Three soldiers followed him into view. Lastly was dragged the stumbling Lako, wrists tied behind his back.

"Pūku'i, my *ali'i,*" whispered Olohana. "A high chief of Ka'ū."

"Let him come," Kamō'ī instructed.

The quintet crossed the shallows, water swirling around their calves. Lako staggered and fell on the slippery stones and was yanked roughly to his feet by his captors.

Kamō'ī stepped from cover. Pūku'i, bending to climb the bank, looked up to confront the giant monarch a few yards distant. For a moment their eyes met and held then Pūku'i fell to his knees. Behind him the startled soldiers prostrated themselves on muddy earth. Lako sprawled on his knees, his head hung, whimpering.

"My *ali'i,*" Pūku'i said.

"Why do you come?" Kamō'ī asked.

"I am returning the warriors of Ka'ū to your service, my lord."

"You men of Ka'ū deserted me with a traitor."

"Our orders were to follow him, my *ali'i.* Not knowing his treachery, we obeyed."

"Where is Manu?"

"Here, *ali'i.*"

Pūku'i grasped one end of the kapa bundle and, with a sudden lifting motion, unraveled and opened the package. A grimacing, mud-crusted head rolled out on the turf, bloodless and gray, its black hair snarled. The lips were drawn back and a stubby dark object had been forced between its teeth.

"What is in his mouth?" Olohana heard himself ask.

"The *uli* of our lord, Koa, the man he killed," answered Pūku'i.

"It was I who sacrificed your master at Kohol *heiau*," said Kamō'ī.

"Yours is the way of kings," answered Pūku'i. "This we understand. But it was Manu who did the deed. Thus it was he who paid."

"Where are your men?"

"Against the far side of the valley, *ali'i*. We await your command."

"So be it," said Kamō'ī. With his spear he scornfully poked the grisly object on the ground.

"We leave this to the rats," he said.

"You—swine," he addressed Lako. "You shall have time to think about dying. Go to Pule. Tell him we will finish this in the old way. Until then I will find and fight him with numbers equal to his own." He made a gesture to Kai. "Release this dog."

"I have never been disloyal, my *ali'i*," Lako whined. "Manu forced me, under threat..."

Kai arrested the speech with a stunning backhand slap at Lako's mouth. The stout chief reeled and fell under the blow.

"Say no more," spat Kai. "Go and do as the *ali'i-nui* commands."

The two mile long gorge of Nu'uanu was steeply walled and generously watered.

This was one of the grandest valleys of all O'ahu, rich in the valuable produce of Hawai'i highlands. Breadfruit, bamboo, plantains and sugarcane grew in profusion. Myriad birds fluttered through its glades and its streams were alive with fish and fresh-water shrimp. At higher elevations there were yam and *kalo* patches watered from the falls dropping over the steep and furrowed cliff-sides.

Now the huts of farmers, woodgatherers and bird-catchers were abandoned, all having fled the warring soldiers of Kamōʻī and Pule.

For three days Kamōʻī drove his foe back and up.

Fighting was a drumming, deadly exhaustion through the jungled valley floor; a fitful, bitter struggle over terrain broken by ravines, cross-hatched by streams, tangled with growth and uphill all the way. In retreat the men of Oʻahu fought tenaciously. They killed from deceptive cover, hitting hard with muskets and sling stones, then backing to dig in and repulse again. Always they were merely yards ahead of Kamōʻīʼs advance. Only rarely were they seen in significant numbers.

But Kamōʻīʼs progress was persistent. The Oʻahu fighters were being forced back to the massive cliff at the valleyʼs head like mullet into a net.

Puna pleaded again: "Let me go with you, Olohana."

Stone weakened. Perhaps it would be safe enough... "Only if you remain well behind the forward line. Is that clear?"

"I can fight, *aliʻi*. Better than some of the older men."

Stone thought: I would have laughed at this before I saw him kill a man...

"Life will provide all the fighting you need," he said. "This is a deadly business. One only loses once."

"ʻAe." Obviously Puna was not impressed.

"Listen, my hearty. You have already proved you are a brave and clever young man. There is no need to run stupid risks."

"Kamōʻī will not see me as a warrior."

"Dear God. You are here, with us! That is enough. You are but thirteen years old!"

"Near fourteen," Puna countered.

On the morning of the fourth day of the valley battle, the inexorable advance ended.

Kamō'ī and his companion *ali'i* peered through slitted eyes into the gusting mists of Nu'uanu. Some three hundred yards ahead low clouds raced through a yawning gap in the razorbacks of the Ko'olau peaks. At this out the valley walls ended in a pali plunging over a thousand feet to the windward O'ahu flatlands below—the same cliff Manu and his troops had scaled several days before. Backed into this rough V-shape Pule and his men awaited the final encounter.

Kamō'ī called Olohana to his side.

"No cannon, no guns," he said. "We will finish this in the Hawaiian way."

"Christ! He will have guns, my *ali'i*. This is not wise."

"No, Olohana. I have sent a messenger. Pule has agreed."

Stone's face mirrored his disapproval.

"This is necessary, my friend," said Kamō'ī. "For both Pule and myself. We desire to fight as kings should."

Terminal peaks of the long valley were obscured by scudding clouds. Ribbons of water plunged over cliff-sides to be caught and spun into lacy spray by harsh winds. Stunted trees thriving on the valley floor had been bent into grotesque shapes by lifetimes of the lashing gusts.

The armies faced each other in silence across a rocky clearing. Soldiers clustered wherever they could find vantage points to view the royal duel. By hundreds they gathered on rises, stony outcrops and in trees, tensed and waiting. The scene was eerie in the gray light, the wind keening and watchers silent. There were murmurings as the kings appeared, Kamō'ī with the long valley at his back, Pule framed against squalling sky above the plunge of the *pali*. Both stepped forward until there was scarcely a spear´s length between them. Except for *malo* both stood naked. Their eyes met, taking the measure enemies never before seen.

Kamōʻī spoke first, "You will die with honor, Pule, as you have fought."

"Breathe my Oʻahu air deeply, Kamōʻī. It is your last."

Olohana stood with Billy Pitt, fixated on the two monarchs. With a shock he became aware of Puna among the nearby soldiers. Anger surged with a desire to shout, scolding the boy for his disobedience. Such an outburst would only disconcert Kamōʻī and Stone held his tongue.

The now silent scene was charged with anticipation. Against the trees behind Puleʻs back Pono and Lako were visible, their faces tight and apprehensive.

The spears of the two kings went up and touched briefly. Both stepped back. Assuming a slight crouch they began a slow circling. Pule was first to essay a thrust. Kamōʻīʻs thick lance whipped up in block and the battle began.

Veterans of hundreds of such joustings, both were masters and deadly dangerous. For long minutes the fight was balanced, with equal parryings, lungings and quick footwork.

Slowly it became evident that Puleʻs age would take its toll. His will to fight remained passionate but the signals from brain to limb grew increasingly sluggish. Pule carried the weight of failure, a kingdom slipping away, his army nearly destroyed and family in shameful hiding. The cause now danced before him—ten years younger and harder, faster, surer.

Sensing his power Kamōʻī ventured closer, stabbing.

It was an almost fatal mistake.

Pule dug in countering viciously, refusing to give ground, his spear whistling and slashing. A roar of defiance tore from his throat as he blasted into an offensive. Kamōʻī was forced back, parrying frantically under the violent attack. The Oʻahu king threw every ounce of his strength into a gargantuan effort to end the fight in a burst of power, discarding caution in a savage attempt to catch and kill.

But he could not and the intense effort left him gasping.

More slowly Kamō'ī moved to the advantage, prudently this time, great bulk moving sinuously and his spear taking Pule's cuts and thrusts. Pule was clearly weakening, backing a foot or two, fending new attacks clumsily. Again he cried out, this time in rage and frustration.

Then he chose to make a stand. He stepped back and planted his feet firmly. His torso bent forward.

For an instant only Kamō'ī paused, assessing. Then Pule lunged.

It was the final act of the O'ahu monarch. Seconds later he was dead on the cindery earth, Kamō'ī's spear through his heart.

A frenzy of sound and fury followed as the deed crashed upon the watching soldiers. Kai's great shout exploded first, spear held high over his head. Cries hurtled into the wind—despair and sorrow from the ranks of O'ahu, praise and joy from Hawai'i battalions. Kamō'ī's warriors milled forward as he stood over Pule's body. Olohana was transfixed by the volcanic power of the charge—then horrified as a slight form darted past him into the wave of soldiers.

Puna raced toward the O'ahu line, his spear upraised.

"No!" Stone screamed. "No! Come back!"

His voice was near lost in the thunder of other shouting. Unhearing or unheeding Puna raced on. Olohana dashed after him, bellowing. Instantly he was surrounded by charging comrades and buffeted from side to side. He stumbled and fell on the slaggy lava, unfeeling of its ripping at his hands and knees. On his feet again he lost sight of the boy in the shambles ahead.

When he saw him again his heart stood still.

Puna was sprawled on the ground, boyish limbs twisted and awry. A spear was being tugged from his chest by a burly O'ahu warrior.

Horror and rage hurled Stone at the man with insane purpose, his fists lashing out in stunning blows. The O'ahu fighter was taller and stronger but had no defense against such crazed fury. Stone's hands closed around his neck and the soldier tore at his fingers. He might as well have been plucking at steel bands. The warrior fell to his knees, eyes bulging and body in spasms before he collapsed. Olohana seized a stone and slammed it into his face. Again and again he pounded until the head of Puna's killer was a bloody pulp of bone and flesh.

The final battle for O'ahu exploded in an avalanche of Hawai'i men pouring into the valley head. Like writhing spirits in the swirling mist, warrior met warrior in horrifying clashes on lava and in thickets. The Maui chief, Mohu, found and killed Pono, adding new stature to his rank as the island's governor. Lako met an ignonimous end, disemboweled by the dagger of an ordinary soldier.

His regal duty accomplished, Kamō'ī remained motionless over Pule's body, watching the charge with a steady gaze.

Knowing their ultimate victory was at hand in a matter of minutes, the big island fighters could not be stopped. Vainly O'ahu forces battled to hold a ragged front. But Kamō'ī's troops were a roaring wave of bristling spears and daggers and brutal flesh, crazed with success.

In minutes scant yards remained between Pule's defenders and the terrifying pali at their heels.

Soon the struggle raged to the very edge of the precipice. O'ahu's warrior fought with frantic desperation but the assault was overwhelming. Both sides battled over a ghastly strewing of bodies, stumbling over the dead and the wailing, contorted wounded. Kamō'ī's

army had become a crushing might with maniacal drive.
The end came in final moments of horror.

Backed until they could no longer stand, hundreds of
O'ahu men were driven over the jagged edges of the
awful *pali*. Scores of their comrades chose the same fate,
dashing to hurl themselves over the great cliff-a cataract
of humans tumbling to their deaths on the stones below,
their screams floating up on the wind.

Less than an hour after their leader's slaying Pule,
Kamō'ī's forces stood victorious on the windswept
heights.

Triumphant shouts waned to silence.

Solemnly the care of the wounded and burial of the
dead began. Olohana wrapped Puna in *kapa* and laid him
gently among his comrades, later to be covered by stones.

Priests began removal of Pule's bones for honored
burial at the Lē'ahi *heiau* of his dynasty. Kamō'ī ordered
the K-stone brought forward that his warriors might see
and give thanks to the source of their bravery and skill.

In the wind and rain the brows of the Hawai'i victors
touched earth in prostration before their god.

In the afternoon the winds lessened and sunlight
glowed palely through the gray blanket, softening the
scene.

Kamō'ī and his men began the long march back down
to the now largely abandoned plain of Honolulu.

PART XIV

*K*ona nights were long and quiet and Olohana was usually astir before dawn.

He came to wakefulness slowly, liking the solace of the resilient mats and snug warmth of Namo at his side. He savored these moments, listening to the sounds of the sea and breeze, his senses adjusting to the morning and its moods.

Invariably he slipped from their pallet and started a small fire for tea and comfort. First hints of daylight outlined the swellings of the big island, but it always remained cool until the sun appeared over Mauna Loa.

He sat, watching the diminutive dance of flames, enjoying the perfumed hot liquid and pleasant bite of pipesmoke. Shadowy figures moved among the trees and along the shore—fishermen and other early risers preparing for the day. Spent waves hissed, dying on the sand. Soon Namo joined him, saying nothing but reaching to touch his face or shoulder, knowing he relished the morning silence. She would pierce a coconut for drinking or poke a plantain or yam into the coals. He knew great contentment in her presence, feeling her tenderness, seeing her smile. The sight of this golden beauty, large and ripe with his child, her breasts and shoulders glazed by soft firelight, never failed to move him.

"Where is Olohana now?" asked Keōpū.

"With our master," Kahu answered. "They are fishing off Hoʻokena. The *ōʻpelu* are swarming, a rich harvest this year."

"And his woman?" asked the sacred queen. "Is she well?"

"'Ae, my sister. But she had awkward moments now and then." Kahu shrugged and smiled faintly. "I wish I might experience such discomfort."

Keōpū did not respond. She no longer cared to even think about her—or Kahu's—barrenness of sons. Of late, Kamō'ī's visits had been less frequent. A few nights before he had ventured near insult.

This had happened at an 'aha'aina in honor of Kai, who was visiting Kona to report on his temporary governorship of O'ahu. At the feast a comely young girl had danced a new hula, representing the gyrations of a virgin mounting a stiffly erect king. When she finished Kamō'ī had loudly ordered that she be sent to his sleeping house in order that she might experience the real thing.

Such extra-familial romps were condoned, of course, but never flaunted. Kahu had shared Keōpū's embarrassment and annoyance at the king's thoughtlessness.

"When do they return?" asked Keōpū.

"A few days, my lady. Kalani-Pitt says the fishing is an opportune time for Kamō'ī to talk to Olohana, urge him back to activity. The king wishes him to take the command of O'ahu."

"Will his woman have the child with us?"

"'Ae. She will go to the birthing stones at Keauhou."

"Is she being cared for?"

"Yes, my lady. Well cared for, by our master's orders. Hina, Tweed's woman, is by her side, and the kahuna of birth stands near."

"Many young men were killed," the king said. "I must sorrow for each."

"None were as young as he," said Olohana.

The two men watched fishermen in a neighboring canoe scatter redolent chum over a submerged net.

"I did not come to know him as you did," said Kamōʻī. "My interest was selfish. Beyond my sorrow for you I can feel only guilt."

"You have none, *aliʻi*. The blame is mine for not sending him to safety."

"What might have been lies dead with the boy, Olohana. It is two months since Oʻahu. What we do now is of proper importance. I need your help."

"I am ready, *aliʻi*. We will leave after the child is born."

"A time well chosen," Kamōʻī mused aloud. "The beginning of new lives, for you and your infant."

"*Ae*, my lord."

"Kai is dedicated and faithful," Kamōʻī went on. "But his rule on Oʻahu is that of a conquering soldier, impatient and demanding, inclining to harshness. This attitude has served in establishing my dominance but it is now time for a more moderate and compassionate hand—a governing by thought rather than reaction. Pule was a reasonable man and many people remain angry and resentful about his death. Their ability to make trouble must be identified and minimized. Several *kāhuna* appear to be particular threats but we should eliminate them only if we see no other solution. In the most ideal circumstances we will have no more killing. I depend upon you to encourage such conditions."

"In every way I can, my *aliʻi*."

The king continued, reflectively, "Our younger people wonder what the future holds for them. They are troubled and confused. The reasons are clear. Their world is not what they were taught it would be. They are threatened by customs and beliefs they do not understand. The temptations are great and the gods and *kapu* are being questioned. I must lead Hawaiians as one people, for everyone's good, with the ancient laws as our strength. But we must also give ear to complaints, making more equal use of lands, water and fishing rights. You, Olohana, can help by seeing that haole do not harm, cheat, or shame our people. Do this in my name and with the force of my authority. One day soon I will join you. Kalani-Pitt is not well and I would stay with him."

"Yes, my *ali'i.*"

"On O'ahu the district called 'Aiea will be yours, from the mountains to the sea. It is fruitful, well watered, and with many people. The area also includes Pu'uloa and Wai Momi, the pearl harbor."

"A great wealth, heavenly one. I am grateful."

"My debt to you is greater. I wish you long years of health and happiness and many children on O'ahu. But I desire that you settle first at Honolulu, on the harbor."

"I understand, ali'i."

"See that proper houses are built for my visits."

"There is a good site, ali'i. A point called Pakaka, commanding the entrance to the bay. It would also be the proper place to mount guns, should they ever be needed."

"Maika'i," very good, the king said. He was pleased that Olohana was thinking about the future.

Almost every morning Alec Tweed came to visit, sip tea and chat of days current and days ahead. Talk of the past was rare now, as if their lives had begun with the *Nahant's* disappearance over the horizon. In the first black weeks after the O'ahu battle the big Scot had been a great comfort, his gruff good nature frequently banishing Stone's depression over Puna's death. Now Tweed was a glow with plans to build a small shipyard on the calm at Honolulu, once Olohana was settled. Fair-sized sloops could be constructed for Kamō'ī's fleet, he said, not to mention profits from minor repairs on visiting traders.

When not expounding on this enthusiasm Tweed frequently extolled the virtues of children to a man's middle years. He now had a tiny girl by Hina, another wife about to deliver and two others approaching fruition. The din of one's own bairn, he told Olohana, took a man's mind off almost everything else. He was pleased that Hina would accompany Namo and her midwife when she traveled to the ceremonial birthing stones.

"It'll be a bonnie day, John," he grinned. "We'll break open a bottle of the best and have a celebration." The midwives, he assured, were highly skilled. Stone need have no worry.

"These lassies are remarkable contrivances, John. A ruddy wonder."

"Come," greeted Billy Pitt. "Sit by me."

Olohana had not seen Pitt for two weeks and was surprised. The old man looked wan, drawn and very tired. Stone settled at his side as Pitt ordered tea and brandy. A *kāhuna* of medicine, dispatched to Pitt's service by the king, looked on from respectful distance.

"You are taking my place," Pitt said softly.

"Nonsense, *makua*. There is not a man in all Hawai'i who could take your place. Nor would I dream of designs upon it."

"You are kind, Olohana, but misunderstand me. I do not doubt you and I hold no envy or bitterness. What has happened is in the proper order of things. Our king learned everything I was able to teach him long ago. Then you came and were chosen to help. You have served with loyalty and courage. Now you must be his guide and adviser. To do this best there is something you must know."

He paused before continuing, his breathing labored.

"There are times when his certainty is a shield, concealing doubts. He is a man under attack, between our Hawai'i of the old ways and the new world of vast lands, great wealth, curious customs and numbers of people beyond imagining. Often he is secretly appalled by the weight of what he does not know—and this is the only fear he has ever tasted. He has hinted these troublings to me and I feel Kahu also senses them. Now you also know. In days to come, Olohana, you must anticipate his doubts, give him confidence, offer the help he will need in these strange new times. It is a *haole* world he will rule in and deal with. My use to him is at an end."

"Don't talk so, Billy Pitt. You are the rock he stands on."

"No longer," Pitt smiled. "But I have known a fine life at his side. I am an old man content in memories."

They came to camp near the small inlet of Keauhou two days before Namo's time was signaled.

There was damned little happiness in this occasion. Olohana reflected. No celebratory air of anticipation—only the fervent wish it was over. Namo's discomfort was constant. She did her best to be quiet and uncomplaining but the whimpers escaping her lips attested to pain. Hina was always at her side and a massive midwife hovered in mute solicitousness. The gaunt *kahuna* remained aloof. His function began at delivery with an appropriate chant of welcome, a prayer that the child would be worth of the hallowed site upon which it entered the world.

The seven birthing stones varied from three to six feet across and were of a dense gray basalt alien to this cindered coastline. All were smooth and convoluted, embedded like miniature islands in a flat clearing of water-worn beach pebbles. Ten generations of kings and numberless lesser *ali'i* had been born on this site, taking strength and *mana* from these sacred boulders. The origin of their potency was vague even in legend, but its presence never doubted. This was the honored place for *ali'i* to be delivered to earth, the proper stage upon which to launch a life of honor and accomplishment. The clearing lay near the ocean in a landscape of stark lava, its only greenery a few coconut and hala trees ringing the stones. Scattered brooms of arid grass trembled in warm wind. Inland the ashen desert wandered to far foothills. About fifty yards distant, the sea licked lazily at low bluffs.

"You must not worry," Namo said.

"It is frightening to see you suffer so."

"I think only of the joy to come."

"Is there nothing I can do?"

"Yes. Stop fretting. I am in good hands. The midwife is expert and Hina gives me great comfort."

"I will be near, my love."

"'*Ae*, dear man. I know."

She gasped. Her face twisted and her fingers dug into his palm.

"You must leave now, *ali'i*," the midwife insisted. Hina nodded to Olohana and moved to Namo's side. The two women helped her to her feet and began walking her toward the stones. Olohana watched as they eased Namo to rest against one of the larger boulders. The *kahuna* joined the trio, staring with clinical interest as the women moved to make Namo comfortable. He held two wooden calabashes, one with herbs with which to clean the infant, the other with oil to anoint the child.

Hina looked up and flicked her hand impatiently at Olohana, bidding him to go away.

The sun came up over Mauna Loa, the Long Mountain.

He sat on an outcrop a few feet above the sea, staring at the rise and fall of crystal water. Small striped surgeonfish and purplish wrasses darted in the swells, nibbling at weeded coral. A mottled moray snaked across the sandy bottom, dark and sinister. Elegant white fairy-terns flashed overhead on their way to deep water. But these movings were on the periphery of Stone's awareness. Other thoughts jostled: of Namo's tortured face, his own inadequacy to help; the bleakness of this setting for new life and recollections of their pleasure in anticipating the child. It had seemed so easy—brief discomfort then great joy. This would be the first of many, she had said. She would give him four, six—perhaps eight boys and girls—strong, beautiful and intelligent. And they would grow, loving and happy and close. People would look with love, respect and envy on the noble family of Olohana...

He waited. Sunlight rose higher to dance upon the sea.

The murmuring of water and piping of sea birds were the only sounds. He stared vacantly at the distant sliver of a canoe breasting swells as it entered open ocean from Keauhou bay. Puna walked his memory. He thought, a life taken, a life given. The name Puna denoted spring, source, beginning... He and Namo had talked long about names for the new child. Hawaiian *wahine*-names were euphonic, musical: Maile for gentleness and peace, Lani for heaven and Malu, for shelter. Or the goddess-names: Laka of dance, Hina of the moon, Pele of fire...

But he had determined that if the child was a boy he would be named for his grandfather, David Stone-Olohana. It had a pleasant ring, he told Namo, remembering now how he had to explain what this meant... And with the name, other memories flickered: his father's calm and leathery presence, his mother's loving face chiding him over lessons, autumn apples and sweet cider... Most vivid was that final horror of flame and the loneliness that followed. North of Boston. A litter of black ashes in snow, a fieldstone chimney standing stark in smoking rubble...

Time crawled. The canoe was lost on the brilliant sea, the birds gone.

When the screams came he leaped to his feet, chilled by their intensity.

Rooted with fright he stared inland but the tossings of lava obscured his view. Again the hideous cries slashed the air, then abruptly died. His breath arrested, Stone waited, tensed and fighting the urge to race to Namo's side. There was nothing he could do—and he did not wish to watch her agony.

Minutes moved interminably.

Hina's figure appeared on the waste, picking her way carefully among the ragged stones. The squalling infant in her arms was swathed in cotton.

"A man-child, Olohana," she said softly. "A beautiful man-child." A wizened little face yawned up at him and tiny fists thrashed impotently.

"And Namo?" he asked.

Hina lifted her head. He saw her stricken eyes and began collapsing inside.

"She is dead, Olohana."

The tremulous chant of the *kahuna* wavered above the child's cries and the brushing of the sea. The priest was burying his son's umbilical cord, a rite binding the boy forever to the land and his people.

"The ship is supplied?" Kamōʻī asked.

"Yes, aliʻi." answered Olohana. "Everything I need to settle comfortably."

"I have money for you. Spanish and American dollars. It may have use in the days ahead."

"*Ae*, my lord,"

"Is the little boy well?"

"He thrives, heavenly one, thank you."

"Your old companion, Kimi, wishes to accompany you."

"He has become restless, my *ali'i*. The life of a landlord has not pleased him as he thought it would. He will be David's guardian."

Kahu followed the conversation, smiling faintly. She admired the quiet strength with which Olohana had borne his grief.

"Our grant of the O'ahu lands is a small gesture," Kamō'ī continued. "A gift which does not inconvenience or tax me and demands no sacrifice. I remain in your debt, Olohana."

"I am happy to serve, *ali'i*, and am more than satisfied with the reward."

"But I am not," Kamō'ī said pleasantly. "Listen well, my friend. You need only ask for everything it is in my power to give."

In time to come, thinking of the next few moments, Stone would be appalled by his answer. Perhaps the words erupted out of his precious and irrevocable losses, a desire to see how far he could push the king. Or perhaps they surfaced out of some ugly perversity he had no idea he harbored.

He stared boldly at Kahu.

"Anything, sire?"

Kamō'ī stiffened. Kahu's eyes rounded and her mouth dropped ajar. She looked sharply at Kamō'ī then incredulously at Olohana. The silence was charged with tension before the king replied, "Yes, Olohana, by my vow, anything." His voice was low and tight, his eyes narrowed. More seconds plodded past.

"You do me greatest honor, my *ali'i*. I desire nothing more."

The king's shoulders relaxed almost imperceptibly. Kahu exhaled audibly and her gaze dropped to her hands. A servant appeared with wine and the moment was past, the tenseness broken.

"Take this, Olohana," Kamōʻī said. He removed King George's gift-watch hanging on a braided cord around his neck.

"I am not comfortable with *haole* time," he smiled. "Accept this as a small token of my great esteem."

Olohana heard his child mewling in the dark below decks.

"Davey wants his breakfast," smiled Tweed.

"Aye."

The two leaned against the *Little American*'s taffrail. Gray light of dawning outlined Oʻahu off the bow. The sea wisped along the schooner's sides and her sails snapped in erratic breezes. Tweed grunted instructions to his Hawaiian helmsman and Olohana lighted his pipe. A few dim glows from fires were visible in the dark along the shore. High above the Koʻolau peaks were crisp and black.

Olohana heard the nurse's soothing song. The infant stopped his fretting.

"We'll lay off the harbor," Tweed said. "You take the longboat in. I'll wait for high water."

Kimi appeared with tea and bread. He smiled at the two, but said nothing, respecting their reticence.

When he left Olohana spoke, "You'll stay for a few day?"

"Weeks if you like. Long enough to see you settled, then board Kai and his lot." Aleka studied his friend's face in the half-light. "Tell me squarely, John. Are you all right now?"

"I've accepted, Alec. The going's easier."

"Good. You'll have your hands full here, for a fact."

"I welcome it. And then I'll be welcoming you from time to time."

"Aye," said Tweed. He peered at the quiet shore. A feathering of coco-palms was taking shape in bluish light.

"A bit different than last time," he observed. "With a spear or musket behind every bush."

Many things were different, Olohana mused. He realized that he and Tweed had been conversing mostly in Hawaiian.

He climbed down into the longboat to join his son, the nurse and Kimi. Tweed smiled down from the schooner's rail, leaning on his thick bronzed arms. Olohana waved and the Scott returned a jaunty salute. Oarsmen began pulling for the island.

The sun was now above the mountains, warming lee shores as they approached the harbor's mouth. Stone turned to look at the *Little American*, her sails glided, nodding languidly on a slate sea. Tweed was still at the rail, hunched and watching. Olohana felt the powerful lift of swells as the ocean surged against the O'ahu shelf, lifting them toward the channel entrance. Ahead the splendid long valleys of Nu'uanu, Kalihi and Mānoa were carved deep by morning shadows. Several *'iwa*, the bandit birds, soared out from land, their thin swords of wings etched sharply against an ice-blue sky.

Shores of the area called Honolulu were lifeless.

The boat eased past the blunt peninsula starboard of the harbor mouth. To the left ebbing surf roiled shallows beside a broad and low islet of exposed coral. Beaches inside the bay were few, dark sand mottled by threatening boulders. Surrounding flatlands were arid, a few lonesome trees and shrub growths, with more luxuriant clusters around the Kawaiaha'o spring and the Nu'uanu river entrance. He saw no signs of dwellings or habitation. Apparently the residents driven away by the O'ahu battle had not yet returned to the remote community. The squat platform of a small *heiau* near the point was the only evidence that men had lived here.

The head oarsman spoke, "Where do you wish to land, *ali'i*?"

"There." Olohana pointed. "Nu'uanu." Clear, clean water tumbled down from the valley where the stream entered the bay. Coco-palms, *hala* and breadfruit trees promised solace of shade in the serene landscape.

The Hawaiians rowed easily on the calm. David gurgled contentment, tugging at his nurse's nipple. So much needed doing, Olohana mused. Houses to be built, supplies to be brought, canoes to be acquired and food to be planted. He would begin by building his own quarters, then a storehouse and an appropriate house for Kamō'ī's visits. Eventually the fishing families who had lived here would return. Others would be attracted by the activity and promises to trade. In time the haole would come, too. He wondered who and when. In years ahead there might be a small village here. One could easily envision a settlement along the shore path—or on the seaside trail to the bright sands of Waikīkī. It wold be pleasant to have a little shelter on Waikīkī beach. It was a lonely and beautiful strand. He and David could swim, fish and have long talks as the boy grew...

A diaphanous rain fell, a truant sunshower blown seaweed from the Koʻolau mountains. Kimi turned, grinning, his face up to its refreshment.

"Good sign, Olohana! We get big blessing!"

The mist settled lazily, a gossamer cloud jeweled by sunslants.

The shore neared. The rich grove around the stream mouth looked cool and inviting. David bubbled blissfully in his nurse´s plump arms. Olohana spoke to the woman and held out his hands.

He wanted to be holding the boy when they stepped upon land.

Against his breast the infant gaped a captivating baby-grin and flailed his doll-like arms. His tiny fingers caught and tugged at the sennit string holding Kamōʻī´s gift watch. Olohana removed the timepiece, hefting its weight, thumbing the oily silver smoothness. He held it to his ear.

Silence. He had not bothered to wind it.

He remembered Kamōʻī´s words when the watch went dead, "Nothing else stopped. The sun and clouds traveled and the sea rose..."

He cupped the disc in his hand over the gunwale and stared at it for a long moment before relaxing his fingers.

It flashed only once in the water before being lost in the dark deep.

EPILOGUE

Excerpts from
Three Voyages to the Sandwich Islands
Admiral Sir George Courtney, Royal Navy
Greenwich, London, 1819

We raised the islands on the 31st of December but the perverseness of northeast winds forced us to make long runs in the lee of O'ahu for the afternoon and night. On New Year's day, 1816, we stood off Honolulu Bay and I was unprepared to see the masts of three other vessels in the once-unknown harbor. This was merely the first of several surprises awaiting me at these landfalls I had not visited for some twenty-four years.

What had been an almost deserted shore where I had once paused for canoe trade was now a community of about three hundred dwellings. Most were the grass huts of natives but sprinkled among these were a few modest structures of European flavor. All were dispersed without plan among narrow lanes on a dry and dusty plain under patches of coconut, plantain and paper mulberry trees. Chickens, pigs and goats strayed among the human greeters as we came ashore.

Olohana John Stone was at the landing to welcome us and escort me to the queen. I recognized him immediately, tall among the dusky throng, hatless and clad in white cottons. He was now in his sixties, I assumed, not without vestiges of his youthful handsomeness, but with his hair bleached and skin scarred from decades in the sun. His manner was open and friendly but his discourse gloomy. King Kamōʻī and Queen Keōpū had been dead for five years, he said, and his friend, Alec Tweed, for three. Kahu remained as premier until Kamōʻī's son by Keōpū was older and wise enough to rule. This young monarch was now nineteen and Olohana Stone's son, David, served as his equerry and companion.

Remembering Mr. Tweed's bulk and vitality, I asked how he had died.

Shot, was the answer, by an Oʻahu chief whom he had cuckolded. It would, Stone said wryly, have been one of the ways in which the Scot would have chosen to go. "Almost twenty five years with Kamōʻī," he said, "and Alec became more a Hawaiian than many born here. A happy man too, in his family and the king's generosity. I still miss the rascal..."

The royal pavilion was large, of white washed planking, with glass windows thrown open under a high-peaked grass roof. Queen Kahu greeted us on its long verandah.

She was no longer the bare-breasted, assertive and jovial dame of long ago but carried her sovereignty with a resolute and quiet dignity. The years had treated her kindly. She was now approaching fifty, I reckoned, and considerably slimmed from the imposing fullness of her youth. She wore a pink cotton frock from her neck to her ankles which accentuated the radiant chestnut-glow of her skin and did not hide a still seductive form. There were traces of silver in her jet hair and tiny lines at her eyes and mouth. Her gaze was quick and inquisitive and her speech brisk and pointed. Her adoring handmaidens scurried to serve us tea, brandy and biscuits, then arranged themselves on the boards like plump puppies to monitor our conversation. She remembered me well, she said, as a visiting captain who gave valuable gifts to her people rather than taking things from them. I thanked her for her kindness in receiving me and offered the compliments and best wishes of George IV. After an exchange of such pleasantries her air went to melancholia.

All dead, she rued. Kamōʻī, Keōpū and Mister Tweed. And all within such a short time. Kamōʻī and Keōpū had succumbed along with hundreds of their subjects to the measles, an illness against which the Hawaiian had no resistance. The king had died at his beloved cove in Kona, with Olohana weeping by his side. A ship's doctor had been brought from Honolulu but could not save him. The mourning and wailing had gone on for weeks. Thousands of people had come from all the islands. There had never been such a tribute to an *aliʻi*.

I expressed my sorrow. Perhaps I could attend Kamōʻī's grave, to appropriately pay my respects and those of my king?

Stone answered. This was not possible, he said. By his own command Kamōʻī's body had been taken to a secret place for entombment. He, Olohana, was the last surviving member of the burial party and only he knew the resting place. He and the queen exchanged glances.

"When Olohana dies," she said, "no one will know."

Kahu's mood changed abruptly shrugging off gloominess. She desired to know what brought an English ship back to the islands.

Britain had thoughts of placing a consul at Honolulu, I informed her, with the aim of establishing a stronger and more active relationship with Hawaiians in years to come. The growth of commerce in the Pacific and the need to discourage Russian and French aggression in the area also made an official presence desirable at this mid-ocean point. I had been chosen to make representation for the Crown in the light of my previous—and most agreeable—experience in Hawaiʻi. I begged her favor in considering the application. It was John Stone who answered.

The gesture was late, he said, but welcome neverthe-

less. Such a presence might serve to give pause to troublemakers. At the moment a man claiming to represent
the Russians was creating an annoyance on Kaua'i island,
inflaming its high chief with thoughts of a revolt against
Kahu and the young king. Stone added as if to himself, "I
shall have to go and have a chat with this bastard."

He talked on about other problems encountered since
Kamō'ī's death. Kahu watched him over the rim of her
teacup.

The traders in furs were fewer, Stone said, and sandalwood barter had greatly languished. Many chiefs had
accepted payment for wood they were unable to deliver
as the mountainsides became denuded of the precious
trees. The cattle I had introduced so many years ago had
been allowed to run unchecked. Their progeny, along
with those of the sheep and goats since brought to
Hawai'i, had been consuming the islands' sparse greenery with similarly shocking speed.

The coming of whaling ships escaping arctic winters
had brought welcome trade, he said, but the troubles they
created often appeared to outweigh any profit.
Frequently there were as many as five or six of these vessels in Honolulu harbor at one time, spewing their drunk-
en and lecherous crews ashore and causing vile scenes.

The queen shook her head. The wretched traffic in
women sometimes became livelier than all other trade,
she deplored. The ships rang their bells at dusk to summon the *wahine* aboard, then again to drive them off in the
morning.

We sipped our refreshment and stared over the straggling settlement. Dugouts and skiffs plied back and forth
to the ships from wagons along the shore. Stone identified the two wooden structures along the harbor trail as
warehouses of Honolulu merchants. One belonged to
Tom Cox, representing his father's factoring establishment in Boston. The smaller was owned by a Chinese
who had appeared a few years back. A farther collection

of sheds was Alec Tweed's little shipyard, now operated by his sons and dealing in chandlery, repairs and small boat construction.

Two of Stone's former gunners, a white and a negro, ran a ramshackle saloon and rented pallets to sailors and their paramours in an annex. Most Honolulu whites were drunkards and lechers, Stone said, but a soberer few had gained respectability with skills of carpentry, sailmaking and smithing. A Spaniard from Mexico had brought seedlings of many vegetables and fruits and worked a flourishing farm above the town. This man also rolled passable cigars, made a decent wine and had introduced roses, carnations and other exotic blossoms to O'ahu.

It was now time for her midday lie-down, the queen stated. Her tone was firm but pleasant. We would join her for supper, she said, at which time we would talk of the consular possibility and other interests. She offered her hand, which I kissed, while thanking her for the audience and the invitation. Olohana Stone bowed slightly and touched her hand. Her fingers curled in his, briefly pressing, and her smile for him was intimate and confiding. I felt certain that something more than an old friendship existed between them... Stone then walked me back to my longboat...

He was candid and obliging and remembered our last visit with gratitude. This made it easier for me to ask questions about the queen and her circumstances. In England, I told him, news from the Pacific had been infrequent, sketchy and unreliable.

Kahu's mourning for Kamō'ī had been intense, he said, but she had lost no time in asserting her power. In a gathering of the high chiefs she had proclaimed Kamō'ī's dying wish that she serve as regent until his son was mature enough to rule. There had been mutterings but no man had dared dispute this declaration and she had easily taken the royal reins. Only a few months later she had

openly defied the *kapu* against women eating with men
by sitting at a banquet of the chiefs. Kahu had persuaded
the young king to join her, thereby bestowing royal
approval on the deed. This rash and ruinous act had
served to destroy the power of the ancient *kapu* system.
The death of this major *kapu* meant contempt for all others.

The turning point, Stone said. And it was soon clear
that Kamōʻī had been right—it had been the abiding faith
of Hawaiians in the gods and laws of antiquity that kept
them strong and united. In abolishing the *kapu* and denying their deities they had made an appalling mistake—re-
jecting their heritage for a way of life that would spell
their doom. As Kamōʻī had predicted, the seductions
became stronger, the Hawaiians weaker as more and
more strangers came. Now there was no stopping the
flow: whalers, adventurers, traders, thieves and the
human rubbish of the seven seas.

"I conduct the queen's business and handle affairs as
best I can," he said. "But one must compromise, make
adjustments to these changing conditions. I try to deal
fairly with honest men and minimize problems with others. Frequently it is difficult to tell them apart."   He
smiled without humor.

"Often I feel I am steering a rudderless ship.
Sometimes I fear it is only the queen's strength, and the
love of her people, that keeps us functioning. The Hawaiʻi
we have known is no more. It died with Kamōʻī."

Our return to the boat followed a lane twisting along
the bay. Naked children gamboled in tide pools and there
were shouts from the draymen and canoe people servic-
ing the whaling ships. Russet colored women lolled on
the pebbled porches of grass bungalows, smoking pipes
and smiling greetings. The establishment of Cox and
Pinkham, Ltd., occupied a substantial shed with a brass
bell hanging in a tiny cupola on its roof. The warehouse

also served as a place of prayer meetings, Stone said, though Tom Cox´s congregation could be counted on two hands. A trickle of men issued from its doors, bearing hogsheads and other burdens for transfer to the boats. A few native men sat listlessly, watching their laboring kinsmen, and a rib-skinned dog worried some object in a swarm of flies.

A few yards farther we came upon a newer and less imposing structure which Stone identified as the Chinese man´s store. Three white men in ragged seamen´s garb lay around a small cask from which they were drawing sustenance. All were stupidly intoxicated and scarcely glanced up as we approached. Olohana Stone waved to the proprietor, who was standing in his doorway. The aging Oriental lifted a hand in response. His face was bland, except for the glaring white welt of a scar across his nose...

Nearing the boat there was a commotion ahead. A small carriage, drawn by a lathered horse and containing two young men plunged toward us on the narrow trail. The man on the reins jerked his trembling animal to a halt as we neared. These two were the king and his own son, Olohana Stone said. I would have known the youth instantly as a lean and handsome copy of his father but for his burnished brown skin. He wore only nankeen trousers and a red kerchief about his neck. The smile on his sharp and even features was nearer insolence than amiability. The young monarch at his side tended to corpulence and was naked except for a breechcloth and the whaletooth pendant of his rank. He swayed, eyes closed and grinning vacantly and it was clear he was quite drunk. David Olohana was sober. His father made introductions.

Young Olohana nodded curtly. I bowed to the king, who stared blearily, then tossed off the dregs of a flask and flung it to the stones. Stone moved closer to speak to

David. He lowered his voice but I could hear him berating his son for permitting the king to become drunk. From his words I deduced that this was not an extraordinary occurrence.

Young Olohana stared at him coldly. "You mind the white man´s business, father," he said. "I´ll take care of this fool."

He viciously whipped the little horse into action and the carriage careered off down the path, scattering chickens, children and other pedestrians before it...

I spent several hours on ship´s business then released half my people with the stern reminder that we represented the Crown on a commission which could be endangered by any mischief. I than enjoyed the luxury of a fresh-water bath in preparation for supper with her highness.

In late afternoon I took a cigar on the stern and sat, staring over the harbor scene. The almost still air was heavy with the stench of dead leviathans butchered by the nearby whalers. Cloud cover added a gloom to the waning light, a few small boats plodded back and forth to the larger vessels.

Inland a smoky haze from fires hung over the aimless scatter of grass and wooden huts. Low tide revealed an ugly litter of rubbish from the ships and the bloated carcass of a cow along the shoreline.

There was the pealing of a bell. Mr. Cox, I assumed, summoning his sparse flock to evensong. Moments later another sound arose, raw male voices in a sea ditty—probably from the saloon operated by the retired gunners. Farther along the shore a bursting of sparks flew from the forge at Captain Tweed´s shipyard. The clang of steel upon steel could be heard and the sharp squeak of winches.

All these sights and sounds bespoke change and progress, I reminded myself.

Still, they left one wondering about the dubious blessings of our modern times.

Photo by Ronn Ronck

Ed Sheehan
1918-1992

About the Author

The late Ed Sheehan, came as a young man from Malden, Massachusetts in 1940 to work at Pearl Harbor as an iron-worker. His presence there on December 7th, 1941 resulted in a first eye-witness book of the attack.

He was a radio personality for twenty one years, a film actor, a television performer and a public relations director for a major ad agency in Hawai'i.

His columns in the Honolulu Advertiser were reprinted in U.S. Wide Metropolitan papers and magazines. In 1984, Ed was the winner if the Benjamin of Tudela Award presented by the State of Israel for the best article that had been written about Israel. In 1986, he won the Lowell Thomas Travel Journalists award for the best travel book among the Society of American Travel Writers.

Ed was considered the unofficial poet laureate of the islands. His previous books include THE HAWAIIANS written with Gavan Daws, DAY OF '41 - PEARL HARBOR REMEMBERED, and the award-winning HONOLULU. He was commissioned to write the book KAHALA for the Kahala Hilton's 25th anniversary.